DEVILS

John Klawitter

DEVILS

DOUBLE DRAGON

Dedication

To Lynnie, the Light of my life…

And where is my light, the light of my life, my love?

Prologue

<u>Limboland</u>

Sally Jensen-Harris woke to her own bitter tears. She had been weeping for what seemed like an endless time, and for what she knew was good reason; after all, everything she loved had been taken from her. Her sense of loss was total and complete. She had fallen down a black hole of despair, a place from which there would be no hope or salvation. But it was more than just a sense of loss, for whatever she had become—all that remained of the living, breathing person she had once been—was here now with her. It was disorienting because there didn't seem to be any difference between *inside* and *outside*. There was just the blackness, the loss, and nothing else.

She could sense the frightening, palpable *nothing,* the ether in which she floated. Reaching out made no sense because she knew there would be nothing there. All around her was blackness, void, empty. She wasn't cold or warm; she was only aware that her own physical reality had disappeared, along with that of her entire known world. All that remained was the pain of her loss.

After a time, in the same way she was aware of the hopelessness of her situation, Sally also became aware that her daughter Anne Mae was nearby. She couldn't see or feel her; she simply was *aware* of the familiar loving and needful presence of Anne Mae in the way of all

7

mothers that goes light-years beyond anything of logic.

Before this *nothing-time*, everything had been different. Once Sally had been a self-contained person and a scrappy fighter, tough and independent ever since she'd been a little girl. She hadn't been afraid, even as she remembered the last real things from her life— the burnt rubber smell, the squeal of tires, one brief flash of chrome teeth in the headlights, and last, her daughter's long, trailing scream into nothingness. But even in her despair, she knew this sense of no-being wasn't right; it had an almost alien strangeness. She hadn't expected to wake up at all, much less to find herself lost in this nothing world of no light or life or sensation.

Perhaps there was a personal angel who guides each of us on our path. Sally couldn't be sure, but from that first moment when she woke in the dark void and resolved to control her weeping, she was somehow aware that things had gone very wrong, although at that time she had no idea how off course she had drifted…actually, been *herded*.

And yet even then her pervading sense of gloom couldn't overcome a faint flicker of curiosity. This new place could not by any stretch of the imagination be the logical extension of the terrible accident that had happened to her and Anne Mae. Heaven? Hell? She was well acquainted with the classic Christian beliefs, thanks to years of indoctrination by the nuns of St. Bonavita boarding school, an isolated and difficult high school calculated to garner a certain number of applicants into the sisterhood itself. Their seed had fallen on the rocks of doubt, and the system of eternal rewards and punishments hadn't taken with Sally; but if it did really exist, she was sure hell was nothing like this. Could she be in purgatory, that place in high Christian belief where sinners were sent to wait out the time until their souls were cleansed by fire? She doubted it. Where were the flames, the purging?

With nothing but an endless string of moments on hand, she pursued this line of logic a little further. There were those Christians who believed purgatory was simply a place of waiting; if so, actual flames might not be necessary. She dismissed the thought with a fearful little attempt at a laugh.

Sally tried to look back realistically at their lives and who they had been. She and her husband Mica had enjoyed their talents and their great love; but on the greater scale of things, they were fairly ordinary people living normal lives without any real exception. They had both come from broken families, but that had only encouraged a tighter bond between them. And their daughter Anne Mae had been well-adjusted and caring. Sally would readily admit that maybe she herself had committed bushel baskets full of garden-variety sins in the old sense of sin, guilt and the attendant penance, but Anne Mae was barely ten, and her daughter would never end up in a place like this.

Sally forced herself to believe she wasn't going to wallow in endless self-pity. But as she fought hard to push down the overwhelming sense of loss for everything she had left behind, she was aware of a new feeling, a growing dread for what might lie in store for her and Anne Mae. Too easily her mind could become a pinwheel of frightened thoughts. *Where are we?* she asked herself. *And who did this to us?*

CHAPTER 1
Ferngate

<u>one</u>

Dr. Railsbach sighed and tried to stuff back his boredom. Once you grow accustomed to the pitiful mewling of lost souls, you are supposed to be able to withstand anything. That's why they have a special school for it. One could get over the pity, but never the crushing sense of the inconsequentiality of it all. *Simpering Satan, who cared what happened to any particular homo sapiens, much less the entire lot of them?* Railsbach paused, struggling with the fact that the troubled house he was visiting was the only place remaining in the entire *sap* world where they still performed the dance of the dead. He shook off his quirky moment of sad bemusement; he was impatient to get back to his work on the 21st floor of the obsidian tower adjacent to Cedars-Sinai Hospital, and figured he was not entirely responsible for his thoughts. Still, he was an old and experienced player, and he knew he wasn't going to get away from the party without performing at least the obligatory bowing and scraping.

Dr. Railsbach was nearly six feet tall, well-groomed, with healthy pink skin and a full head of snow-white hair. If things were as they appeared, he might have been in his late sixties; and, were it not for a small, foreign glitter in

11

the remote depths of his light blue eyes, he would have the look of a benign pharmacist, a man you could trust to dispense antibiotics or point you to a hot water bottle. But in Railsbach's case, appearances were only skin-deep. He had been spawned nearly six hundred and fifty years before; his body coating cleverly hid a dark gray carapace that was both insect-like and demonic in appearance, and his perfectly modulated voice emanated from a cybernetic voice box designed to produce the impossibly light sounds of human conversation.

Railsbach moved away from the shadow of Sir Albert's house, savoring the heat of the distant sun as if it were brimstone's own nectar. The structure itself, for all its elegant looks, gave him the dry sweats, reeking as it did with the passing smudge of generations of doomed human spirits. He knew he was supposed to enjoy the scent, but he didn't. Just another of his little quirks, a disquieting shibboleth he kept to himself lest it bring him unwanted attention or—Hell help us—remedial action.

Railsbach was well aware of the fact that this wasn't the kind of place where one would expect to find demons of any sort. In the first place, the huge home was located in Southern California near winding Mulholland Drive, on a level pad above the dry sage and stunted oak slopes north of Beverly Hills. *Beverly Fricking Hills, for Bub's sake!* as the new spawn would say.

Not that Ferngate wasn't unusual, in and of its own right; a looming English Tudor is as out of place on those oxygen-drenched and sun-scorched slopes as a fig leaf on a rock star's crotch. Railsbach bit down on the subject, realizing the extent of his boredom. He wanted to get back to his offices so badly, the sulfur was curling in his brain, back to his wonderful few rooms where the critical experiments of his long and generally not very rewarding career hung in the balance.

Railsbach reluctantly turned away from the broad green lawns and the gardens and made his way back inside, heading toward the festivities and idly glancing as he went at the dark walnut wainscoting, the heavy old cut crystal chandeliers, and the deeply carved Jacobean tables and sideboards.

He returned to the study just as Speth the assassin swung by, a graceful picture of lean menace. Railsbach tried to pretend an absorbing interest in the nearest oil painting, but Speth snagged him neatly, approaching too closely with the translator's dare and handing him a glass frothing with hot, dark liquid.

"Old Albert sure knows how to desecrate a room," Speth sneered.

Railsbach wanted to reply that Speth's own tastes ran more to *sap* nudes painted in Day-Glo on velvet, but he bit the thought off sharply. *Nothing good comes from angering an assassin.* Instead, he retreated to a polite stance just out of lash range and spoke politely.

"I think there is some merit in some of these..."

"'Some merit in some of these'," Speth

13

echoed, his voice heavily coated in mockery.

"I think so," Railsbach said, moving on to inspect the next painting, which was of a Renaissance picnic in the roofless ruins of an ancient palace. To his dismay, Speth moved with him. The oversized oils were painted in the manner of Thomas Coventry, English countryside scenes with ant-like peasants diminished by gigantic boils of ancient forest stands and threatened by enormous, mushrooming death-white clouds. Railsbach paused before a notable rendition of a pack of pitiless hounds tearing at something that might have been a fox or a small *sap*, and another depicting somewhat larger wolfhounds swirling around a bloodied brown bear. These paintings were darker than their original intent, as over the centuries they had become smoke-dried and varnish-cracked. Railsbach moved on to study a faded tapestry featuring a naked, dreaming lady with floating hair and one hand cupped coyly below her abdomen, the ornate stitchwork laudable for the vague sense of peril which oozed from the too-big cabbage roses and the fence of thorns which made up its border.

"I'd love to eviscerate her in Cupid's name," Speth growled, spitting into a nearby potted fern.

"Come on, Kelp," Speth said impatiently, calling Railsbach by his old otherside, or hellside, name as he moved inside range and took his arm, "Let's go plague Felney." They were old flankers, and Speth casually broke the

14

common rules of space and courtesy that his kind had built up over the ages to keep from killing each other. And worse, from Railsbach's point of view, Speth the assassin talked in shorthand. *Go, No Go. Hit, Run. Translate, Rollover.* Railsbach liked ornate language, disliked the fact that Speth had effortlessly gotten close enough to invade his space and encircle his arm, and most of all hated being called Kelp, which was his ancient spawn name. But as usual he said nothing, and Speth easily led them through the dancers.

two

At the far end of the ballroom, which also doubled as a study, a great fire roared in a huge floor-to-ceiling fireplace of foamy pinkish-gray marble carved in the intricately detailed manner of the medieval cathedral craftsmen. Railsbach, who had never really taken the time before, now noticed it was crafted in ornate swarms of human heads thick as bees, the *sap* eyes and mouths gaping wide at unknown horrors as they swam around the rim of the fiery furnace. A closer look at this carved pattern of doomed soul heads revealed not marble, but intaglio designs cast in thin, translucent porcelain with the cream or antique white color of *faience fine,* a clever surface that had assumed a lifelike rose-colored flush from the flames which licked behind them. The incised, silent *sap* howlers gave Railsbach the eerie feeling that, as he moved, they slowly turned and stared back at him while the writhing life of the fire gave the figures themselves a hellish animation.

This room was the center of a social event that most of the *saps* who had showed up vaguely remembered as being long on their calendar of *must attends*, though in reality that was anything but the case; were anyone to ask, not a single one of them could actually tell precisely why they were here. It didn't seem to matter. They danced and chatted and nibbled and sipped while a string quartet delivered a chilled Mozart and caterers in striped white-on-white silk vests chummed platters of creamed sardines, gray pot stickers and blackened calves' livers circled in nearly raw bacon, and poured a fine smoky Fume Blanc from light green bottles. More *saps* were constantly arriving through the high front doors, thrown open now to the afternoon heat. And just as regularly, they were leaving again, although none of them back out through the front doors.

There was a costume-party froth in the air, undercut by the hint of smoke from the giant fireplace, a scent whether slightly of pitch or brimstone, which lent the hint of a rougher medieval ambiance to the festivities. The guests made up an odd speckle of humanity, everyone dressed as-you-were in a variety of attire from pajamas to dinner clothes to bloody butcher's overalls.

"Aren't you going to drink that, Kelpie?" Speth asked, gesturing to the glass in his hand.

Railsbach bolted down his nasty jolt as they arrived in the corner of the room next to the fireplace where the little clerk Felney, Sir Albert Fern's right-hand man, was busily plucking souls. He was at his usual seated position behind a huge, old wooden swing-open banker's desk. Even with the party at full blast, the regular business had to be attended. Soul trapping waits for no one, as the old saying goes. It was proudly said of Felney and his Southern California troop that they had a sixth sense for that right moment. *More Hellside Propaganda,* Railsbach thought uneasily. Lately, doubting fumes had more and more

17

drifted unbidden across the darker tunnels of his mind. For some years now, Railsbach and his fellows had eagerly scrambled across a line that now he personally was beginning to believe should not have been crossed. Of this he said nothing; he simply shrugged his *sap* coat and turned his attention to Felney and the scenes at hand.

Much of the original desk at which the little clerk sat had been gutted and altered; the inner face and the open wings were neatly stuffed with banks of monitors, so clear they were like little mirrors of life itself. Keypad in front of him and face shield over his eyes, Felney punched away as if there were no party, no wine and *hors d'oeuvres*, no last dance of the lost souls. Railsbach knew the bulgy little fellow sometimes fancied himself fate's clerk, Charon at the crossing, the counterpoint to Peter-at-the-Pearly-Gate. And, in truth, Felney and others in his station had become far more than simple scribes since Railsbach and his dark team had uncovered the knowledge to nudge *sap* destiny towards their own destruction. Mankind may have slept since the fall, but their oldest enemy was back with the same old attitude—and the help of Father Science.

three

The party was approaching its climax, the music was taking on a wild and knife-glitter edge, the looks in the dancers' eyes were wide and hopeless. A young man in ragged jeans and a tattered T-shirt swung by with a woman in a gray business suit. The young man's shirt joyfully shouted CARPE DIEM in letters composed from colorfully designed surfboards. The young man's hair was dusted with fiberglass, a dark stain oozed from the corner of his mouth and his ribs were strangely caved. His partner's face seemed composed, though her hue was an unhealthy greenish-white and her lips were dark and purple. Railsbach had to duck to avoid the swing of their arms. He lightly slapped once at his own face, bothered by a minor annoyance. Just one little tap for control, and then he coughed and looked for a place to set down his empty glass.

Speth, who saw everything, chuckled a characteristic spitting gargle, the sound that Railsbach found particularly annoying. Speth never had any trouble with his own coat. He was angular and lean, dark, sardonic, always ready, a coiled spring with nails of steel sheathed inside an expensive Italian suit. Railsbach hated him in a way simultaneously genetic and personal.

Back when he had chosen his own coat, Railsbach had gone for a kindly, old fellow look, by inclination that was more instinct than thought. In his white lab coat he looked like he should be on cable television pitching hemorrhoid cures or liposuction. He and Speth shared little but their mutual impatience with boss Fern's old-fashioned style. *The cause made for curious bedfellows.* Again, the flicker of an unbidden thought. Speth in bed would be dominating, cruel, quick and done with it. *Speth in bed!* Railsbach shuddered. He would have to think of going back under, taking some lax time, getting a groom or even submitting to a semi-clamp. Of course, that would be impossible, now with his lab fully funded and his own EMO Project on full engines forward.

Speth sneered with enough punch so Felney had to overhear, "Back in force, out in the open for the first time since the fall, and we throw *going-away parties*..."

Railsbach tried to defuse, to disassociate, "Don't get your blue fellows in a pincher, Speedball. It's all a write-off to Sir Albert..."

Speth's answer was little more than a half-sneer, half-snarl. Railsbach shifted away from him, turning his attention to the rows of monitors facing Felney inside the desk. There he could see the scenes of daily human life played inside the bright rectangles, the entire wall of monitors a wash of human soapies. One monitor beeped, the flashing LED at its side attracting attention. Behind their shield, Felney's eyes flicked to the screen, that small motion combined with a twitch of his left eyebrow flicking it over to the main monitor directly in front of him. Railsbach, more than a little aware that his boredom had reduced him to watching a common *sap* melodrama, noticed that it was a kitchen scene. A black woman of about 40 was washing dishes. Railsbach looked at the blue-and-white checkered curtains in the windows behind the sink and wondered for the hundredth time why humans were so impractical. Before he could begin to form an answer, an angry black man came into the scene, yelling, "So, Doris—you had to let that skunk have his way with you!" His fist shot out, catching the woman on the side of the head and staggering her nearly out of the frame. She recovered and went on washing dishes, as if ignoring her furious attacker was going to solve her problem.

"Answer me, damn you, you bitch!" the black man shouted, pulling back his arm to punch her again.

A super in bright yellow letters blinked on at the bottom of the screen. It asked simply, "ROLLOVER OR TRANSLATE?"

Felney hesitated only a second, and then his finger hit a red button marked TRANSLATE on the keyboard in front of him.

The black man screamed, "Doris, you screwin' aroun' wit' the wrong man—!"

His thick-muscled arm was already coming out of cock, shooting forward to deliver a stunning blow to the back of Doris's head—but the blow never reached its mark. Instead, the black man grabbed his chest and went wide-eyed as his mouth formed a gaping hole in his face. A tortured gargle burst from his lips. He gasped for air, fingers clutching the dress of a startled Doris as he crumpled to the floor.

Speth shrugged, talking to Railsbach, but eyeing Felney, "The rumor is, the success rate is just about the same as it was before we had all this." He waved one hand, as if the bank of monitors was just so much trash.

Felney, his head shielded by his clear plastic shell, said nothing. His eyes continued to rove the bank of smaller monitors, which were clicking from scene to scene at a furious rate of ten or fifteen every second. Doris was calling 9-1-1 on the main, but Railsbach knew it was no use. *Translated is as good as dead.* Another scene bleeped. Felney's left eyebrow flicked the new moment to center stage and Doris's little life drama was ancient history, replaced by a shot angling down on an intersection somewhere in a battered urban ghetto. A black cop and a white cop were standing next to their squad car, confronting a street gang made up of a half-dozen sullen teens. A hulking black kid dressed in Oakland Raider silks led the gang, slouching with menace. The super appeared low on the screen, ROLLOVER or TRANSLATE?

"Trans 'em, man!" Speth urged impatiently.

But Felney hit ROLLOVER. On the screen, the gang hesitated, and then walked away from the confrontation, leaving the two cops in a state of thankful disbelief.

Felney replied for the first time. He spoke in his clipped way, his mildly sulphurous manner showing he took no *mundungus* from anyone, not even from Speth the hit man,

22

"Hardly a wise choice, sir. We would likely have gotten the white policeman who has a string of corruption, and the big black kid who once drive-byed two teenage girls."

Speth shrugged, "Two out of eight."

Felney's eyes were black coals. "We have plans for them both. And my bet is we'll get at least half of the rest."

"Huh." Speth nodded his approval. "Deeper than I thought."

But Felney, clearly showing that he didn't need Speth's goodwill for anything, had already turned his gaze back to the main, where a new scene was bleeping for his attention.

four

It was a setup in a grungy bar, and a slight Hispanic man was talking to a burly Italian dockworker, yelling, "When you say, 'Chicaaa-no' to me, you got a mean look on your face."

Felney smoothly flicked the TRANSLATE button with the side of his thumb.

The big dockworker moved in closer until his face was a fraction of an inch from the smaller man's nose, "You don't like how I talk to you? *Mange me*—uhh!"

Those were the last words the larger man would utter. His eyes went wide, and he looked down to see the blade of the slight Hispanic's knife buried deep in his stomach.

Speth looked at Felney, "Well?"

Felney kept his eyes on the monitors, his attention on a corner screen featuring a man, a woman and a young girl walking down a mountain trail. "Actual capture rate, sir?" Railsbach noted the word "sir" sounded like an afterthought or an oxymoron falling from the little clerk's lips. "I wouldn't know about that," Felney concluded.

The spitting sneer that bloomed across the assassin's face told Railsbach that Speth's failed buttering up of Felney had fanned his bad mood. The assassin was a few degrees away from steaming out of the room, but instead he turned back to the screen where something had caught his eye. He studied a simple family hiking scene, which Felney had eyebrowed across to the big screen, "What's that?"

Railsbach looked as well, and recognized the *homo saps* on the screen. He was careful not to say too much, "One of my EMO's."

One of Speth's eyebrows raised a fraction, "Who?"

"The man," Railsbach said, his tone of voice indicating he didn't want to talk about it.

"EMO is sapcrap," Speth sneered.

"The argument is *over*, Speth. I have been allocated the resources to continue my project."

"You and your *ubermensch*. You can't create a supersap. It's all sapcrap."

Speth's attention wandered back to the party. Railsbach eyed him with relief, knowing Speth had no interest in drawn-out conversations, much less any capability for a debate on the EMO Project. Speth was bred for the hunt, trained to unleash savagery, honed to move in for the kill. There wasn't a sap born, from Samson to Bruce Lee, not even any of their mythic warriors like Batman, Spiderman or the mighty Electra Assassin who could stand for 30 seconds against him. It would take an angel, or an aware and unblanked human...again the uneasy thought flickered through Railsbach's mind like heat lightning. *The angels were gone, and no human would ever be unblanked or aware again. It couldn't—could not—happen.*

Dr. Railsbach eyed Speth obliquely, from the corner of his face so not to draw a stray lash. It was common knowledge that, if the EMO experiments lived up to their promise, the day of the hunting assassin would be no more. There would be no chance of a rogue human breaking loose, no possibility the species could ever again present even the whisper of a threat. When that new age came, Speth would be promoted to the rank of noble hero...and promptly clamped, downgraded and given some shuffling task back Hellside. And they both knew it.

26

<u>five</u>

Tumbling through the dark nothingness, Sally Jensen-Harris pushed back her fear and tried to think. There was no way to tell how much time had passed since she had awakened. Was it seconds? Minutes? Hours? She had no way of telling.

Still, nothing else had happened to her. She and Anne Mae were simply stuck here in the dark. Was she blind? In a hospital somewhere? She had no sensation, no sense of up or down, no pull of gravity...how did she know she was tumbling? Worse than anything, there was an awful stillness around her.

No, she told herself, she was wrong. She wasn't tumbling, *couldn't be* tumbling. And, impossible as it seemed, the minute she had the firm resolution that she was stable and not tumbling through space, she settled into a rock-steady state.

But it was only a moment before a new panic set in—*what if she wasn't anywhere at all?!* This unusual and frightening thought brought on a new wave of near-hysteria. She had to be *somewhere*. She recognized the small presence of Anne Mae, sleeping at her side, and this calmed her. *No time for panic.* She was the Mom. She had to be strong and smart. She had to figure out where they were and what had happened to them.

Sally's thoughts raced back to that last day, the glorious day of the hike when she and Mica and Anne Mae had charged happily down the mountain trails of Northern California, without a care in the world. Maybe the answer lay there, somewhere hidden in that last day of her normal life.

28

CHAPTER 2
Under The Redwoods

<u>one</u>

Like a bright original of one of the dark and musty oils on Sir Albert Fern's walls, golden sunlight streamed down through huge redwood trees onto the curving downward trail that made up the Tamalpais Mountain nature walk. The scene was far out of Fern's territory because the EMO, Mica Harris, had traveled north on a weekend getaway with his family. Still, with the help of boosters, the liquid digital reception in Fern's study was flawless. Looking down from a camera angle through the trees, the vision was that of the pantheistic neo-classicists, the family looking small and insignificant in the majestic woods and under the flaming twilight sky.

Racking in for a closer view, the demons observed Mica Harris, apparently lost in his thoughts as he walked behind his wife and young daughter. Mica was Railsbach's most advanced EMO, the prize of his collection. The human male had just turned 38. He was lean and intense, a Sting look-alike who was often stopped in the streets of West L.A. for his autograph. Ironically, he was just as well-known as the famous pop singer, particularly among the young affluent, for his creation Horny Hamster, a funny little character he drew in the loose style of Thurber or Groening.

In his formative years, Mica had endured enormous personal deprivation and pain under Railsbach's program, and he poured into Horny all the pointed sharpness of his sardonic cartoonist's vision of the human condition. The complete irony was, the more he pointed out their weaknesses, their faults and shortcomings, the more the *saps* loved him.

And there in the frame was Mica's wife, Sally, the faithful companion he thought had just loomed out of nowhere to fill his life with meaning at the precise moment when Railsbach had pushed him so far that he had the pistol to his mouth. Railsbach had been reluctant to give him the comfort of a wife and a companion, and, of course, the daughter had been another terrible accident, but these were temporary intrusions, and soon to be whisked from Mica for the greater cause.

Sally had been chosen from a limited field of three young females, each first-generation and yet believed to have been isolated beyond repair through natural parental neglect and abuse. The first had been a semi-reformed hooker working as a sandwich girl. The editorial offices where Mica sometimes worked was on her route. The second was an embittered Jamaican girl whose mother and sister had both been brutally shot in the face by corrupt policemen while she watched. This one was beautiful in *sap* terms, but black as Satan's butt, potentially a drawback to a *sap* mating. Railsbach had her introduced to the head of the art department, put it in his head what a wonderful addition she would be to his staff. And then there was Sally—surly and smart, a freelance writer who took no crap from anybody and came and went as she pleased, even while grubbing for assignments and angrily living off the dole from her parents when the pickings got slim.

Sally's parents had been ambitious, in their own way. Born and raised in Rockford, Illinois, they had used the big profits from grandpa's car dealerships to concentrate on climbing the Rockford social ladder, all the while dropping Sally off to grow like a wild weed in a series of girls' schools. The girl was expected to show her carefully scrubbed face for holidays and social functions, and by the time she was in her preteens, she figured relationships were about money, and little else. One way or another, Sally always had her hand out, and by the rulebook, Railsbach figured she wasn't capable of any sort of giving relationship. The root of it was expediency; they had needed a diversion to keep Mica from killing himself. Faced with limited resources and no time at all, they'd simply lined up the three of them and thrown them at him.

Soon Sally and Mica *had become an item*, in the quaint *sap* phraseology. She possessed a slight female frame and pretty smile that only hinted at her hearty spirit and an inner strength, traits unhappily not uncovered by the EMO Project until far too late. It was odd how she had blossomed in all the wrong ways after starting her affair with Mica. They had wanted

31

a lusty diversion, and no more. What they got was a genuine rival and a constant block in the progress the EMO program had charted for him. Her unexpected strengths had given Railsbach continuing concern over her choice as Mica's spouse, but when working with semi-wild humans, one didn't have much latitude—it seemed to be all or nothing. Now the doctor could see she was walking in front of Mica and keeping her eye on impish Anne Mae, who was jauntily leading five yards out in front of both of them as they wandered down the well-worn trail.

The daughter, ten years old, bright-eyed and laughing, jumped the creek by a small waterfall. Railsbach watched her look back at her parents with a grin on her lips.

"Sure you're not too old for this?" Anne Mae taunted them. Railsbach felt a twinge of regret. Someone with all that energy could be of use to the cause. It was terribly unfortunate, but there were too many risks involved. He reminded himself that, without blanking, dangerous *ubermensches* would be everywhere. He had to stay focused. The EMO Project was designed to create the *schwarzen ubermenchen,* the dark fanatic who would have the uncaring charisma to lead the rest of the *saps* to their destruction like lemmings off the unforgiving cliffs of earth. It was a carefully thought-out program, with absolutely no use for freebooting along the way.

Sally paused by the gnarled trunk of an oak tree and smiled at Mica. "It looks like we're prehistoric, as defined by wretched youth."

"It's not fair," Mica complained, "You're lighter, Anne Mae, so you've got less to carry."

Anne Mae thought for a moment, "But my legs are shorter. It makes up."

Mica squinted into the distance, hoping they would get to the bus by sundown. "Well, it's downhill. I think we'll make it in time."

As Railsbach knew, Mica wasn't very comfortable in the outdoors. He had asthma and horrible memories of the countryside, courtesy of demondom. The poor *sap* obviously did this for his family and no other reason. Railsbach figured Mica was probably thinking that, if they could get to the bus, the drive back up the mountain to where they'd parked their car would be a snap. Railsbach shook his head, studying the screen. *After today, the Harris family would be no more. After today, Mica Harris would be set on a course as relentless as fate itself. He would be driven to mate with the black Jamaican woman both he and Sally thought of as their best friend. From them would be born a son, and, after the black woman would be forced to leave them both, this young half-breed sapiens, warped and twisted by Mica's bitterness, would become EMO's first true schwarzen ubermensch, the beast-man from the darkness.*

two

The golden sun of late afternoon glowed on the wandering forest path. Mica slipped as he underestimated a little jump across a stream. He ended up with both feet in the cold, shin-deep water. Anne Mae paused, not saying anything, then grinned and went on ahead when she saw he was all right. Mica took Sally's extended hand. Anne Mae's voice came floating back to them, "Yeah, you're okay so long as you've got Mom to keep you out of trouble!"

Mica had to laugh in spite of himself. She'd never said anything more true. Before meeting Sally, his life had been a melodramatic mess. His parents had died when he was five, died in a high-speed auto accident. Mica had been flung through a side window on impact. He'd survived and had been patched up and taken in by a grim old uncle and aunt who lived in semi-isolation on a small farm in Minnesota. The old couple, bitter at their own lack of children, had been cruel and taunting. Chores were endless, food was intermittent, and there were no holidays, no school, no relief from the constant barrage of punishments they called "life's little corrections". That had lasted until the uncle chose to sodomize the terrified young boy under the approving eye of the aunt. There was a scuffle and, with Felney's able assistance, Mica escaped while the barn burned to the ground with both uncle and aunt still in it.

After that, Mica had been rescued from being a ward of the state by a clause in a will he'd never read; there were apparently enough resources in the will to send him to a series of boarding schools, and finally to college. But, everywhere he went, tragedy dogged him; his friends moved away, switched schools, or died from illness or accident, until he was sure every misfortune and ill turn was, somehow, his fault. He was the bringer of pain, bad accidents and death. He had the curse, some kind of pure evil that rubbed off on others while leaving him smoldering but intact.

As a teenager, Mica had begun his long but necessary pull away from human contact. He burned the midnight oil and became one of those brilliant, emaciated students with the hollow, sunken eyes who take a fatal dose of aspirins or start shooting random targets from high windows. And yet, something like that would never happen to Mica Harris. It couldn't, for the energetic Dr. Railsbach was very, very careful. With such an investment of time and energy, the easy out of an overdose or a slashed wrist simply couldn't be allowed. So just when it seemed that Mica was at the end of it and everything would snap, Railsbach introduced Sally. Beautiful, wonderful, giving Sally. Unfortunately for the good doctor, as the relationship bloomed, that was more or less what she turned out to be.

As for the daughter, Anne Mae, Railsbach always thought of her as *the horrible accident*. It had been one of those full-moon nights when

35

all of *sapdom* seemed to go crazy, and Fern's resources were spread so thin they just hadn't been able to prevent it. The monitors had made Railsbach aware that Sally was pregnant weeks before she knew it, but despite a series of close calls, she had carried the child nearly to term, and even endured a 72-hour labor. The woman had unexpected inner strength, and her aura had proven impenetrable, another disturbing addition to the new layer of knowledge Railsbach's generation was gathering: *Even blanked humans had disturbing and unknown layers of spiritual reserves.*

<u>three</u>

After a short time of light hiking, the family came to a clearing and happily entered a broad down-sloping meadow bursting with flowers. Railsbach watched impatiently from the other end of the state of California as Sally and Anne Mae seemed to find it important to stop and plop themselves on the ground to weave crowns of daisies. Mica was content to sketch his wife and daughter, and they stuck flowers in his hatband for his reward.

The sun was now low against the horizon, and as the little family moved into a final stand of redwoods, red-gold bars of light streamed through the trees. Anne Mae and Sally held hands and danced in a circle.

"Magic, magic, magic!" Anne Mae shouted.

Sally chanted, "Elves to the left, elves to the right, elves in the trees all around!"

They plumped down next to Mica, looking at the sketch of themselves dancing while Anne Mae took a big swig from her bright yellow plastic water bottle.

"Daddy, can this be our place forever?"

"I don't see why not."

She held out her hand to him, and another to her mother. While Railsbach watched, the three of them swung around in a magic little circle, maddeningly elusive in the hard shell of their love and so utterly, foolishly convinced that nothing bad or evil could ever get to them.

<u>four</u>

Sally Jensen-Harris learned her first simple post-normal life lesson when she decided to put an end to her own spinning through the dark void. She had stopped gyrating out of control simply because she had willed it. The spinning motion, which she decided had been formed of her own indecision, came to an end. There was no crashing halt. It simply stopped, and she was steady and firm in her space.

After that, her brief moment of elation had been followed by lengthy periods during which she alternated between fear and boredom. There was nothing at all—no sight or scent or sensation—to give her any further indication of where she was or of what had happened to her family.

After a time, since there was nothing else to do, she set to thinking again. Since there was no up or down, no pull of gravity in any direction, she decided it was logical to assume she was a dot. A dot was a point of light, and could be expanded into a circle. Since the circle would have two halves, one might be considered a top and the other a bottom. So much for up and down; once she decided which half was the bottom, gravity naturally had to be in that direction.

A quick check convinced her of the presence of Anne Mae, still asleep at her side. She returned to her review of their situation. *Bottom half* and *top half* were unsatisfactory descriptions, for these terms didn't really describe or define what she knew of the human form she had so recently possessed. She willed herself to remember, and the circle of light shaped, carved and sculpted itself into the glowing body of a young woman. She studied the hairs on her arm, perfect in every detail. In a sense, she had become her own memory of herself.

Looking to her side, she quickly concentrated on the small point of light until the sleeping form of her daughter resolved itself. Because Sally could and because she wanted to, she selected her best underwear and a flowery summer dress for herself, and a favorite pair of jeans and a T-shirt for Anne Mae.

Having puzzled through that, she held out a hand toward her daughter's soft hair, wondering at the gentle glow of light that emanated from their skin. The light surrounded them like a warm blanket or cocoon, and quickly faded into the surrounding void. And then something else occurred to her. Gravity couldn't exist in a total void, could it?

This is not logical, she thought, imitating one of Mica's favorite Star Trek characters. *There has to be something under me.* Immediately, an irregular segment of plane illuminated under her. It too faded away from her into the dark void.

This latest success brought her to an altogether different level. She took her successes for clues as to her particular state of being. Perhaps she was living in a dreamworld.

But, if so, she could take comfort in that it was still some form of world. *I think it, therefore it exists. And therefore, I exist.*

This sort of *constructive reasoning* came naturally to her. She'd always had a flare for architecture, and an ability to see spatial relationships. Trained in fine arts in college, she had learned how to construct perspectives in her paintings. In a painting or her favorite watercolors, she simply reconstructed her own little world on canvas. It didn't seem odd to her that she was now able to, in some limited form at least, re-create the things she knew in this void. Fear can be a terrific motivator.

Then too, her husband had an almost rabid curiosity for modern physics, which he called the true basis for science fiction. She would scoff as he explained the scientific basis for wormholes in space, time travel, warp drive, and alternate universes.

"Don't be afraid of what isn't immediately obvious," he would say, looking at her over the wire rims of his glasses. It was a look he affected that made him seem wise beyond his years.

Not wanting to be left out of his conversations, which could get abstract and impossible, she had leafed through most of his books, puzzling through the works of Einstein, Lederman and Hawking, and she had pondered over his well-thumbed copy of J.T. Fraser's Time, The Familiar Stranger. Mica, who could be grumpy and reserved, had been surprisingly encouraging.

40

He quoted from Richard Feynman, a favorite of his, some lines about how ordinary people could understand extraordinary things, if they set about it with confidence.

"You're saying I'm *ordinary*?" she had shot back at him.

"Not at all," he had replied patiently. "But you're not a nuclear physicist."

"I never heard of him."

"He was in New Mexico with the team that invented the bomb," Mica said, as if that explained everything. "Feynman said that anybody—you, me, anybody—could understand the basics of really tough concepts like the theory of relativity."

"Oh, sure, right." She remembered grinning and kissing Mica lightly on the cheek.

"No, maybe not the math and calculus part of it," he replied, slightly annoyed that she wasn't taking him more seriously. She was reminded that the modern scientists were Mica's gods. He frowned and continued, pointing what she always called his *serious-idea finger* at her, "You can get this stuff. In fact, that's just what the so-called experts are afraid of. They realize how little difference there is between you and them. They spent years becoming professionals and working on their post-doctorate crap. They don't like the fact that you might be able to understand something important on their level."

Something about that appealed to Sally. Shortly after her half-serious conversation with Mica, she began leafing through his scattered library of textbooks.

She'd even tried some of his science fiction. Although most of it left her terminally bored or gasping in laughter, she had found something haunting and real in Jack Finney's romantic Time and Again and the lesser known If I Never Get Back by Darryl Brock. Now, considering her present state of affairs, she wished she'd read more of those fanciful pulpers about other dimensions and alternate states of being.

She didn't think her answers lay in organized religion. Her own personal belief system contained a healthy skepticism for a hereafter of fertile green valleys where the lions lay down with the lambs. Still, she had a deep and abiding faith in Something and Someone, in unknown things she called the mysteries. It was almost as if, in a way of thought similar to that of rogue priest Pierre Teilhard de Chardin, she was comforted by the notion that *all things were on a journey from the few, the simple and the dark to the many, the complex and the light.* It was a path she believed led to this Thing called God.

After a while, she was tired of just sitting there, thinking. She decided to try to light up her void with the comfort of a night sky. But this proved beyond her capabilities. Perhaps she didn't know the stars well enough to be able to fling them across the sky from a blanket, as had the tricky coyote of Navajo legend.

Anne Mae stirred in her sleep. Sally sat on her glowing ledge of indeterminate slate and wondered what she could do to cheer the place up and make it more homelike before her daughter awoke. Glowing skin was going to be hard enough. There had to be more for the kid than a six-foot slab of rock in the middle of nothing in the center of nowhere. And yet, even as Sally stared at her own translucent arms and wondered what to do and how to do it, her thoughts drifted back to those last terminal seconds in that other place she now thought of as *the real world*.

<u>five</u>

Jerry Bliney wiped the sweat from his eyes as he hunched over the wheel in the stuffy cab of his dark blue-and-chrome Peterbilt, aware of the heavy drag of the double-double burgers he'd gobbled down a half hour before and even more aware of the dead weight of tons of giant logs strapped over the spinning wheels behind him. Jerry yawned, rubbing the bleariness from his eyes. He'd picked up some bug down the road. He should have passed by this run, slept out his fever. His eyes ached, and oncoming headlights had that starry effect that seemed to blow all definition from the rest of his view.

"Goddam," he said, working his left eye with the knuckle of one fist. He missed his line on a shallow curve and had to overcompensate by sweeping through the oncoming lane. *Lucky thing it was a short run and a nearly empty road.* He'd get to the mill in under an hour, dump his logs and settle down his stomach at the local Trucker's Pit Stop with a big plate of ham and eggs before sliding between some clean sheets.

"Christ-o-matic," Jerry said, blinking awake in time to jerk the wheel and correct his line the other way. He opened a window vent, but the wind blew the triangular glass pane shut. He drove one-handed, holding the vent open with his left hand and leaning over so his head caught the full blast of the warm evening air.

Just another hour or so, he'd be crawling in

between those wonderful cool sheets. He rubbed his eyes, trying to clear them as he saw the glaring lights of a car rounding a distant curve.

Jerry was filled with sudden overwhelming fury. "Jesus, turn your brights on, why don't you?" he snarled angrily at the approaching car.

six

Although it was barely evening, the afternoon party for the lucky batch of departing souls had finally ended. Dr. Railsbach had left long before, as soon as he had decided it was acceptable to slip away. Fern's study was deserted, lit only at one end by the roaring fire that was framed with its lifelike intaglio horror masks, and in another corner by the eerie glow from the old desk. Felney was alone at his desk, still working with calm precision. He had dimmed down the flicker of his ordinary transactions, and all the screens were muted, except for two. One of the bright screens showed Jerry Bliney the trucker, yawning and stretching first one arm and then the other as he fought to hold back sleep, while on the main screen a tracking view, like that of a giant owl, followed Mica and Sally in the front seat of their cream-colored Fiat Spyder. The two of them were singing along with Anne Mae, who was lying on the small backseat.

The little girl sleepily sang, "Forty-two bottles of beer on the wall, forty-two bottles of beer..."

There was a glow of an approaching vehicle.

"Car coming," Sally said.

"Got it," Mica replied automatically.

Cresting a hill in the middle distance, the brights of an enormous truck came into view. Mica squinted, "Got his brights on."

Fern studied both screens as they

simultaneously lit up with the question, ROLLOVER or TRANSLATE? At that moment, a voice behind Felney said matter-of-factly, "You know, old Gurpler, you've got an implant there..."

Felney couldn't resist a momentary twinge of anger, even though it was his boss, the mighty Sir Albert Fern. Felney gave a split-second glance away from his screens to input the image of Fern, splendid in a maroon silk evening jacket, pipe in one hand and bubble of cognac in the other. *What did Sir Albert know of the timing it took to neatly translate a sapiens?* But Felney bolted those feelings and swallowed them whole.

"Another of Dr. Railsbach's EMO's, Sir Fern", he replied with a dead calm to his voice. "It's all vectored into the equation. The implant will be rolled over; the two females and the trucking man are translated." Even as Felney spoke, he knew his annoyance showed. He'd been doing this all day, and it was his specialty and it was blessed tough and nobody gave a hallelujah in the first place.

"Sorry, Felney. I should have realized you'd be on top of it."

Felney nodded once, his attention back on the screens. The trembling index finger on both hands reached for the Translate buttons. He paused for perhaps three seconds, and then pushed.

It looked like the two vehicles would clear. But then, at the last possible moment, the truck veered directly in front of the small roadster.

And after that, in the last possible second, Mica actually jerked his steering wheel the wrong way, squaring the little Fiat with the oncoming flare of lights like a moth drawn to a flaming brand.

Sally only had time to give him one brief, bewildered look. "Mica, No—!" she cried.

From the backseat, Anne Mae yelled, "Daddyyyy—!"

And then the truck plowed mercilessly into the Fiat, flipping it high in the air like a killer whale tossing a hapless bloody seal.

Felney shrugged and looked up from the screens. Sir Fern gave him the briefest nod of approval and turned away.

CHAPTER 3
One Year Later

<u>one</u>

Sally was increasingly depressed in her void. It seemed logical that the plane where she sat and Anne Mae slept might be extended, yet her every attempt to create a night sky was a dismal failure. She couldn't even create a roof, a ceiling or a cave wall over their heads.

Maybe something more familiar, she thought to herself. *You don't start a shelter with the ceiling. You need a foundation. And for a foundation, you need a base.* She started by imagining the slab on which she rested actually extended to a distant horizon. It took a few false starts, but she finally got it by determining the horizon and then working backwards. She stood and slowly turned in a circle. There it was, her horizon extending in whatever direction she looked.

Since a flat surface seemed unnaturally harsh, the shape and form of the rolling hills behind their old house came to mind. She worked her thoughts around the idea until, nearly effortlessly, the landscape became as she imagined, a computer-like landscape, a smooth and rolling skin that lifted to form a soft and rounded horizon in the near distance. That was progress, but she found it still not satisfactory.

For a while, Sally struggled with the notions of cold and hot, and finally settled on *warm wind, springtime, flowers, high green grass and dewy morning. Amazing!* She stared in wonder, recognizing that she had re-created the rolling pasturelands to the north of their house. It was a view from the kitchen that she had loved and lingered over. And she had walked those hills until they were old and dear friends.

As a last touch, she set up easels with blank canvases, and brought out boxes of watercolors. Painting watercolors with her mother had been one of Anne Mae's favorite pastimes. Sally stood in the middle of the meadow, gazing around critically at the beautifully lit scene of spring. She added a few sycamore trees with fresh green leaves, and a graceful stand of eucalyptus in the distance, and then gently bent over to wake Anne Mae from the hollow of fresh grass where she slept with her favorite sweater for a pillow.

The little girl yawned and stood, slowly taking in the scene around her. She smiled at her mother. And then the smile froze, and she howled in terror. She clutched at Sally's waist, burying her face in the folds of her dress.

"Mom! Mommmmm! There's no sun!"

Sally managed to place a glaring orb in the sky even as she cursed whoever had done this to them. There is no force quite like the sudden rage of protectiveness that overcomes a mother when her child is threatened. *Someone*, she vowed, *someone somewhere was going to pay. She would make sure of that.*

But then she heard an unearthly music, a

deep chant that came from nowhere and everywhere. *We need you, We need you, We need you,* the chant softly demanded, *Go to sleep, We need you both. Together now, you'll help us. Give a little help here, We need you. Sleep, Sleep, Sleep, We need you.*

In seconds the spring day across the bright meadowlands had faded to nothingness. For a moment more, the glowing apparitions of the mother and daughter turned and spun slowly, unconscious in the void. Another mark of time and they were spheres, and then only points of light. And then even those tiny sparks winked out and were gone, like two fish suddenly scooped from a bowl.

two

The bland, oddly lilting voice of the Scandinavian tour guide assured Mica there were two things he absolutely had to see in Copenhagen. The first was the bronze maiden riding the dolphin. She would greet him in the harbor. The other was the Gefion Fountain, named after a hoary Scandinavian legend of how the land came to be. He had seen the lady on the dolphin, and was now seated by the Gefion.

Viewed in a slow spin from above, the bird's-eye view of the Gefion was a water world, a sparkling, three-tiered pond peopled with heroic bronzes. As Mica took in the bright warm sun and cool breeze, pigeons clattered in a loose formation across the public square. Mica paid no attention as he made small, unconscious circles in the cold water with his hand. He felt isolated, as he had throughout this entire trip, which he now realized was a terrible mistake. Tomorrow he would hop back on a plane and in twelve hours or so he would be back in Los Angeles. Not that that would matter, either. Mica was lost, so utterly lost he no longer had the will to take the pistol from the bureau drawer and hold it to his head. He couldn't even join the ones he loved.

Maybe he'd taken this foolish trip—he wasn't really sure—because Sally had told him once that, long ago, her folks had emigrated from a forgotten little burg somewhere near Copenhagen. Sally Jensen. He could kick himself for being so stupid. What had he expected to find, a country full of light-haired, golden-throated, loving and laughing Sallys?

Two elderly ladies were seated next to Mica on the curved concrete slab which rimmed the fountain, discussing matters of importance in Steger, Illinois, a small town about 40 miles south of Chicago's downtown Loop.

Lucy sucked a bit of pancake that had become stuck between two of her teeth and looked over at her companion. "Did you bring the tickets, Tillie?"

Tillie's eyes, quick as a sparrow's, darted to her purse. "Of course, I brought the tickets, Lu. How else do you think we are going to get home?" Tillie wasn't really miffed; she just had a naturally spunky way. She pulled the tickets from the big blue purse and waved them to demonstrate her point.

This didn't set well with Lu, who had seen enough in life to know that only country bumpkins flashed their tickets in public. "Well, I didn't mean show them, Tillie! You never know who might pick your purse."

Tillie was thinking of something to say to that when a soccer ball took a thump and bounced right on by them. Lu nodded as if this proved her point. The ball rolled up to the young man seated next to them, bumping his left leg. If he noticed it, he gave no sign.

"Kick it back," Tillie advised, "Give it a good one!"

Mica started, his mind a world away.

"Huh?"

"The ba-allll..." Tillie enunciated as if she was talking to a retarded student.

"She wants you to kick the ball back," Lucy said helpfully. But before Mica could respond, a teen wearing Team Italy's red, black and green on a faded T-shirt came over and took the ball away.

"Oh, he's a helpful one, this prick," the boy said over his shoulder as he hustled away.

"What did he say, Lu?" Tillie asked.

"You've known me your whole life, Til. I don't speak Swedish."

"What did he say, young man?" Lucy asked. Maybe he was just foreign. She hoped he was. It would be nice to know that he wasn't backward, and also to hear what the soccer player had said.

"Huh?" Mica said. He looked at her, and then back at the ground, then back at her again, and then at her friend. "He said, umm, 'You can't get here from there.'"

But they could see he wasn't paying attention. They both felt he probably had just told them a lie. In fact, he was looking around the fountain as if seeing it for the first time. Who knew, Tillie thought, he might even be one of those thieves Lu was always so concerned about, or worse, a dangerous drughead. They tried to follow his gaze. What could a young American—they were sure he was a countryman—be so distracted about on such a simple, sunny day? There was absolutely nothing out of the ordinary, so far as

54

they could see. There was the usual ant-scramble of tourists and the scattered bunches of local citizens enjoying the sun. There was a balloon seller, and one of those clever vegetable carvers who could make flowers out of radishes without the $39.95 tool you could buy on The Shopping Channel. The soccer teens continued to boot their grubby ball back and forth, annoying almost everybody.

Because of Tillie and Lu's keen curiosity, they saw the woman and girl across the pool at almost the very moment Mica did. The elder of the two was a beautiful blond woman, maybe in her early thirties. And the other was obviously her young daughter, a girl of nine or ten. Both of them were ecstatic, waving, jumping up and down in their eagerness, their shouts riding over the hiss of the fountain. They were clearly waving at the young man and shouting his name. The name sounded like Mica, but pronounced with a hard "e" sound, like "meeka", not mica like the clear stone sheets Lu and Til had known as isinglass in the long-ago days of their own youth.

"Mica! Over here! Micaaa!"

The young man leaped to his feet, the words ripping from his throat in a cry of incredulous joy, "WHAT?! Sally!! Anne Mae!!" He was gone in a rush, pushing through the crowd.

"He found his family," Tillie said, the note of approval obvious in her voice.

<u>three</u>

Dropped like eggs in boiling water into the bright push and clatter of a world they thought they'd left behind, Sally and Anne Mae fought like tigresses to break out of the mind clamps imposed by Dr. Railsbach's technicians. But they were fighting a bewildered, one-sided and doomed struggle, without much chance of success.

It was daylight; the woman and her daughter were dressed as they had been in the void. Their bodies felt real; and so did the smells of the rich, warm urban scene, a scent of lilacs and salt sea in the air. The sun was warm on their faces, and everything should have been wonderful, but for the realization that they had no idea how they'd gotten there.

Sally could see they were in a foreign country, yet the people spoke a language she understood instantly. She found herself uttering syllables in response. People nodded, satisfied, and turned away. Anne Mae, more or less dumbfounded at her side, had yet to speak a word. She tugged at her mother's skirt with an increasing urgency. Sally dropped to one knee, brushed a curled wisp of honey-colored hair from the little girl's face and looked directly into her light blue eyes. Sally realized she couldn't even say her own daughter's name.

Real words failed her. She struggled harder, reaching not for the easy language ready at her tongue, but for the invisible one she knew lurked just beyond her understanding.

An invisible music started from somewhere, soft and sweet. The inviting strains beckoned her back to a dreamworld of forgetfulness. *No!* her inner voice shouted, *No, there is no music to replace that of my real world!* She found herself staring at Anne Mae's blue jeans. *My name is Sally Jensen-Harris! And this is my daughter, Anne Mae! Nothing can stop or change the facts of reality!* No sooner had those words of pure revelation tumbled from her mind than the clamping pain dropped away from her head. Mother and daughter remembered everything and danced for joy in the warm sunlight by the fountain—and just when they thought their happiness couldn't be any more complete, they spotted Mica on the other side of the laughing pool of water!

four

Albert Fern shook his head, groggy from being lagged halfway around the miserable oxygen-laden planet. His coat felt slippery and unmanageable, as was usual under the circumstances. He wasn't worried about his entry; if any stray human had accidentally observed him phasing into this scene, they would have already been spot-blanked by the ever-observant Felney from his post back in his study. Fern moved instinctively away from the splash of the pool. He spotted Railsbach and moved quickly toward him.

"What the Bub is going on, Railsbach?!"

"It's part of the plan—but it's getting out of hand."

"What plan, idiot?!"

"My EMO. Mica Harris. To drive him mad...I've written it all up. It was approved by council. You signed the order—"

"Railsbach, I can't look at every..." Fern saw that further conversation would be useless. Railsbach had never been much of an operator in the field. He saw he'd arrived late, indeed, and the situation was coming to boil. Mica Harris, the doctor's prized EMO, had already spotted his wife and daughter and pushed halfway through the crowd in a desperate attempt to reach them.

Fern glared in the direction of the blond woman and her daughter, who were not ten feet from them, fairly leaping with joy as they waved and shouted across the fountain.

"They don't look like trances."

"They've broken out of their clamps. Nobody ever expected—I mean, I really had no idea this was possible—"

"Not now, Kelp. We don't have time."

Albert Fern laid one hand on Dr. Railsbach's shoulder, bending down to partially shield his face from the general public, and in that same motion, Fern's facial features smoothly transmogrified from those of an elderly, well-groomed captain of industry into a bushy-haired, scholarly old professor with rubbery lips. He spoke into the palm of his hand, "Felney, I could use a little interference here." Fern could almost see old Gurpler back at his desk in the study, scratching the thin hair on his skull as he tracked various views all around the fountain. Felney would have Mica, the blond woman and her daughter, Railsbach and himself, and a dozen others, all on the monitors.

"I think I have something, sir," Felney's voice whispered dryly in his ear.

A plump American tourist, a man of about 40, backed into Mica while trying to take a shot of his unhappy wife and their antsy twin boys, and he and Mica stumbled to the ground, their arms and legs tangled. The demons were lucky as the camera tripod caught between Mica's legs and further complicated his progress.

Fern, now in his guise of a scholarly professor, moved over to Sally. He bumped into her and excused himself, taking her and Anne Mae briefly by the arm. He stared

59

intently into their eyes and spoke a few words in an ancient tongue, which seemed too guttural and broken for the human throat. There was a nasty millisecond of rebellion, and then the joyful thoughts rushed from mother and daughter as from open-ended balloons.

After the briefest of moments to reinforce his dominance, Fern let go of their arms and brushed past them to sit nearby at the edge of the pool, the proximity to which he clearly felt was distasteful. He was confident his few words would be enough with the *sap* females. The ancient silver threads were woven, a web that would have been difficult to break out of even in the old days, when humans still retained their natural powers. The race had been blanked for too long, and the bond was too firm for any *sap* to withstand.

five

Meanwhile, Felney was still hard at work. Mica disengaged himself from the plump American only to back into a pair of porcupines, a spiky and irate elderly couple. No sooner had he made his apologies to that old man and woman when he found himself in the center of the soccer game, facing a handful of sneering teenagers. Hands up and palms forward, he backed away until at last he was able to rush up to the blond woman and her daughter.

"Sally! Anne Mae!!" he cried, knowing he was crazy to believe this could happen, and at the same time so far gone in his desire for them that he was beyond caring what anybody thought.

They calmly turned and looked at him. Fern's intent was on the blond woman and her daughter, his gaze never wavering. Railsbach took a hesitant little breath of hope. As long as Fern held control, it was obvious to Railsbach that the two of them were back in the bag.

A look of panic came over Mica.

"Sally! Sally!! It's me—Mica! You—you just called me, from over there. I was over there." His arms gestured, pointing to where he had been, showing where they were, when he first saw them.

The woman and the young girl shook their heads. The woman spoke in a strange and broken language, laughing in a slightly embarrassed way and shaking her head. After a

61

moment, her daughter did the same.

Mica stared at them, his glance flashing back and forth, his words choked up inside. The blond woman gave him a slight bow, and, taking her daughter by the hand, began to walk away.

"No—wait..." Mica looked wildly around, seeking help, "Does anybody—does ANYBODY know that blond woman and her daughter?"

No one answered. It was as if he was living in a dimension of invisibility. A young couple couldn't be bothered. The old couple he'd bumped into a moment before now glared angrily at him. A businesswoman with her blond hair cut in a short, greasy ducktail gave him a look that meant he'd better not try anything cute.

"Anybody know them? Anybody at all?" The blond woman and her daughter were moving further and further away from him, moving out of his life, and he could do nothing about it; it was as if he was frozen in amber. "At least, what language were they speaking?"

Albert Fern couldn't resist showing off a little in front of Railsbach. He gave Mica a scholarly look and spoke in heavily accented English, "If I had to say...17th century Nordic?"

It was a mistake; he miscalculated how fast Mica might move, and in a flash the young *sap* male was at his side, grabbing at his tweed jacket.

"Be serious!" Mica shouted in his ear, so close he caused unpleasant static in Fern's carapace. Fern, uncomfortable at the mad gleam in his eyes and the sight of the saliva flecking the corner of his mouth, now wished he hadn't said anything.

Fortunately, good Felney mustered a rescue. In another second, a burly hand descended on Mica's shoulder, and he was roughly pulled back from the professor.

"What's going on here?" a wide-shouldered policeman asked. He looked for answers from the crowd, which had gathered to watch Mica's outburst. Emboldened by the presence of the law, the elderly couple moved forward. The old man poked Mica in the shoulder.

"An American pest!" he shouted.

Mica shoved the policeman in an effort to see which direction the blond woman and her daughter were taking. His actions irritated the big officer, who yelled at him in broken English, "Okay, mister—what is your troubles, here?!"

Mica doubled his efforts to see around the policeman, and this earned him a sharp crack across his hand with the officer's nightstick.

"I said, what is going on?!"

Mica, holding his injured hand, still tried to get around the bigger man.

"I just—I have to—"

But before he could explain, the policeman poked him hard in the stomach with the stick. Mica doubled over and fell to the ground, gurgling and gasping for air.

Fern looked about, careful that no one was watching, and quickly transmogrified his appearance back into his more familiar human coat.

Railsbach was already whining his apologies, "I don't know what went wrong. We haven't had something like this since—"

Fern glared at him, finishing his thought for him, "—since Orpheus charmed us with his lute? Since Persephone slipped the bounds of Hades?"

Railsbach shuddered at the ready sarcasm in Albert Fern's voice. Sir Albert's punishments were legendary. The scientist could only listen and hold back his panic as the boss's tone deepened into a thick menace, "You find out what happened, Dr. Railsbach. These are new and dangerous times..." Albert's voice hissed and became the spray of the fountain as he himself faded into air. Railsbach waited several beats to assure the energy drain was off the system, and then he also lagged back to California.

Tillie, already on overload from the beating she'd seen the policeman give Mica, actually saw the elderly man in the white dentist's coat dissolve into thin air. Speechless for a moment, she raised one hand as if to stop him, and when that didn't work, turned to tell Lu.

"What, Til, what?" Lucy asked, thinking from the whiteness of her friend's face that she had eaten something rotten.

But by that time, Tillie had forgotten.

six

The one person Sally longed for more than anything else in the world was Mica. She missed the warmth of his body and his quick smile. She knew she could rely on him for a hug on a cold morning. After Anne Mae had caught the bus for school, he would sit over a cup of coffee in the kitchen and watch her paint or listen to her talk about her day. He never said much, but when he did it showed he had been listening, and that he cared. Sometimes, if the day was lazy and she didn't have to go anywhere and he was caught up with Horny, they would wander back to the bedroom for a few wonderful hours. Mica was a slow and thoughtful lover, with wonderful hands and gentle caressing ways. God, how she missed those mornings!

For what seemed like a long section of eternity, Sally thought of Mica while she stayed snug and safe in the comfort of her tiny pinprick of light, safe from the darkly sweet music that had ended in a roar of pain as it plucked her from the little world she had created out of nothing, safe from dread and fear, safe from the waste and bother of human emotion, retreating from the pain which convinced her she could never again leave this one location in the huge and dangerous void that had somehow reached out to pull her down into its black web of nothingness.

Here within her tiny spark of consciousness there was at least the cold comfort that they—whoever they were—couldn't take anything more from her. The truth was simple but harsh, and she had to face up to it; her former life, her previous human body, her many passions both intellectual and physical, her quirky, dour genius of a husband and her elfin sprite of a daughter, Anne Mae, the light of her former existence, were all gone. All that was over now, removed so far from her prison that to even think of reaching out was to bring her a pain so intense she feared it would snuff out the last glimmer of being she clung to. *Why not, in fact, just let go? What was left worth hanging on to? A few worthless scraps of memory?*

But even as these final thoughts came to her and she was about to give up everything and drift off into the chaos and nothing that surrounded her, the small hard thought came to her that she shouldn't be giving up, she should be angry. The reasons why didn't matter. Even the pain didn't matter. She didn't deserve whatever was being done to her. She was an unwitting victim. She should be furious.

And then, in a painful yaw of recognition, Sally sensed rather than heard Anne Mae moaning at her side. She recognized the extent to which her helpless little daughter was unutterably frightened and lonely. And in that moment, Sally was swept up in the beginnings of her own great and terrible anger. Maybe existence hurt, and maybe it sucked, but those people had used her and Anne Mae to hurt Mica.

With one swift mental backhand, like a warrior recovering from a bad fall, the small spark of her being broke out of the metallic clamps holding her captive. Flexing her anger, she felt herself growing, taking up space. Soon she was once again a glowing replica of her human form, sitting on the dull gray slab of slate, glaring out into the nothingness, and once again the image of Anne Mae slept fitfully at her side.

This time, before going on to re-create a place where her daughter might feel more comfortable, Sally tried to remember exactly what had happened to them in this last strange and bitter event. They had been in her reconstructed vision of the rolling meadows and hills behind her kitchen in Southern California. And then there was a sound of sweet music, and they were lulled away. She remembered being given other memories...or had they come from deep within her own spirit? For the moment, it didn't matter. They had been taken away to a strange location, somewhere in Europe. There was a waterfall with heroic bronze statues, and the day was bright and clear.

On seeing Mica, they had, if only for a moment, been able to break through to their true selves. For perhaps a minute of earth time they had truly been Sally and Anne Mae.

No, Sally realized, thinking more carefully about what had happened. *That couldn't be true. They had not been alive, in the sense that ordinary people live.* But something very close. And then the old professor with the beard had sung to them, snared them once again in his sweet web, and they had been forced to walk away from Mica, breaking his heart.

What manner of people were these, who could be so cruel and heartless? Were they pure evil, if such a thing existed? Were they possessed by evil? And, if so, what was their purpose? Sally realized she didn't have enough information to venture a guess. But she'd seen enough to know they had some very strange powers. She was sure they had a plan, and Mica, Anne Mae and she were all being used.

<u>seven</u>

Another time, letting her thoughts wander, Sally found herself remembering a paper she had read on the human spirit. The spirit, the article had said, could be visualized as a sphere of strength that could only be defeated through weaknesses, which appeared like cracks in a smooth surface. Evil, like a cancer, could invade the cracks, spreading and causing still further weakness. Sally slumped forward from her sitting position until her head rested on her knees. The glow of light coming from the shale slab and from her body itself seemed to weaken with her admission of almost certain defeat. *If that vision of the spirit was correct, she had so many weaknesses that the cracks would be everywhere. How could she ever hope to defend herself in a situation where she had no power and the invaders had everything?*

Still, her daughter was with her in this, and the realization that Anne Mae's fate was tied to her own gave her the beginnings of resolve and a will to try to fight. She had an idea that she might try to construct her own defenses.

With both her fists and eyes clenched tightly, Sally used every ounce of her determination and forged one small, hard kernel of self, one tiny space where she resolved she could go to make her last stand. No matter what words or songs they used to lull her away, she told herself she would always be able to retreat to that space to keep her own free will. As an additional thought, she willed that it be invisible to any and all invaders, to anyone who meant harm to her and to those she loved.

She was a fast learner; although she wasn't sure how it worked, she already knew the void could be made to respond to her wishes. And she hoped that this brave little core, this new little kernel of resistance that she had created, would prove as impenetrable as she imagined. It was going to have to; she was getting the deepening feeling that whatever reserves she could draw upon were going to have to surpass anything she currently could imagine.

Sally instinctively knew Mica was going to need her help, too. They were linked in some way in a dangerous struggle. This went beyond normal love; some evil was threatening the eternal bond of love that she knew existed between them. This evil wanted to control them, and would think nothing of snuffing out their very being, of simply erasing them forever. Although the reasons why escaped her, she had no doubt as to the seriousness of their situation.

She had to find a way to talk to Mica, or the three of them would be lost forever. She had no idea how that loss would come, but she recognized that when it did arrive, it would be total and unending. And only she could stop it…if only she could figure out what to do.

CHAPTER 4
Sympathy for the Devil

one

From a helicopter pilot's slow-spinning point of view, the intersection of Interstate 10 and the 405 South looked like the center of a dusty beige spiderweb. The smog-filtered sunlight of Los Angeles glinted from the cars, which raced along the concrete strands, drivers seeking safety from some vague menace, from the fear of being late for the appointment of their lives, or perhaps that secret spider in all their lives, the dread of losing an unknown fortune that existed just off their fingertips.

Mica had no thoughts of impending doom, even while driving his late model but battered and dusty Alfa sportster, even though the Doc had warned him this car was too much like the fated little Fiat in which he had lost his family. When he and the Doc had that little talk, Mica had laughed a short, barking sound, a cough that was almost not human. For him, doom had already happened. How could he tell Doc that he wanted to be reminded, to never forget, to have this faint fragrance of the joy and beauty that had rushed into his life with the coming of Sally Jensen? How could he, now the ultimate *isolated man*, tell anyone that?

As he drove to his appointment, Mica beat his hand on the black leather-strapped wheel, tapping lightly in rhythm with the *hoot, hoot,*

hoot of the Rolling Stones' "Sympathy for the Devil". *Please allow me,* Mick-the-Devil sang, *to introduce myself/ I'm a man of wealth and taste.* At that moment a blue-black Mercedes 500 tried to edge the Alfa over and take a cut into his lane. Mica briefly eyed the other driver, deciding he looked like any other wanna-be movie producer—he was probably a successful glasses frames salesman or a rack jobber headed for the garment district. The sleek coupe, top down and snorting into the hot wind, drifted within inches of Mica's front fender, and the chubby little guy honked, gesturing the Alfa over and flicking Mica off in the same movement. Mica, in his own world, ignored him, and the guy had to back off while the devil sang, *I've been around for a long, long year/ Stolen many man's soul and faith.*

The glasses frames salesman was so certain that he could bully Mica over that he missed the cutoff. He sailed on east on the 105 while Mica took the Overland off-ramp and cut north toward Beverly Hills. He was off in another world; he liked the rumbling sound of his little Spitfire engine and the guy in the Mercedes had given him an idea for a new Horny Hamster cartoon strip. Horny, the soiled innocent, tries to sell a movie script to a highly successful Hollywood agent who looks like a successful glasses frames salesman. In turn, the agent tries to sell Horny a vial of crack. In the last frame, Horny looks out from his cartoon rectangle with the sadly pained expression of understanding that was his trademark.

Mica knew that over the past year his ideas had drifted into the bittersweet, to where they were darker, biting, often more sardonic than funny. It didn't seem to matter; if anything, his syndicate felt that since his accident he had developed a meaningfulness, a special edgy awareness they were pitching as *L.A. Immediacy*. Maybe they were right; readers liked Horny, and the strip was spreading like an octopus across the land.

Mica spotted an empty parking spot in front of the medical building, which rose like a black obelisk on 3rd Street. He had already zoomed in nose first before he noticed another car had been waiting to back into the same spot. The other car was an old beige Chevy with its left rear light bandaged in cloudy red tape. Before Mica could back out again, the Chevy honked angrily and drove off in a cloud of dark gray exhaust fumes. *AND the horse you rode in on*, Mica muttered to no one in particular.

Mica sat for a moment until the Stones' last *hoot, hoot, hoot* faded, and then turned off the high-compression four banger engine, which had already started to overheat. He slid to the passenger side and hoisted himself over the door without opening it. It was almost the perfect move, but on landing, he stumbled awkwardly over a pair of legs covered in dirty gray work pants. Off balance, Mica staggered and nearly pitched forward on the sidewalk.

"Sorry, boss," a softly contrite voice said.

Mica regained his balance and saw that he'd stumbled over a bum's legs. The man was wearing no socks, just ratty, flap-sole gym shoes. He was just another old black guy sprawled across the sidewalk. The bum's wide white eyes were staring out of a frayed cardboard Motorola television set box which sheltered the upper half of his body. The man was lean and stoop-shouldered and, with his thin legs projecting at odd angles from the box, he reminded Mica of a hermit crab.

Mica had a quarter for the meter already in his hand, but he dropped it as he was reaching to insert it in the coin slot. The quarter rolled about six inches from the bum's left hand.

Mica didn't even go through the motions. It was the only quarter in his pockets. *Pay the meter maid at twenty-three bucks a pop? That wasn't even a choice.* He scooped up his quarter, fed the round little box and twisted the time dial. *Ching!,* the meter said, giving him a lousy half hour. Not enough for his appointment with the Doc. Mica remembered some coins had been rolling round on the floor of his car a few days before. He leaned back over the bum's legs, scooped between the bucket seats and found a dime and another quarter. *Ching, ching!* An hour and ten minutes. That might do it.

Mica leaned against his car again, reaching into the backseat and wondering, *Christ, can't this guy move his damn legs?!* But that, Mica reminded himself, was the dictionary meaning of the word *bum*, a guy who couldn't or wouldn't help himself. He wondered if he could do a strip about it, his little horned hero arguing about the meaning of life with a wino who wouldn't move his legs so he could get past. He wondered what the snapper might be; maybe something like, *What's life like down there, anyway?* He reached into the backseat and got a hand on the Horny drawing he'd had Jimmy, the office gal Friday, frame for the doc.

As he pulled the framed cartoon from the backseat, the bum gave him a strange look. The old man's eyes went even wider, and he retreated deeper into his cardboard shell. He gave a sign, crossing a finger from each hand, a simple movement that came through to Mica as *warding off evil.* It was a mild gesture, like an old habit rather than something sharp and effective, but for no reason in particular, it made Mica angry. *Stupid bum!* He thought, *Can't work for a living, but has to have an opinion about everything!*

Almost in defiance, though he couldn't have said of what, Mica turned the drawing so the bum could have a better look. There was Horny with his famous expression of resignation, saying, "Why me, Lord?" He'd signed it *To Doc B. Thanks for everything. Mica Harris.*

The bum shrank as deep as he could into the shelter of his cardboard box. "It don't pay to fun wit' de debil," the old man mumbled with a shake of his head.

Mica grinned. He was going to have the last word.

"Actually, it pays quite well...but you wouldn't know about paychecks, would you?"

75

"We all pays one way or the other, boss...", the old bum answered.

Mica couldn't think of anything to say to that. He gave the old black guy a funny little salute, half wave and half flick-off, and headed for the black glass doors.

two

It was a short walk, but there was a thin film of sweat on Mica's forehead by the time he reached the chill of the lobby. He stood for a moment to settle down, looking back the way he'd come. He could see outside to his car. The bum hadn't moved a muscle. From this angle, Mica could only make out one side of the frayed cardboard box and the man's long, skinny legs. Mica leaned his framed drawing against his own left leg and flapped his arms a few times, feeling sticky in his short-sleeved cotton shirt. *Maybe the Santa Anas wouldn't come at all this year. Southern California would go right from smog to cold rain as the winter wet moved in.* He wondered where the black bum would go then. *What do you do when winter comes to paradise?* Mica shook his head; *It was definitely not his problem.*

He shifted his thoughts to the seventh floor. Doctor Bruce would be up there, the same old frantic, hyperdrive medical man, running hard to keep all the balls in the air. His predictability was reassuring to Mica. *See Bruce run.* The Doc didn't know it, but Mica had used him in a Horny or two, drawing him as a blur of capitalism, somewhat like and yet unlike Warner Brothers' animated Tasmanian Devil or Charlie Brown's friend Pigpen.

Mica headed for the elevator. He would check in; and, if history was any precedent, the Doc would be glad to see him.

77

three

Dr. Railsbach watched through the one-way plasma as Sally, aided by her daughter, constructed what looked like the frame of a small clubhouse in a big oak tree.

"It doesn't exist. None of it does. Not really," one of his white-coated assistants said. His entire staff had deferred to his tastes when it came to their *sap* exos, and so there were nearly a dozen gentlemanly old fellows wandering the lab. They looked so nearly alike that Railsbach relied on his sharp sense of smell to tell them apart.

"How long has she been doing this?"

"Well, she made up that meadow place before…"

"I mean since she was lagged back from Copenhagen," Railsbach snarled.

The assistant carefully moved back out of lash range. "Not long at all, sire. A few minutes of earth time, at most."

"We had her clamped down tight before we lagged her," Railsbach said abruptly, the memory of his recent failure in Sir Fern's presence still very much on his mind. "Old Fern himself spun her down."

"Yes, but…" The assistant shrugged his shoulders.

"I tell you, she should not be able to do what she is doing in there."

"We would have called you if we thought there was any danger, sire," another assistant said, scratching his thinning white hair. "She's

78

double-vacuumed in total isolation."

Railsbach hissed and spat into a wastebasket, then caught himself self-consciously.

"It is true we've isolated her…but what we know of chaos would fit in a brimstone finger-cup."

"Sire, all aspects of the EMO project are totally thought through and approved."

Railsbach found little reassurance in that notion. After all, he was in charge of EMO, an idea he'd stolen from his father. He'd found it in the old man's papers after tearing out his hearts. Unfortunately, if it failed, his father had nothing more to lose.

"Am I surrounded by idiots? Do you know exactly what that female sap spirit is up to?"

No one could give him any better answers, so he sent them all back hellside to try and come up with some ideas. He sat alone in his offices, gazing through the one-way plasma. He was certain it was sheer coincidence; but as he studied her, the elder sap female looked in his direction and for a long moment seemed to be returning his gaze. Before he could suppress it, a feverish shudder ran down his thoracic joints.

Railsbach found himself so uneasy that he had to look away, his gaze falling to the strange whorled texture of the curved arm of the wooden chair in which he sat. It was an odd 19th century Victorian chair of heavy oak with the carved faces of a pair of snarling demons on the ends of the armrests. The sap artists had imagined so much that was real—if they only knew! But such thoughts did not comfort him. They only made him worry more about what his trapped subject might be thinking. If she only knew, at that moment her dear husband was in the same building...about ten floors close, and yet an alternate dimension away. It was a gulf Dr. Railsbach was firm in his own exoskeleton she would never be able to cross. Still, he looked forward to the return of his research staff. He'd like some answers, and sooner would be better than later.

four

The waiting room to Suite 725 was the same crowded nest as always, full of sad old bugs squinting at worn copies of *Sports Illustrated*, *People*, and *Time*. Receptionists—three of them—were outlined behind frosted glass windows which slid open at rare intervals to accept paperwork and announce graduations in the waiting line. Mica knocked on the glass and was waved in right past the angry geezer stares, by reason of his long-standing relationship and just maybe his celebrity status.

Janie, the pretty receptionist with wide, innocent gray eyes and long straight blond hair, smiled as she waved him through. She laughed, showing even white teeth, and pointed at the drawing under his arm, "Come on, Mica, let me see."

He held it out for her approval as he walked past.

"How about one for me?" Giving him that sexy half pout, half smile of hers, the girl next-door come-on look.

"Nope. You have to save my life, or something."

Her smile brightened, showing dimples in both cheeks, "How about we could work on the *or something?*"

He smiled back, but smooth.

He wasn't serious, she thought. *But there was always that chance. You never knew. A Mica Harris was worth your best shot any day of the week.*

He could see she was thinking of some snappy line, but by that time he was past, in the tow of a cute and chubby young nurse with Peggy on her nameplate. Peggy had his huge file under one arm, and as they came to a room, she slid it into a holding slot on the door. It was so big it almost didn't fit.

"You're in 2 today," she said. She caught a glimpse of his Horny drawing. "Ohh, that's sweet!"

He automatically turned it so she could get a better look and by that time they were in Exam Room #2, the one with the splashy South Coast seascape painted with thick slabs of color, coastal chunks of green and beige, an odd spray of dark green poinsettia leaves in the foreground between slices of deep blue sky and sea. There were six examination rooms, and Mica had been in them all so many times he knew them by the paintings on the walls.

"The doctor will be right in," Peggy said.

"Yeah, sure," Mica replied with a little snort.

"Now don't be a curmudgeon." Peggy was chunky and short, with curly brown hair and a shy look. She gave him a grin as she closed the door.

"See, Horny," he said to his drawing, "Nobody's afraid of me. Nobody."

Mica leaned the Horny out of the way in one corner and hoisted himself onto the exam table. *No big news, the Doc was nowhere in sight. The guy overbooked his patients like a Las Vegas whorehouse on the Fourth of July.*

<u>five</u>

Mica lay back and looked up at the tan ceiling tiles, idly scratching his thumb as he wondered why they paid somebody to poke all those little holes in the tiles. He was surprised that not thirty seconds passed before Doc Bruce pushed in through the door. The Doc looked as busy as ever, not even watching where he was going as he shuffled in while looking at the top sheet on the bulky Mica Harris file.

The Doc was a little Jewish guy with probing dark eyes under thick black eyebrows and a quick, bright flash of teeth. Mica saw him as the ultimate professional hamster, running hard on the little exercise wheel of his life.

"Hi, Mica," the Doc said. He gave his patient a quick glance, a quick grin, and then his eyes flicked back to the file.

"Hi, Doc. How ya doin'?" Mica liked to play it casual with the Doc. Breezy. Jaunty. *I don't have a care in the world.*

The Doc answered without looking up from his studies, speaking in an accusatory banter, "Last time YOU forgot to leave a urine sample."

"Maybe YOU didn't ask for it." Mica grinned, pleased the game was well begun.

"Highly UNLIKELY," the Doc replied, head still buried in the chart, but Mica couldn't miss the quick smile, come and gone like a winking star and then the Doc solid again, back to business.

"X-rays okay. Blood test results came back. Triglycerides a little high. Lay off all that ice cream."

"I'm only 37."

"38. It's BAD for you."

"I LIKE ice cream. It's my only vice."

"AND chocolate." The doc giving him a mock-severe glance over his reading specs.

"Well, yes, chocolate, too. But who are you to talk?"

"I'm your DOCTOR."

The conversation string ran out and a dry but not unpleasant silence slid between them. Finally, the Doc said, "Any more...trouble?"

"Like?" Mica asked, avoiding any reference to the mess his life had become.

The Doc just looked at him, waiting him out.

Mica shrugged, rushed into it. "Okay, once, a few weeks ago, I actually thought I saw them. Honest, Doc. I thought I *saw* them! That's where I got this." He held up his bruised hand.

Still, the silence and the Doc looking at Mica. Finally, gently, the Doc asked, "And... was it...them?"

"...No...", Mica answered in a little mouse voice. *How very unlike me*, Mica thought, hearing that tiny answer escaping from his own mouth.

"How did you know? How were you sure it wasn't them?" The Doc was patient, talking in his probing but understanding way.

Mica looked at his hand, studying the blue-

and-yellow bruise that hadn't quite faded away.

"I got talked out of it."

The Doc waited a beat, waiting for more words that didn't come. Finally, he handed Mica an empty urine sample bottle.

"Well, here. Don't forget this time."

Mica took the bottle. He reached down and picked up the Horny cartoon and handed it to the Doc.

"For you."

The Doc's face lit up like a kid's. "Oh, wow! Mica, thank you! This is WONderful!!"

The wall telephone rang. The Doc picked up the receiver while he was still looking at the cartoon. Mica shrugged inwardly. *That's how the Doc's life was, speeded up and full of overlaps, hit-and-run and on to second base, until the day when he would keel over stone dead from a busted pump.* Still, for a moment, there had been a genuine look of pleasure on his face.

Doc carried on a conversation with the receiver, "Uh-huh? Oh, sure, I'll talk to him." He looked up from the Horny and pointed to the sample bottle in Mica's hand, waving him out of the room, "Down the hall. Unisex washroom. Go. Go. Go."

Mica was halfway to his destination when he spotted a nearly full box of Winchell's donuts sitting on a shelf in the hallway. Peggy, the girl in white who had escorted him to his room, was passing by.

"Hey, Peg," he asked, "whose donuts?"

"Doctor Bruce brought them in." Her perky smile invited him, "Have one if you want."

"Did the Doc himself consume any of these fat bombs?"

"Oh, sure! He likes the sugarcoated ones with the jelly inside."

She walked on past. He gave her a brief glance to be certain she wasn't looking, and then took the entire box. With one quick motion, he closed the top and whisked it into a big cabinet marked "Specimens".

"A doctor of medicine," he muttered to nobody in particular, "should know better than to eat this stuff." Mica whistled a few bars from Rodgers and Hammerstein's "Everything's Up to Date In Kansas City", flipping the empty bottle up in the air and catching it as he continued on his way to the bathroom.

<u>six</u>

Sally sat with her back to one wall of the tree house, looking out over the meadow as dusk softly turned to night. She wondered if the stars were going to come out, but that problem was solved when a heavy fog rolled in. It was so thick she could barely see the base of the tree.

"When are we going home, Mom?" Anne Mae asked sleepily from the pile of blankets under which she rested.

"Soon, Honey-bird."

"But when, Mom?"

"Soon as I can figure it out, Anne Mae. Until then, we'll be safe enough here."

"Cool. We get to sleep in the tree house...?"

"You bet. Try and get some rest now. Mom has some thinking to do."

Sally crossed her legs and sat more erectly. She closed her eyes and tried to sharpen her focus; there had to be a way out of this strange little world in which she found herself. If she could concentrate on their situation, perhaps some answers would come. But time went by and nothing came to her. Finally she leaned back against the rough unfinished cedar planks of the wall that she and Anne Mae had so recently hammered together. Supplies and food hadn't been difficult at all. If she could remember it, she could conjure it out of nothing. Just think the thing, and it was there. She found herself a warm blanket and wrapped it around her shoulders. She stared up at the loosely flapping canvas roof overhead. After a while, her thoughts strayed back to Mica. Where was he, and what was he doing right now? She tried to conjure up his image, to bring him to her, but this desperate experiment failed miserably. She was alone with her sleeping daughter in a chilly tree house that didn't really exist.

More lonely than ever, she fell into a fitful sleep. She reached out for Mica, and was rewarded with a sudden image of him. He was in a doctor's office. The office was staffed with people—no, *not people*—with creatures who were disguised in human flesh! Mica didn't seem to recognize this. He made his little jokes, just like she knew he always did, to overcome his awkwardness and unease at being in a doctor's office.

She saw he wasn't in immediate danger. But she could see in her dream that the creatures were in control of his every movement. They could do anything they wanted to him, and he didn't even know it. She looked at Mica more closely. There was something wrong with him, a large bruise on his left hand. Sally's attention centered on that hand, almost as if she was focusing with a microscope. The skin went in and out of focus—no, she was able to see *under* the skin. What was important about flesh, tendons and blood vessels? And then she saw the small object tucked next to the bone near the joint at the base of his thumb. He had something inside

88

him, some abnormal growth or implant. Working in great leaps of logic, Sally recognized that in some way she had been drawn to the exact source of Mica's danger. She pounded her fists against her knees in a gesture of silent frustration. She had to warn him! For a moment, he did seem to hear her. He felt the spot at the base of his thumb, saying something to the doctor about it. *No, Mica! She silently screamed, He's the enemy! Don't tell him about it!* But the doctor, who was a busy bee of a fellow, didn't seem to take notice. He simply handed Mica a bottle and motioned for him to go out the door. After that, Sally's mind went blank. She had lost her connection, her train of thought, her dream, or whatever it was, to that other world she had left behind.

At that same moment, Railsbach broke his gaze, turning away from the intense staring contest in which he'd found himself engaged. He rose from his chair and stretched his limbs in an exaggerated version of the oriental Tai Chi movements that had been designed to renew the outer human padding that covered his exoskeleton. The sap females had been flung into an alternate dimension. According to every scrap of knowledge the masters had wrenched from ignorance over the centuries, those two were completely and totally isolated. No demon could live for more than a few seconds in the chaotic dimension; in fact, few saps lasted longer than a day or two. Fundamentally, Sally Jensen-Harris and her daughter were one small step from total unraveling disintegration into the chaos from which everything had been formed. Yet Sally was in there, spinning out her little fantasies without a care in the world. As deeply puzzling as Railsbach found the continuing existence of the sap pair, one small matter troubled him even more. It was this curious staring contest in which he found himself involved. *How could the elder sap female know the exact location of the one-way plasmic window? How could she?*

seven

The bathroom was a little gray-walled unisex room with gray tile on the floor, a big, businesslike white porcelain next to a stainless steel basin. A wide mirror ran entirely across one wall. Mica unscrewed the cap on the plastic urine bottle and tried to fill it, but the act wasn't happening so he turned the water on and stood there, looking at his sad and tired eyes, which were staring back at him from the mystery side of the mirror. After a while the splash of the water in the silvery bowl reminded him of the Gefion Fountain and he was back in Copenhagen, reliving that first wonderful moment when he saw them waving and screaming his name, impatiently jumping up and down in their eagerness to be reunited with him. *He couldn't have dreamed that, made that up. He COULDN'T have...*

Still looking in the mirror, he was startled back to reality by the warm urine running over his fingers. Mica jumped back with a *DAMN it!* He sighed and poured some off the top into the toilet bowl. Then he set the bottle down and screwed the cap back on. He carefully soaped first the bottle and then his own hands, rinsing and drying and getting out of there quickly without looking back at the big yellow puddle on the floor.

eight

Exam room #2 was empty when Mica returned. *No big surprise.* He closed the door and bumbled around while humming under his breath, *hoot, hoot, hoot,* in an aimless echo of the Stones. He looked over the rough slab seascape painting and studied the neatly lined up bottles of antiseptic. Betadine, Normal Saline, and Hydrogen Peroxide, hand-labeled on small plastic bottles. Hibistat. Phisohex. A somewhat larger brown bottle of alcohol. His gaze wandered over the bottles containing cotton balls, tongue depressors, gauze pads and Q-tips. There was a plastic tray of various odd instruments of the trade; Mica recognized the tuning fork and the rubber ball peen hammer. He saw other small instruments. There were cutters, pinchers and scrapers—he defined them in an offhanded way—all resting in a neat little row in their own small metal tray.

The door opened, and *wonder number two,* less than a minute, and here he was, the Doc was back again! But it was only the physical half of the portly little physician, the attention half was talking over his shoulder to an assistant on the other side of the door, "Three hundred Mg's is enough. I simply will not give her anymore."

Mica spoke up, "By the way, Doc, I've got a nasty bone chip. A fascist pig hit me with a nightstick."

The Doc looked at him oddly, "I don't follow."

"In Copenhagen."

Mica held out his hand, palm down.

"Right there, on the back of my right thumb. Mica took Doctor Bruce's hand and pushed his index finger on the spot, "Here. Feel it yourself. Tucked next to the bone."

The doctor frowned, dismissing his hand with a little shrug. "I don't feel anything."

The phone was ringing again. Mica felt the spot for himself.

"Come on, it's right there. What do YOU think it is, Doc-boy-wonder?"

"Oh, I don't know, Mica. If anything, a broken-off bit of pencil lead. Look here, not even a scar. You probably got it when you were a kid."

Doc reached for the phone, still talking to Mica, "Could have happened years ago. Completely healed. Forget it." By then he had the phone to his ear. The Doc listened briefly; then responded, "She's on the phone now?" A mildly exasperated expression crept over his face. "Yes, all right. Put her in here." There was a moment, and his voice changed to that of a concerned parent, "Yes, Agnes, it is Doctor Bruce. What? No, you cannot. No. You have to trust me, the flutters are normal for a few days. Yes. Yes. No, it's perfectly normal. Bless you, too, Agnes."

Mica noticed the Doc had trouble saying the last sentence. Maybe, Mica thought idly, because the Doc was Jewish, he didn't believe in people saying, "God Bless you." Or maybe, as a scientist, he didn't like too much God around his office. Whatever it was, he wasn't comfortable saying it. Mica started to work on a Horny scenario in his head, Horny trying to talk to God, but of course he couldn't, being a little devil himself. *Naah, too on the nose*, he thought. Maybe Horny says, "Bless you," and has to have his mouth washed out with soap. There was something there. *It wasn't quite right;* Mica figured he would have to work on it a little bit.

The Doc started to turn back to Mica, but Peggy poked her head in the door.

"Doctor Railsbach on line 3."

To Mica, the Doc looked disoriented, like he was coming out of a trance.

"He said it was urgent," Peggy said.

"He's always upset about something." The look of bewilderment was slowly leaving Dr. Bruce's face.

Peggy grinned. "I've never actually heard him scream before."

The Doc didn't think that was funny. He reached for the phone, hesitated, looked at Mica and said, "Be right back."

Mica shrugged his agreement. He tried to whistle the *hoot, hoot, hoot* as he walked around the room, prepared for a longer wait this time. But it was only a matter of seconds and the Doc returned again. He picked up the file and began to scan it. "Where were we? Oh, yeah, the triglycerides. You've got to—"

Mica grinned, holding up his hand and waving it back and forth. He never thought he'd see the day; the Doc was actually on overload. "Doc, you're losing it. I keep telling you you're doing too many things at the same time. What about my pencil lead? Couldn't we just pop it out of there?"

"Too damn much going on at once here..."

Even as the Doc grumbled about his workload, the phone rang again. He held up a hand for Mica to wait, and picked up the line. He listened for a moment; then spoke in a semi-bewildered voice, "Agnes' MINISTER is on the phone? Wait. Just a minute." The Doc punched the hold button, indicated to Mica that he'd be right back, and headed out the door.

nine

Once again Mica wandered around the small examination room, but this time his attention was on the little bump he could feel on the back of his thumb. He eyed a small, shining scalpel in the middle of the neat row of instruments resting on the tray, and it seemed to call out to him. He moved over to the table and picked up the miniature knife.

"Come on, Meekie-boy-wonder," he muttered softly to himself, "this is just a grown man's Boy Scout knife." But he set the shining blade down carefully, exactly where he'd found it, without doing anything. He glanced at the door, wondering how long it would be before the Doc came back. *How embarrassing would that be if he were caught cutting himself open in the Doc's office!?* But after a minute or two, the Doc still hadn't come back. Making up his mind, Mica placed a few paper tissues on the chrome pan on the small side table, yanked the stopper from the brown bottle of alcohol, dipped the little knife in the liquid, and pushed the triangular tip of the blade in under his skin. The first blood drops oozed out, bigger and rounder than he had expected, and quickly formed a small red stream that ran down his thumb and onto the tissues. He gritted his teeth, more against the revulsion to what he was doing than to the pain. He saw he was going to have to do more damage. *It wasn't so bad; it was just pain*, he told himself. *And we all know I'm really good with pain.* He whistled some tuneless little hoots as he methodically dug deeper, making a small half circle around where he thought the pencil lead was buried. He went slowly. It wasn't that he was encountering resistance; the Doc's knife was super-sharp, but he just wanted to be careful. Bad enough that he was doing this stupid thing in the first place. The Doc would probably walk in on him at any moment and there he'd be, looking silly as a fox with bloody feathers in his mouth.

He was a half inch deep and had the tip of the knife on the lead or bone chip or whatever, but the damn thing wouldn't budge. He sawed back and forth to give it a little room. By now, he'd made a circular incision about as big around as a dime. There was a flap of skin in the shape of the letter "c", but when he worked the knife under it, nothing happened. He took a pinchers and, after dunking that in the alcohol bottle, tried to dig in under the skin flap. There was too much blood, and he couldn't see anything that the pinchers might be able to grasp.

He decided to give it up, figuring he'd done enough damage. Maybe the Doc's "foreign object" had somehow attached itself to bone, or lodged itself under a tendon. Mica cleaned the knife and lined it up exactly where he'd found it, and then returned the stopper to the alcohol bottle. He stripped a few more napkins out of the box and got them under his thumb. There was much more blood than he would have imagined. It quickly formed a big red blot on the tissues. He took more tissues and cleaned up the spots of blood covering the surface of the table.

And still, no Doc. Mica lifted the bloody tissues and peeked at his jagged incision. He felt more frustrated than scared. *Maybe he'd quit too soon. Maybe the damn thing was just ready to come out.* He grimaced and squeezed the skin, working to pressure the imbedded object. Nothing. He squeezed harder and the blood ran in a little rill down his thumb and streamed over the tissues, spattering the table again. Still nothing. The old squeeze-a-zit method was failing him. *Oh, what the hell,* Mica thought. *Over the top. Go for broke.* He picked up a knife that had a little spoon on the end and stuck it in the cut he'd made, pushing it under the object and trying to lift it out. After a few moments of seesaw prying, there was a small sucking noise. He heard one little *pop!* and then a tiny silver capsule less than one quarter inch long and as big around as a pencil lead showed itself as it dropped from his skin. He only had one quick look at it as it rolled on the table top and fell to the floor.

Mica set the scalpel down and bent over to pick up the small object. He had it halfway back up to the table when he realized it was burning his fingers.

His lips formed an involuntary *Ouch!* and he dropped the slippery little silvery cylinder on the instrument tray. In seconds, the thing glowed red, redder, and then white-hot. He managed to throw up his hands just before the

tiny capsule flared blue-white and disappeared
in a blinding flash of light.

CHAPTER 5
Unblanked

<u>one</u>

Mica blinked, trying to resolve the spots in front of his eyes. There was just a small, tarnished hot spot on the tray where the capsule had been. It took only a few moments to move the instruments around to cover the grayish discoloration, wad the tissues, wipe up the blood specks on the table and the tray, clean off the knife and the pinchers, and then stuff all the tissues in his pocket. His hand was still leaking blood, so he wadded tissues around the incision, wrapped that awkwardly in gauze and shoved his hand in his pocket.

And just in time; there were only a few heartbeats before the Doc returned, his attention automatically going back to Mica's chart. By the time he looked up, Mica was leaning against the wall.

"What's the matter?" The Doc was giving him his friendly-but-concerned look.

"Oh, nothing." Mica laughed unsteadily. "Didn't you feel that tremor? I think we had a four or a five."

"Naah," the Doc scoffed, "just the elevators. Everybody thinks quakes all the time. It's actually just cheap construction." He had started writing something on Mica's top sheet when Mica saw the blood drops, three of them, not six inches in front of the Doc's foot.

Mica moved closer, like he wanted his own look at the chart, and managed to turn one shoe sole on the spots, grinding them into the floor tiles like he was putting out a cigarette.

"Anything new and significant?" he asked.

Doctor Bruce shook his head, holding out the latest notes for him to see, "Nope." The Doc paused, "Almost a year and a half since the accident, already..."

Mica stiffened. "Yes," he said.

"Any more headaches? Migraines? Dizziness? Spells of disorientation?"

Mica answered no to each. There was a particularly long pause before answering to "spells of disorientation", but the Doc let it pass. And he didn't ask the usual ones about illusions or hallucinations. He closed the folder with a little shrug.

"Disgustingly healthy. Call me next week for the urine results. DON'T FORGET."

"It isn't ME that forgets," Mica responded, gamely getting back into the wisecracking mode.

"And remember, eat vegetables. Fruit. Certain kinds of fish. You EAT LIGHT—"

"—and you EAT RIGHT!" Mica finished for him.

The Doc handed over a brochure with a picture of a salmon, an apple and a bunch of green celery on the front panel, "It's all in here."

Mica nodded.

"What?" The Doc was looking at him.

Mica could see the Doc had radar. He was

smart, picking up that there was something else unsaid.

Mica looked at his little hamster of a doctor, thinking how crazy it would sound, him operating on himself, and then the silver thing popping out and then disappearing like a tiny supernova. Crazy or not, he was going to blurt out the entire thing, but the phone rang again. The Doc sighed, gesturing to the phone, and waving goodbye.

"Thanks for the drawing, Mica. I LOVE it!!"

"No prob; anything for a guy like you, Doc."

Mica waved with his good hand and managed to get out the door. He blinked, looking around in the hallway and suddenly overwhelmed by off-balance sensations. He felt like his systems were running on overload, too hot and too cold at the same time. He wasn't sure he would be able to get out of the office, much less to the elevators and out of the building. He bumped into the wall. A blur moved by; it was only Peggy, head buried in a stack of files, not looking up, but still teasing over her shoulder. "We found where you hid the donuts, naughty boy!" she said.

Mica gave her a weak smile, but it wasn't necessary, she continued on past with her own little stack of problems. Ten huge, yawing steps and he was at the front desk, definitely having problems now looking out on a room that was streaked and blurred with colors and images that were disjointed and not at all what reality was supposed to be. He was glad he'd worn dark jeans because his hand felt soaked in his pocket.

"Need a check?" he managed to ask Janie. She put her hand over the receiver for a moment and shook her head. "We'll bill you," she said, and she smiled.

He started past, but she held up a small white card and waved it at him. He managed to get over to it, taking it from her with his good hand.

"Your next appointment on the front," she said. She pointed to the card, "My home phone number on the back." He hoped his face was friendly enough to pass as he thanked her and somehow made his way out of the reception room, past the antediluvian insect stares from the ancient ones still sunning themselves under the reading lamps while they waited for their turn with the Doc.

two

Once he was outside the waiting room, Mica staggered down the hall toward the elevator, weaving and bouncing off the walls like a Mission Street drunk. He fell to his knees, crawling for a few yards before he was able to regain his feet. For him, reality and fantasy were interwoven in a rough and frightening texture of new sensations. Daylight poured in from a window at the end of the hall, impossibly bright liquid gold bouncing off the gray slush-textured walls. Sounds that were colored like an unruly English garden pouring from the other side of a wall fronting a New Wave exercise clinic, and from himself came the booming rhythms of heartbeat and blood flow, the snap of neurons, the unsteady thump of his own footfalls. He could see clearly now, but he couldn't focus in a world which had gone mad with an excess of definition and detail. He could follow footprints in the carpet, hundreds of trails, by the shape and pattern of heel and sole long passed.

He staggered toward the elevators and wondered at the fingerprint whorls on the metal plates around the elevator buttons. He pushed the down button, wondering as his own imprint overlapped and partly replaced the one before it.

There was an immediate gong like a brass temple bell, and the doors slid open. He walked into the elevator on what felt like twenty-foot-high stilt legs and pushed the button marked "L" for lobby and a burning white square lit around the letter. The doors closed and the elevator continued up. He jabbed the "L" button, but it was no use. The elevator whirred like a robot eagle, carrying him up toward the top floor, which was listed as "21".

When it finally stopped, the doors slid open and a white-coated man entered. He was tall, with a shock of snow-white hair and pinkish skin, which seemed to glow in ruddy good health. Probably in his late sixties, Mica thought. The man didn't push any of the buttons on the elevator. Instead, he looked over at Mica and smiled. Mica frowned, looking away, gazing at the incredibly intricate patterns on the floor.

"Get some sugar in your blood," the white-haired doctor said, flicking an imaginary hair off his white coat. "You'll feel better."

Mica realized he must look worse than he imagined. "How did you—?" he started.

The man shrugged and gave a confidential chuckle. "I'm Dr. Railsbach. You either gave blood or you had the full rectal inspection. Take two aspirins and call us in the morning. Ha-ha." He gave a dull little laugh at his own joke.

Mica was clearly in no mood for mild banter. His vision blurred, and the man took a closer look at him as he staggered against the wall.

"Wait a minute. You certainly do not look well, young man. And look, your hand is bleeding. Maybe you better come to my office. Lie down a minute." If Mica had been in better shape, he might have paused to wonder that the doors of this elevator, which had gone up when he wished to go down, now refused to close.

"I'll be all right..." he muttered. His tongue felt like clay; he was barely able to get the words out. He pushed his shoulders back, took a deep breath, tried to rally. But the man reached out and touched his arm, and Mica felt enveloped in physical weakness. He fell into the man's arms, his knees giving way as darkness collapsed his vision into a long, narrow tunnel.

The white-coated man with the white hair caught him neatly, supporting him and leading him off the elevator. Somewhere in the back of his mind, Mica heard singing, a sweet boys' choir, and as his feet dragged his numbing body along, the music kept telling him everything was going to be well.

<u>three</u>

The hallway was dimly lit and deserted. Mica staggered along, one arm around the man's shoulder. They stopped before a door that was like any other, and the man half-propped him against the wall and leaned against him while he fished in his pockets and came up with a large key ring. He found a big brass key, inserted it in the cylindrical lock and swung open the door.

The deserted reception room was dark and musty. The white-coated man half-dragged Mica through it and down a dimly lit corridor that seemed vaguely familiar. Mica could see it was the same floor plan as the Doc's suite, the examining rooms in an outer circle that took advantage of the windows, and the services in the center core.

Mica was feeling weaker and weaker, as if contact with the man was draining something vital from him; now he couldn't even stand without support. He allowed himself to be half-carried into one of the examining rooms. On his second fuzzy impression, Mica thought it looked more like a surgical room. There were big circular lights over a table, lights that were off now, their blank gray lenses staring down at him.

"I'm sorry," Dr. Railsbach said, "that we don't have more comfortable accommodations. You can rest here." He helped Mica onto the table and leaned over as if he were about to adjust something. At that moment, a phone jangled in another room. Mica noted that a light winked on the phone in their room. *Efficiency in repetitive design.*

The phone continued to ring. The man hesitated, seemingly annoyed by the interruption. He eyed Mica, his look seeming to say, *You going to be all right for a moment?*

"Get the phone," Mica slurred, giving him a sloppy wave of his hand. "Doctors always have to get the phone." His lips felt numb, the words sticking to his tongue.

"Mmmm. Guess you're right." The white-haired man gave him a speculative look and, apparently satisfied by what he saw, hurried over to the phone. He picked up the receiver, which was on a long cord, and went into the next room, closing the door as far as it would go with the cord in the way.

After a moment or so, Mica heard muttering from the next room. *Doctors,* Mica thought to himself, *see how they run.* He was going to have to do some more Horny strips featuring the Doc; there was a wealth of material there, just waiting to be mined. He sighed, feeling a little stronger.

Mica rubbed his eyes and looked around the room. He shifted a little on the table, trying to find a more comfortable position. He finally rolled over on his back, and as he did so, he heard a metallic clunk. He swiveled his neck to see a heavy arm strap. It had fallen from the table and was swinging in a little arc below him. Mica jerked his arm away and raised his head a fraction. There was another strap in the

108

middle. That's what had made him so uncomfortable. He saw a third wide strap down near his ankles. He tried to sit up. In his condition, he nearly rolled off the table and fell to the floor. He overcorrected and fell on his back, knocking the second strap off the table with another harsh little clunk.

Come on, Mica-boy, he urged himself. *You're a creative guy, do something creative.*

He propped himself on his elbows and sat up slowly and carefully. He managed to get one foot off the table and then the other, letting go too quickly, standing there duck-legged with his arms out like a drunken monkey, flailing for balance. The dizziness subsided. *There. He had it.* He lurched around the room, giving bleary attention to an intimate painting of an orchid, up close and personal, pale yellow stamen and pistil thrusting from the softly vulnerable yellow and purple petals.

"Ha Hoo, the sex life of the orchids," he muttered to no one in particular. "Penthouse for plants."

The low conversation interrupted his scatterbrained thoughts. He'd completely forgotten the doctor in the next room. The white-haired man was now arguing on the phone. Mica lurched to his side of the door and listened. The man's voice carried through, sounding peeved and impatient.

"Yes, I've got him RIGHT HERE, RIGHT NOW...no need to worry...look, he's my EMO..."

That was enough for Mica. He stared

wildly around the room and noticed for the first time that there was a door on the opposite side. He staggered out this door and made his way down the hallway, circling in the opposite direction.

<u>four</u>

Mica had nearly reached the reception area. He only had to cross one pool of bluish light coming from an open door, and he was there. As he passed the doorway, he glanced into the room—and was astonished to see his Sally, centered on a flat TV monitor that glowed in the center of the otherwise darkened room!

"Sally...and Anne Mae..." he whispered in awe. With a will of their own, his feet carried him into the room. He slowly approached the screen. All he could make out was that they were in a dark space. The only illumination came from their figures, which radiated strangely with a soft glow.

He touched the screen with his hand. "W-what has happened to you? What have they done to you?"

As if in response to his fearful whispers, Sally raised her head and looked directly at him. Then she reached out as if she too would touch the screen from the other side. But before she could complete the gesture, there was a sharp bark from behind Mica.

"No!" Railsbach yelled. "What are you doing, young man?!"

"That's my wife and daughter! You've got my wife in there!"

Railsbach snapped off the monitor and turned on the lights in the same gesture.

"You're really sick! You're hallucinating!"

"I saw them!" Mica shouted.

"Here, look. I'll show you." Railsbach's voice took on a placating tone. His fingers made a blurred movement over a keyboard at his side, and the monitor snapped on again. A woman and her child appeared on the screen. There might have been a vague resemblance to Sally and Anne Mae, but they were obviously different people.

"It's a simple isolation experiment," Railsbach said. "You've had a bad shock. Come, please now, lie down in the next room."

Mica retreated as he advanced, until the only thing between them was the thin monitor mounted on the wall. With one quick movement, Mica moved to pull it from the wall.

"No! That equipment is priceless!" Railsbach shouted, but it was too late. The plasmic window crashed to the floor and smashed into shards that softened into gel and bubbled fiercely, letting off acrid fumes. And in that instant, Mica ran out the door and down the hall. Rather than following him, Dr. Railsbach chose to hover over the computer keyboard. His fingers briefly danced over the keys, shutting off any possibility that his two female captives might escape. Once that was done, he started after Mica.

It was only a lead of a few seconds, but Railsbach's floor plan was a duplicate of the Doc's place, and Mica quickly made his way back to the elevator. He pushed the elevator button, and to his enormous relief, the doors opened immediately. He lurched inside and pushed the "L" button.

five

The door mechanism whirred and the silvery doors themselves began to close. But at the last second, just when he thought he'd made it, a hand slipped in. The doors stopped and reversed themselves, and the white-haired man stepped in the elevator.

"Ah-Hah! *There* you are!" He spoke with a hearty joviality.

"I feel *much* better now." It felt like a parody of his banter with the Doc, but Mica's words dropped like bitter acid from his mouth. He didn't feel like playing games.

"You don't *look* better," the man said.

"Well, I *am* better."

"I don't know. You'd better come back to my—"

Railsbach was interrupted by the doors, which now began to slide shut. He reached his hand out to press the OPEN DOOR button, and was surprised when Mica knocked it away. It was a feeble gesture, but just enough to knock Railsbach's hand off target. Railsbach angrily jabbed again, but his motion was a fraction of a second late. The doors had shut and the elevator now accelerated smoothly downward.

Mica moved to the opposite side of the little cube. Railsbach eyed him for a moment, rubbing his fingers where Mica had slapped them. "That was rude."

"I didn't hurt you."

Railsbach made up his mind, starting forward toward Mica.

"You stay over there." Mica's voice sounded hoarse and threatening in his own ears. Railsbach paused.

"Why?"

"You just stay over there!" Mica realized he was shouting. He could feel the elevator moving steadily downward. He sensed that every second now was in his favor. The too-bright numbers overhead were counting down from 21.

"That's ridiculous," Railsbach said, taking another cautious step toward Mica. His hand started to come up; he was going to touch Mica again. Mica cowered back as far as he could, bunching himself into the corner.

And in the next moment, before Railsbach could touch him, the elevator stopped and the doors slid open. Mica looked at the numbers overhead and his heart sank. *They were only on 16!*

But then two doctors stepped into the elevator. They puffed pipes and held thin briefcases, their attitude daring anyone to question their right to smoke on the elevator. Mica quickly slipped to another corner, jostling one of them as he went by. The man frowned and brushed an imaginary ash from his sleeve, but he didn't say anything.

Mica stared across the two newcomers to the white-haired man who had called himself a doctor. Even as he jockeyed to keep distance between himself and Railsbach, he wondered what he was doing. *What the hell was wrong with him? Had he just hallucinated again, the same way he had in Copenhagen? Maybe the poor guy was just trying to help.* But then, even as Mica's feelings softened, a weird *happening* occurred, something that shook his belief in his own eyesight. As he gazed across the elevator at the face of the kindly old white-haired doctor, something terribly wrong began to happen to Railsbach's face. There was a physical *chattering*, a loosening of the flesh which caused a bewildering warp of the man's features, almost as if they were being tugged alternately and swiftly between two poles.

Even as Mica watched, Railsbach's face was changing from that of a kindly old doctor to another face, that of a coarse-featured man in his 30's. This second face was swarthy, and heavily bearded. This face had bad teeth and a bald spot setting off an unruly mop of black hair, while the other one had perfect white teeth and waves of snowy hair. *Doctor-worker, doctor-worker, doctor-worker,* the features warping back and forth like tortured putty, like a warped and oily vision of a popular shaving commercial for one blade does all faces. Speth, the assassin, would have been smugly amused—he'd long argued earthside was no place for amateurs.

For his part, Mica was sure he was losing his mind. He stared, wanting to scream. This was Copenhagen all over again, only a thousand times worse. He was convinced the hallucinations were creeping in, surrounding him, and driving him mad. *He should give up now, before he hurt someone. They should put him away. They would put him away.*

Railsbach saw the look of bewildered alarm on Mica's face, and with that, a frightened look came over his own features. Railsbach quickly lifted one hand to his face, pushing and slapping. After a moment the chattering subsided, and he looked like a man who was simply rubbing his own jaw. He shot a triumphant glance across at Mica. But the damage had been done; he could see his prey was beyond recall and would have to be reeled in by force. He tried to push past the two doctors, but Mica circled away from him, and Railsbach found himself still with the two doctors between them. Worse, the two men were now visibly annoyed; and since the white-haired man had made the last disrupting and antisocial move in their cramped quarters, they focused their angry attention on him.

"What is your problem, anyway?" one of them rumbled disagreeably. When the white-haired man didn't answer, the doctor addressed a larger audience, "Rude people, I tell you. What is this world coming to?"

His companion, obviously agreeing, gave the white-haired man an icy stare. It was more than enough. Railsbach glared at Mica for a moment, and then he crumbled, realizing by Mica's horrified stare that his face was twitching again. Railsbach slapped a hand to his forehead, as a woman might try a quick fix on a fallen hairdo, but he could see it wasn't going to work. The chattering was on the upswing again, this time broadening into

117

something Mica could hardly comprehend, sliding from doctor to worker and then through to a demonic presence the horror of which many artists have attempted to draw but none have ever captured. *Doctor-worker-demon, doctor-worker-demon, doctor-worker-demon,* the man's tortured features flickering back and forth under a now unruly wig of white fibers that waved like thin and dangerous undersea worms. Mica saw the creature—whatever it was—hit the buttons, all of them, with the flat of its hand, a hand that now chattered back and forth between normalcy and a twisted and clawed paw. The elevator stopped and the thing rushed off in a panic.

"Say, what was that all about?" one of the doctors asked, aiming his question at the air and studiously ignoring the one person who could have answered.

For his part, Mica sagged against the wall in his little corner of the elevator and tried to slow his own ragged breathing.

"I can't wait," the deeply tanned doctor said, "to retire. Two more years of this idiocy and I'm in Carmel, tending my CDs and putting for birdies."

"Lucky you. I've got another ten, at least."

Doc Tanface nodded sympathetically, "Bitches will set you back." They were old friends, they could shorthand around each other's lives.

"Do you—," Mica started. "Have *either* of you ever heard of EMO? A project, maybe, or a disease...?"

118

His voice trailed off, squeezed to nothing by the hard looks they gave him. *They were doctors, for Christsake, they didn't dispense free advice and information to sweaty riffraff on elevators.* The elevator gong sounded and the doors slid open, revealing the marble expanse of the lobby. The doctors retracted their bleak stares and walked away, not having said a word to him.

six

Without a warning light or bell, or a moment's hesitation, the elevator doors swiftly and silently began to close. Mica managed to jam one hand in to stop them, and had to insert his body between the doors and push hard to gain a necessary few inches so he could squeeze through to the lobby.

He spilled out onto the dark marble square floor. It was a moment before he could manage to regain his feet and make his wobbly way to the directory. He dragged his finger over the dark glass, whispering to himself, "21, 21, 21, come on, hit me. 21. Lucky Lady, 21st floor." By that time his finger had wandered through the list to the end of the directory. "There is no 21st floor."

Badly shaken, he looked around the lobby. It was nearly deserted. There was just an old man in a gray uniform with darker gray piping down the pants, standing by the information desk. One puffy-faced nurse, dressed in white, hurried in through the revolving doorway and made her way toward the bank of elevators.

Mica realized the elevator he'd just left was still there, standing like an open invitation. As the nurse moved quickly toward it, he forced himself to go back, to have one last look. She was holding the Door Open button for him.

"Get in," she ordered.

Mica poked his head in, saw that somehow, unaccountably, the steel rows of buttons now only numbered up to 20. He ducked back out as she made her move. One strong hand grabbed him, the fingers like steel, pulling him inexorably into the mousetrap.

Again, instinctively, he lashed out at the hand, which had snared him. She recoiled as if scalded by hot lead, letting go of his arm and screaming as she clutched her own, though there wasn't nearly enough force to warrant such a reaction.

"No 21st floor," he stammered, feeling stupid and lucky as he backed away from the elevator. He got halfway across the lobby, walking backwards and looking all around as he went. He was nearly to the door when the lobby man slipped smoothly out of the shadows to confront him. Mica sensed hesitation in the fellow's movement. As he raised his fist to backhand the lobby man, the old man's chin quivered and he moved aside. Mica moved forward like he was going to complete the blow, and the man jumped backwards. And in the next moment Mica bolted through the door and half staggered, half ran toward his waiting speedster. As he got in, he dimly noted that the old black bum and his portable cardboard house were now nowhere to be seen. *Not that the ancient derelict would have been any help in the first place.*

121

CHAPTER 6
Road Kill

<u>one</u>

The multiplex grid of overhead cameras pulled in an image of Speth for the lackeys in control, catching his speeding vehicle from the tiny view-scam camera stuck on a graffiti-laden freeway sign. Half of the screen was filled with NORFDICK SPAN sprayed across reflector-light white letters 10 EAST. Still, it was easy to spot the *Old Speedballer* as he flashed through the bottom half of the view. Speth the assassin was enjoying his heavily modified gray 700 series BMW sedan, as he did all the luxuries his class and rank provided him. The expensive Italian suits. The thin gold watch. The $400 Swiss-made shoes with leather soft as butter. Speth delighted in the irony; he was steel wrapped in human flesh and then sheathed in fine-spun cottons, wools and silk, the best this world had to provide.

Speth pushed his hair and examined his coat in the flip-down mirror. He approved the narrow face, hawklike nose, smooth olive skin, and the low hairline. His hair was short and oddly blond-white, lifted up in a crew cut on top and swept back on the sides in a longer affectation that resembled the old ducktail of the 1950's.

Speth had Berlioz turned up until the wonderful chords made his carapace shudder under his human coating of flesh. *The Symphonie Fantastique, what a wondrous musical thunder! That and Wagner's Rings. They could take their sweet Mozart and their mechanical Brahms—give him Hector and Richard at their best!*

Speth wondered once again if all the great *sap* musical madmen had translated to the light, or if the dark masters had a few of them locked away in some secret chamber, spinning hour after hour of incredible harmonics for the pleasure of the select few. There was no way for him to know, not at his level. Still, over the eons he'd heard a pendragon or two grumbling and grunting their way through some unknown melody, and it had been cause enough for suspicion.

The overheads locked onto him, and control beamed in with a discreet beep and a soft announcement flare on his instrument panel. He could have used mind-lock, but his habit was to employ the more cumbersome sensual links provided by his human coat. *Live like a sap in sapland.* He turned the music down and picked up the gray, fist-sized telephone.

"Speth here."

Control rattled on and on with inconsequential details. Speth shook his head. "Get to the point, drones," he snarled. Not that he needed to know more. Some incompetent had let a sheep out of the pen. And not just *some incompetent! This time, the smugly scientific Dr. Railsbach had his own blue*

123

cahones in the pincher! Unless his analog was wildly inaccurate, Speth figured it was another of Railsbach's precious EMO's. Railsbach—or Kelp, as Speth thought of him—believed he was so blessed clever; yet Speth figured the fusty little bio-demon had at least a half-millennium to go before his highly theoretical experiments would begin to show results, if ever. How Kelp had gotten Fern's ear and the attendant massive funding for the EMO project was beyond his wildest imagination.

In spite of all the nasty whisperings about how the conflict was soon to be reduced to a human whimper, Speth knew at the base of his two hearts that it was all the same old story: another rogue human was on the loose and the time had come for the wolf man to reel him in.

Speth cut out the reception, replacing the phone receiver and hitting the isolation shell before control could handcuff him with their stifling special orders. Railsbach would have put out a Treat-Kindly, trying to preserve his experiment.

Special orders! Speth's lip curled and he spat involuntarily, the acidic glob of moisture bubbling and steaming as it ran down the inside of the window. *Don't do this, don't do that, handle it this way!* Speth knew, by the very fact that control was calling him, they'd run out of other options. *Didn't Sir Fern understand, rogue humans with their unpredictable powers fueled by their runaway emotions were the only real threat that existed?!* Apparently Fern did not...for while assassins and jailers all over the planet expended enormous resources to keep the human race blanked and null, Fern had empowered Railsbach to do just the opposite, if only in a limited scope. Speth believed Railsbach had fallen under the spell of ancient rogue spirits like Machiavelli and Richard III of England, and more modern emotives like Hitler, Stalin and Pol Pot. Railsbach's scheme was to create a so-called *super-rogue,* the *ubermenchen schwartzen,* the Prophesied Dark One who would lead billions of saps like lemmings off the cliffs of fury and despair to their own destruction. *Sapcrap,* Speth muttered to himself. *It was all sapcrap.*

Translation for an assassin was simple. It was a form of one-on-one combat, a battle which, once enjoined, was never lost. Speth, for all his scornful madness, had a certain grudging respect for individual *saps.* In his younger days, there were humans—several of them—who had crept out from under the blanket. One had even showed the audacity to damage his coat with a bronze battle-ax before he'd been able to squeeze the poor creature's mind to pulp.

Forget fancy experiments like EMO, sweet trickery promising to tumble untold masses of humans down into the black fold. It was all too much for Speth. He only operated one way. *Run down the sheep.* Find a way to cut their throats, drink the blood of their final agony, and then flog their stunned and startled spirits on the downward path before they could collect themselves and think to fly. Let the final

125

weigh-in (if there ever was one) sort out who deserved to rise or fall. And on to the next assignment.

Speth's car accelerated effortlessly with his thoughts. Traffic was light, and he soon flashed along at over 90, the BMW slipping easily as a gray shark through the slower traffic. He swiftly passed a black-and-white, giving the two policemen a casual finger as he raced by. The police were even more heavily blanked than the general population; they ignored him, as he knew they would. *Stupid sap cops! Pigs, they were called by many of their own citizenry. The term of derision seemed oddly inappropriate to Speth, the pig being a hoofed animal and hence in demonic lore suspected of at least some degree of superiority.* Still, he didn't like the fact that the arm of the law, weak as it was, was so close to the action. Blanking could only do so much. A blood-splattering such as he had in mind would jerk them back to reality, and they would be on the scene sooner than he'd like. He shrugged off his reserve. *One way or the other, it made no difference. Surely as Lucifer had dared the pearly gates, he could null them into lumps of obsidian if he had to.*

He turned up the Berlioz and hit the gas, and found himself thinking about the other side as the music churned up memories of a dark slide and the bubbly pits of his youth. *Burn bags, but that had been a long time ago!* Nothing back there for him any longer. Better the cold alienation of this oxygen-poisoned world. Here, he had his fine clothes, his car, his golden trinkets and obsidian jewelry. Here was his high-rise apartment, looking out over the western sector of the city, and his job, making this outpost colony a safer, better place for those who would follow to scrub the planet clean and make it ready for joyous, open sulfide-methane breathing.

Speth imagined the newly unblanked EMO in his little Alfa speeding along not a mile in front of him. He could visualize that little car spinning and rolling out of control, until all that remained of the rogue human was a quivering and broken puppet that had been dragged in a red smear for 200 yards or so along the unrelenting cement pavement. The image pleased him. Speth put his mind to the metal and his big gray sedan leapt forward.

two

For one brief moment, Sally had seen Mica's face looming at her out of nowhere, his hand outstretched. It looked like he was peering over one edge of the wall of the tree house, in the few feet space where the boards stopped below the canvas roof overhead. He looked rattled and bewildered. She had sensed the presence of someone else in that area before, someone she thought of vaguely as *the doctor*. Now she was certain she and Anne Mae were being observed.

She wondered how she might be able to see better, and the idea came to her that a television set projected distant images. In no time at all, she imagined a television set swinging like a planter with an ornate macramé hanger that she herself had woven in the months while waiting for Anne Mae to be born.

Images started to flash across the screen, along with a scattering of narrative voices whose transmission overlapped and interfered with each other. The images were from all over Los Angeles and the surrounding area, and the voices were speaking a language so guttural and alien that she wondered if it was speech at all.

Anne Mae, who had been stirring restlessly, sat up and rubbed her eyes.

"Cool, Mom," she said in sleepy surprise, "You brought out the little TV from the kitchen."

"Not exactly, honey..."

"Some car chase movie…Look, Mom, *Dad's in that car!*"

"I see him."

"He's not driving too well." Even on the small screen, it was easy to see Mica was flying across lanes like a bug who'd been sipping too much wine.

"And it looks like somebody's after him. We've got to concentrate on helping Daddy."

"How do we do that, Mom?"

"I'm not sure, Anne Mae."

Anne Mae was on her feet, yelling at the screen, "Daddy, look out!" She stamped her foot in frustration, "Mom, that dark car is going to cut him off!"

Sally and Anne Mae watched the small screen in hopeless dismay as the bloody accident poured itself all over the highway.

three

Now less than a half mile ahead of Speth, Mica's small car was weaving across the lanes as the Alfa unsteadily butterflied its way west, heading toward the underpass where the freeway turned into the heavily congested Route 1, a four-lane highway that ran north along the ocean at the base of the crumbling Santa Monica cliffs. Mica had missed the last two off-ramps, had forgotten his intention was to go into the office where he would settle down and try to churn out his latest Horny idea. There was no way that was going to happen now.

He saw the freeway as a blurred stream of traffic, an impossible tangle of streaking colored shapes and glittering chrome punctuated by super-loud horn blares. Hard-slapping semi wheels, higher than his head, churned by on both sides of the car. There were 18 wheelers on both sides of him for a moment, and then he was alone again as they whizzed past, air horns blasting in protest. He jerked the steering wheel as a Dryer's Ice Cream truck hedged its bets by giving him two full lanes on the left and it nearly wasn't enough, the Alfa sliding behind the square zebra-striped truck with inches to spare.

Speth's BMW approached and then was gliding alongside him before he saw it. At least, for a moment, there was nothing, and then Mica saw some sort of fuzzy, dark presence. He was able to brake, and the BMW slid into the lane in front of him, and then crossed over and went on ahead.

In the lane directly in front of Mica, a battered old pickup truck chugged along, the only vehicle on the road going slower than he was. It was faded robin's egg blue, one of those south-of-the-border numbers engineered with high hopes and sagging, home-built plywood sides. The bed of the truck held an unsteady load of moisture-dense logs and flailing green pepper tree branches that were taller than the truck itself was long. The *dos obreros* were driving along, minding their own *enchiladas,* and then there was the vague dark shape again, cutting in front of the pickup, and suddenly the old truck was veering directly into Mica's path.

Mica yanked the steering wheel, and the Alfa spun wildly out of control as the faded blue pickup toppled over, spraying the freeway with soft, heavy pepper tree logs and a screen of branches.

In a flash, the road was littered with bloody mayhem. A log rammed through the window of the pickup, and another through the front windshield of a gray Saturn, impacting with a middle-aged woman, blood and pearls flying through the air. Logs rolled under car wheels and bounced off grills and metal roofs. The *obreros* were caught full force by a heavy black Cadillac, both vehicles painting an oil smear on the road and then belching into flame before they came to a halt.

In his rearview, Speth caught a glimpse of Mica's Alfa, which was spinning wildly out of control, in the center of the death and violence. It finally flopped over on the pavement just as the assassin imagined it, sliding and skidding off the road into an ivy covered embankment. It rested there, upside down with its wheels spinning.

"Yesss!", Speth hissed in delight, pumping a fist in the air like a successful pro quarterback. He quickly braked and swung the BMW to the center divider. He rolled down his rear window to get a better look at the damage.

As he had expected, the humans were fast getting to this one, swarming like bugs on *sapcrap*. A helicopter was fluttering overhead in tight circles, radioing in the damage and calling for fire and police backup. The copter pilot feathered in lower, trying to get a bead on Mica's car.

Control had tapped the overhead camera, and Speth watched the feed from his console. Smoke was boiling from the overturned Alfa's engine. It looked bad. Speth's screen clicked over as an angle from one of their own pole-mounted mini-observers gave a closer view, the lens cranking in to a fairly tight shot on the passenger side door. And then an unexpected and very bad thing happened.

It caused Speth to gape, and yellowish spittle gathered unnoticed on his lower lip. The door on the passenger side of the Alfa was being smashed open, an inch at a time, from the inside. It was a methodical hammering, the effort of someone still very much alive. Finally, the door flew open, a pair of legs

132

showed briefly, and Mica tumbled out. He staggered to his feet, looking battered and bruised, but otherwise not much the worse for wear.

four

Speth got out of his own car, staring back at the accident with a lingering sense of disbelief. *He'd vectored that accident, himself. No one could just walk away from it.* He had a brief, uneasy suspicion of intervention, but quickly pushed the bad sulfur out of his mind. The white ones were long gone and far away. *It was simple,* he thought scornfully, *this was one of those sap sheep with nine lives.* He stood erect, taking his time. *Let's see if he has ten.* He turned sideways, raising one arm full length and pointing his fingers. It was an out-of-context stance and a seemingly odd gesture for that time and place. But no one stopped to say anything. No one even noticed him from among the ant swarm of drivers and passengers in the cars that were negotiating their way through the maze of logs and shattered debris. And that was blanking as it should be.

With all the deliberation of a skilled hunts-fellow, Speth lined his arm, pointing straight, two hundred yards back along the freeway to where Mica stood. He was about to translate the rogue EMO once and for all when an onlooker stepped in his direct line of energy. Speth barely noticed who it was—some old black guy dressed like a bum. And then a beefy CHP officer replaced the first onlooker. Now both of them were talking to Mica, a barrier of human flesh between Speth and his prey.

Speth lowered his arm, suddenly impatient

134

for this to be over. *Too many complications!* In the old days, when the battle was full-pitched, it would have signified other operatives were in force in the area. Knowing that was impossible couldn't entirely ease his mind. Old habits die hard; he had scars from the white ones that would never heal. He blew out a quick breath of the thin, poisonous air and spat with the ease of old habit on the roadside gravel. He had to grab a little calm here. *He was being crazy superstitious! Crazy as an old breed-bitch! Crazy as a prophet-loon, wandering in the bubbling plains of Neb!* He sighed, looking at the ground to clear his vision for another shot. He looked up, zeroing in on Mica once again. And what he saw this time upset him more than anything had since he'd squeezed into this assignment a full 1,400 sun cycles ago.

Mica Harris, the rogue human, was looking his way. It was a direct, significant stare. Worse, he was pointing in Speth's direction, pointing across the freeway directly at him! The CHP officer was shaking his head like he didn't see anything. But the CHP didn't matter to Speth. *Not an hour since Mica had plucked the cylinder from his thumb, and the rogue human was already shedding his blanking! Mica Harris could see him!* Feeling naked and decloaked, Speth unconsciously retreated a step, bumping into the door of his car. He cursed as he felt the back of his coat catch on the metal corner of the open door, the expensive fabric tearing before he could pull away.

"How can he—?" he asked of no one. "Merde, merde, *MERDE*!" Speth jumped into the BMW and mentalled the gas. The car squirreled a little, the tires smoking as they went from the loose roadside gravel to the solid bite of the pavement.

This was not good for many reasons. Now there would be the endless reports, the hateful grilling, the layers of soft-hoofed officialdom whining, *Why, Why, WHY?!* Speth realized he should have forced the translation by dropping the intervening *saps* and zedding the rogue when he had the chance. He'd never have such an easy shot again. Now silly Kelp, the disgusting Doctor Railsbach, would be back in the picture with his precious EMO this and EMO that and all his fancy hoof-step airs. Speth wound down his dark gray window and spat. Long ago, his sire had taught him the only good *sap* was a dead *sap*. He'd have to be more careful, but the good Doctor Railsbach's brand of modern thinking was going to endure a serious setback. When all was said and done, this rogue *sap* was going down the old way.

CHAPTER 7
Demon Love Song

one

From a hawk's-eye view a thousand feet overhead, the hills of the Santa Monica Mountains above Brentwood resembled a fairyland in the last witching moments when dusk intermingled gold and ebony shadows and the sun's last burst comforted the darkening land, giving a magical haziness to the castle-like mansions and the wide formal gardens carved between the raw stone outcroppings and the brush-clotted ravines. This evening the dying sun set last, as it always did, on the Fern estate, coating the huge brick manor and the outlying servant's quarters, the stables and the motorcar garages and all the expanse of rolling grass and hedges in tones of red-gold and ocher. The sunset blaze was wasted, however, on those who lived there, for those inside were of the inclination that fire, real fire, was of molten stone and smelled rich with fetid sulfur, sweet arsenic and the multiplex wonder that was brimstone.

Inside Albert Fern's oak-paneled conference room, in a somewhat smaller room just off the huge study that had passed for a ballroom not long before, ten elders in expensive dark suits were pushing back from a long mahogany table, ready to walk away from what had been a long and intensely grueling

137

meeting. They stood on their feet, their exos creaking and ancient coats chattering slightly from what was for them an extended contact with the noxious oxygenated atmosphere. They each maintained balance, however, attempting the impression that the long meeting had been nothing; it could have taken twice as long, they would have endured, for to show even the slightest weakness was to risk subsumption, no one to be carried for blind pity when the cause was so thinly stretched across this dangerous new territory. And so they stretched their carapaces with exaggerated nonchalance, shuffled their papers carefully and placed them in their dark leather cases before hurrying to make their exit.

Sir Albert rose to his feet as quickly as possible, without seeming to rush them. Throughout the entire meeting, he'd only listened to their usual nettling wails about costs and effectiveness with half an ear. Of course, by now the Copenhagen affair was common knowledge, but he'd been hoping against hope that news of their unblanked EMO hadn't leaked back otherside—and, apparently, it had not.

Now standing, Albert pulled down his vest, which had a tendency to ride up over his coat. He coughed politely, "It has been long, and not all pleasant, but thank you for attending."

He was rewarded with a handful of nods from the dozen. The rest were silent, deep within their shells and not available for reading. Still, they were old rivals, and Albert knew how to decode this pack. He was going to have to stiffen them. "Please recognize your material presence will be required one month hence, as usual." He spoke with the command tone, no waver or hint in his voice that there might not be another meeting, no acceptance of the fact that it was entirely within their discretion to strip him of everything.

This time there was a mutter of assent from his guests, a few more nods. Albert began to feel his luck was still holding; he was going to squeak through this one. He closed his tired and burning eyes and listened to the sound of their blackskin briefcases snapping shut and the shuffle of their feet on the parquet floor.

As they started to file out of the room and into the adjoining study, Albert judiciously invaded personal space here and there to shake a hand and clap a stoop-shouldered back or two. After a brief, discreet pause, he and Felney followed the last of the Old Ones. By the time the two of them rounded the corner into the study, the large room was already empty. Still, he glanced around, pausing for an additional moment before opening up to Felney. No one remained but Zilch and Nilch, the twin guard dwarves, who were playing roughhouse with a little white dog they had plucked out of the brush somewhere near the west ravine, sparing it from a quick death at the jaws of some wild earth coyote or wildcat.

Albert's gaze lingered on the huge, roaring fireplace, which dominated the far end of the study. *Odd, how the Twelve's lingering old-*

demon smell could penetrate the fabric of his confidence! He gazed at his thin little helper.

"Felney, how think you, Old Gurpler?"

Felney paused for a moment, reflecting. "They are never very grateful, sire."

"Will I last until crop cutting?" Albert used the seasonal cycle analogy, the language of his father, for whom Felney had worked in those faded times now so distant as to be legend.

"They couldn't replace you, sir. Who could they possibly manufacture to fill your space?"

Felney's surface was openly indignant, and Albert had always accepted his coat at value. *A fawning little fellow, but steady in his loyalty, allowing that every rock had its melting point.* As for the fawning, a little less of that, and he might be a threat. *You can't have both worlds.* That had been his sire's advice, and he'd always listened to and loved his father, even to the day he'd hacked out his two great beating hearts and snatched the obsidian rod of power.

Albert sat in his favorite wing chair, the one with the crimson flower brocade print. From his position he could watch the last shrill vibrations of the sun retreat before the calm and massive beauty of the night. Felney rolled out a wooden chair and sat at the old rolltop desk. He inserted a worn brass key, and the desk swung open to both sides, revealing the marvel of electronic screens and displays. Adjusting his chair so he could easily work any of three keyboards, he programmed the necessary sequence and took over the sector watch from

140

control. Now all of Fern's vast command from the Colorado River to the ocean was under his watchful eye. He sighed, looking at the long column of upcoming translations crowding the preview screen, and winked up an ugly confrontation, two men arguing over a fender bender from the center divider on the intersection of the 101 and the Harbor Freeway. His hand hovered over Translate, waiting for the exact moment. The early evening promised fog, and high-speed crashes would play prominently in the night's events. By dawn the freeways would be speckled like a war zone with the blackened hulls of burned out cars and trucks. The two settled into their coats, Fern watching and puffing his pipe as Felney played across the lives of the *saps* foolish or unlucky enough to live in Southern California.

two

Sitting in the north-facing fork of the ancient California oak tree which spread its rigid, clawlike branches above the driveway of Mica's rancho, the minuscule auto mini-cam device looked down as an owl might on the informal old hacienda, the tiles of which were intermittently drenched in light and shadow as the moon dipped in and out of the low misty fog drifting in from the Pacific to this hilltop in the oldest section of Granada Hills. The rancho was located in the broken, rolling foothills north of the San Fernando Valley. The house and grounds made up 20-odd acres, very private and unimproved, the last parcel remaining from old-time movie actor James Cagney's original hunting lodge. In addition to the main house, which was *Spanish cozy* rather than rambling, there was a barn, a stable, a separate guest house, and a corral. Several neglected horse paths were overgrown with tall mustard grass and tumbleweed, the bushes drying to tinder balls at this time of year. The stable sagged, and although it still seemed serviceable, it now leaned to the southwest. Down the main trail was a small, spring-fed stream. The property continued on the other side of the stream in a series of rolling, grassy hills seeded at various random places with oak and eucalyptus trees.

Mica was sitting in the dark, in a rustic chair, not conscious that he was under the porch overhang and so out of range of the electronic peepers. He was sipping a beer and looking out over his pastures, over the tan September grass all silvery-gray in the light of the full moon. A dusty old radio on the tile patio floor next to him softly played the Righteous Brothers, singing, "You've lost that lovin' feeling..."

A horse whinnied. He looked up, heard Sally's faint, mocking laughter.

"Mica's a chicken, Mica's a chicken. *Bawk, bawk, bawk.* Chicken, chicken, chicken. I had chicken salad for lunch today..."

Mica stood and finished off his beer. He felt uncomfortable and off-guard. Sally had that unpredictable air about her, that way of goading him into things he didn't think he really wanted to do. He walked the short distance to the stable, and there she was, stunningly beautiful, backlit in the moonlight, her hair a blond halo around her face. She was radiant and so very, very alive. It was Sally, riding bareback and naked as the day she was born.

She smiled the moment she saw him, wheeling her horse around, and even got it to do a little prance for him.

"There you are, little man," she purred.

"Come on, Sal..." He was asking her to calm down, be a little normal about things; after all, he was supposed to be the slightly crazy artist. Still, he walked closer with the dust of the corral feeling cool and smooth on his bare feet, an odd sensation for him, and the timothy weed tickling the backs of his calves.

143

She chuckled. "What's the matter, oh Great Creator of the mighty Horny Hamster? Afraid you'll hurt yourself?"

"No, of course I'm not afraid." He felt he sounded like a pouting little boy. He would never admit it, but Sally was much more comfortable on a horse than he was. Flat out, she was a better rider.

"Well, then?"

He shook his head, giving her a rueful grin. His own horse waited patiently nearby, probably wondering what kind of game this was from these two special people in his life who were so full of complicated tricks and games. He prepared to throw one leg over the horse's back.

"Nuh, uh," she shook her head. "No, no, Mica-boy wonder. The bet was *au naturel,* my brave warrior."

Mica nodded slowly, staring at her, hands on his hips. Then he stepped out of his cutoff jeans, carefully folding them on the top bar of the fence. He gathered his nerve and leaped to a chopping block, and from there onto the back of his horse.

Sally had already spun her mount and was galloping away. He was mildly surprised to find he hadn't ruined himself for life.

"Come on, Blumper!" he cried. He slapped his horse on the flank, and took off after Sally. It was a sloppy ride for him with a lot of sliding around, but Blumper was huge, smart and patient, and content to ride on after Sally.

After the first thundering gallop, she

slowed down and he caught up to her, and they rode like a dream through the moonlight, light as feathers, laughing and talking. He shivered with delight when he looked at her, riding through the moonlight like a savage princess. It was a moment to remember for his entire lifetime; he had never felt so complete, so whole as he did at this moment with her.

Topping a rise, they sat their mounts and looked down over the entire San Fernando Valley spread out like a jeweled web below and in front of them, with the jutting solid black of the Santa Monica hills beyond. From where they watched, they could easily see the single heavy golden thread, the 405 Freeway, running over the distant ebony rise and through the Sepulveda Pass.

"Nifty, huh, little man?"

Sally leaned over to kiss him. But it, too, was a tease. Their lips brushed, and then she had broken away once again.

"To the brook!" she yelled over her shoulder.

They raced with the cool night air against their skin, topping a round hillock and plunging on toward the wooded wrinkle in the hills where the thin stream ran over smooth rounded stones. Sally did beat him, but not by much, and he was content to have escaped with his manhood as they dismounted to water the horses.

They threw their reins, letting the horses browse at will, and lay in the grass, close and warm and willing to take and be taken, to let the wonderful madness of their love roll on, to give and be given to, to let their bodies send their souls soaring skyward. Mica stirred to the fire of her closeness, drew her to him, her firm breasts against his chest, and they flew skyward, skyward, finding the patterned rhythms of the old sweet song made fresh and new with each tender kiss and caress. Their spirits reached higher, higher, higher, until they both felt they floated among the stars.

Mica and Sally circled the moon, left the solar system to thread the wonders of the Milky Way and storm the constellations scattered across the heavens, the night sweet Anne Mae was conceived. Not sure, but hoping, they rested together, looking up at the stars.

"Chicken salad! You have a cruel tongue, Sally Harris." And full of tender, scoffing love, he bent over and kissed her soft blond hair.

She smiled, but her thoughts were light-years away. "I don't ever want to leave this place."

"Who's going to evict us?"

She said nothing for a while, looking at the bright starry path spilled with reckless abandon in the sky above them. After a while, she spoke again, "Do you think a person could ever be too happy?"

That one was easy for him. "No, because then you'd be sad."

She rose on one elbow, leaned over and ruffled his hair. Even then it had been ash-blond. He couldn't remember a time when it wasn't.

"Behold," she said, "my rational artist!"

"Rational?! Galloping across a prairie full of gopher holes in the dark without any clothes on!"

She just grinned and leaned over to kiss him full on the lips. He gathered her into his arms, and never in his life had he felt so content as at that moment.

And then Mica started awake. He had the soft feel, the smell, the taste of her still warm in his mind but retreating now, pulling away from him. She wasn't there. She was gone. That joyful moment had been over ten years ago. He had been dreaming.

three

The realization of his hollow present blasted through Mica, leaving his mind aching with agony and old, unhealed grief. He huddled in the chair on the porch, chilled by a night mist which had moved in like a thin, diaphanous veil over a quarter moon tacked over his sagging stables like an upside-down horseshoe, pale, distant and out-of-luck in the blue-gray light of early morning.

Aching in every joint, he launched himself unsteadily to his feet and stared at his three-day growth of beard in the rusty old Bianchi Gunleather mirror hung on the porch. His ash-blond hair was now streaked with darker brown. *Odd...his beard was coming in darker, too.* He stretched and accidentally hit his hand on one of the low beams stretching under the eaves. The pain was excruciating. He grabbed his arm, studying the thumb on which he'd performed his crude surgery. No big surprise, it was swollen and infected. He sighed and looked around for his shoes; then decided he'd better shower and find something new to wear.

One hour later, from the owl's-eye view in the great oak in front of his hacienda, Mica could be seen swinging his legs into his battered Alfa and driving unsteadily down his potholed stone drive. The view swung to follow him. The Alfa coughed in early morning agitation; then disappeared around the bend in the road, heading down into the Valley. But no owl would ever sit in the crook of the tree, looking down on whatever it might see from that vantage point.

four

Mica was bent over his art director's desk while sensations and emotions streamed in a wild riot through every sense and inch of his physical being. Last night he'd dreamed for the first time in years, dreamed of things he'd pushed from his mind since Sally and Anne Mae had left him. In a curious way, he'd never felt more alive. Since he'd cut the little cylinder from his thumb, living had assumed the nature of a dangerous flame. He could feel himself as part of the pulse and flow of the lives around him, the interlocking mesh of friendships, the grind of unpleasantness. And yet the cynical hope-in-hopelessness of Horny Hamster had begun to feel trivial, the devilish little creature's supposedly insightful adventures now seemed banal and of little consequence. *Writer's block*, Mica told himself.

He sat at his desk, aimlessly rotating a 2HB pencil with his left hand. The white 14"x17" sheet of 32-pound acid-free layout paper that he'd taped to the slanted artist's board in front of him was slowly filling with aimless doodles. As the morning dragged on, the doodles grew more jagged, disorganized and meaningless. Still, Mica filled up page after page, and then crumpled and bounced them on the floor and taped down another that was fresh and clean.

Word went through the cramped offices of the editorial department that Mica Harris was to be left alone. Phone or fax or e-mail does not send a message like that. It drifts, seeps through the pores of an office, travels by osmosis and ESP. Nobody bothered him until towards noon, when Jimmy Moneypenny, the lean black Jamaican girl production assistant, poked her head in the door.

"Good friend of yours that I am, even I wouldn't dare intrude, things being what they are..."

"But...?" Mica glared at her from under lowered eyebrows.

"But it is my job."

He went back to doodling, studiously ignoring her. She gave him the hesitant beginnings of her perky smile and spoke in a throaty contralto, her voice all smoky, bantering tease.

"Mon," she said. "Hey, mon. You, dere. WHITE mon."

"Whaaat?" A snarl from the genius.

"Oh. The beast answers. Fling him fresh red meat."

"Okay. What you want, Jimmy?" He wasn't going to make it any easier for her.

"Hey, mon. You got anything for me?"

She stood in the doorway like a bright-eyed grackle, ready to wing away before he could chuck anything heavy or hurtful in her direction. When he didn't say anything, she tried a new approach.

"Hey, mon. You did your hair. I think I like it." Mica's hair had, over the course of only a few days, gone black from the roots out, until it was just tipped with white frosting.

"Thanks, pal." He gave her a haggard look. "Hey, look; it's just not happening for me here, Jimmy."

She shrugged, "I'll pull one from the pot. You're still three or four in the black." She came closer and ran the long and graceful fingers of one hand through his hair, "Not to worry, mon. Hair like this is to die for."

Mica nodded without looking directly at her. He was in his own world, but where that might be, she couldn't tell. She thought she'd try a wild shot, "How about Il Fornaio's tonight? Beeg-a party, mon. You could bring your new hair."

He blew out a long, extended breath intended to convey the extent to which she was bothering him. But she only retreated back to the doorway and the silence lengthened between them while she stood there. Her concern—and *love*—for him vibrated openly in the air like the pealing of a bell. *How had he come to read his fellow humans so easily? He passed them on the street and in the hallway and they were open psychology books—hateful, greedy, needy, loving, caring.* Finally, embarrassed, he muttered, "What's the occasion? For the party, I mean."

"Behold, the wonder! It speaks!"

"The reason for the party?"

"Well, if you need one: ICM Splinter Group Forms New Talent Agency. Hollywood Agog."

"Spare me." Mica returned to his doodle bugging, conscious of her concern as she stood

152

there, framed in light in his doorway.

"Come on, sooner or later you got to get back in circ, Mica-boy." She was teasing again. She'd picked up that *Mica Boy Wonder* stuff from Sally. Best buds, they used to be, back when the world was young and he was whole. "Here you are, all prettied up and nowhere to go."

He said nothing to that, and so she gave him pert, one hand on her jaunty hip, "Don't those little sperm-things die if you don't use them up?"

"Beat it!"

The quick grin broadened, "That's not the best way, am it, white boy?"

He threw one of the many wads of balled up paper at her, wincing at the effort.

"Woah," she said, pointing to his infected hand. "You better do something about that, hon!"

"Get out of here, Jimmy," he muttered.

Mica looked at the angry black line running up his swollen wrist. Reality swarmed around his heightened senses with a thousand new sensations both pleasurable and painful, and yet he couldn't figure a single reason why he should care.

five

Dr. Railsbach's five look-alike assistants returned from their little hellside junket with a bald zero to offer in the way of consolation or scientific data. They did return with a finely scraped piece of advice; if the silly and fantastical rumors of an unblanked human could in any way be laid at the cloven hooves of the EMO project, there was going to be dust and clamp enough to go all around.

Once he saw his pecking little clones had returned without a clue, much less any useful answers, Railsbach barely gave them a cold puff of inattention. He couldn't remove his gaze from the plasma screen and the continuing curious antics of his two sap female captives.

Apparently having decided the tree house wasn't sufficient for their needs in chaos, the elder had set about to reconstruct an exact replica of the old Spanish style house they had lived in. Sally obviously knew a great deal about construction, for in no short order the tile floors were in, the structure was outlined by 2x4s, and the curved reddish-orange roof tiles were stacked by the front door, ready to be applied. True, she put the wallboard up before adding the electricity and plumbing, but, as mistress of her own reality, that wasn't much of a problem. At her bidding, the pipes and electrical wires found the right pathways as if they had a mind of their own.

Few sap spirits had lasted longer than a few days in chaos, and no demon volunteer more than seconds. The auto accident and her translation was now over a year past, and yet Sally seemed to be thriving…and pulling her daughter along with her. From the jabbering of the one cloven they had managed to retrieve before he spattered, Railsbach knew no sense of time existed in there. Using the slaved spirit of a depraved sap, he had also been able to impose his will in a crude way on environments such as the one Sally was building around her. *Foggy doubt and earthquakes of despair*, he'd proudly reported, the grand sound of his own elation ringing in the Hall of the Elders. But he was secretly worried, knowing even to the meshed cycle of his twin hearts that it was always easier to destroy than to create.

Since Sally had left the roof until last, Railsbach imposed on the depraved sap to leave off his senseless whimpering long enough to send a rainstorm her way. This tentative little experiment was an out-and-out failure; not only were the clouds dissipated as the first wisps crossed her horizon, the depraved sap experienced a fierce sting for his reward. Shortly thereafter, the sad creature lost whatever it was that enabled him to exist in chaos, and he dissolved into nothingness like the rainstorm he had attempted.

CHAPTER 8
The Golden Locket

<u>one</u>

Sally and Anne Mae sat in their newly formed kitchen, sipping hot cocoa in celebration of their housewarming. They had their favorite cups, Sally a fat little cup with feet, and Anne Mae a porcelain Mamma Bear.

"You know, Mom, I've been thinking..."

"What, Anne Mae?" She brushed a lock of golden hair back from her daughter's face.

"We don't know where we are."

"That's right, honey-bird."

"But you can do anything, right?"

"So could you, if you tried it."

Anne Mae shook her head stubbornly. "Not me, Mom. I couldn't." The little girl frowned and blew into her hot cocoa.

There was a dry snap somewhere in the room, and Sally's attention was drawn to the kitchen floor. One of the tiles had a crack in it, a dark line that ran diagonally through the ochre square. She was sure that imperfection hadn't been there a moment before. The house had been flawless. Sally took a quick breath and quickly willed the tile whole again.

"Mom..." Anne May continued, "There's something I don't get...but...I'm kind of afraid to ask."

"Ask me anything, honey-bird."

The girl looked up from her cocoa, and

Sally saw a tear running down her cheek.

"If you can do anything, why don't you make Daddy come here?"

Another crack appeared in the tile, only this time it ran in a jagged line across the room, running through the grout and disappearing under the wallboard in the direction of the master bedroom.

Sally's voice was quivery and uncertain, "I can't do that, honey. Believe me, I've tried."

"Oh." Anne Mae's answer sounded small and disappointed.

Sally knew she had to do better. She was the adult; she had to find some reserve of strength to pass on to her daughter. "But he's coming for us," she continued, trying to sound sure of herself. "He'll be here any day now. We just have to be brave and strong until he gets here."

"He better come soon." Her small voice had a tired note of finality to it.

"Don't think about it now, hon. You want to help me fix the tiles?"

Anne Mae shook her head no. She quietly sipped her cocoa and watched while her mother replaced the tiles one by one until their floor was perfect again. She was rinsing her bear mug in the sink when she thought she heard the same weird dark singing they had heard before approaching in the distance. She shot a frightened glance in her mother's direction, and the jagged crack Sally had just repaired ran through the floor once again.

Sally moved quickly to her daughter's side

157

and held out a shining golden heart locket on a chain. "Take this, Anne Mae. Wear it for me."

The girl's eyes went wide and she started to protest, "Grandma's heart locket! I couldn't—"

"No time now! We'll share it. Right now, I need you to wear it for me." Sally put it around her daughter's neck. "Tuck it in so nobody can see."

"Why, Mom?"

The singing was louder now, their visitors only a few heartbeats away.

"Because it's a *secret* locket, honey-bird," Sally whispered, "Only you and I know you've got it. Nobody else in the universe."

There wasn't time to say anything more, but it didn't matter. Sally's secret kernel of resistance was nestled in the safest place she could think of, buried in the sweet innocence of a young child.

two

The small white toy terrier yipped and yapped and raced across the floor, darting under the legs of the heavy wooden furniture, sliding across the polished parquet to carom off the ornate wood-paneled walls, feet spinning madly as she set out on a new course. She was being chased by the two heavyset little dwarves, Zilch and Nilch. Albert Fern watched in growing annoyance as they lumbered after her with the relentless pursuit of dwarf ogres. Try as they might, the two of them couldn't seem to bring an ounce of grace or manners to their earthside coats.

They sang together in their high-pitched voices, "Lollypop, Lollypop, Oh my Lollypop; Lollypop, Lollypop, Oh my Lollypop!" The screechy lyrics were repeated over and over until Fern was sure they must have been sent directly from ancient hell as his personal cross.

"And they say translating is easy," Fern sighed, turning his attention back to Felney. Evening had long faded into night, and still Albert and his indefatigable assistant worked on at their task of choosing, selecting, translating or turning over the hapless and the unfortunate of his assigned territory while the endless canine torture went on in the background.

Just when Albert was sure he'd reached his limit and was resolving to frostbite his two darling little guardians, they switched the game, Zilch snatching up the little dog and running in crazed circles.

"William Josef fades back to fire a pass," Zilch screeched. "He seeks in the end zone for his favorite receptor!"

At the same time, Nilch ran a post pattern, nearly tripping on a long Persian rug patterned with hunting scenes that the visiting triparch of the New York territory, as Albert's equal in rank, had bestowed on him as a gift epochs ago, and dodging a priceless vase that had been neatly lifted from the Getty museum when the curator had a sudden case of highly selective memory loss. Zilch managed to fling the dog in a high, wiggling arc, and Nilch pulled it in just before it disappeared into the roaring flame of the fireplace. They fell to the ground, laughing and pounding at the dog.

Albert's stern voice carried across the room, "Zilch. Nilch. No outdoor games inside the study. How many times do I have to remind you?"

Attention diverted for the moment, they allowed the dog to escape. It quickly ran and hid under a Jacobean secretary of heavily carved oak overlaid with varnish that was nearly black with age. Zilch and Nilch were instantly after the dog, pouncing down on their bellies to peer under the legs of the huge old desk.

"Ha-ha," Zilch whispered, "Himself is having a bad coat day."

"Oh, yes, having myself already noticed," Nilch whispered back. His quick hand darted out, and he snatched at Lollypop, who growled and bared her teeth. Nilch quickly pulled back his hand, but Zilch took advantage of Lollypop's momentary distraction and grabbed one of her hind legs, neatly pulling her out and holding her up like a dead rabbit.

Nilch was already considering new frontiers, "Let's do toss-across-the-pond!"

"Okay-dokay, holay smokay," Nilch replied, just as eager to get out of the house and the parental constraints of Sir Albert. They wandered from the room, Zilch still carrying the struggling Lollypop by one of her hind legs and swinging her in a disheartening loop whenever she got twisted around enough to threaten his arm with her sharp little teeth.

Felney sighed in relief as the two dwarves waddled out through the wide French windows, which were open once again to the noxious night air as per his boss's instructions. Albert, he knew, was putting on the big "this land is our land" bluff, but all their internal scrubbers were working overtime to purge the oxygen and keep their systems relatively functional. It was working up to a *pendragon's purge* of a night; Felney was accommodating his boss by translating the old-fashioned way, reading a series of 9-digit numbers from one of the monitors. After completion of each series of numbers, Albert would ceremoniously pronounce *rollover* or *translate*, his human voice rumbling from his slumped position in the big padded wing chair.

Felney finished the current file and did a wrap/save and then punched in a new batch.

As he waited for the codes to line up on screen, he leaned back and hunched his shoulders.

"Doesn't it feel odd to verbalize instead of just winking them over?"

"Not to me," Albert replied. "I prefer the old way."

"Every soul his due," Felney quoted from the Black Book.

"Amen, old Gurpler." Albert nodded his agreement, sucking to revive the last embers in the ornately carved ebony-and-silver pipe in his hands. Discussions of modern progress were an old topic between them.

Felney wondered how Railsbach and his merry clutch of scientifics had ever wrested the energy from this man to go forward with their experiments. It was part of the puzzle that made Sir Fern unpredictable and had kept him on top of the clawing heap for so long.

"All too typical, I'm afraid." Fern had started up after a long silence. He'd obviously been thinking about it. "Penny-wise and pound foolish."

"What, sire?"

"The board of advisors."

Felney nodded again, his thoughts going back to their last meeting with the Elders—the *Dusty Demons* or the *Dusty Dozen,* as they were known to their backsides.

Fern was drifting, his thoughts going from the present to that approaching great day of total conquest. He found himself more and more scatter-minded these days, perhaps because of the excitement attendant to their great strides forward, perhaps because of the advancing number of his days. Soon he was going to have to pass over the active reins of power, join an overseers team as one of the dottering and fusty ancients who met with him once each lunar cycle. Maybe even breed himself, and have the boldest spawnling rip out his own hearts and stalk off with the rod of power. But not yet, not yet. Albert carried himself forward with just one wish, to grasp the completeness of his triumph before he had to hand over a single nub of his power. It was a forbidden desire, this wish to personalize their victory; yet Albert knew the directives were driveling foolishness, concocted by frightened old hooves. Personal triumph was what drove the empire.

Fern glanced at the screens, but Felney had pushed his chair away from the desk. "Sir..." he began in that petty whiner voice that Albert had come to recognize as signaling one of those canny conversations about some matter beyond repair, and hence, a waste of nitrogen. Still, Felney had to be Felney.

"Yes, go on, old Gurpler." The pipe definitely out, Albert sighed and began to dig for his silver cleaner, finally finding it in his vest pocket, where it always was.

"Sire, we're making mistakes."

Albert Fern gave the hopeless topic his most solemn and reflective look of concern and nodded in agreement. His coat showed none of his inner impatience. *Damn fool, what did Felney conjure, that everyone with longer horns than his own was a blathering idiot? Of course they were making mistakes—but look at the ground they'd gained!* But he said none of this, only pursing his lips thoughtfully.

Felney continued, the concern sprouting instant acne across his face, "And they notice..." His eyebrows twitched, indicating the fireplace through which the elders had earlier departed.

Albert nodded, blowing through the pipe stem to dislodge a nuisance sprig of burnt tobacco. *Of course they noticed, old Gurpler.* Still, Albert said nothing.

"I don't know what they expect of us anymore!" Felney wailed.

Albert widened his eyes a trifle. This was a major outburst from his little fellow. In a way—in an important way—Felney had his finger on the pulse. He was to be commended for his loyalty.

"We are much too thin throughout the ranks."

Albert rewarded his servant with a grave nod. "Like that mad little *sap* genius Napoleon racing towards Moscow," he responded. "Or the great Hitler, himself."

Fern picked up a little silk bag and deftly fingered a small amount of pungent Caribbean Tar into the bowl. They both knew that smoking, which all demons craved (and recognized as the only human contribution to civilized behavior), demanded the ultimate mesh between human coat and demonic inner frame. Albert's smooth and easy manner

164

demonstrated his skills with the social art.

"Point of order," Albert continued as he poured the proper amount of tobacco into the carved bowl and tied up the precious bag, "Where's my new detail man?"

As if on cue, the door chimes rang out the haunting first notes of Brahms' "Variations on a Theme by Hayden".

"That could be him now."

"Wouldn't that be pleasant?" Albert replied, tamping down his pipe. Lighting up, he rose with Felney, and they walked through the large and opulent rooms together.

Felney squinted out of one of the diamond-shaped wedges of heavy cut glass in a long and narrow panel set to one side of the massive oak doors.

"I believe it IS, sire..."

three

The outer sides of the front doors were plain and massive and made of dark stained oak, with simple curled black ornaments stamped of flat wrought iron; but the interior of those same doors were of ornately carved exotic tropic wood, the design of which composed a sea-field of thrashing fish, netted all in a panic. Felney knew these front doors were, from floor to high overhead arch, tall enough to allow passage of a troop of chain-stooped ogres marched side by side, for he had personally seen it.

He quickly unlatched the heavy iron bolt. The doors opened smoothly and easily, belying their huge size, and a young person stood on the dark slate flagstones of the entryway. He had the look of a patrician's son, a graduate of perhaps Yale or Oxford, a young gentleman of taste who knew what clothes to wear and what wines to drink. *Perfect coat,* Albert thought to himself with just a touch of envy. *But what else could he expect from the loins of old Bacchalius Gravely?*

The young man appeared to be in his mid to late 20's. He had curly dark hair, a slight cleft to his chin and a happy twinge of the old satyr to his ready and optimistic smile. He was dressed in an expensive, tasteful and yet dashing sports jacket of blue-black cashmere, and tan linen slacks. There was a touch of colored silk at his throat.

He stepped forward, presenting his right

hand as a show of subjectivity. "James Gravely, at your service, sir."

Albert was hard-pressed not to show his pleasure at the sight of this young man, the son of an old comrade with whom he'd shared the ups and downs of earthside campaigning. He cleared his throat, quickly accepting the hand and wrapping both of his around it in turn. He assumed the properly gruff tones, "So, young Gravely...so very good of you to join us."

Still, for all the necessary gruffness, Sir Albert's warmth showed through. He needed no motivation other than this being the first spawn of his oldest ally. "Come in, James, come in."

He eyed the young man, liking what he saw. *A well-tempered fellow, sure to fit in.* He'd read the reports, of course, or Bacchalius be saved, the kid would have been assigned somewhere else. *Keen eye and quick wit,* the an-logs had reported. *A sharpster, destined for the high ride.*

Albert clapped his new man on the shoulder, "Coat fitting well?"

The young man touched a tentative hand to his small, well-groomed moustache, "Yes, thank you, sir. Quite comfortable."

"Good, good."

Felney had moved on ahead a discreet distance, making his way back toward the study to continue the endless list of translations. They followed after him.

"I knew your sire," Fern said. "We were quite good confederates, actually."

167

"He has oft growled fondness of you, sire."

Fern nodded. *A nice touch. The boy knew the old patterns, respected past phrases and ancient ways.* Content that he could down-guard, he called ahead, "Felney, if you could continue, I'm going to brief our new man."

As Felney walked on, Fern took Gravely's arm and led him to the nearest open French window.

"Come," he invited, "the gardens."

Gravely hesitated, showing his newness. "Too much air for me, sire?" His tone was still polite, but with just a touch of concern in his voice. The academy, if nothing else, was thorough in its drill on the agony of oxygen poisoning.

"Nonsense," Albert chuckled, brimming with confidence, ready to show the younger man the true way of the outlanders. "So much of what you learned will prove to be nothing more than old bitch tales. Oxygen, in the proper dosage, is good for you." His throaty voice deepened as he saw the young man bring his disharmony under control, "It keeps the scrubbers in top shape."

They strolled together on a closely clipped lawn. The grounds were walled-in high fences of dark, ropy lava imported from Hawaii. Flower beds were skillfully woven in and out of the grass runway, with groupings of exotic teas and tobacco plants and stands of imported coffee and cork trees sprinkled about to provide earthly pleasantry no matter where one looked. The statuary tended to depict ancient

Mediterranean gods entangled with *sap* men and women in stony, violent embrace. Leda struggled to escape a powerful swan whose stone wings beat high above her bare breasts and frightened gaze. And there was Pasiphae, wife of Minos, with her arms and legs wrapped lovingly around a bull of white marble. Hercules stood with his drawn bow, ready to shoot a fierce horse with the head and shoulders of a man. Eve gazed into the distance, enraptured by the snake coiled around her voluptuous waist.

James listened attentively, and said little. Thinking back at a later date, Albert would remember one tiny incident from that stroll. Young Gravely spotted a ladybug that landed on his shirt cuff. Albert watched him examine the little bug as it crawled onto his index finger. He inspected it momentarily, and then put it to his lips. His white teeth crunched down on the creature, mincing lightly as if to test the flavor. He sniffed once and gave a slight shrug, as if mildly disappointed. At the time, Albert had taken no exception to his behavior, continuing with his fire-'em-up pitch. But in retrospect he had time to reflect that the academy might do well to establish a residency program, a halfway house for the newly coated. Humans, to his knowledge, rarely ate bugs that way.

But for the time, James had his bug, and Albert went on with his rolling thunder. The night was pleasantly dark, and beneath them the blessed black was interrupted by the curved flash and glitter of the Los Angeles basin,

169

which only stopped at the darkly beckoning lip-edge of the Pacific Ocean.

Young James gathered his courage through some moments of chitchat, and then timidly dipped his hooves into the local politics, "Sir, I've heard rumors..."

"Yes?" Albert managed an encouraging smile.

"There have been some...lapses...?"

"Yes. We nearly had a historic moment. The spirits of two *Sapiens* females attached to one of Dr. Railsbach's EMOTIVES actually found their way back to earth."

"How is that possible?"

Sir Albert shrugged, "Well, we provided the avenue. There's no way they could have come back unaided. What we do, from time to time, is allow them back under heavy clamp."

The young man was clearly astonished, "Why ever would you do that?"

"When it serves our purpose. Shock value, misdirection, confusion...we've found, if handled correctly, the image of a lost loved one is enough to drive a blanked *sap* over the edge of madness."

"Isn't that dangerous? I mean, it's against everything we ever—"

"James. While in the operation, the *sap* spirit is on a very heavy leash. And as part of it, we make certain their subconscious takes over. While back earthside, they are whomever we say they are. We operate them like puppets. A million little strings everywhere, attached to everything they do and say."

"Are there...many things such as this which we don't know?"

Fern nodded and puffed on his pipe. "Unfortunately, young master, great leaps forward of necessity cover new ground." He decided to take a risk. "I can tell you this. The rumors you heard regarding the Copenhagen incident were correct. But the reasons one should be concerned are not properly interpreted."

"I don't understand, sire."

"As I've just told you, the two *sap* females didn't somehow escape to earth—we sent them. Our concern is that they found some means to break out of their clamps."

"Unblanked humans?!"

"Just their spirits. Remember, they weren't alive."

"Still, sire..." Gravely shook his head and blew out a breath of the noxious air, a sympathetic gesture, much used by the *saps*. Albert wondered that his new man's coat handled complexities of this order with such grace. *Or was it a clever ploy? Had the boy been sent to presage his downfall?* Forcing his hands to remain clasped behind his back, Albert willed the steel claws in his fingers to retract. This was, after all, Bacchalius' whelp. *Et tu, Bacchalius? Then die Albert.*

"Yes," Albert nodded, "they actually burst their bonds, and we haven't one fume in a stench why..."

"Bad fortune, sire," young Gravely said.

"I do not believe in fate," Albert replied,

conscious that when things bothered him he talked as if he was eating, alternately chewing the words and spitting them out. "I believe in careful planning."

The young man nodded respectfully, his presented attitude showing things were as they should be.

His nails now fully retracted, Fern regretted suspecting his old ally's whelp. *Still, suspicion was the crown jewel of respect.*

"What became of the two?" James asked.

"Which two?" Fern blinked, realizing his mind had been wandering.

"The EMO's women."

"Oh. No problem. I lagged over and reeled them in. Railsbach isn't really very good in the field. These new scientists. You know, he doesn't even know elemental incantation…Anyway, I got them back to the lab and once we had them back there, he tethered them in a state he calls 'limbo'."

"'Limbo'?!"

"Yes. He calls it an altered dimension, I believe. The *state of limbo.* Why do you ask?"

"Nothing. It's just an old sapiens concept. Limbo was a mythological place where *sap* souls were supposed to wait until they were pure enough to get into heaven."

"Humph. Interesting. Another word for purgatory." Albert puffed on his pipe for a moment. "On any account, with what we've learned over the last few days, Railsbach believes we're about to take another great leap. Others are not so sure."

172

"And what do you think?"

Albert's claws started again, and he had to self-clamp to will them back in.

"I think," he said with great deliberation, "We have the situation well in hand."

As they continued walking, Albert's gaze wandered past the profile of the clean-cut young man, across the lawn to a distant dark patio skillfully painted in dappled black and silver by the moonlight, to where could barely be seen the outline of a blond woman and her young daughter, the apparitions quite as solid in appearance as if they were real flesh and blood. The two were quietly sitting on a bench, looking out over the night city. They were as motionless as the stone statues, frozen in their ecstatic horror, absolutely stone quiet except for the light breeze playing with their hair. Young Gravely, who was quietly consumed with controlling his newly adapted coat and fighting the unaccustomed oxygen overload, didn't even notice they were there.

Albert decided it was time to cut to the twin hearts of the matter, "What are they saying about the rogue EMO, back-side?" he asked.

"The rumors are everywhere, sire. The idea of an unblanked human caused a good spatter of initial panic, but *pater* did some digging to your good."

"Ah. I owe him yet again."

"He says he owes you, sire. Old debts he can never repay, if offspring may quote their loins."

Albert nodded, at last content that the

173

ancient compact with his old ally held.

"I heard the assassin Speth voted the quick out, sire."

Fern could see Gravely had done his homework. He laughed uneasily, "Ha-ha, yes, *Speedball* Speth. I've often regretted I ever gave him a vote. Now he will be your problem as well, won't he?"

They turned to face a distant shout. It was Felney, huffing under the bright crescent of the moon as he rushed down the combed gravel toward them, his outstretched arm holding a cellular phone raised like a bugle or a flag.

four

Young Gravely showed his concern, turning toward Albert with a look of alarm, "What can it be?"

"Whatever. It is not good news. You can count on it."

Another moment and Felney was next to them, puffing and out of breath. "It's Speth, sir. He's been trailing Mica Harris, and begs sweetly permission to translate."

Sir Fern's mouth clamped shut, and he spoke as if he were chewing tough meat, "Transmit at once: Lord Fern denies him."

Felney continued, "Apparently our rogue EMO is heading for some sort of *sap* celebration. We should have the perfect opportunity to re-implant him, if Speth doesn't *go maniac* on us."

Fern shook his head, "All Speedball thinks is *blast away*. Transmit my wishes that he stand down *immediately*." Felney nodded and broke into a low sputter of native tongue on the phone.

Young Gravely was on the opportunity in an instant, "I have a few entrapment ideas we might try."

"Excellent! You're the man in charge!" Sir Fern voiced delight, but his gaze wandered back to the earthly apparitions of the two women, still unwavering in the ghoulish light rising from the distant city. He would have Felney bring their presence to Gravely's attention in a way that would make whatever followed seem like the young man's own idea.

"You don't want to hear what I have in mind first, sir?"

"This is a mighty fast track, young man, but I'm betting you're up to it. I will want you to review with Felney; his assistance, as I've found many times, can be very helpful." Albert showed clawless and clapped his new assistant lightly on the shoulder, "Not ten minutes in town and already your first assignment. Welcome to *Los Angeles*, James."

The way Fern said it, with just the right touch of irony, was not lost on Gravely. *The City of Angels.* The younger man paused, not quite as wonder struck as he'd been some days before when, still in the sanctuary of the academy, he'd learned of his incredible fortune to be assigned here. He allowed himself a moment to wonder about the twin forbidden concepts that always struck like a double heart attack—bad luck and fate. But just a moment, and no longer for thoughts like that. He was a very eager young fellow, on his way in a hurry down to the core.

CHAPTER 9
The Trap

<u>one</u>

The Il Fornaio restaurant had the look of instant heritage that can be acquired by flinging outrageous amounts of money in the direction of Beverly Hills interior decorators. High ceilings, dark wood and plenty of brass and marble, big windows so the crowds passing by outside could catch a glimpse of the real *show biz*, of movie deals being consummated, stars with heads bent close as they whispered love and commitment, the wealthy clinking glasses of bubbling Italian white and rich, dark red, and nibbling on endive salads sprinkled with pungent hard cheeses and a variety of pizzas disguised as *haute cuisine*. Young Italian waiters in white shirts, black vests and bow ties rushed here and there with trays balanced on uplifted arms, secure in the knowledge that they worked at Il Fornaio's, the heart of the heart of the young working film and video moguls' Beverly Hills.

From the ceiling, the scene in the room was crowded with little square tables with black-and-white checked cloths. From this overhead view, all was patterns of human movement and swirls of color. An out-of-period party was in full swing, and it had attracted the same clump of young and desperate *avant-garde* who always gathered

177

with their kind at these sort of events. In one corner, a swing jazz band was thumping its way through a thin but hot and happy version of "Stompin' at the Savoy." The polished hardwood floor on the bakery side of the restaurant was packed with dancers.

As Mica wandered through the room, he was thinking the party was an enormous waste of energy. Here you found nothing more than a bunch of carefully selected young people trying hopelessly to imitate a fearless age now long gone. *How do you capture innocence fled?*

In near desperation to dampen the flood of information rioting through his sensory system, Mica had found a half-used bottle of double strength codeine pills left over from a bout with the summer flu. He'd popped two, and with the workday nearly exhausted, had managed one Horny, a barely funny strip wherein his little hero was confronted by a hopeless black bum. The idea was that poor Horny had everything but didn't know it, while the clever old bum had nothing; but when he got to the last frame, the lines that came to mind all made the worthless old bum the hero, as if he had something precious that Horny didn't, and since that wasn't right, Mica left the last balloon blank, a round empty airspace over Horny's quizzical, pained expression, the first unfinished Horny since he'd been syndicated. Mica had given in to the inevitable, erased the balloon, and made the bum the hero. And then he had taken two more codeine pills, washing them down with ice-cold coffee from a half-filled cup he hadn't touched in days, and fled into the street. He was halfway home before he realized he wasn't ready to return to the rancho—*couldn't* go back so soon after his recent dream of his beloved Sally in the moonlight. That left two choices: driving around aimlessly until he became too numb to care, or the party at Il Fornaio.

He moved on through the crowded room, greeting a few people he recognized. He waved at an agent who was trying to get Horny into an animated series, an effort Mica was convinced was doomed to failure. And, although even in his deepest thoughts he tried to deny what he was doing—or rather, what his brain was doing to him—everywhere he looked, he was still on his hopeless search for his lost Sally. He recognized the senseless trip to nowhere, and yet there was nothing he could do about it. *Look, LOOK! There—over there!* There was something in the delicate curve of the neck of a short-haired brunette that reminded him of Sally. *No, here—look here!* And here he saw a hint of Sally's sweet smile in the look tossed his way by a wonder with a beautiful oval face. *And there!* A bit of the challenging thrust of Sally's old hand-on-hip stance in that of a Vampira look-alike across the way, the cigarette dangling from her deep purple lipstick nearly as light as her dead-white skin. *Everywhere he looked, he saw a part, a glimpse, a bit of his lost Sally!* And yet she was nowhere, gone into nothing, disappeared along with his other love, his daughter, the sweet Anne Mae who would now have been nearly

179

eleven, a young lady in her own right.

The band started up a slow dance number, the piano running through the opening lines while the clarinet player put down his instrument and stepped forward to croon the old classic, *"I'm moonin' all the mornin'/ Moanin' all the night/ And in between its nicotine/ And not much heart to fight/ Black Coffee...!"* Mica spotted Jimmy flirting with a young waiter, one of those gaunt European wanna-be Robert DeNiros. He caught himself thinking the guy looked raw enough to have just stepped off the boat from Palermo or Ragusa, and then he wondered why he should care.

He'd had his fill of the Il Fornaio scene and was already moving toward the door when he spotted the blond woman and her daughter. They were sitting alone at a table near the back of the room, and his heart skipped a beat. His sheer momentum kept him going a moment longer, propelling him toward the door. But then he stopped short, forcing the crowd to mill around him.

"Hey, blockhead, move it!" somebody said, and a giggling twosome squeezed past him and out the door.

And still Mica stood looking backward, one foot actually out the door but with no chance of being followed by the other leg.

two

They hadn't seen him. The two of them sat quietly while the party chattered and swirled around them. They were wearing shiny silk dresses with straight fronts and swirls of fabric around the knees. The Sally look-alike (for even with all the codeine, he knew it couldn't be Sally) was wrapped in silver foil. The Anne Mae double wore a red dress that flashed with bright crimson sequins. Both of them had affected the Roaring 20's look; although the theme was correct, they were the only people who had bothered to come in costume. They were perfect in every respect; their blond hair was bobbed in the pageboy look, they wore cloche hats and clutched their beaded purses.

Feeling like a hooked trout, Mica let his broken emotions reel him, tattered and bloody, through the crowded room and over to their table. *What crazed new fantasy was this? This wasn't reality. This was just like Copenhagen and he was crazy as a loon and so desperately lonely he didn't even care. Could he get to them before the men in the white coats carried him away?* And yet, they looked so much like who they were supposed to be! When you've known someone intimately—a father, mother, sister, brother, lover, wife, daughter or son, you can spot them anywhere, even after twenty years of separation. You can easily tell them from a look-alike with that first, fleeting impression. He drew close, and still the false vision held; these were not look-alikes, they

181

were the real thing.

They looked back at him with bright, friendly stares. *Friendly, but they didn't recognize him.* He nearly panicked and fled. They were just a woman and a girl at a party, looking up at someone they didn't recognize, but just might like to talk to. In that same moment, it was and was not Sally and Anne Mae.

He could have, should have, left then. He should have run out of there. But that was impossible. Ask the rainbow trout or the shy and wily albacore, hook set deep into the bony roof of its mouth.

"M-may I sit down?" he asked.

three

Unknown to Mica, miles away in a mansion high in the hills, a dozen pairs of eyes glittered. In that distant study, a pair of hands rubbed together and a quiet chuckle was overheard. The game of all-or-nothing had begun.

At Il Fornaio, the woman replied, *"Mais oui,"* with Sally's voice. "We were just saying, no one wishes to talk with us."

Mica's mind was reeling. *Sally's voice but with a heavy French accent.*

"My name is Mica Harris." He looked around for Jimmy, who had laughed and spent the good times with Sally. *Jimmy would know!* But Jimmy was probably back in the kitchen, rolling around under the butcher-block tables, sending the flour dust flying with her new Mister Italy.

Mica was struck with a sharp pang of fear, and would have rushed from the table, but at that moment the woman who was and wasn't his Sally held her hand across the table, reaching to take his own, "Pleasant to have your acquaintance. I am Amy Ferrasont. And this is my darling Zoe."

Zoe gave him a clear, frank appraisal. There was a little nod, saying nothing, and then she flashed a quick look of approval to her mom. For some reason, Mica felt he was in with the kid. Sometimes you just clicked, right away, and you knew it.

He settled into an empty chair across from

them and took a deep breath. "You both...look so much like...some people I knew."

The Amy-person laughed, and it was Sally's full, rich, warm laugh, the only laugh like that which had ever existed in the world, and Mica knew he was truly lost. Not that his one true love could ever be replaced, but somehow, in some impossible way, this was truly her. He simply *felt* it through the incredible contradiction, felt it across the indestructible lines of space and time, of life and death, of his own common sense and madness—this somehow was his true and eternal beloved.

"So," his Sally said, with the accent of Amy Ferrasont, "we have a doubles."

A shadow clouded Mica's features, remembering the horror of that last shattering moment as the chrome truck grill loomed in his memory and their blood splattered—NO!! *This couldn't be. None of this could be!*

When he finally spoke, it was through gritted teeth, "Well, you did have. They...they had an accident some time ago. A car crash."

Amy impulsively reached across the table, and for the second time in as many minutes took his hand in her own. "I am sorry. They were some people you cared for."

For a moment he allowed himself her touch; then pulled his hand away. *This was crazy. Walking this path would lead to madness.*

"My wife and daughter," he muttered, his voice barely audible above the crowd.

There didn't seem to be anywhere to go with the conversation after that. But he saw that it didn't matter. They looked content and at ease, and pleased to be here, to be with him, to speak or not speak. After a while, it came to him that he was acting like a fool. *All right, so it wasn't Sally and Anne Mae. It was two people so very much like them that in his present state he couldn't tell the difference. In his madness, they had become the forms of his beloved wife and daughter. Did that mean he had to sit here, saying nothing? Say nothing, and he would never find out any more about them.* His brain raced, trying to find connectives, trying to figure out this impossibility. The here and now was different than Copenhagen. There, on that sparkling crisp day beside the splashing pool, at least at first, the two of them had recognized him— there could be no doubt, they had waved and called his name. Here, these two were friendly, but distant. Here, in the heady mix of foreplay that was the Il Fornaio by night, they didn't even know him. *What could that mean? Why didn't they know him?* Mica felt it was important, but the codeine and the strain of the moment numbed his brain, and he couldn't find any combination to unlock the puzzle. *Still, he couldn't just sit here.*

"Where—uhh—where do you work?"

Her smile was bright, her answer immediate, "At the new May Company department store. I am very good to sell *les belle fragrances Francaise.*" Never much of a

185

shopper, he vaguely remembered talk around the office that May Company had merged with Broadway, Robinson's or Macy's. He decided she must mean one of the stores that had come out of that merger.

<u>four</u>

The table lapsed into another long silence. *Improvise,* he chided himself, *Improvise!*

"Would you care to dance?"

Her smile seemed to light the room. "I would love to cut ze rug with you. But, to leave Zoe...it is impolite..."

Mica insisted, "Come on, it's the Charleston. We can all dance."

Zoe was on her feet in a flash. "Hot dice, Mom! Can we?!"

Her mother nodded her approval, and they made their way through the crowd and onto the dance floor just as the drummer did a roll and the crooner started into *"Five Foot Two, Eyes of Blue/ Has Anybody Seen My Gal?"*

Amy and Zoe were nothing less than fantastic. They were easily the best dancers on the floor. They glided, they floated, they played, laughing all the while. They gave Mica, who thought of himself as a good dancer, a real challenge.

He stopped dancing and stared at them. Amy came to a halt, a little out of breath, and looked back at him.

"What happens?" she asked.

"My wife and daughter could dance like the wind..."

The chorus came along, and she swung back into the rhythm. "You live too much in your old history. Dance. Dance."

He told himself he was making too much of the chemistry, of the magic that happens between people. But even as his thoughts wandered back to how perfectly these two matched his lost Sally and Anne Mae, he realized the chemistry was right here, not between the man and the woman, but between the three of them. For a few brief golden moments, they formed a unit on the dance floor, and Mica felt whole again, complete in a way he had not since his beloved family had danced their sacred dance in the redwood forest on the golden afternoon before they left him.

He attempted the bees knees, did it badly, and a laughing Zoe showed him the true way. Amy broke free for a solo that brought cheers from the crowd that gathered around them.

And through it all, one small, unbelieving part of Mica was attempting to get back to reality, was eyeing the crowd, looking for Jimmy. But Jimmy was still nowhere to be found.

Laughing, the three of them headed back to their table.

Mica slumped in his seat with a big sigh. "How about something to drink?"

Zoe's laugh was a bubbly delight. "I would like zee float root beer!" she cried.

And Mica was unable to believe his ears. Amy, seeing his look, said, "What is this seriousness, written all over your puss?"

"Nothing." He tried to cover up, to act normal. "Well...something. Root beer floats were my Anne Mae's favorite."

Amy smiled, patting his arm, "And mine also. The universality of ze float root beer. It is a principle widely accepted in intellectual circles."

Mica had to laugh at his own foolishness. He raised his arm, caught the attention of one of the waiters, "Three floats."

The woman and her young daughter chatted while they waited for their drinks. They seemed delighted with everything, as if they were seeing the world fresh with new eyes, or perhaps after returning from a long trip. They commented on the clothes, the women's shoes, the fashion watches and frosted hair. They teased Mica about his own frost-tipped hair.

Mica, watching them, became self-conscious. He looked up, he didn't know why, at the ceiling and studied the whirling fan overhead. It was a white fan, but it was too high to be easily dusted, and was topped with a fuzzy layer of dust caught in a tan sheen of grease. *How much do we see?*, he thought uneasily.

"We make you sad?" It was Amy, staring at him, breaking his chain of thought.

"No," he said. But he spoke too quickly. He didn't know how to express his own feelings, didn't know what to say of the jumbled fall of thoughts and emotions pouring through him. He was confused. He was upset for his own sanity. He felt utterly lonely and alone. He was swept up in sweet nostalgia.

"It's so many things," he started. "I just can't think anything through right now. You look so much like my wife and daughter, and

189

yet you're from—"

"—Paris. Gay Paris."

"How did you—?"

"We came by boat. On the Queen Mary. To your New York City. And then the train.

Traveling by boat seemed a little odd for such young people, but he supposed someone with money and time to burn might still do that. And then the train. Maybe she was phobic; maybe she had something against airplanes. He didn't know how to ask that directly, fearing he might offend her.

"You took a train?"

"Yes, we took *le chemin de fer*." She smiled, gentle mockery in her eyes. *So it must have been she didn't like planes. Her teasing ways so reminded him of Sally! He was lost, lost!*

The root beer floats arrived and were consumed. He said nothing, though Zoe ate her ice cream first, while Amy stirred hers into a thick soup and then ate it with the long silver spoon, the exact way Anne Mae and Sally used to eat their own root beer floats. *Ze universality of the root beer float,* he had to remind himself, barely holding on to the waterlogged life raft of his sanity.

They filled the air with small talk about the long, extended summer and the autumn rains, which seemed never to arrive. He mentioned his job, and neither of them had ever seen or heard of Horny. He drew one for them on a napkin, Horny just a little rakish, winking, saying, "Hi, pretty ladies!" He signed his

190

name. Zoe wanted to keep it, and he gladly handed it over. Amy carefully folded the paper as if it was a little treasure, and, looking very serious, said she would have it framed as a keepsake for them both. And then she looked at her watch and said it was time to go.

Mica was caught off balance. It was too soon; even while he knew it was craziness on his part to want to know them better, there were a thousand questions he had to ask, a thousand things he wanted to say. The only words he could think of tumbled automatically from him, "Do you have a ride?"

"Oh, no," Amy shrugged, "We do not need a conveyance. It is a close place."

"Well, if you insist on walking..."

"We do insist." She gave him a fetching little smile. *The old Sally come-fetch-me-if-you-dare look. He was lost, lost, lost!*

five

The micro overheads caught the three of them coming out of Il Fornaio, and watched through a variety of down angles from the tops of nearby buildings, from streetlights, telephone poles, billboard scaffolds and palm trees. Amy, Zoe, and the lost one with the frost-tipped hair, engaged in animated conversation as they walked down Beverly Boulevard and headed south across Wilshire. A moving shot from a silent night bird showed the three of them pointing in store windows. A fuzzy view taken from a location tucked in the shadow of a tubular transformer tracked them as they turned down a side street, heading away from the bright store windows and the still busy traffic on Wilshire.

There was an unaccountable blank span, and then they were picked up from another angle, this one through the dense cover of a leafy ash tree as they walked through a quiet residential neighborhood, the closely spaced duplexes and quads artfully disguised to look less crowded by great clumps of shrubbery and rows of tall trees with branches hanging over the street and brushing the walls of the buildings.

Walking along with them, Mica could feel the numbing effects of his last codeine wearing off, leaving him light-headed and on edge, wary that the strange, streaming flood of sensations would overwhelm him once again, just when he was trying to concentrate on Amy and Zoe.

He was surprised at the brooding stillness of the night. Nature itself felt out of order; things were too quiet, ominous and listening. *Something was out there, watching, waiting to pounce!* A large bird, probably an owl, flew overhead. When he looked up and saw it, it hesitated and then wheeled away and was gone.

"Oh, God!" he groaned out loud, sure he had gone off the deep end of his emotional reservoir once again.

"What is it?" Amy asked.

"Nothing," he said through gritted teeth. "Just a headache, coming back to haunt me."

"I have some medications." She pawed through her purse and handed him a small brown plastic pill bottle.

Without thinking, he unscrewed the cap and shook one out in his hand. *Odd that she would have codeine tablets.* He glanced at the prescription. They were made out to Amy Ferrasont, the strength more than double the ones he'd been taking. He palmed one, screwing the cap back on and handed the bottle back to her.

But instead of gulping the pill dry, he carefully placed it in his shirt pocket.

"Need water," he explained. He half expected her to pull a warm can of Coca-Cola out of her purse, but it was Zoe, taking a small bottle of Geyser water from a pocket of her sweater. He took the bottle, but something in the night air bothered him. There was a hesitation, now just a touch of chill. He heard a distant rumble that might have been a truck on the expressway.

"Aren't you going to use my water?" Zoe asked.

"Here, you have some."

She shook her head solemnly, "No, it's for you."

"Thank you," he said. He noticed she was watching him with a sharp look, like that of a little sparrow. It was something more intense than what he knew from his daughter, as if she were being driven by some secret inner mechanism.

"Here, hold it for me for a minute." Zoe reluctantly took the bottle back.

"He isn't going to take the pill, Mom," she said. "He doesn't trust us."

"Hush, dear," Amy said, clearly embarrassed.

"I—I like your perfume," Mica said. After that, the conversation died for about a half a block.

"Bell a la Nuit," Amy finally said with a small half-smile.

"Bells at Nightfall," Zoe translated, bright again as if she'd forgotten all about the incident with the water. "It's Mama's favorite—'cause she sells more of it than anything else!"

Mica could see they were slipping away from him, just as they had on that fresh and sunny day in Copenhagen. *This time would end, they would leave him, just as Sally and Anne Mae had removed themselves from his life, just as everyone he ever knew had deserted him.*

"It is not much farther," Amy said, the sad note in her voice only confirming his deepest fears.

"Are—are you staying with relatives?"

He knew he couldn't let it end like this. He had to see her again. He had to work the conversation around until he could figure out a way to set it up. *Normal people did this. It wasn't odd or weird or perverted. He could do it, too.*

"No," she answered, "not with relatives. Not much more distant, now."

The night felt close and still. It was warm, but occasionally there was a cold gust, as if a misdirected blast of air conditioning had gotten loose on the night wind. Mica heard another uneasy rumble in the distance. Thunder seemed an unusual explanation, considering the bone-dry summer spell had shown no signs of relenting.

"Huh. Heat lightning, I suppose." He shrugged, *Who could figure the weather?*

She smiled at him, not commenting. He thought he caught a glimpse of something immeasurably sad and vulnerable in her expression, some indefinable loneliness behind the softness of her gaze. Zoe, too, seemed to have caught an attack of the pensives, looking down at the sidewalk and attempting to step on every crack as they walked along.

"Just a few more houses," Amy said.

There was a nearer rumble, and a flicker of heat lightning.

195

"Just in time. I think it's going to rain."

She said nothing, and he plunged on with the courage of the damned, "I—I'd like to see you again..."

Her answer wasn't a direct response, and yet later he would reflect that it perhaps said more than it seemed. "This has been such a nice evening for us," she said. "So very long, since such as this...."

He was still thinking about how he could set up a date, about how he might persuade them to see him again, when she paused and indicated a house just ahead and on their side of the street. He saw that it was an ordinary quadplex, just like all the others. He couldn't see a number, but on the far side past the building there was an empty lot where construction was about to begin, where an older building had been razed to the ground and the harsh light of a bare bulb shone from a post that had been raised over square piles of 2x4s and stacks of cement bags.

She unexpectedly extended her hand and took his.

"Thank you for a lovely moments," she said.

Zoe snatched his hand from her mother, pulling him unexpectedly down close to her. "I'm not really mad about the water," she whispered. "Ze devil made me do it." She gave him a wink and a quick, warm peck on the cheek. "I liked that root beer," she said with an intense and shy eagerness, so much like Anne Mae that his reserve melted, his heart crying out to her. And then she reached for her mother's hand again, retreating from him.

He didn't know what to do next. The two of them were walking toward the front door. But to him it was as if they were walking out of his life forever. He stood frozen in his pose, helpless to stop them.

They reached the front door, hesitated, and then began to walk across the damp grass around to the side of the house, in the direction of the empty lot.

"Did you forget your key?" he wondered out loud, using the opportunity to gain a few more precious seconds with them.

They didn't answer or look back. They simply marched steadily away from him, around the side of the house, and then they were gone. The grass where they had walked was high and in need of a cut, and he saw the imprint of their footprints in the lawn. They had to be confused; there was no reason for them to walk around the building that way; there was no path, nobody went in that direction.

There was a louder thunderclap, much closer now. *A real storm,* he decided. The electricity in the neighborhood flickered. The streetlights, porch lights, the lights in all the apartments dimmed and then came back up to their former strength.

"Wait!" he yelled, "are you sure this is the right—?"

But it was too late for the question. The two of them were already gone around the corner of the house and he was left talking to the bushes. He ran after them, and with one brief sprint he was around the corner.

And then he stopped short. He was dumbfounded, faced with the absolutely amazing. What he saw was incredible, not possible in the normal, sane universe where a man took a 9 to 5 job messing with computers, stocking shelves in a supermarket or even drawing a zany little hamster-devil. He knew that he was now, beyond all shadow of a doubt, 100% totally insane.

six

The thing Mica saw in front of him was steaming, and some parts of it were still spinning in a complicated way. Lights flashed, and it sat on its haunches, striped and gray and somehow reminding him of the grin of the famous Cheshire Cat from Alice's Wonderland. It was a flying saucer.

Impossible, but there it was; a plump round disk of a little spaceship that glowed slightly as it balanced on four little legs, presumably after a rush across interstellar space. It wasn't very big, and yet it filled the vacant lot nicely, settling as it had behind and a few feet away from the stacked boards and cement bags.

A flat beam of light extended like a ramp or a runway from the lit outlines of a doorway, which led into the spaceship. He saw two aliens backlit in that same door. One was tall and the other short. They were the almond-eyed aliens of popular cult mythology, and they were beckoning. And while he stood there with his mouth open, Amy and Zoe walked steadily toward the ship and started up the lighted ramp. The blood drained from his face. No matter how odd and unbelievable the present circumstances were, he couldn't bear the thought of losing them again.

"Noooo!" he shouted. "Wait!"

And in that moment, Zoe turned to him, seemingly broken out of whatever shell it was that had ensnared her.

"Daddy!" she cried, "Get away, quick!"

Anne Mae! Frozen no more, he took his first step to race after them. He had no idea what he was going to do when he got there. *Tackle them? Take on alien hordes?* He didn't think it through. It didn't matter, because before he had taken his second step two things happened to him, nearly simultaneously, like an absurd one-two punch.

First, he tripped over the legs of someone sleeping in the bushes. And, a split second after he fell in a heap to the ground, a beam of intense light swept the spot where he'd been. The light raked the bushes like a bright steel claw, and then it was gone.

Mica tried to get up, intent on rushing the spaceship and pulling Amy and Zoe out of harm's way. He realized he had to get there before they made it to the top of the ramp. But he was hopelessly tangled in blankets and what was left of a battered cardboard house.

"Git *off* me, man!" an outraged voice demanded.

Mica untangled himself and rose to a standing position, peeking out of the thick shrubbery. He saw nothing but swirling mist. The lone bare lightbulb, which had been strung to a raised 4"x4" to discourage thieves suddenly popped with a little spray of sparks. But there could be no doubt, the spacecraft was gone; it had vanished without a trace.

Mica looked into the night sky, which revealed the dark gray and ballooning underside of a storm cloud about to break over his head. He turned toward the bum, and

200

recognized him as the same old black man he'd seen before. Mica had tripped over the same set of legs twice in one week. *Like the rest of his life, totally absurd and unbelievable!*

"You!" Mica shouted. "What are you doing here?!"

The bum shrugged, concentrating on flattening out his frayed Motorola box. He managed to fold it over so he could carry it under one arm.

"Ev'ry man gots the right to sleep somewhere," the bum said. His tone was soft and gentle, the quietly remonstrative voice of an aged Negro who just wanted to avoid confrontation and get on with whatever was left of his quiet life.

The bum wedged his grimy blanket and flattened cardboard box under one arm. He slung a double-bag of black plastic over his shoulder and walked away from Mica without a backward glance.

"Wait!" Mica followed after him.

The bum paused and turned back to give him a look as old as history.

"What, boss?" the old man said patiently.

"Did you—didn't you—see *that*?!" Mica pointed toward the vacant lot.

"What, the lightbulb poppin' like that? Nothin' lasts forever, boss. Will there be anything more right now?" He studied Mica a moment longer through eyes that were yellowed with age, and when Mica didn't answer, he turned and began to shuffle away.

Mica ran after him and grabbed the corner

of his cardboard box. The box and the blanket fell to the grass.

"You SAW it!" Mica demanded. "I know you saw it!"

The man stopped again, and this time returned Mica's look with a heavy sigh. He set down his plastic bag and bent over to carefully refold his cardboard box and the blanket and replace them under his arm.

"No, boss," he said. "I didn't see nothin'. A few flashin' lights, maybe. Could'a been the po-lice, lookin' for poor ol' bums to haul away to jail. Could'a even been maybe an ambulance, flashin' by here wit' some poor broken people they gonna take to the emergency room."

He slung the plastic sack over his shoulder again and walked away.

"Wait!" Mica ran after him and held him, this time grabbing him by the arm.

The bum gave him a distasteful look and tried to pull away. "Git away from me, Mister Make-Fun-Wit-De-Debil! I don't need your kind of trouble. You can make your own messes!"

Mica let go, recoiling in pain; maybe it was because he'd grabbed the man with his infected hand. He couldn't be sure. He felt dazed, almost as if he had been brushed or swatted away, or perhaps hit with a stun gun.

He watched the old bum limp down the street as the first drops of rain began to pelt down from the sky, darkening the sidewalks and chilling his head and shoulders. The new

202

season, the wet, was going to come without the cleansing Santa Anas to blow the old, smoggy air away.

CHAPTER 10
Until the Messiah Comes

<u>one</u>

Sally and Anne Mae Harris came aware all at once, like mice dumped out of a box. They were again standing on solid ground, as had happened to them countless times before, standing in the densest fog that could be imagined. It was neither night nor day. The fog was too gray to be milky and too light to be a night fog. But unlike the previous times they had been returned to their void, Sally was no longer overwhelmed.

In previous times when she and Anne Mae had been returned to this place, they had no memory of where they'd been or what had happened, or even how long had been the interval in between. This time Sally remembered the horror of her last few moments on earth. There had been a brief moment before the crash, those last few microseconds when the probability of their own deaths became so immediate and clear. *The crash!* It came back to Sally for the millionth time, the nightmare flooding her consciousness. It replayed across her memory once again, the sudden impact of wheels and a huge chrome grill, the semi-truck broken from its track and flying across the yellow lines at them. A flash of white light, and then the white fading into this endless gray nothing. *Had Mica actually tried to steer them directly between the oncoming headlights?* No, she could never bring herself to believe that. He must have panicked along with her and Anne Mae, must have tried to skid them into a spin, a last desperate maneuver to avoid the inevitable.

She struggled to remember. There had been some things since then. Smoky wisps of important events that had occurred teased her, just beyond the fingertips of memory. *Mica was not here. There was something important about that. They had met by a fountain, somewhere in a prince-land with old buildings, somewhere in Europe.* Or was it all a dream? She sensed that much had happened since the crash, to Mica and to her and Anne Mae. But it was just a feeling. Where there once had been impressions and memories, now her mind felt a dull weight, a blanking depression. And a little more; the feeling that things were not right, that balance and order had been lost, that it was somehow wrong that they were held captive in this unending blanket of fog.

Yet here they were, she and Anne Mae, standing in a soupy warm nothingness, still wearing the clothes they'd worn on their last day, the day of their happy hike down the mountain—the clothes they'd *died in*?! It didn't make sense. Death was clouds and glory or pitchforks and agony, but not this endless waiting. It wasn't *right*!

"Honey-bird," she said to Anne Mae, "let me hold Grandmother's locket for a moment."

The golden locket felt warm to her touch.

The moment Sally had it in her hand, the fog began to lift into predawn light, and a tangible *thing* began to form in the blankness. *Funny, she hadn't seen it before.* It was the skeleton of their house, framed in 2x4's. She watched with a small feeling of anticipation as the framing for a roof materialized over their heads. They were standing in the kitchen of their rancho, the dream home she and Mica had selected after all those months of searching for the house that was, as the loan company brochures breathlessly exclaimed, Just Right For Them.

Anne Mae's arms formed a tight circle around her waist. The little girl's eyes were wide with alarm.

"Mommmmmm," she wailed, "Where are we, and how did we get here?"

"It's going to be okay, Anne Mae."

"You didn't answer my question, Mom!"

"Anne Mae. I need your help. Try to help me, hon. Look, it's getting lighter."

In truth, it was. As Sally spoke, the first true rays of dawn came in through the newly formed window casement, slanting through the fog. Now the walls of their old, informal kitchen-cum-family room were solidifying, plaster forming itself and familiar fixtures appearing at the same time she could see the bare outlines of their hilly pasture. *Impossible, but true. Believe it or not, by Ripley, Sally and Anne Mae.* Sally gave her daughter a smile she hoped was reassuring.

"See, it's not so bad."

"But—it's not real...this is the same thing

you did before." Anne Mae was walking around the room, fingering an empty cereal bowl on the table and touching the paint set by her canvas, which was set up next to Sally's larger one by the big bay window, before she returned to plop down in a chair by the table where she glumly eyed a chess game which looked newly begun, several of the pawns on both sides advanced in beginning gambits.

She gave her mother an accusing stare. "You build this place out of nothing."

"We have to stay here for a little while." Sally's tone was more confident than she felt; inside, she quivered and shook with fear. This was a weirdness she couldn't hope to understand. Yet, even as she quailed before the vision of this house, which was and wasn't there, she had a feeling of *deja vu*, as if she and Anne Mae had come through the fog and reconstructed this same house, stood and talked in this same room, again and again and again.

She gave her daughter a smile she hoped was reassuring.

"I'm sure of one thing. We have to stay here for a little while." She forced her mind to push on, trying new sentences as she came stumbling to the end of the last one. "Just until Daddy can sort things out and come pick us up." She didn't know where she got that idea; it just popped into her head. Yet, once it was there, she knew it was true. And with that came a rush of new understanding, tumbling in as if the fog was lifting from her mind as well. *Mica could save them. They were being held against their will, against some ancient law or covenant. There was a great danger here, a personal danger to them both.* Sally sensed an even greater universal wrong that cried to be righted, but it was the clear and present sense of urgency for the safety of her daughter that swarmed her instincts, grappling with the fog and pushing the unformed chaos further and further from them, replacing it with the order of remembered things.

"Daddy will be here soon," she repeated.

Even as they watched, the intensity of light surrounding them was increasing, bringing with it wallpaper and painted walls, pictures and familiar utensils, the common dust of their old life in the rancho.

Anne Mae picked up her battered old Raggedy Ann doll, staring into the blank button eyes. "Mom, how did you—?"

"It's not me, Anne Mae," she replied. "It's both of us, remembering."

Anne Mae let go her mother's hand long enough to walk across what had become their familiar Italian marble tile floor. She touched a wall and picked up one of Mica's HB2 drawing pencils off the artist's drawing table he used.

"Don't you...isn't this scary?" Anne Mae's voice was small and pinched.

Sally went to her, on one knee in front of her, and gave her a big hug. "Oh, Anne Mae, Anne Mae—remember, it's as strong as we are."

Sally held her daughter in her arms and sang a snatch of an old blues lullaby that had been one of Anne Mae's favorites when she was a baby, *"Love, oh love, oh careless love. Oh love, oh love, o careless love. / You've broken the heart of many a poor gal, but you'll never break this heart of mine..."*

And with the wavering and tentative notes of the song, the first golden light of the sun streamed in through the blue-and-white checked cotton curtains tied back country-style from the windows. Insects sounded in the backyard meadow and a friendly nicker carried up from the stables. God was in his heavens, everything was right with the world.

two

Railsbach sat on his black leather chair watching Sally and Anne Mae on the video screen, much as human scientists might observe their favorite test monkeys through wire mesh. He found their reactions to being placed in the strangeness of chaos utterly fascinating, and more than a little chilling.

His predecessors had stumbled on the pre-dimension the ancient Christians called *Purgatory* after years of researching forbidden Catechism studies; it had taken eons of poring over musty old hand-drawn fictionaries, curious saintly scrolls and even vaguely superstitious cuneiform slabs of unfired clay for clues and bits of information to help the cause. When translating the notion of limbo to a scientific inquiry, they had tumbled into the realm of the unformed chaos, which was certainly forbidden or at least little-known and vastly misunderstood territory to demondom as well as the so-called *modern progressives* who ruled *Sap* thinking. In short, there was a purgatory after all, a chaotic dimension of nonbeing that was outside and somehow bordered on both hellside and earthside.

And so the dark side experiments had begun, open-ended tests characterized by an enormous appetite for electromagnetic energy. In the end they had brought demondom the capability to warp reality in both the demonic and the earthly dimensions, and finally provided Railsbach and his fellows with the capability to deposit living souls in that newfound chaotic dimension. Speth called it *a lot of scraping for very little meat,* but Railsbach felt like a minor Lucifer, courageously lifting a dark wing into the unknown.

Limbo itself was proving to be a strange and forbidding place. So far, only random human spirits had proven capable of withstanding the isolation. Most of them slowly shriveled into nothingness, while some few dissipated instantly in shrieking horror; on the other hand, every single spawn volunteer placed in the chaotic state had quietly inverted, their physical presence swiftly deteriorating in a process Railsbach's team suspected was fundamentally molecular, deteriorating in a matter of only seconds until they were lost spawn in the void, a state at least the equivalent of the common ground-into-dust punishment. *Yet here was this simple earth-woman and her daughter, spinning a memory out of hope and dreams, and thereby in some manner capable of survival in the same environment where the toughest of his brothers had withered and disappeared!*

Railsbach was on the cutting edge of the new wave, of those who suspected this surprising *sap* toughness was somehow related to their human emotionality, to the incredible outpourings of love and hate, anger and pity, sympathy and terror, of which members of the *Sapiens* race were still capable in spite of the heavy universal blanking which covered 99%

of the populated areas on the planet.

Although detractors continued to rail that EMO was an enormous waste of credits, effort and energy, Railsbach and his team had been able to shape some worthy little monsters out of young *saps* who displayed a certain charisma combined with (an often masked) proclivity for violence. Ceausescu in Romania. The Marcos in the Philippines. Edi Amin in Africa. Cambodia's Pol Pot. The new leadership in splintered Yugoslavia.

But those experiments were fundamentally flawed; too impatient once again, leadership had demanded instant results, forcing Railsbach's team to push forward with already living *sap* stock. Hence the fool killers, religious fanatics, political anarchists, and the drive-by shooters. Add to that the occasional crazed celebrity slayer, distressed student or hopeless post office worker. Railsbach saw early that direction was not going to yield the planet.

Project EMO had been designed to place the breeding-for-violence program on a course of predictability. The experiment itself was deceptively simple; a handful of selected humans who had registered extremely high peaks of emotionality even under blanking had been weaned out of the general *sap* population at birth. Mica Harris was one of these. Isolated with cold or cruel foster parents, a situation that had been determined would almost always foster alienation or at the least, anti-social tendencies, they were being reared not to

212

dominate the world but rather as the gene pool for those who would follow—a true race of mighty *schwartzen ubermenchen*, a new subspecies, *Homo Sapiens Monstrus,* who would lead their fellows like lemmings over the edge of the final cataclysm, cleansing the earth for the new reality.

Over the years, Railsbach had been convinced the only thing that could stop him was—once again—the impatience of his own leaders. But now, watching Sally comfort her young daughter in the strangely resilient yolk of the little nest of reality she had spun, he wasn't so sure. *Temporarily sent into the madness of chaos, her spirit creates, no matter how fragile or temporary, an image of her past reality.* He knew that no demon could ever do that. *A* treacherous and forbidden thought hovered at the back of his mind like a dangerous white scorpion—*what if some humans, even a few, had a little piece of THE GREAT IT in them?* The heresy implicit in that thought was so enormous that, Bub-Bub-Beelzebub, he instantly self-blanked it from his mind.

But as the long night wore on, and Railsbach studied the amazing sap female and her spawnling, he formulated the beginnings of a dangerous but uniquely exciting new experiment. He got the idea from his longing to wrest the golden locket from them. *There was something important about that locket, he was on to the scent of something there!* It infuriated him that he couldn't just reach out

213

and take it. What if, relying on the strength of the earth woman's spun illusion, he himself visited her in chaos? And that little notion led to a greater plan. *Using slaved humans to control limbo by building their own little worlds, might it be possible to tame limbo as well?*

three

The light of a bleak gray morning found Mica in a room that had the same shape and form and identity as the one in which Sally and Anne Mae waited for him. But he was alone in his kitchen, and while the idealized memory his wife and daughter had constructed in their world was crisp and clean and full of loving memories, the actual room that he occupied was dark, dusty, and layered with accretions of bachelor living. The kitchen sink sprouted pots and pans, and Mica had spread three days' worth of newspapers across the room, covering the table, the chairs, the sink counter and even the Italian tile floor.

He paced impatiently back and forth, kicking the newspapers that settled wearily behind him. He went to the telephone, punched in numbers and asked a set of questions, which by now had become standard.

"No one reported ANYTHING?! I find that hard to believe!"

He threw the phone down. The plastic receiver bounced off the table and scudded across the tile floor like the stiff corpse of a dead gray rat.

Mica stalked angrily out of the room, kicking at newspapers as he went. After a moment, he returned, retrieved the phone from under a chair and placed it on the table. He looked briefly around the big kitchen, shaking his head in disgust.

"I've really made a mess out of things,

haven't I, Sal...?" he asked the empty room. He closed his eyes and stood motionless in the quiet of the room, not really expecting an answer. He tried to push all the events of the past few years out of his mind, to go back to those earlier, happier times, the golden age of his life, and for a moment he felt he almost *was* there. The memory of his wife and daughter was so real that he imagined he could actually reach out and touch them. *So close, so close, and yet forever far, fading and untouchable.* And with that thought, the spell was broken; they were a billion miles away, they were nowhere, lost into air. He kicked at a fallen pillow that was in his way and slammed his way out the back door.

From the owl's-eye view in the old oak tree in his drive, he could be seen making his way to the car. He leaped into the battered Alfa, wincing at the pain in his arm, and zoomed down the hill. Once he passed out of range, other micros picked him up from a telephone pole, from a branch in a heavy old peppertree, from two more telephone poles, and then he was on the regular hookups down-beaming the freeway as he made his way into town.

216

<u>four</u>

Felney, watching the monitors from his customary position behind the desk in Fern's study, had turned over his normal translations to Control and upgraded his surveillance from intermittent to steady. He didn't share Railsbach's nonchalance about unblanked humans. Mica Harris had been selected for the EMO seeding, and that meant he was capable as well as unpredictable. If they needed any proof at all, the mess he'd made of Gravely's clever entrapment attempt was there for all to see. Sir Fern referred to it politely as *the UFO Incident,* but behind his back Speth, who already had Gravely on his excrement list, was calling it *Foolsgate.*

At the morning's brief requesting, Speth had put in his usual demand for immediate translation, but Railsbach had raised a fuss of the first order, pulling up graphs and charts on not only Mica but also on his assistant Jimmy and two unidentified females. According to the plan he outlined, each of the three would, at the appropriate time, sexually intersect Mica's path, resulting in three perfect, wonderful little children that, nurtured with the proper amounts of pain and isolation, promised an excellent source of holocaust leadership. How could they lose all this simply because the EMO had become unblanked?

Fern had denied Speth; still, he asked for a deeper review. Railsbach explained away the earlier incident of the two translated females breaking out of their clamps in Copenhagen as a matter of the somehow inexplicable pull of human desire. He quoted from their storehouse of knowledge about Orpheus, arguing that this *sap* capability was a rare but already known quantity. Further, it was simply bad luck that the burly policeman had struck Mica on his implant hand, causing the capsule itself to become a low-level, unconscious irritant. Doctor Bruce had been severely flayed and clamped for bringing it to Mica's attention; there was no truly adequate explanation for his confused actions other than fume poisoning, and he had been earthside considerably longer than was recommended. Here Railsbach gave Felney a significant glance. The balding secretary sniffed and frowned, silently looking down at the table.

"The necessary adjustments have been made," Railsbach assured them all. "Nothing of this sort can or will ever happen again. All that remains is to snare one unblanked *sap*."

Speth was not mollified. "You say his life hangs in the dicey balance; I say we cut him now."

At that point, just when Railsbach was running out of nitrogen, young Gravely stood. "I don't think we should pull in our horns on this one."

"We're not pulling in our horns!" Speth sputtered furiously.

"Shortsighted to terminate him now." Gravely pointed the fully extended claw of his left forefinger at Speth, confident the width of the table had him out of lash range.

For a moment the assassin looked like he might leap across the table, but then his rage subsided and he contented himself with clawing the underside of the table.

Gravely, showing signs of the incurable romanticism which had been his father's mark as well, stood in Railsbach's behalf, spouting out a long-winded and somehow poetic speech about dark destiny.

Fern was impressed. "So, James, your first operational decision is for scientific progress..."

"Dr. Railsbach is the hope of the future."

Sir Fern's eyes flicked in their heavy gray lids, in turn marking each one around the table. For long moments he didn't say anything.

Even as Gravely had finished and settled back in his chair, a hot dry wash flushed through Railsbach's system. He had the most to lose, and realized his boss was taking an exceptionally long time to resolve what should have been open-and-shut. *So Copenhagen wasn't gone and forgotten after all. And now he could pile the UFO Incident on top of that.* Gray foreboding shadowed his thinking, and his breath became shallow. Sir Fern's so-called *rewards for inadequacy* were legendary. Railsbach realized that, for the first time since he was spawned, he would be wise to give some attention to a personal exit plan. He mulled this problem with a strange fascination, and a little chill erupted somewhere under his *sap* coat, deep in his silicate exoskeleton. Rogue demons were as rare as rogue humans.

219

The penalty for even being suspected of *desiring* the leap was instant dust. Still, dust was dust, no matter how you got there. He'd rather go down clawing than to one day be aimlessly wandering about one's business and hear Speth's oily voice asking him in a friendly way if they shouldn't go out and take a little walk in the rocks together.

Railsbach's attention snapped back to the present. In the face of the bright new man's plea for a little more time, Sir Fern was granting Mica an extension of translation, what he called a brief respite on a very short leash. The decision had young James Gravely grinning ear to ear, the hairs of his moustache twitching unaccountably until he gave them a little pat with his hand. Dr. Railsbach coughed out a little bark of relief. Felney accepted without a word, but Fern's decision sent Speth spitting and fuming from the hall.

"You'd better have a chat with the Old Speedballer," Fern said to Gravely, watching the assassin as he slammed his way out of the room. The meaning was clear, *Take charge, young man.*

Speth came back a few minutes later, as he always did. Sir Fern delivered a brief but explicit reprimand and took his exit with the others, leaving Gravely alone with the famous assassin. After a brief thrill of fear, Gravely noted he was again protected by the wide width of the conference table, and plunged right in.

"I don't want to step on your hooves, but under Sir Fern, I now claim full responsibility.

I don't want or need you stamping about, showing your displeasure at my desires."

"I didn't—" Speth started to spit out, but Gravely cut him off.

"Perhaps, in the olden golden days, hunters had more self-determination in the field. But there is a new order, and you are simply going to have to conform."

"I see." Speth nodded, pulling his fury in behind a cold and wary veil.

"You had better see. I have reviewed the record of your freeway chase after the EMO, as well as your tailings over the past few decades. You cut transmission with control over forty times in that period."

Speth, who had been about to mention the famous flying saucer failure, now found himself on the defensive. "Wave link is never dependable—" Speth protested.

"Over *forty* times. In urban areas where the blanket is rarely suspect. It doesn't cut flesh."

"No one's ever complained before..." Speth pushed his feet straight out, slumping in his chair and pulling in his chin until he looked like a turtle.

"Not that you *know*...", Gravely replied, letting the implication hang in the air like a raised claw. He paused for effect, and then continued in his sternest voice, "Now that I am here, here is what you are going to do..."

Gravely watched his assassin carefully as he laid down the law. Speth gave terse and instant agreement to everything he demanded, but the young demon wasn't taken in; Speth's cool body temperature gave him away. *The old assassin was masking his inner feelings with the clear contempt of detachment.*

The more Gravely talked, the more upsetting he found Speth's attitude. *What did Fern expect of him, that he convert an entrenched assassin?* Gravely found himself worrying about a blotch on the first page of what he had hoped would be a spotless career. Was any of this really his problem in the first place? After all, he had joined the fray in mid-eruption, so to speak. They could never blame him for the Copenhagen Incident; he'd been taking his final test in Coat Management at the time. If only the rewards weren't so promising, he wouldn't have taken the risk of siding with the doctor.

He wondered if he'd have made the same choice if he'd seen Sir Fern's cold stare *before* he'd decided. Gravely squeezed that small white clot of doubt out of his own mind. Decisions of consequence were to be made, and he wasn't going to let his boss's reputation—or an old reptile like Speth—fork him out of the way. After all, he comforted himself, Speth already had something to answer for, his failure when he had his run at the rogue human. *Too long without a groom,* Gravely said to himself, resolving to take a look at the schedule and have Speth in for remold at the earliest clamp. Still, that would have to wait. For now, they had to reel in the rogue EMO.

CHAPTER 11
Reeling in the Rogue

<u>one</u>

Two days later, James Gravely, Zilch and Speth were sitting at an indoor table in the eating area at the Sherman Oaks Galleria. Zilch was bored and Speth showed characteristic signs of impatience, but Gravely was gaping in openmouthed wonder at the human shopping carnival he saw before him. Speth had to warn him for the seventh time to stop staring.

"Where's Doctor Railsbach?" Gravely asked, more to change the subject than any desire to have a fix on the doctor's whereabouts.

"Call him Kelp," Speth spat gloomily. "You don't know it, but there was a time when our renowned Dr. Railsbach was little more than a translation clerk like Felney."

"That doesn't answer my question. Where *is* he?"

"He begged off. Said he had to observe the two females, and he had a promising new batch of EMOs to analyze." Speth spat into a nearby pot of miniature bamboo. "I told him we could handle this." A small column of acrid fumes rose from the greenery.

Gravely had to bite his lips shut. He suspected Railsbach had set this up; the doctor had been analyzing the tapes from the Il

Fornaio, and for some reason only he knew, Mica Harris would pass by this section of this shopping mall sometime today. They were to drive Mica to the brink, get him into the shock mode, if possible, then inject him into submission and hustle him into a waiting ambulance where a maximum strength blanking capsule would be rammed into his thumb. It was to have been Dr. Railsbach's operation, but with Railsbach —or Kelp —out of the picture, one of them would have to get close enough to operate the capsule inserter. For Gravely, that wasn't the twin hearts of the matter; the trouble was that now the responsibility for success or failure lay squarely on his shoulders.

Feeling neatly outplayed, Gravely accepted a stiff paper plate of slimy, warm organics from Speth.

"But it's *dead*," he protested.

"Oh, fold yourself," Speth reprimanded him.

Gravely stifled a dry rush and looked more closely at the mess on the plate.

"What is this?"

"The humans call it pizza," Zilch said, his high, fruity voice carrying a nonchalance Gravely found suspicious.

"Didn't you do well in eating?" Speth asked with mock politeness.

Gravely stiffened his coat and took a bit of the cold stuff in his mouth. He made a terrible face and spit it on the floor.

Several shoppers stared at them and

hurried on by.

"*Enfold* yourself!" Speth reprimanded, this time more severely.

"What was *that*?!" he asked.

"Vegetarian," Zilch shrugged sympathetically. "It's better with meat on it."

"*Sapiens* flesh?"

Zilch shrugged, "I don't know. Probably not. Probably some beast."

"Right. Like a rat, horse or dog." Speth grinned.

Gravely was bug-eyed as he tried to clean out the inner lining of his mouth with a paper napkin. Speth handed him a drink in a plastic cup. The assassin shot a quick warning look at Zilch as he did so.

"Here. Liquid. Wash it out." Speth sounded sincere, and Gravely gratefully accepted the cup, but when he took a big gulp, the color of his face shot from red to true purple. The veins on his coat stood out and his moustache twitched like it had been hit by heavy voltage. For a moment, Speth thought he would pop his coat. Gravely spat the liquid out in a huge shower, struggling to get the hair on top of his head back under control.

Speth grumbled under his breath and looked away like he wasn't part of the scene. Hazing the new earthsiders was old fun, but even he could see things had gone too far. Passersby were starting to stare. It really wasn't good for business. *But what in Hades were they teaching the new graduates these days?*

"What—was—THAT?!" Gravely managed

to sputter. He had to endure Speth's wry smile.

"Lemonade," Speth said.

Speth raised a cautionary hand before Gravely could curse him. "Wait. Work to do."

Gravely could do little more than glare and try to recover. He went into calm-tek mode, smoothing and settling his hair and patting the wiggling strands of his moustache into quiescence. There was time for nothing else, for Mica Harris was walking through the mall. He was advancing in their direction, head down and self-absorbed with the same abstracted look Gravely had seen on his face in the Copenhagen tapes. *Railsbach had been right! Here he was, the vaunted EMO, the rogue human himself, just ripe for the picking!* It was one thing to review textbook operations, but they were in the real *sap* world with its unlimited possibilities for advantage or failure. A moment ago, Gravely had been full of brine and brim for the overflow, come what may. But the young demon suddenly found himself quailing in the face of the actuality, of what his instructors had called the *"nowness"* of the event.

"What do we do?" he whispered.

Speth was more than a little pleased to take over.

"Do?! We improvise," he snorted happily.

226

two

The mall was crowded for one of those big three day sales, this one announcing the beginning of the school year. Speth projected the image *30% off on sheets* at a blond woman who could roughly pass for Sally from a distance.

"30% isn't much," the woman was thinking.

"50%. It's 50%," Speth projected.

The woman abruptly turned and headed in the right direction.

Speth found a slight teenager of about the right proportions and placed her in step with the blond woman, this time with the whispered promise of a new rock band due to make a personal appearance at the local Wherehouse.

Next, Speth tried to imprint Mica; but without his implant, the human seemed oddly disinterested in even the most lurid suggestions. Still, Speth got lucky; Mica spotted the blond woman and the teenager at just the right moment. He fell for the ploy, rushing up to them and grabbing the woman by the arm. He spun her around and went wide-eyed, seeing through Speth's illusionary veils instantly and recognizing it was the wrong woman.

But she was precisely the right woman from Speth's point of view. She was newly bleached and divorced, a tough, angry lady in her early forties with a wealth of emotional handles Speth could use to twist and turn her at will.

Mica saw the teen girl wasn't a close look-alike, and that she didn't even know the blond woman. Speth tried to get the younger woman to scream, but she was too deep in her rock star fantasy, and his suggestion slid off her psyche like a dead slug. She gave Mica a wide-eyed look and backed away, the best Speth could do with such obdurate material.

"Whoa, dude!" she said in valley mode talk, "Chill, man!" She waved the palms of both hands as she backed away, still on autopilot in the direction of the Wherehouse, shrugging as if to rid herself of the incident, and then turning and half-walking, half-running away, as fast as her tight jeans would allow.

But by now Mica was in trouble with the blond woman. Speth imprinted Mica's shape with a quasi-image of the blond's former husband, a vacuum-brained surfer dude who ran a bicycle shop and had peddled off into the sunset with his round-bottomed young assistant.

"My GOD!" the woman shrieked, clutching at her big silvery purse, "What are you after?! Leave me alone!"

Mica put his hands in the air, also palms outward, and started to back away.

"I'm sorry, I'm sorry, I'm sorry," he repeated. "Wrong person. I'm sorry."

Speth smiled, easily working the woman into a nasty hype, winding her up for a big scene. *Your ex-husband's a pig. He wants your money. He's been following you,* he imprinted. *All men are alike. Just another pig.*

"You're supposed to stay away from me!" she screamed.

"I thought you were someone else," Mica replied. Still backing away, he was running into as many passersby as Felney, helping long-distance from the study, could throw in the path of his retreat.

Brows lowered, the woman stalked after him. "A not-very-likely-story! You come back here, you rapist pig! I'm not even started with you!"

But in spite of everything Felney could do to keep him at the scene, Mica was now thirty feet away and back-pedaling rapidly. Felney managed to lure a black security guard away from his coffee and half-eaten donut with a vision of a big promotion, but the man had a tough mind, and went for the woman instead of Mica, taking her arm and impeding her progress in the course of his simple little investigation. All he had to do was give the unblanked EMO a little rap on the back of the head with his big black flashlight, and in a few minutes they'd have Mica in the ambulance, strapped down for reimplantation. But he didn't. Felney should have known, *sap* security guards didn't go for the source of the trouble; they avoided personal danger by mollifying the injured. Meanwhile, Mica was slipping out of the scene.

Their tap into the crude mall security black-and-white overhead monitors caught the entire story of what happened next in jerky skip-frame motion. There was Mica, turning and walking swiftly away toward the far end of the mall, while over there, the irate blond woman making a scene, trying to get past the security guard, actually pelting him with her purse. Speth didn't help matters, making sure she caused one of the guard's ears to bleed under the rain of blows. At that point, she dug in her purse to find her wallet. After making sure nothing had been taken from her, she turned her wrath on the guard, demanding his name, telling him his business, and gesturing furiously in the direction Mica had taken.

Even as a frustrated Felney watched the action on the monitors from his vantage point in the study, Speth, Gravely and Zilch saw everything close-up from their seats in the resting enclosure in the mall. Gravely looked at the lemonade container in his hand, frowned and set it on the piled boxes belonging to a lady shopper who was sitting nearby. Speth glazed her with weariness and got her concentrating on her tired and aching feet, or she would have seen the lemonade cup and they would have had another incident. As it was, he gave the young Gravely a look as if to say he was the biggest incompetent ever spawned.

For his part, Gravely clapped Speth on the back, quietly and surely pinning the assassin with the failure.

"Too bad, but Rome wasn't built in a day," Gravely shrugged.

"Gomorrah was," Speth responded, giving him a vicious glance and spitting on the nearest potted fichus tree. For all Gravely's onward and upward attitude on the old coat, Speth wasn't buying the new recruit's projection of *comradeship*. The *spavling* would have to be watched carefully, and if he became a real threat, he would have to be dusted. There was nothing in Speth's personal code of ethics to prevent it. Young lieutenants were always catching their coats under the stones of life. Out here, nobody raised much of an inquiry when such tragedy struck.

three

The overhead black-and-white monitors continued to track Mica, who had paused at the far end of the mall. To his left lay the freedom of the parking lot. To his right, the uncertainty of a big department store. After the briefest of hesitations, he entered the store and made his way to the fragrance department. The overheads, which were not rigged for sound, recorded him asking questions, and saw him receive several negative shakes of the head from pretty young salesgirls. One of the young girls behind the counter pointed toward a nearby bank of elevators. Mica took the escalator instead, vaulting up the moving stairs three at a time. On the next floor, he made his way to the personnel department, where he asked his questions again, and again was rewarded with negative shakes of the head. He returned more slowly, shuffling down the steps one at a time. He passed the fragrance department again, this time looking like he was on his way out of the store.

He was almost through the wide doors and back out into the mall proper when the girl behind the counter saw him.

"Oh, sir—did you find her?" She gave him her bright smile.

"No. They never heard of her." He was about to go when he had another idea. "Bells in the Dusk," he said.

"I'm sorry, what?" The girl gave him her best, the hundred percent pure honey smile.

"Did you say something to me, sir?"

"It's a perfume. Bells in the Dusk."

"I don't think we carry it." She was disappointed; she'd done as much as a girl could do. *Oh, well, Subway sandwich and a cold Bud again tonight, sitting in front of old Seinfeld reruns...*

He was turning to go when the department manager, a well-dressed lady in her mid-forties, looked up from waiting on a woman perhaps twenty years her senior. She eyed Mica sympathetically.

"No one has carried that scent in years," she said. "I'm pretty sure."

"How many years?"

"Bells at Sunset?" The elderly customer cut in, "I think my mother wore it...or my grandmother."

"I know now," the department manager said, giving him a triumphant look, "I remember from a management course. Not the course; actually one of the teachers had been in accounting and then moved to marketing, back before they called things *creative* or talked about *marketing a brand*. Bells in the Dusk was one of the first great branded scents to make it in America."

"When?" Mica held his breath, knowing this couldn't be true, and yet anticipating the answer.

The department manager thought it over, "Ohhh...maybe..."

"Roaring 20's?" The elderly customer threw in her best guess.

233

"Hmm. Yes. Probably. *Bell a la Nuit*, wasn't it? Something French like that."

They nodded in agreement and smiled, pleased to have solved his arcane little difficulty for him.

Waiting in the parking lot in the white-and-orange ambulance with a human driver who looked so over-blanked he might not ever be able to drive, Gravely tried to avoid Speth's brooding presence by talking to Zilch. As it had so many times in the past few hours, the conversation turned to the botched spaceship job. The bait had done their part, and they'd thought they'd had him, neat and clean. But when they'd snapped the net, Mica somehow wasn't in it. No one had been able to figure it out. *Not a nice way to start a tour.*

"Humans want to believe in aliens. It's a basic," Gravely hissed for what felt like the hundredth time.

"Well, sure..." Zilch was fawningly agreeable, but Gravely didn't care; he kept talking to the ugly little gnome. Anything to keep Speth off his scales.

"It was a classic lure movement," Gravely continued.

Speth could hardly hold back his disdain. "Classic, but it didn't work." He spat, more an expression this time than actual expectoration. "I understand you and Kelpie are having trouble with the two women as well."

Gravely could feel the coat tighten over his lips. "They are not what we were led to believe. It is Doctor Railsbach's theory that—"

"Bub's balls for every theory he's had! You let Kelp lead you, and you'll find his tail behind you when the project fails."

"Fails?! What is that supposed to mean?"

"You've burst academy. You go figure."

The two eyed each other, locked in silent fury. Zilch, who knew Speth better and who also recognized that James Gravely dusted would be no advancement for anyone, was relieved to see Mica exit the mall and stride toward his beat-up Alfa.

"Where's Nimrod going now?" Zilch piped up, pointing toward Mica. It had the desired effect of unlocking the horns. Being a very good fool, he recognized what he would have to do next. Now he had to play the clown to excess, so they wouldn't direct their anger toward him. Speth's car was in the opposite direction from the Alfa. Zilch ran off toward the BMW, doing a cartwheel and singing out loud in his shrill dwarf voice, *Naughty Marietta, come be good, say she; Mais No, say me!* Their recent bitterness stamped into the background, Speth and young Gravely retracted their over-blank from the ambulance driver, who slumped without a sound to the floor of the ambulance, and they followed after Zilch, convinced the dumpy little sharp-tooth had gone insane.

235

CHAPTER 12
Discovery

<u>one</u>

It was her kitchen on a bright, sunny day. Sally, who knew it better than anyone, looked it over and saw that it was perfect in every detail, even to the view of the hills outside and the sound of the wind in the trees. *Just don't throw open the door, because there was nothing but fog out there. And, of course, there was no Mica, grumbling like a bear because he'd lost his favorite pair of pants or couldn't remember where he'd set down his morning cup of coffee.*

She was keeping Anne Mae busy, baking chocolate chip cookies. They had one batch finished. The delicious hot chocolate smell was filling the air, and they were kneading the dough for a second batch when there was a knock on the door. Anne Mae gave her a fearful glance, and for a moment the light dimmed, not on the indoor lights, but the light everywhere as if the scene was lit by an electrical sun on a rheostat. The dimming effect held only for a moment, and then the golden light was once again pouring across the rolling meadows of their little estate and in through the wide kitchen windows.

Sally gave Anne Mae a reassuring look.

"The door, hon. I have to answer it."

She opened it, and there, standing in the fog, was a white-haired man in a white pharmaceutical coat and a short, ugly dwarf-like creature with long, curled fingernails. The man seemed vaguely familiar, but she couldn't place him.

"Hello," he said, and his cheery smile reminded her of someone she had seen on television selling nose spray, "I'm Doctor Railsbach. And this is Snivler, my assistant..."

Sally didn't know how she was expected to act, so she started right in on the Doctor, "Where are we and how did we get here?"

Railsbach, who had prepped himself for hours, rehearsing the possible responses to every situation, chose a polite reply, "I'm sorry. How very unfortunate, but I'm not at liberty to say."

"So," she said, her eyes narrowing, "We are someplace."

He recognized his blunder at once. Until that moment, the human female could have thought she was delusional or in a coma. She could have thought anything.

"Well," he tried to recover, "you don't know that."

"So there is a me."

He went wild-eyed for only a moment, got a hand to the human coat on his face, which he knew was flushing red in an inadvertent response. *Salvationable woman!* This was all new territory to him, one of those unexpected avenues of opportunity down which the EMO experiment was leading them. It had seemed, at the time of their translation, an excellent idea to bottle the two of them in the little-known

237

chaotic state. Most human spirits lasted in chaos about seven earth days, after which they shriveled up and disappeared. It was a mystery where they went, but as they were never seen or heard from again, it was a good dumping ground for troublesome mistakes. But instead of withering, the two had formed some sort of metaphysical shell that had at least a degree of permanency. After nearly a year, Railsbach's team postulated that the two *sap* women were surviving through some sort of encapsulation in their most cherished memories. But that wasn't a lot to go on.

Even though it seemed to be working, Railsbach felt the first pangs of regret for this bold move on his part, to enter chaos protected by the sap women's cocoon. He reminded himself there was little danger to him personally. He was on a very secure channel, and could be yanked to safety in a twinkle.

"I'm sorry," he said, "I am not here to answer your questions."

"Why are you here? And, by the way, where is 'here'?" Her voice was surprisingly tough, and he realized the implications of the old wisdom that the soul itself could not be blanked. He had long argued that a human spirit without its body was as impotent as a thousand year reptile, but the way she bristled made him wonder. *Could she be dangerous to him?*

He took an inadvertent step backwards, placing himself within Snivler's protective range. The little demon recognized the move

238

and his unpleasant grin broadened.

"What do you want?" she demanded, seemingly oblivious to any danger from Snivler.

"Just to examine you," he replied. "Think of me as your doctor."

"That will be the day." She tossed her head defiantly, her golden hair shining in the false sunlight.

He reached out to touch her, and then pulled his hand back. *Time enough for that, he told himself.*

"Perhaps later. For now, perhaps we could just have a friendly chat."

"I might have been expecting a lot of things," she said in a voice that was like ice, "but not that we would have to entertain."

<u>two</u>

The white-coated man shrugged and walked around the room, followed by Snivler, who hunched along as if every limb had been twisted and broken not once, but many times. When his huge, plate-like eyes took in Anne Mae, they glowed in anticipation. His gaze shifted from her to the cookies, and he shuffled over and helped himself to a handful, which he shoved in his wide mouth.

"Hey!" Anne Mae regained her wits quickly. "Get away from those!"

Snivler didn't have Doctor Railsbach's reservations, and he snarled at Anne Mae. His fangs were set in reddish, warty gums. He picked up a kitchen knife by the blade, examining it like he'd never seen such a wonder before, or perhaps as if he was in awe of the damage such an instrument could perform. He flipped the gleaming knife in the air, grabbing it easily by the handle, and eyed Anne Mae, making an obscene gesture with the knife, illustrating how easily he might pierce and then gut her in a single motion.

"Get away from her!" Sally screamed, and she moved quickly between her daughter and the little creature. The dwarf grinned, raising the knife to thrust it into her chest.

For Railsbach, there was a moment when the experiment, indeed his entire future, was held in the balance. He couldn't control Snivler once he'd caught the killing fever; nobody could. He saw his witless apprentice raise his weapon for a plunging stab wound. The blade gleamed in the air. There was just a brief flash as it made its arc—and then it was gone!

"Snivler!" he shouted. He used the voice of command, and he let loose a string of words in a language too coarse and broken to be formed on the human tongue. Snivler heard, and understood perfectly. Still, as he retreated, he eyed Sally's hips, which were on a level with his eyes. He licked his flappy lips, shifting his gaze to savor her breasts, within easy reach of his clawed hands. Then he skittered back to a spot near the door and flopped down like a dog, bright-eyed and attentive, his unwavering attention back on the girl.

Doctor Railsbach shot him a warning look and then turned his attention back to Sally and Anne Mae.

"Don't worry," he reassured them. "Your little daughter is safe. You're both safe." Again Railsbach tried to rally his shaken confidence, to take assurance from the knowledge that he and Snivler both were tied with electronic jerk-backs, so they could be pulled back to the lab at a moment's notice. The thought was interrupted by Snivler, who was chuckling to himself, a soft, oily laugh.

"Ignore him. He hasn't any manners." Railsbach wandered around the kitchen for some time, looking at the coo-coo clock, feeling the radiation from the still hot oven.

"May I?" he asked of Anne Mae. After she looked at her mother and nodded yes, he tried a small nibble of one of the cookies. A little white pang of fear passed through his frame. *Creating reality out of chaos, wasn't that what the two human females had done here?*

He was no expert on earth food, but if there was a difference between the chocolate chip cookie and one baked on earth, he couldn't tell.

"Very good, really," he said. With his insides churning, he set the cookie back on the tray, "for what it is." Anne Mae gingerly took the cookie off the tray, handling it as if it was tainted, and threw it in the waste can. The cookie was an awful wonder to the man in the white coat—not for its taste, but for the fact that it existed at all, and the real marvel was what had become of the knife. Somehow, the woman had caused it to disappear. That meant she was, should she ever realize it, the absolute mistress of this unstable little world she had created. You couldn't even chant her down while you were in her house, because the incantation would destroy the nest that was protecting him.

Maybe they had learned enough for a first visit. Maybe it was time to be getting out. Railsbach shook his head, fighting down his desire to be gone at once. He spotted a chessboard, set up on one corner of the table. "Ahh, chess! Do you play?"

Sally and Anne Mae exchanged a wary glance, certain they were in the valley of the crazies.

three

Over the next few days, the winter rains retreated once more, and Los Angeles returned to the hazy, eye-gritting air of late summer. The overheads looked down through the shimmering heat and the late morning smog, easily following Mica's Alfa as he took the 101 downtown, got off the Harbor Freeway at 3rd Street and made for the fat little Egyptian obelisk that was the city hall building. Felney and the new batch of translators, who had been added as Mica's rogue status continued, followed the banks of monitors easily as Mica found parking and trudged across a broken concrete plaza and into the hall of records.

"I don't like this," a new young observer said, looking up from his single monitor at Felney's side.

"It is not for you to like or dislike," Felney replied, a bit haughtily, hiding his own inner fears. Nothing had gone right with the EMO project from the beginning. It was one of those long-range plans at which devildom was historically not very good. *Lucifer was always in the details.* While they watched from the monitors, Mica walked steadily through the antiseptic old halls of the city building, hearing his own footfalls echoing away from him. Mica gave the elevators a wary glance and took the stairs instead, down into the basement. A gnomelike human peered over a counter; then, after hearing his request, beckoned him inside to a small reading room and sat him at a worn

243

wooden bench in front of a table. The little man disappeared behind rows of stacked books, only to reappear with a small cart loaded with tattered and dusty old record books.

"Nothing this old is on the computers," he apologized.

"Not your fault," Mica shrugged. He accepted them all and took them to a nearby table where he began to pour through them. It was slow, thick work, trailing his finger on the dusty pages with their handwritten entries. He kept at it for three hours, drawing his finger down each page to be sure he didn't miss a name. 1921. 1922. 1923. He had covered the entire decade of the Roaring 20's through to 1927, and was three-fourths finished with that year when his tracking finger trembled and came to a halt. He saw the words hand-printed in a blocky registrar's signature: AMY FERRASONT, DIED OCTOBER 3, 1927. AUTO ACCIDENT. Mica's hands trembled so violently he placed them under his thighs for a moment, sighing and rocking back and forth in grief. And then he went on to the next entry, reading softly out loud, "ZOE FERRASONT, DIED OCTOBER 3, 1927. AUTO ACCIDENT..."

The demons watched. Even as they zoomed in to make certain of what they already knew, they saw Mica pull his finger away from the thick book. His head slowly lowered, to rest like a prayer or a fallen dove, directly on the page, and the things called tears worked their way into an irregular Rorschach pattern that pooled and ran across the ancient, faded lines of printed information and slowly seeped into the fabric of the paper, a small and insignificant amount of liquid that would in time evaporate, leaving its own forgotten stain, just a curious brown blot on a page that, chances were, nobody would ever open again.

Felney nodded, watching the visible collapse of the unblanked EMO's spirit. He admitted to a grudging admiration for young Gravely's patience. A rogue *sap* who was morose, brooding and emotionally crushed would be that much easier to net. And if the plan collapsed, there was always the assassin. Nobody really liked Speth, but he was the very best crusher alive. And Speth was at Gravely's side, eager for a chance to slash and maim. Felney recognized that Mica's time as a free *sapiens* was now very short, indeed. He would have allowed himself a brief chuckle of triumph, but at that moment the sap jerked up from his chair, knocking the books to the floor as he ran from the room.

Felney toggled his team, "Gravely. Speth. He's coming out fast!" But an answering crackle showed he hadn't gotten through. He cursed Speth under his breath, working his way through the incantations. The assassin had cut them off.

four

Speth and Gravely were taken by surprise as Mica rushed out of the city hall building. They had been arguing next moves in tones that were becoming increasingly shrill. Now the rogue *sapiens* was suddenly right next to them, close enough to skewer with a picket or crush with a sporting bat. All morning they'd been nipping at Mica's flanks, hoping for the lucky snap of the jaws to bring him down, and now here he was.

Speth knew he'd blocked control transmission, at least until they upped for an override. *There the rogue human was, not ten feet away!* Sensing immediacy would override any command the young academy grad could come up with, the assassin took his dueling stance and raised his hand. And in that moment, before he could reduce Mica to dust, a tottering old black man wandered into him, bumping him just enough to where he had no clear shot. It was the lunch hour, and in the next moments, hundreds of workers on noon break poured from the building to take their sun and open their brown paper bags in the cement courtyard. Speth cursed and looked around to ossify the old clown, but he was too quickly swallowed up and lost in the milling crowd. He was a very old man, and couldn't have gone far. Speth, his snuff instincts aroused, took a few steps as if to follow.

"Wait!" Gravely said, coming to his senses when he realized how close they had come to dusting Railsbach's singularly prized EMO, "Stay with us, Speth! It could be a diversionary tactic!"

"Diversionary tactic!" Speth spat in disgust. "Sapcrap!" But the old instincts were too strong, and he returned to stand with his back against the other two in the traditional outward fend-off-danger poise.

Felney, seeing that Mica was not yet captured, took measures to assure that immediate exits available to the EMO were blocked with a wall of humanity, all of whom had stopped to chat for a moment, tie their shoes, or otherwise perform some routine *sapiens* custom. But Felney ground his sharp teeth when he saw in the next moment that the enormous outlay of energy was entirely unnecessary; Mica had chosen a low cement bench and was sitting there like a big, shiny fly on a white chintz curtain.

Felney now had overcome Speth's electronic block enough to low-emission transmit the *sapiens* position to Gravely, and the message, *Waiting instructions.* He would continue his link, even though the drain to get through that jumbled mass of downtown buildings and *sap* flesh would create an energy peak and be another nasty subject at their next monthly fun-and-games with the Dusty Dozen.

Gravely's reply astonished him. *Rollover; hurry, prepare for capture.*

Felney's face bloomed bright red, and he felt a tick in his left eye, a slight chatter he'd had under total control for at least a generation.

The young spawn had no right—!

"Sire! He's supposed to take him down *now*!" But Fern apparently shared none of his concerns.

"Brilliant," Sir Fern's velvety old voice bubbled over his shoulder. "You see why I chose the lad."

"No, I do NOT see," Felney shot back.

"Gurpler, Old Gurpler," Fern soothed, using his subordinate's private name, "He's in proximity with the first rogue we've entertained in generations, he's got old Speedball to contend with, and he hasn't forgotten our directive was *Capture.* I see now why he was so highly recommended."

"I'm not so sure we shouldn't translate."

"Then why did you help him with the interjection of the ancient Negroid *sapiens*?"

"That wasn't me!"

"Ohhh..." Sir Fern's voice trailed off and he felt for the comforting shape of his ornate old smoking pipe. His attention was drawn back to the screen, where Mica sat on an outdoor bench.

The rogue EMO was breathing hard, looking around wildly, just waiting to be plucked. He didn't know where to turn or of whom to ask help or even what to do with his next movement.

And in that moment a cute, curly-headed kid of perhaps ten years or so sat on the bench next to him. The kid was dressed in fashionable homeboy style, in designer baggy pants and the appropriately off-kilter Raiders baseball cap.

Felney cursed, "Eternal Salvation—*Zilch!*" He looked wildly at Fern, who shrugged, "To my knowledge, no one authorized him."

"Should I sting him back?"

Fern thought for the briefest of moments, then shook his head, "No. Let him play. Perhaps it's Gravely's idea. We'll take it where it goes."

five

By now, the Zilch-kid opened the wrapping on a junk food hot dog and, his tolerance for earth food being very low, took a small nibble off the end of the squashy bun.

As Mica sucked oxygen and tried to calm himself, a voice appeared in his head, clear and quiet, like an echo chamber. Mica looked up in alarm. The voice wasn't emitting from a loudspeaker or coming from any passerby. It was in his head. As he glanced around with a jerky, wild-eyed stare, the voice spoke to him in the warm tones of a best friend.

"You didn't really love them," the voice said.

Mica jerked to his feet, quickly looking in every direction like a frightened sparrow. He saw nothing but a kid sitting next to him who was ignoring him in favor of some junk food wrapped in bright tinfoil. Mica spun around, desperate for an explanation. Commonplace images from the ordinary lunchtime scene poured through his brain in a jumbled assortment; three plump young Oriental women jabbered merrily at each other in Cantonese while they ate salads from little plastic boxes. Two East Indian kids played Hacky Sack. Three black women studiously poured over yellow legal pads while they munched thin turkey slice sandwiches on white bread. A plump little white man with a thin moustache read a fuchsia-covered paperback with fuchsia tiger lilies on a brocaded fuchsia background,

Star Flight by Phillis A. Whitney.

Felney, who had no idea the little dwarf was running short-range transmission, had lost all patience. "What's that silly little incompetent *doing*?!" he fairly screamed.

Fern, who had actually been the one to teach the technique to Zilch, patiently training him as one might teach tricks to an earth dog, nodded, "Good boy. He's going to drive our poor EMO right to the edge of madness. And when Mica Harris is all foamy-mouthed and blathering, Gravely will be right there with the net."

Back in the sunny square at the flanks of the city hall building, the quiet voice in Mica's head continued relentlessly, *"You see, you didn't REALLY love them. No. Not really."*

Mica jumped up and violently shook his head from side to side, punching at his ears. He staggered and nearly fell, desperate to understand how it could be that he heard voices out of thin air. It had to be the last phase of the madness that had been growing in him since Sally and Anne Mae left him, since Copenhagen, since their dance at the Il Fornaio had ended in the crazy flying saucer scene. Of course, it made sense; the final phase of his loneliness would be *An Attack of the Voices*. They would squeeze his brain, steal the life out of him, leave him lying on the concrete slab with cold, staring eyes and a dark mass of blood pooling from his mouth.

"What?!" he shouted, "What do you want of me?!"

A few people glanced at Mica and kept on walking, or returned to their conversation and their peanut butter and jelly sandwiches. Nobody stopped or dared to stare at him.

"If you loved them," the voice in Mica's head persisted in a reasonable, comforting tone, *"you surely would have saved them. You wouldn't have let them die like that, you know, in such horrible agony. Their bodies were burned beyond recognition, weren't they? At least, that's what the papers said. You did read the papers, didn't you? You did at least read the papers that said those things about the ones you say you love?"*

For a moment, Fern believed they had a chance. Mica stared in every direction. The *sap* was twitching, saliva actually drooling from a corner of his mouth in the traditional manner of imbecilic *sap* madness. He was ready to ram his head into the nearest wall, to take the obligatory dive out the nearest window, if he'd had a gun, to shoot himself— anything to make the voice in his head stop, to give him a little peace.

"Go away!!" Mica screamed, banging his fists against his ears. "Who is it?! Who's doing this to me??"

Even distanced by the overheads, Felney and Fern could see Mica was in the final stages, ready to be led back to his implant. *Now,* they knew, *now was the time to pull back Zilch and move in by pretending to be Mica's friends, the time to gather Mica into a dark and deserted corner of the building. Slip the implant gun*

252

from a pocket, one quick Pffttt! and the rogue would be back in the blanket.

But Zilch was having too much fun. *"Come on, admit it,"* the quiet voice started up again in Mica's head. *"Let's have no denial here. We're friends—friends! Sally was an object, something you got off on. Anne Mae was your possession. Come on, now, 'fess up! You only love yourself!"*

Mica trotted in a little circle, hands clamped over his ears, screaming so loud the spittle could be seen flecking from his mouth, "NO! WAIT!! THAT'S NOT TRUE!!!"

It was an excellent time for Gravely to make his move. The typical humanoid circle had begun to form, the herd ready to cast out one of their own who had become a menace from within.

253

<u>six</u>

At the end of the month, in the review, the committee analyzing the views from the overheads easily recognized the critical moment. They pointed to and endlessly chattered over the turn-point when Mica gained cognition, though not a one had any field experience or even the vaguest notion of what had caused the victim to suddenly become aware.

Whatever it was that inspired him, Mica stopped raving when he shouldn't have, pausing when he should have begun to flee. In short, he gathered in when he should have spilled over the last edge and gone flail-legged into the abyss. Mica obviously never knew what happened, and if anyone else knew, they weren't telling.

To the Council of Elders, it seemed apparent that, for no discernable reason, Mica simply calmed himself. And looking around in a less agitated state, his attention unfortunately centered on the homeboy sitting on the other end of his bench.

In honest appraisal, the committee conditioned that under Mica's gaze the kid did hesitate, just a flash. It could clearly be seen on the retro. And, in that flash, Mica seemed to catch the kid's eye. Mica was seen to look away, still searching for his sanity, and then he was observed looking back again. And this time, something formidable and ugly was forming in the rogue *sapiens'* psyche.

At that moment, as Mica watched the young homeboy, the kid's features began to bobble, to warp back and forth, much as had those of the white-coated man who had tried to intercept him on the elevator. The face flashed back and forth between that of the homeboy and some sort of ugly little dwarf. Homeboy to dwarf. Homeboy-dwarf, homeboy-dwarf.

Zilch, having the good sense to understand he had been detected, jumped quickly to his feet, throwing the hot dog at a nearby trash container. His aim was off, and the human food hit the lip of the can and fell to the cement pavement.

In Zilch's defense, the committee noted, it had been centuries since any of them had been uncovered in their true form by a *sapiens* in a public place, and the procedures for it were so ancient as to have drifted into ritual. Panicking, Zilch slid from homeboy through his dwarf coat and straight to demonic. Now his coat was chattering between dwarf and the hunched little demon dog that he really was. Dwarf to demon-dog. Dwarf, demon; dwarf, demon.

Suddenly, unexpected by any of them, the human roared at Zilch.

"You!! Stop!!" Mica shouted.

Zilch froze in place, though his coat continued to chatter between dwarf and demon. Again, in the defense against dusting the little demon, he was used to obedience, and not used to interrelationships with unblanked humans.

Zilch slowly turned to face Mica. And in so doing, he panicked and broke the first rule—

he lost his sap coat entirely. He stood naked in front of Mica, almond eyes shining his panic, his classic badger-like body hunched forward on his powerful forepaws. He was black as coal, as pitch, as obsidian. It was Zilch the devil-dog, the Egyptian guardian of death, the Mayan keeper of the seasons, the Greek and Roman guardian of the gates of hell.

It lasted for only a few seconds, and then Zilch had the presence of mind to break whatever spell had come over him and to dart away.

Mica was stunned by what he had seen, and could barely speak as a security policewoman pushed her way through the crowd and took his arm.

"That little punk swipe something of yours, mister?" Mica could see the empty aggression in her attitude. She wasn't going to chase; it was a formality, part of her job.

"Didn't you SEE him?!" Mica whispered, as he pointed after the retreating back of the little alien.

She misunderstood his awe for choked-back anger.

"I see 'em all the time." She gave him an efficient grin. She was Mrs. Cop, one hand on her hip, all bustle and efficiency. "They're a real pain around here."

Perhaps they still could have taken him, nulled the security female and walked him away. But Speth and Gravely were glaring at each other rather than concentrating on their prey.

256

Mica was about to start after Zilch, even though he was around the corner and headed for a long stairway that led deep into the stacked cars in the parking structure. Felney was able to divert him with the hot dog. Mica saw it out of the corner of his eye, a half-eaten black snake trying to wiggle out of the bun. The snake cleared the bun and headed for some nearby bushes, leaving a little wiggle of bloody glop in its trail. Mica reacted as Felney had hoped, heaving violently into the same nearby bushes.

And still, Gravely and Speth were going after each other, rather than move in on their prey.

"I give you no authority to translate!" Gravely, red-faced, pulled himself into the rage stance.

"Oh, yes," Speth hissed, "you just know the right way to do everything!"

"Stupid, blundering, jerk-brine translatiac! I said *rollover!*"

Speth was not at all forked in. "Some day, little Grackling," he hissed, "your noble-skinned sire's name, and rank, and reputation is going to do you absolutely no good at all."

"Go for it, Speth," Gravely taunted.

For a moment it looked as if Speth was going to call down wrath, skewer himself and everyone else on the jagged point of his own spite. But the canny old war-trump only jammed his coated claws in the pockets of his expensive gray suit and turned away, spitting on the nearest bush as he walked away.

"You're so good," he said over his shoulder, "reel him in yourself!"

Gravely, who was extraordinarily quick on the lash and had been the academy champion, retracted his claws with a sense of bitter disappointment. He felt sure Speth would have learned a brief and final lesson. Now, the game between them would continue, distracting him from his real work. He watched the old assassin walk away, thinking *Double-dangerous the demon who can withhold his strike*. Gravely sighed, patting his moustache back into submission. He would walk quietly until the monthly meeting, and then strike to remold Speth without mercy. He looked around, intent once again on his mission. But by this time Mica Harris was nowhere to be seen.

CHAPTER 13
Snivler's End

<u>one</u>

To Railsbach, the phenomenon of the woman who could create a kitchen out of nothing was as deep as the primal mysteries of light and darkness. It may have been her own little security cocoon, and seemed to be unconscious on her part, but he was drawn to it as an aspect of the same complex set of wonders which had lured him to scientific studies when he was just a raw spawnling. Fresh from the nest, something seemed to attract him to gape in admiration at the vastness of dark space and the limitless possibilities of crossing dimensionality, caused him to first ponder the so-called *Other Plane States*, which had become the very heart of their drive to blossom on the new anti-earth into which they had pushed their way.

That dimensionality itself had laws he did not doubt, and he sensed that, in establishing their outposts on the poisonous, oxygen-heavy lands of the *homo saps* they had somehow broken through a thin, hard shell of order. But none of the angels of ancient lore had driven them back, and he also believed that existence had a higher law, that of survival. To paraphrase in *sapiens* terms, a cancer didn't think of itself as destructive; the cells were simply hungry new organisms trying to maintain their own existence. To a cancer cell it was natural that the host was destroyed, if they even thought of it at all. *And when all the world came to be deliciously ravenous carcinogens, was that not the new order?*

The *sap* females' kitchen, it seemed, was in perpetual bright daylight, and would remain so as long as the two of them had the energy to maintain it. A total oddity, the sun dependent on humans! And where did that energy come from? *Lucifer, but he loved the mysteries!* Even under his humanoid coat he felt the little thrill of wonder shiver the hard shell of his carapace.

He walked around the brightly lit room, took another nibble from one of the unbearably sweet cookies the younger female had made, which had now cooled to room temperature, apparently their normal state. His moving around the room had a second purpose. He had started a game of chess with the mature female, and she had swiftly harvested most of his pawns and now had his bishop hopelessly pinned.

"Can't figure a way out, huh?" she prodded him with a grim satisfaction.

"Mommmmmmmm!" Anne Mae complained from a nearby chair.

Railsbach was having misgivings about bringing the lower-life, Snivler, along with him. Generally the *saps* found them distracting or even terrifying, and he'd thought it might more easily give him the upper hand in close contact. But the crooked little orgone brought out a strength and hard anger in Sally that Railsbach wouldn't have believed possible. Snivler was lying on the floor, clicking his long nails and trying to look up Anne Mae's dress, showing the ageless mix of disgust and wonder that demons, who chose their own sex more or less to suit the moment, had for human organs and their mating rites.

"Will you get that ugly little creature out of here?!" Sally shouted.

Railsbach was about to play the scene out, see what the woman would do, when the relay buzzed in his pocket. He snapped his fingers at Snivler, who scrabbled across the room away from the girl.

The relay continued to buzz. He didn't want to answer with the earth woman in proximity, but the insistent sound continued in the pocket of his white jacket. He asked himself, what harm could it do? There was no way she could know the phone was his lifeline, that he had been hardwired so they could jerk him back from this chaotic dimension the moment the pocket of security around them began to dwindle.

"You stay over there," he said, pointing a finger at Sally, who was still sitting on her side of the chess game. He turned from her, extracting the phone-like relay from his jacket pocket and hunched in a corner facing the stove.

"Kelp, here," he said in a low voice into the phone. He looked over his shoulder to check that she was still sitting in place. Snivler had

261

started to creep across the floor towards Anne Mae, but Railsbach froze him with the lancing image of a merciless flailing.

two

Felney's voice, strangely booming, came across the line, detailing how Mica had gone to city hall and tracked the origins of the blond woman and the girl who had lured him into the spacecraft trap.

"But you have him now...?"

"Still at large, Kelp. And he's growing stronger. He saw through Zilch's coat."

"That was foolish to—"

"It was Sir Fern's idea. At least, he went along with it." Even at great distance Felney's voice had that superior pitch, that *don't blame me, I only work here* attitude that Railsbach detested.

"All right," Railsbach responded. "But...I wasn't there, either. You're not saying that Krath-Net-Ja-Pur believes the failure to capture was *my* fault?!"

"Sir Fern didn't directly accuse you. Just keeping you informed, dear Doctor. Mica Harris is your EMO, and even though you weren't there, it was your operation."

Railsbach snapped his little transceiver shut with a little click. It was clear that he was being set up. He realized again that his own dusting might be at stake. He returned to the chess game in a glum mood. The *sapiens* woman was eyeing him with a speculative look on her pale face.

"Kelp," she said. "I thought your name was Doctor Railsbach."

The blood rushed to his face and he

263

slapped his cheek to prevent the chatter he knew was coming. *She knew his name!* He had to fight down the ancient superstitions. Well, so what, he told himself. She didn't know the significance or what to do with her knowledge. That gave her the potential for dominance, but not necessarily the capability. Knowledge, after all, was everything.

"Just an old schoolboy nickname," he muttered.

"I'll bet," she said softly. "Who were you talking to?"

"I can't answer that."

"I'll bet you can, *Kelp,*" she said. Her voice was quiet, but the sharp cut of it when she intoned his name could not be denied.

What did it matter? The information was useless to her. He found himself answering, "It was a certain Mr. Felney. Assistant to my boss."

"Come. Let's continue our chess game." He sat in time to witness her wipe out his second castle with the diagonal sweep of a white bishop across the board.

"And what's his name, *Kelp*? Your boss's name?"

It wasn't so bad, opening up to a helpless *sapiens.* After all, he had her in his laboratory, out in the center of nowhere.

"Albert Fern," he said softly. "Sir Albert Fern. He's a hard taskmaster, old-fashioned and does things by the book."

"Oh. The one you called Krath-Net-Ja-Pur."

The blood seemed to drain out of his face and his coat began a chatter he knew he wouldn't be able to suppress. *What had he done? What a foolish, ridiculous blunder!* And then blessed relief flooded his mind. They were in the chaotic zone. There were no monitors. No one knew. And, chances were, even if she recognized the significance, now that she had been boxed she would never meet Albert Fern face-to-face.

"I think I met Krath-Net-Ja-Pur once," Sally said, as if she could read his mind. "No, make that twice. Once in Copenhagen, and then at that big, gloomy mansion in the hills."

"What does his name mean, in my language?"

"Cut of the Dark Knife."

"A pretty scary fellow."

Railsbach nodded, lips pursed, and decided to say nothing more. On the chess table, Sally's little band of white pawns was marching steadily forward, and he had to collapse his few remaining troops around his king and queen.

"Where are we?" she asked.

"I don't really know," he answered honestly enough.

"Is it some sort of experiment?" He nodded that it was.

"Who do you work for, *Kelp*?"

"I already told you, though in all honesty, I could be ground to dust for that."

"I mean, what side, what team?"

"I don't understand."

"You understand. What bunch of creeps

265

would do what you've done to Anne Mae and me?"

He tried to bluster his way through it.

"We didn't do anything. I mean, you *died*..."

The sunlight, the air, the very fabric of the room around them seemed to shiver and dim as if struck by a reality quake. Railsbach couldn't be sure, but as it slowly recovered, it seemed more insubstantial, less warm and secure than it had a moment before. Anne Mae, who had been staring at him in white-faced silence, now began to cry softly. Her mother put her arm around her and gave Railsbach a bittersweet smile.

"So," was all she said. "Excuse me for a moment."

Snivler had started to crawl back across the floor, panting like a dog, his shiny silver-dollar eyes on Anne Mae's hips. Sally stalked across the tile floor toward him.

"Snivler!" Railsbach saw the danger, shouted a warning.

Sally lined the little demon's round head up with the experience of a soccer mom and gave him a hard boot in the left ear. The evil little creature rolled into a corner, hissing and extending his claws. He bounded back like a ratty beach ball and headed for Anne Mae, intent on scooping her stomach before anyone could do anything about it.

"Get away from her, you little vermin!" Sally yelled. Railsbach eyed her with as much newfound fear as amazement. Angry, she seemed charged with electrical energy. She was like a mythical goddess of earthly legend, her features luminescent, her body in the attack mode. Railsbach remembered the old academic warning, *Deadly is the female of the sapiens!*

"Snivler!" she cried, and her voice held the fury of the seven witches of Cibola. Dr. Railsbach gaped at her aura, saw the hair upraised and floating, the glow emanating from her body, and knew he was seeing the first completely unblanked *sapiens* spirit since the mythical angels. But she was too late. Snivler held Anne Mae captive, one of his clawed hands grasping her arm, and he reared back to gut her with one sweeping motion.

Realizing she would never reach her daughter in time, Sally flung out her hands in a furious and futile gesture. But in that moment, something entirely unexpected happened. Anne Mae, struggling with the sudden strength of panic, ripped her arm away from the little demon.

"Don't-you-ever—" the little girl shouted through clenched teeth, raising one hand to point at Snivler's glass-eyed, grinning stare.

Railsbach never heard if she said any more. There was a powerful thunderclap and an enormous emanation of power from the little girl's fingertips. A huge bolt of blue lightning raced across the short space that separated her from her tormentor. There was a flash of white light and Snivler exploded into shredded near-nothing. All that remained was a blackened spot on the tile floor, a few balls of furry matter, and a smell not unlike that of charred pork in the air.

"Moooommmm..." Anne Mae wailed, lost and bewildered for the barest of moments before rushing into her mother's arms.

Sally, stunned by what she had seen, automatically reached out and hugged her daughter.

"It's all right, hon," she reassured her, stroking her honey blond hair. "The evil little monster deserved it. Don't worry. Everything's going to be all right, now."

She stared across the room at Railsbach, her look saying, *He started it!* Railsbach was amazed to recognize his *sapiens* coat was actually sweating. *Of course they hadn't thought to null the two females; how do you implant a capsule in a ghost?* But even as his mind darted around like a spider looking for an escape crack, he realized any hearing by the Dozen on what had transpired would be terminal for him.

Later, in a calmer moment, he would realize the extent of his panic; but for the moment, it was enough if he could just make his way to the door and back to his lab. He put his coated hands up with the palms outward and retreated with the beating of his twin hearts loud in his own ears. He managed to get one hand on the knob behind him and the other on the transceiver in his pocket. And then he was out of the kitchen, and entirely disappeared in the fog.

<u>three</u>

Mica sat slumped over the slanted art director's desk in his cluttered cubicle, staring at a nearly finished cartoon. Horny was playing chess with a woman. He didn't know why. He couldn't find anything funny in it. Horny was looking dismayed as the woman delivered checkmate with her queen. The only line he could come up with was, *You think that's something, wait until my husband gets here.* But that wasn't funny, either. It didn't even make sense.

Jimmy's Jamaican dialect lilted at him over the cubicle partition, "Holdin' for you on 6, Mica-darlin'...Some dude from Ar-i-see-bo, my kind of place, my kind of town."

Mica grabbed the phone at his side, "Hello. My name is Mica Harris. Reporter for the Los Angeles Weekly. I'd like to know if there have been any unusual sightings in this area over the last—"

An educated and impatient British male's clipped voice cut him off, "I don't know what you think we do, old boy, but what you're asking is a bit out of our line."

"But, I heard that sometimes—"

"Dear fellow, you are halfway around the world from us. What would you expect, that we could actually see around the arc of the earth?"

"No, but—"

"We don't credit you Hollywood chaps much in the first place. Probably just some

269

effects clown playing with old leftovers from *Independence Day*. Cheerio." And with that he hung up. Mica clicked off his own phone and wearily sat in his art director's chair in time to see a grinning head poked around the doorway to his little room. It was wearing googly-eyes which waggled down from both sides of a thin, straight nose.

"Yao!" Mica jumped, startled by the eyes. He was in shape to believe almost anything. Radiation birth defects. Mutants. Creatures from another galaxy. *Once you've seen shape-shifting, anything is possible.*

"Hey," the mouth under the eyes said, grinning triumphantly, "it's only me—Jimmy, traffic girl-wonder and head cheerleader!"

"Yeah, well…take it somewhere else. I'm a little jumpy," he grumbled. "Stuff happening even *you* wouldn't believe."

She took off the glasses, "Try me, white boy."

"No, never mind."

She came into the room, her pink-and-white peony patterned silk mini dress showing off the curve of her hips and her long, milk chocolate legs.

"I couldn't help overhearing. Why were you calling Arecibo? Are you a fellow sci-fi lover?"

"Research for Horny," he muttered, trying to put her off.

"Mica," she pouted. She had large, dark eyes framed in a perfect oval face, and a certain wispy, deerlike beauty. Her breasts were so large for her slender frame that the office wags had declared them the products of augmentation.

Mica tried to wave her off. "I know, God is an alien. I don't want to talk about the Raelians again," he said, referring to her latest addiction.

"Naw, naw, man. I just thought you might want to take me on a date."

She handed him a flier printed on lurid lavender paper. The 36 point type headline screamed, COME SEE THE PURPLE PEOPLE EATERS! The subheads continued, *Scores of Exotic Creatures!* There was a crude paste-together of the Creature from the Black Lagoon dancing with the Alice from Alice in Wonderland.

The Annual Sci-Fi Convention; *Weirdos, Freaks and Fanatics of Every Fetish Welcome!*

The thought occurred to him that maybe a lot of people around town were dressing in costume for the convention. But then he remembered the weird facial chattering of the man on the elevator, and his vivid recollection of the homeboy who turned into a dwarf and then a demon. He felt weak and dizzy. If he'd been at home, he would have collapsed on the couch, or popped some codeine and pulled the covers up over his head.

"You don't look so good, mon. You look a little pale—I mean, even whiter than usual."

He kept his eyes on the purple flier, only managing to mumble, "Maybe I'm getting a little run-down."

271

"I've got just the thing." She snapped her fingers and headed out of the room.

"No more google-eyes," he called after her.

She returned with a Sprite, popped the top and handed it to him.

He leaned back and took a grateful gulp. Though the can was icy to the touch, the liquid inside was thick and body-warm. He spit out a mouthful of red blood. They both stared at the can in his hand. Jimmy took her finger and stuck it in the spilled red mess that had spattered all over Mica's new cartoon.

"I'd say we got us a mungo lawsuit here…" she said.

Mica, his world spinning with a sudden attack of vertigo, fell from his chair, hitting his head on a hard edge of his wooden table, and was rewarded with a period of deep, unrelieved blackness.

Jimmy stayed with him until he came around, and no one at the paper related his accident to the strange concurrent incident of the two fame-seekers and their strange little dwarf companion who tried to push their way past the security system and into the L.A. Weekly's editorial offices. Old Jeffrey, the white-haired, mustachioed security guard, was sleeping as usual, and would have missed the whole thing if he hadn't been shaken awake by some itinerant old bum who had lost his way and happened to be in the building at the same time. But once aroused, Jeff had risen to the height of heroism in his eight-year second career in security, the grand moment when he actually unsheathed his gun. Of course, the gun wasn't loaded, but there was a tense moment when the tall, dangerous-looking one pointed angrily at him, and he feared the confrontation might come to blows. But, under the watchful gaze of the bum, who was an old black man, the younger intruder slapped his companion's hand aside, and the odd threesome left without further trouble, allowing themselves to be escorted out of sight by the police.

four

Doctor Railsbach stood in the early morning light that streamed in through the big French windows in Albert Fern's study. He was trembling slightly, for, although Sir Fern had not explained the subject of their meeting, it didn't take much to conjure images of the implacable hater, the dreaded Krath-Net-Ja-Pur, whom he had seen cook many a spawn in his own carapace, and to imagine what he might be up to.

Felney, who never slept, was already hard at work, balancing accounts. Albert Fern stalked back and forth in front of the doctor, who was uneasily shifting his weight as he stood near the roaring fireplace.

"So," Albert started in, "we handle the capture of your EMO with a gloved hand as you requested, and we are made fools of, denied, badgered about by *sapiens* police and louts alike, and in the end..."

Behind Sir Fern, Zilch and Nilch were poking fun at Railsbach, pointing gleeful fingers and puffing their bellies as they imitated their boss. Railsbach snipped off an untimely flare-up of anger, and concentrated on Fern.

He realized his situation might not be as hopeless as he'd imagined. Sir Albert was still talking about Mica, his runaway EMO! They had not been able to override his system and send in sensors of their own to witness his now out-of-control experiment with the two *sap* females! And that meant leadership was unaware of Snivler's untimely dusting!

"Yes, sire?" he said in the subservient posture, breathing a little easier as he moved a touch away from the safety of the fireplace.

Sir Fern rattled on, "...your Mica Harris is still free to wander the highways and gutters of Los Angeles."

Railsbach wondered how much time that gave him. Surely no more than hours, perhaps a day or two. Sooner or later Snivler would be missed at a counting; three absences in a row, and an alert would go out. The orgone would be traced back to the moment they had walked the tether through the void to the two earth females. Railsbach knew he had that much time to plot his own survival. Rumors came to mind, of rogue demons who had gathered earth coin and left the ranks, relying on their wits and luck to live in the shadows until more favorable times, a changing of the order—and even, in rare cases, until sweet clemency had been granted. For his part, Railsbach had only what was in the pockets of his ever-present white jacket, the symbol of his authority. He was the only scientist to ever attain the rank of demi-master. Now he saw how easily everything could be taken from him. What should he do first? The words *build a smoke screen* came to his mind, even as he saw Sir Fern was waiting for him to say something.

"Outrageous!" he sputtered. "I wasn't even here!"

Zilch and Nilch were delighted. Arm in arm, they danced a do-si-do behind Sir Fern,

275

chanting, "Wasn't even there/ Didn't have a care!" until the boss waved them silent with a brief, impatient sweep of the unlit pipe in his hand.

"I suspect, if I may," Felney said, looking up briefly from a monitor where he'd just assisted a young but disillusioned wanna-be movie star to a fatal dose of heroin, "Sir Fern's point is, perhaps you should have been."

"Thank you, Old Gurpler, but I'll speak for myself."

Rebuked by the master, Felney gave them both a nasty little glance and returned to the safety of his translation board.

"It was inexcusable," Sir Fern said, but Felney's distraction seemed to have brought him off his high vapor, "Blight of Salvation, Kelp, where were you?"

"I was off-plane, sire, securing secondary EMOs..." Railsbach held his nitrogen, knowing his coat was already white with fear from withholding so much information and yet hoping Sir Fern wouldn't notice or ask him more.

The two dwarfs were teasing him again, silently mouthing La-la-la-la-la, and gesturing back and forth with their hands and heads wagging side to side like puppets on strings.

A grumbling started deep in Albert Fern's throat. They all recognized from the characteristic ritual of the throat clearing that it was decision time. "Well, alright, then. But from now on you report to young James Gravely."

276

"But—he's a whelpling."

"Report to him on the hour."

"But, my experiments! That's impossible!"

"If I say do it, nothing is impossible. If you're not going to be at his side, you can phone it in. I want him to know where you're at and what you're doing at all times. Is that clear?"

"Perfectly clear, sir." Railsbach bowed and backed away. As he retreated, he walked a little closer to the dwarves than absolutely necessary, hoping to get in an unexpected blow. But Nilch, who had been thinking along similar lines, looked up and bared fang at him, a soft little reminder that they didn't get to be guardians of the gate for nothing. Kelp gave back the same, and then stepped casually into the roaring fireplace.

Sir Fern hummed a sadly off-key version of his doorbell chime, "Brahms: Variations on a Theme by Hayden", and dug in his pocket for the velvet pouch of pungent tobacco which was his favorite. He mused for a moment on the use of smoking among the *saps*. It had sent a generation of dark philosophers skittering along the blind alley that perhaps since the saps entertained this noble habit, they should be elevated as associates rather than considered inferior slave-creatures. Albert Fern's thoughts turned back to his interview with Kelp.

"He's very nervous, our good Doctor Railsbach," he said to Felney. "I wonder, wonder, wonder what he's hiding..."

"We'll find out, sire," Felney said. They

watched one of the monitors as Railsbach popped out of a seemingly blank wall in his office at the medical building.

"I want you to pull Kelp's experiments back otherside," Sir Fern said softly.

"He'll take that as a terrible embarrassment, sir."

"Don't tell him about it beforehand. Just whisk it all back."

"Good idea, sire. Anything goes wrong, we can handle it in our own dimension."

"You think something could go awry, Gurp?"

Felney shrugged. He'd thought the EMO project dangerous from the first time Kelp had proposed it.

"Take the null off a *sap,* and you'll find trouble," he said finally, his lips twitching in a dour little smile as he quoted from the ancient Book of White.

CHAPTER 14
Dr. Bruce

<u>one</u>

Mica was in such a dazed state that he hardly knew how he made his way back to Dr. Bruce's office. He remembered the incident of the bloody Sprite can, Jimmy's look of astonishment, and then blackness. Later, on coming to, he'd rushed out of the office and driven like a madman through the fairly light late morning traffic. He even risked the elevator up to the seventh floor, though he brought a short length of lead pipe that he'd kept under the front seat of the Alfa, and he was ready to jump off and run every time the elevator doors opened to let anyone on or off.

He set the pipe as inconspicuously as he could along the wall, and blond-haired Janie smiled her pretty smile and waved him right in even though a dozen or so old-timers were sitting around, waiting their turn.

The Doc swabbed his infected hand, which was now black and swollen.

"What's going on with you, Mica?" the Doc asked, bypassing their usual banter and cutting right to the chase.

"What do you mean?"

"Look in the mirror."

Mica looked, and saw a wild-haired, wild-eyed young man with baggy eyes and disheveled clothing. His hand was bloated

279

almost beyond belief.

"You have to take care of yourself," the Doc said. "Medicine can only go so far."

"It's been a bad couple of days, Doc."

"We're going to have to lance this, maybe scrape a little, to get the festering out."

"Yeah. Sure. Anything."

The Doc moved around, positioning his body so Mica couldn't see what he was doing.

"Hey, I want to watch," Mica protested.

"I don't want you wincing every time you see a knife or a needle coming."

"I don't wince," Mica said, a shadow of his old bravado returning as he pulled his hand away from the doctor. And then he broke down, blubbering, "I SAW Sally. I—I—I actually SAW her!"

"Mica, Mica, Mica..." The Doc shook his head slightly. "You saw Sally?"

"Twice, now. I know it's not possible. But I did."

The Doc patted his shoulder, helped him on the table. "Here, let's take a break. I can't sew you up with you going on like this. Come on, now. Lie down here a few moments and collect yourself."

Mica broke up, his sobbing filling the room. The Doc felt his forehead, patted his shoulder.

"And then—I mean, so much—it's CRAZY, the things that—I don't know where to—how to explain—" Mica knew he was babbling, but he couldn't stop himself.

The Doc smiled. "It's not necessary, Mica.

Believe me, it's all right. You're going to be okay, now. It's you and me, Mica and the Doc. I got you through after the accident, didn't I?"

"Well, yes you did…"

"And I've always been here for you, haven't I?"

Mica sat up, and saw that the Doc was working on extracting a small silvery cylinder from a plastic tray in which they were imbedded like pills.

"What are those?" he asked.

The Doc looked startled for a moment. Then he recovered, "Oh, these? Just, you know, batteries for pacemakers. For heart patients."

"Let me see one."

The Doc reluctantly passed across the one he'd extracted from the tray.

"Powerful little devils."

Doc's face flushed beet red. "You have no idea," he said.

Mica handed it back. "Here. Probably expensive."

He noticed the Doc carefully set it on the surgical tray.

"Aren't you going to put it back in the container with the others?"

"Oh, now you're the doctor. We going to get at that hand?"

"Only if I get to watch."

The Doc sighed and looked at his watch. He glanced over at the phone; then decided to use one from another room.

"I'll be right back. Take a moment. Relax.

I'll be right in the room next-door."

Alone in the familiar room, Mica shuddered and hunched into a fetal ball, wrapping his arms around his knees and starting his barely audible tuneless, hooting whistle. As he rocked back and forth on the upholstered patient's table, a thick strap fell from under the pad and bounced with a clang against the metal legs of the table. He sat bolt upright, remembering his adventures in the deserted operating room on the 21st floor, the floor that never was.

Mica took a deep breath and whispered a few more hoots from his favorite Rolling Stones song. He saw his own drawing of Horny Hamster on the wall where the Doc had hung it, right next to the horrid seascape with the poinsettia petal palette strokes.

He tried his old attitude, hunching around the room, inspecting things. He took a moment to peer in a built-in closet, muttering, "Hmmm…Nothing in here but...a straitjacket."

Stunned into a wary alertness, he moved quietly to the wall phone. He clicked down on the lit button and then picked up the receiver and held it to his ear. The Doc was talking—he was sure it was the Doc's voice—in a language so broken and guttural it was a shock to his ears. Not Hebrew or anything European. It was like nothing of this earth.

two

Mica slowly replaced the phone and went back to the surgical table to more closely inspect the small plastic case of silvery cylinders. There were 26 in the box, and the one the Doc had removed and placed on the stainless steel table. Mica found a black rectangular top for the box. It looked not much different from the box in which one might receive an expensive wristwatch.

In one decisive move, he picked up the same knife he'd used before and slashed at the capsule on the table, shielding his eyes from the glare he knew would come. But there was no instant flash. The capsule slowly began to heat and to glow dull red. He turned the box with the other capsules upside down on top of the one he'd activated. Mica left the room and was halfway down the hall when the capsules went off like a string of atomic firecrackers.

"Fire!" he yelled. And while the receptionists milled around, he was out the door, down the hall and onto the elevator. The elevator doors closed, and this time it headed down and made the lobby without interruption. Congratulating himself, Mica took a step off the elevator and practically ran into the arms of the man in the white coat.

"I want to talk to you," the man said. His face was steady as a rock. There were no obscene plastic wriggles and no feature shifting. But it didn't matter to Mica, who had already panicked. He ran past Railsbach and out of the nearest door onto busy 3rd Street before the doctor could say another word.

The overhead micros, back on-line after the brief interruption caused by the explosion in Doctor Bruce's suite, tracked Mica as he ran down the street. Felney watched dispassionately as Mica ran up to the aluminum rectangle of a pay phone and fed in coins and then screamed as living black worms oozed out of the receiver, falling to wriggle on his wrist. Felney smiled to see Mica flee in the same direction he'd come, shrieking like the lost soul he was, oblivious, out of his shell, out of his mind, the bloom ripe for the cutting.

Railsbach, who was still unaccounted for several hours later, was commended for his unexpected approach of the dangerous rogue. Mica had escaped, but the doctor had none of the assassin skills and could hardly be expected to bring Mica down by himself, particularly as the rogue *sap* was strengthened by his extended period out from under the blanket.

If they'd had a team available, they'd have hauled Mica in right then and there. But at that moment, Speth and Gravely were being raked over by Sir Fern, and their other units were on their own stakes. It was "rush hour", as the *saps* said it, and by the time a unit was ready, the moment had passed. In retro, it would be seen as the vital path untaken, the little thing that ends up costing the bigger. But retros, as every demon worth his acid knows, are good for little more than chewing and spitting.

CHAPTER 15
The Aliens

one

Mica wandered nervously through the huge hall housing the Sci Fi gathering, sinking into the cheap carnival atmosphere of the convention with its hordes of Trekkies and Tronites, and excessive use of rubber masks, cheap face putty, cracked papier-mache and wrinkled aluminum foil. He tried to find some comfort in the crudeness of the costumes; he kept assuring himself these were ordinary adults dressed like kids for Halloween, wanna-be warriors for Space: Above And Beyond, ordinary citizens dressed and masked and painted to emulate their heroes. There went the Duras Sisters, ridges already cracking in their bad plaster jobs. And here was Spidey in wrinkled, ill-fitting lycra, probably the result of a major washing machine error. And there was a seven-foot Grecian Ghost Warrior with fluorescent bones, his red LED eyes peering from a fake head mounted on top of his real head, the real eyes looking out of a brass-plated chest, his football shoulder pads jutting out at an awkward angle to give the visual trick away. A Ninja Turtle with a clumsy shell cut from half a brilliant blue plastic drum waddled by, waving a wobbly, silver-painted sword. The ever-present Robby the Robot lumbered around, now an affectionate backwash oddity.

Mica tried to imagine the fantasy was all true and real, and his bizarre adventures were just a part of life here among the peoples of the galaxy. But it was a feeble attempt to find sanity in craziness; inside his mind, the cold spark of terror snapped, jerking him along with quick strides and twitchy stares at these strangely outfitted people.

"Hi, there, Earthling. Care to elope to the planet Zurenga for a little neural stimulation?"

He jumped back from the black Power Ranger who had materialized at his side. The shiny jet leotards revealed a lithe, sexy body. The Ranger took off her mask and grinned at him. "It's me, Jimmy, wonder-girl production assistant and part-time crime fighter, at your service, sir. Where's your costume?"

"I'm disguised as a normal person."

"Oh. Good idea." Jimmy took his arm, rubbing against him like a friendly cat. "I thought you weren't going to show."

"It was my last—" He stopped himself, clenching his teeth and looking away from her.

"Mica...I deserve a few answers. You've been acting mighty weird lately."

"Okay, shoot," he sighed.

"Why did you call Arecibo today?"

He was too tired to think of a good lie. "I wanted to know if there were any alien spaceships sighted in L.A. recently."

"Cool." She nodded. "But Arecibo is on the other side of the planet."

"So they told me." He jumped back a step, startled by two slender teens dressed like

286

almond-eyed aliens.

Jimmy followed his gaze. "What's wrong?"

"Nothing. I thought I spotted somebody I knew."

Mica took a deep breath. He jammed his hands in his pockets and took a look around the hall. And saw the man with the dark BMW, the man he'd seen standing across the freeway after his Alfa had been sent spinning by a pickup truck full of tree branches.

"What's wrong now?" Jimmy asked.

"What makes you think something's wrong?"

"Come on, Mica, you're stretched like Godzilla's condom."

"See the man in the dark suit, the one with the mirror shades?"

"Yeah. Sure. Mafia hit man costume?"

"That's the one. He set up an accident that nearly killed me."

"Are you sure?"

"That son-of-a-bitch nearly killed me!" Mica pulled his arm away from her and angrily pushed his way through the crowd.

two

Speth, Railsbach and James Gravely, who had been watching from halfway across the main display hall, saw the unblanked EMO coming.

"I would have thought this distance was absolutely safe," Gravely said, a hint of disbelief in his voice.

"I told you before that he can see us." Speth's lips thinned and he squared around in his duelist stance.

Railsbach's eyes went wide. "Stop him!"

Gravely moved to block Speth's view. "What are you doing?"

"Are you a bunch of clowns? I'll take him right here."

Gravely's voice was that of cold command, "I think not."

Speth dropped his arm and glared at his young commander. "Why not?" His voice was probing and scornful, a direct challenge to Gravely's authority.

The young lieutenant held his own. "This society no longer believes in spontaneous combustion," he snarled in their native tongue. "Or do you intend to convince 10,000 quasi-scientists that somebody at the convention has a real phaser, set to kill?"

"It's everything I've worked for..." Railsbach pleaded.

Speth didn't answer, ignoring them both in his white fury. Gravely's voice went up a notch, attracting the attention of a few

288

passersby as he barked the direct order, "NOT, I said!"

And with that, Speth completely dropped his stance and turned away. Gravely and the doctor followed after him, and the threesome slipped quickly through the crowded aisles. With Felney's help, they were like slippery eels through the packed aisles, while the two clumsy humans pushed and shoved and fell further and further behind.

<u>three</u>

Jimmy managed to get an inky green Star Trek emblem return stamp blurred on her wrist as they pushed out the revolving doors. Outside the hall, the parking lot was filled to capacity. Mica stood in the middle of a wide roadway, staring into the last reddish light of a smoggy dusk as Jimmy caught up to him.

"Did we lose them?" she asked.

"LOOK OUT!" he yelled. He spotted Speth's BMW as a blur rather than a distinct shape, and managed to knock Jimmy aside just as the car bore down on them. Jimmy, taken off-guard, stumbled and fell against the trunk of a two-tone lime-green and white Crosley.

"What the hell's going on, Mica-boy?" she shouted.

"You didn't see that car that almost ran us over?!"

"I didn't see NOTHIN'!" They stared at each other for a moment, and then she turned away, avoiding his eyes. She brushed the dust from her black leotards.

"Mica," she finally said in a low voice. "We know each other a long time. Fact is, time was, I use ta—was Sally's best friend. You gotta talk to me. You gotta tell me what's goin' on with you."

For a moment he didn't answer. Then he started, and the words tumbled out faster and faster.

"Jimmy...I think I'm going crazy. In fact, I know I am. I feel like I'm in the middle of...of a snake pit. I see hallucinations. Everywhere. People's faces change. Demons. Monsters. Crazy things happen to me. Even you saw the blood come out of that Sprite can."

"Yeah," she nodded. "I saw that."

"That was just a little thing. Worms come out of the phone. Hot dogs turn into snakes. People's faces ripple and they change into other people, or disgusting creatures."

She took his arm again, her luminous dark brown eyes taking him in.

He moved away from her, sitting on the hood of the little Crosley. "I don't want your pity."

"Damn you, Mica! I assure you, that's not what this is!"

He nodded silently, accepting her angry stare, and she moved close to him again.

"You said once you saw Sally. In Copenhagen."

"How did you know that?" He pulled away from her, suddenly stiff with fright.

"You're in the cubicle next to me at work, remember? Mica, it's me, the girl-wonder. You were talking on the phone with your doctor. His name is Doctor Bruce."

Mica nodded, accepting her as she moved close to him again and put one arm around his shoulder.

"Well, I saw them again," he said.

"Who?"

Again the words spilled out of him in a torrent. But even as he heard himself speak, he realized how unbelievable it really was.

291

"Sally and Anne Mae. My wife and kid, who I know are dead, and they came back as flappers out of the Roaring 20's."

"When? Where?"

"The other night, at the Il Fornaio. Only, it isn't really them, but some people who look exactly like them, but died the same way, almost 80 years ago. I looked them up in City Hall. Or maybe it is them. I don't know. I've got to get in touch with them, that's all!"

"You're serious, right?"

He slammed his fist—not the infected one—at the nearest car. "Jimmy, I—"

She stopped him with one finger, placing it to his lips.

"I believe you, Mica. Come with me. Please, Mica. I will show you—I know ze exact place where ET called home."

Mica had a sinking feeling throughout his tired frame. While Jimmy was lusted after by the entire male population at the office, she was also the resident kook. Her workspace was crammed with Caribbean fetishes of rag, wood and stone, feathered African tribal masks, and well-worn books on sorcery and other such delusionary madness. He remembered the time she'd brought a pail of sand to the office and carefully sprinkled a line of grains in front of every door and window to keep out, she explained, the evil spirit of a jealous auntie who also happened to be a rival witch. He didn't want to follow after her, but in the final analysis, there was no one else he could turn to, and he could think of nowhere else to go.

CHAPTER 16
The Right Channel

<u>one</u>

Ned's Malibu beachfront home was of wood-framed stucco on three sides, and on the fourth side, sheets of glass faced the light gray surf line, the flat beige sand, and the last dull red glow from a sun which had set an hour or so before Mica and Jimmy arrived. The night was young, but Ned was already in attendance, and the living room was packed with the pseudo and the neo-rich and the nearly, would-be and could-be famous who crowd the lower rungs of the Motion Picture Game. It was a wildly eclectic and mostly youthful bunch; some were lighting up, sniffing and snuffling around a glass tabletop in the kitchen; others were gabbing in a bright little bunch of Hollywood hopefuls around a self-appointed pianist, a chubby imitation Jerry Lee Lewis with a not-too-bad hammer-it-down style at the keyboards. The main gaggle was gathered in wonder or at least bemusement around Ned Parry, psychic channeler to the stars, who was holding court from his throne, a canted-back brown Naugahyde recliner chair in the center of the big room.

Mica took one look at Ned, splendid in his star-studded deep blue and silver silk shirt open to the waist, the golden silk waistband, the silver lycra sweatpants, and he turned to go.

"Oh, Jesu Christi Morris..." he intoned.

Jimmy held him back. "You got any better ideas?"

"No, but—"

"Then shut up and join the team." She took his good hand and pulled him into the circle of the elite. "My motto: *The last shall be first*," she confided with a conspiratorial grin. She whispered, "Ned speaks to us through the psychic connection he has with a departed spirit named Nala. In his previous lives here on earth, Nala has been a galley slave on an East Indian merchant vessel, a rug weaver in Calcutta, and most recently in Rangoon a collector of *pissoirs*, which must be gathered daily and dumped on the fields for fertilizer."

"So he's our low-level connector, no Alexander the Great or Caesar Augustus for us."

"Spirits often take the lowest earthly jobs to practice humility."

"Or maybe they're just lazy," he said, thinking about the old black bum he kept bumping into on the street.

Jimmy had worked their way right next to Ned, who had accepted a pretty girl's hand and gone into his trance. His eyes rolled back in his head and he made an inhuman *Woooo, Woooo* sound that had Mica thinking once more of the Stones' hooting chant, *I was around when Jesus Christ had His moment of doubt and pain/ Made damn sure that Pilate washed his hands and sealed His fate.* All in all, Ned looked like a bad imitation of an epileptic fit until he started speaking in a guttural growl, the words emanating from his throat in a most unnatural and painful way.

"I see...cold gray waves...you are trapped...high in a stony castle...by the cold northern sea..." And then he came out with a few phrases of what Mica took for pseudo-Welsh, "Gunwale, throl gus-Owun sum bzaer bralt..."

The coterie of true believers who were gathered around his head uttered various *ooooh* and *ahhhh* sounds to voice their appreciation and astonishment at this new revelation, and the pretty girl exclaimed, "I have dreams just like that!"

Before Jimmy could maneuver them into a hookup, an Iranian girl managed to hip her aside and place her bangled hand in that of Nala/Ned. Again Ned's eyes rolled back as the spirit of Nala took over. Again he spoke in the deeply tortured Saturday Morning Cartoon Voice, "Ahh Hah. The Casbah of Del Shir a'Rhid Rhannee...you are a very old soul...you have lived many lives...seen many wondrous things in the ancient seven cities...places when the world of mankind was young...young, indeed."

Ned's alter-voice drifted off into silence, but the dark-skinned girl with the heavy eyebrows was pleased.

"See, dip-head?!" she said to her male companion, "I told you!"

two

Ned let go of the girl's hand, and Jimmy neatly moved in. She grabbed Ned's hand, placing it in Mica's even as the crowd's amused attention was still on the Iranian girl. And in that instant, as Mica and Ned's hands joined, the channeler went silent, stiffening a little, as if he'd been jerked away. His eyes were closed, and Mica had the feeling Ned had no idea whose hand he was holding.

Ned's eyes rolled back again, but this time the eyeballs were completely white, the lenses having disappeared somewhere above his lids. He stiffened again, ever so slightly, jerking like a baby roller coaster car that had accidentally been hooked up on the track for the big high-speed run down Colossus.

And then he began to speak, talking not in the stagy Nala voice, but in a strangely calm tone that was and yet was not totally himself.

"Ahh, yes...we are flying...I soar like an eagle, I fly like a dove...over Los Angeles..." He pronounced it the Spanish way, like *City of the Angels*. "Ho, ho, ho, the lights below...Los Angeles. Flaps down to slow, I'm a big, black crow...ho, ho, ho... look at meeee, gang, I'm Santa Claus, I'm Sup-erman!" And he put his arms out like he was flying, dragging Mica's hand up in the air with him.

"This is embarrassing," Mica muttered to Jimmy, trying to loosen the death grip Ned had on his hand.

"Beep, beep, beep," Ned said, "prepare to

dive...we're going down, down, down..."

"What do you see, Ned?" Jimmy had gone to his side opposite Mica and leaned close.

"I seeee...he, he, heeee..." Ned cackled, "I see Los Angeles. We zoom low, low, low, we skim the trees, we fly on the back of a night owl...and now up, up, up...the jeweled city below...up into the hills...we're coming to a big mansion..."

"Yes. Go on."

"Innnnn...we zoom in through an open window...big party...skeleton quartet playing a waltz...real skeletons, heh, heh, heh...odd couples dance but no romance...old man in stained pajamas with the girl with the llamas...taximan with a battered head with a lady dressed in a gown of red..."

Ned's mutterings weren't of much interest to the impatient group around him, each of whom wanted their own past lives revealed. A squat little guy in a blue suit with jet-black hair that threatened to join his heavy eyebrows tried to push Jimmy out of the way. She swung a fist backwards into his crotch, and he grunted and moved away toward the well-stocked wet bar.

"Old letch with a hard-on...wearing no pantsies...dancing with a Sister of St. Francis...there's the master of the nest...pipe in one hand, thumb hooked on his vest...young Fellatio, pats his moustachio—," and here Ned's voice took on different tones, like he was mimicking dialogue, "—*Old Blinkley at the academy felt Kennedy's flaws far outweighed his virtues;* and the old fart replies, *Pah. A*

297

thousand Kennedys for one Hitler, sir. And throw in a Churchill on the side."

"Oh, oh, couldn't last, flying on past, through a flock of old lasses clinking champagne glasses...smiles underneath rotten gray teeth...past twin dwarf duck-fuckers, ugly little suckers, making merrier with a white toy terrier...into the pyre, through the fire...outside again...nightface, some other place...smoky...black fog...LORD..." Here his voice assumed a hushed awe, "Hieronymus Bosch lives..."

"What do you see?" Jimmy insisted.

"Naked humans...whipped, screwed, torn apart by beetles...no, aliens...no, *demons*..."

"What?" Jimmy prodded as he fell silent.

Ned fought to break out of his nightmare, but to no use, "Horrible...old woman trying to fight them off...hopeless...swarming like insects...looking up at us as we pass...we're higher now...city.... black tower...doctor's office...rooms.... drawers.... crashing...no, through wall..."

"What??"

"Kitchen...warm...sunlight...little girl painting a picture...pretty blond lady playing chess with...man in a white coat..."

three

Sally looked up and saw Ned's features as an indentation in the wall behind the creature named Kelp who called himself Doctor Railsbach. Kelp had returned to the kitchen, knocking on the door in a highly agitated state, and had agreed to the game of chess, which she had suggested to calm him down.

Sally smiled radiantly at the wall behind Railsbach. "Excellent," she said to the apparition in the wall, "tell Mica we're waiting."

The white-coated man looked up, startled and flustered.

"What is this?" He turned and saw the impression of Ned's startled face and arms, bulging the wall as if he were sheathed in heavy plastic. Railsbach glared at the woman, "You shouldn't be—"

The woman smiled back innocently, "I thought you said you were our friend."

"Yes, but I can't let this happen."

As he spoke, the man in the white coat raised one hand at Ned, and a red gout of boiling energy rose from the skin of his fingers to burst full in the traveler's face. The image behind the plastic wall twisted, every nerve shrieking.

four

Back in the alternate reality of his own living room, Ned screamed his agony. The crowd around him recoiled in stunned amazement as his body went rigid and levitated several inches in the air, where it quivered and shook in the grip of some unseen and unknown force.

Mica was instantly knocked away, while Ned remained stiff and twitching, held up by thin air, and those onlookers closest to the incredible scene stumbled over each other in their eagerness to achieve what distance they could from him. And then the strange phenomenon switched off, and Ned fell with a soft thud onto his recliner chair.

"Heart attack!" Jimmy yelled. "Call 911!"

Mica was writhing in pain on the floor. Turning him over, she saw the palm of his hand, the hand Ned had held, was burned raw and bleeding. *It was the infected hand*, one tiny part of her mind recorded. *At least he can still draw.* That thought seemed terribly banal and incongruous in the light of what had happened, as if she could find comfort in the ordinary details of her workday. She pulled Mica away from the couch, found a spot by the window and wrapped his hand in a towel heavy with ice.

"She's waiting for me..." Mica whispered. "I'm not sure where, but they're both waiting for me."

The paramedics came, and while seeing to

Ned, one of them bandaged Mica's hand.

"An infection like that," the man said, "and you could lose a hand."

"How is he?" Jimmy asked, hooking a thumb toward Ned, who was being wheeled out in the background. The encouraging sign was that the sheet wasn't up over his blistered and burned face.

"He took a hell of an electrical jolt, but he'll live; at least, that's our best guess."

A squad car arrived, and the police began asking questions. Going over Ned's chair, one of them found a frayed electrical cord.

"Fried in his own chair," the policeman said.

They stood and dusted their hands, the mystery solved, "Bet he saw things he never dreamed."

Jimmy gave Mica a little tug, "Time to go, Mica-boy-wonder."

"Go? Where?"

"You want to do a report? Spend your night at the station?"

By the time the police, who were beginning to piece the story together, had begun looking around the room in earnest, Mica and Jimmy were a half mile gone down Route 1. Mica was behind the wheel of his battered but serviceable Alfa, top down because there was no longer a top, windshield bent back to an angle resembling that which it had before it went topsy-turvy on the freeway. The night sky overhead was black and featureless, but the cold wind cheered him and made him feel alert and sharper than he really was as the little sportster took them back toward the offices of the L.A. Weekly to pick up Jimmy's car.

CHAPTER 17
Thickening Magma

<u>one</u>

Speth wasn't good at routines like the weekly action review, so he let Sir Fern bleat on and on while his own thoughts drifted. Speth's father was *old stone*, from the first magma, from the first batholith, and he'd always identified vice and virtue by hardness, clarity, porosity, ductility. Speth had endured the endless whipping, the scalding baths to the limit of his shell, the isolation walks through endless winding underground molten rivers— had *enjoyed* his testing, knowing that he was one of the last, one of the few purebred snufters still budgeted as the demonic system moved successfully from conflict into management, from hunting to farming, from war to absolute domination.

Speth couldn't detail the philosophic theories of Light and Dark, as could Sir Fern, nor could he discuss in detail the myriad modern theories of the body (both Sap and Demonic) as putty of the everlasting soul, as could Railsbach. But Speth believed to the bottoms of his hearts that all of demondom was moving too fast, that the time of the assassin was nowhere nearly at its end. But who was he to say? Sir Fern certainly never asked him; Speth was just another old-fashioned assassin, a simple snufter of the realm.

And there was another side to the situation. Even as he was being roasted by Fern, Speth didn't think to complain, because there was nothing to be upset about. For the present, he had everything he wanted. With so few assassins imprinted over the last eon, Speth and his few fellows got all the prime urban assignments. He allowed himself a little smile, idly watching the two-inch nails retract and then spring forward from his fingers, allowing the time to pass while Sir Fern droned on and on about the rogue EMO and how much energy the prolonged attempts at his capture were costing.

Speth knew he wasn't alone in his impatience. The small war council which gathered that night in the study of the Fern mansion was in a bitchy, angry mood. Mica had now been unblanked for over a week. The spirits of his translated mate and spawnling (according to Dr. Railsbach's vaguely unsatisfying verbal reports) were showing unexpected talents, and there were many unanswered questions.

By failing to report what he knew of some of these recent developments, Fern had managed to keep his auditors at bay for another month, so the small combat council consisted of Fern, Railsbach, Gravely and Speth, all standing in front of the writhing faces at the rim of the fireplace while Felney sat on a love seat covered in burnt orange paisley velvet with Zilch and Nilch on either side. In sitting between them, Felney's plan had been to keep the two from becoming a distraction; instead, they seemed intent on each getting the last hit on the other, and a good half of their sly jabs and pokes were landing on his knees and thighs.

"But it's just politics..." Railsbach complained.

Speth was disgusted by the look on the doctor's face. He recognized the bitter, weak expression of a born loser right through the coat. *Talc!* his father would have said. *The spalv has gypsum in his shell!* Speth turned away in disgust.

"You really ought to self-immolate," he muttered just loud enough so the doctor could hear him as he spat on the floor.

"Not in here!" Sir Fern said angrily, waving to the acidic fumes and the small hole the spittle was etching in his priceless parquet floor. Fern turned away, knowing even as he spoke that it was useless to yell at a purebred; they spit as naturally as blades cut. Fern looked around him, happy to change the subject.

"James Gravely. Young James, new to us from the academy, bestow upon us your wisdom and your learning. Now I ask you— we have the good doctor here, oddly veiled in his thoughts, concealing only Bub knows what, and yet still wailing for capture of his precious EMO. Flanked and ranked on the other side, we have our noble assassin, and these two—he waved his hand at Zilch and Nilch who were squirming impatiently on the love seat—who are all for dusting the rogue *sap* and isolating his *familia* in the deepest nether. What say you, James Gravely?"

Gravely knew the old snarler had him neatly pinned. It sounded pleasant enough, the wise old man seeking advice of his aides; but now, no matter what, the outcome would be on Gravely's head. Still, he didn't hesitate. *Go for the glint!*

"I think we have to net him," Gravely said. "And we have to do it now, before he can become a serious danger to us all."

Speth made a scornful sound, kicking the white toy terrier out of a sound sleep. The little fur ball ran off, yipping in pain.

"Now see what you have done," Zilch purred.

"Oh, Spethy, go get your own pethy," Nilch added.

Judging Speth's mood, the two of them hopped off their seat and ran behind Sir Fern, who had his full attention on Gravely.

"You're absolutely sure?" Fern asked Gravely. He had to show the necessary concern, even though it was now clearly his young assistant's scales on the griddle.

James Gravely nodded with a confidence he didn't entirely feel. "We either get him first pass, or the poor, miserable rogue will translate himself."

"Translate?! How does that help?" Sir Fern glared angrily from Gravely to Railsbach and back again.

"Either we net him, or he self-destructs. We've found an old scripture to back us; if he willingly disbands his own integration, we believe we can take his sperm."

The twins stopped their bickering, and even Speth came back to the circle.

two

"I've heard nothing of this," Fern said. "There's only been one rumored instance of intervention in mortal conception that I can even think of..."

"Taboo." Speth shook his head.

"No, I think not," Railsbach said, raising his hands and sighing. "It's a new age. We've found scripture enough, if you need it. Self-immolation is unforgivable. The sap loses all. We feel, in this case, we can impregnate his sperm—"

"Unholy blue balls! If that's true—and I say IF—why didn't you simply do that in the first place?!" Sir Fern huffed and roared, clearly not happy to be experimenting with old truth.

James Gravely came to Railsbach's aid, "Sire, it is infinitely more desirable to steer the living *sap* to our devices. We're only saying that we do have a viable backup plan. There is no reason to believe we will fail."

"And the so-called 'immortal spirits' of his wench and spawnling?"

"They must be handled with extreme caution."

Railsbach spoke quickly, perhaps too quickly, and Fern eyed him carefully. "Where did we go wrong, dear Doctor?"

"No, no miscalculation. We're alright. They're harmless for now, isolated in chaotic ether."

"The same, exact state of which we know

308

almost nothing."

Gravely came to Railsbach's aid again, "Sir Fern, if they had any power, they would have risen to light upon translation." Even Felney nodded at this statement of the commonly accepted truth.

Sir Fern was not so easily mollified, "Still, there are rumors of wandering sap spirits, confused and lost, somehow invisible to our nets..."

Speth, who had not been asked his opinion, spat into the roaring fire, turned on his heel and stalked out of the study.

Gravely frowned after him. "I didn't give him permission to leave."

Albert Fern placed an arm on his shoulder. "I've decided to let things run on a bit longer. You've won your case, James. Don't let a little bicker with Old Speedballer spoil your moment."

Gravely nodded, seeing the wisdom in Sir Fern's comment. First they would pop the troublesome rogue human back in the bag; then he would take care of Speedball Speth.

<u>three</u>

The plans that James Gravely had outlined to assure Sir Fern that they had every chance for success—those same plans took a troublesome detour from the very beginning. Dr. Railsbach left for hellside and returned empty-handed from the void; the two *sap* females, he said, were now so weakened as to be unable to accompany him back across the fog from their holding cell. When pressed further, he became testy and would only say they were too close to unraveling, and that there were many things he personally—and surely all the rest of them—did not understand about human spirits and chaos and the rest of reality, for that matter.

Speth grumbled and spat; and Gravely had to be creative, calling on blond-haired Rethan, usually employed as Janie, the 7th floor receptionist in Dr. Bruce's office and now newly re-coated as a Sally Harris look-alike. They would also use Dr. Bruce, a scientist somewhat of inferior rank to Dr. Railsbach, and otherwise known as Maahg. Speth settled in behind the wheel of his big BMW with Maahg beside him, and Rethan and Gravely took up the backseat. Sitting together in a human car demanded constant attention, for the necessary closeness violated every principle of demonic personal space.

"I don't believe I've ever caught your real name," Speth said as they drove north on the 405 over the Sepulveda Pass and down into the twinkling network of valley lights.

"No. I don't think you have," Gravely replied stiffly. Deep magma would freeze before he shared spirit with a raw spitter. "Anyway, I thought you were re-grooved as a progressive thinker. Surely, you don't believe those old power stories, do you Old Speedball?"

Speth kept his eyes on the road ahead, saying nothing. Science claimed to have debunked many of the myths of the ancients, but Speth wasn't buying any of the new way. And he'd never taken the re-groove, just had the records falsified for a bale of earth goods which the low-level recorder had never gotten to enjoy because Speth had buried his nails in the fellow's neck the moment the records were fixed. Speth drove on in silence, wrapped in his blanket of anger and hate.

Gravely finally spoke, giving out a grudging dribble of his true thoughts, "I worry about Railsbach."

"The Kelp-ster!" Speth's reaction was instinctive; spittle ran down the inside of the glass on his side of the car.

"I know you don't think much of him, but we could have used him on this assignment."

"To do what? He was birthed without claws!"

Gravely chose his words with care, "It bothers me that this is the second time he was too busy to come along with us to secure what he claims is the most important experiment of his career."

"So what? He's useless in the field."

Gravely didn't respond, and the silence grew between them.

"You don't think he's hiding something?" Gravely finally asked.

Speth shook his head no. "Kelpie doesn't have anything to hide, the disgusting little worm. You know, he once told me I was going to be replaced by a chemical?! I nearly cracked his shell! A chemical! I asked him, *Which one, a bromide?* He's just a worthless little worm."

four

After a time, Gravely plugged in and checked with Felney, who assured him Mica was still at his office, fallen asleep at his desk.

"I still don't see why you didn't take him there," the little translation clerk said.

"Stop your whining," Speth barked. "What do you know about how it is out here?!"

Gravely said nothing, realizing Felney must not have been able to keep a constant track on them since they left the mansion. *Speth, up to his old tricks again!* Unobserved, they had gone directly to Mica's office. Gravely was surprised by the sudden shocked look that had marred Speth's coat when he saw the little piles of sand that lined the doorway of Mica's cubicle. They had tried to net the hamster at his office, and there he was all alone just a few feet away; but there was no way Speth was going to walk over those silly little lines of silica granules that the Jamaican girl had dribbled around the room. And if Speth wasn't going to cross, nobody else was, either. Gravely had to stifle a sudden moment of weakness, a flash of pity for the supposedly merciless creature at his side. The ancient saying was true; nobody was as superstitious as an old assassin!

CHAPTER 18
Close Encounter

<u>one</u>

It was well after midnight by the time Mica pulled into his drive and parked under the wide branches of the old oak tree. He stomped on the gravel walkway as he made his way around to the back of the house and in through the back door.

There was a roaring fire in the brick living room fireplace. Two individuals stood in the flickering and uneven light. Mica recognized the tall, lean man he'd seen twice before, first at the accident on the Santa Monica Freeway and then at the Sci-Fi convention. The second was shorter and somehow softer, a well-knit young man with a slight moustache.

For a moment panic overcame Mica, and he wanted to run. But he realized it was hopeless. If he was going to flee, that time had been before, when he had gone around the house and recognized the dark BMW pulled up against a wildly flowering bank of ungroomed oleanders. He nodded briefly, and stood watching them.

"You don't seem surprised to see us."

"I saw your car outside."

"We took the liberty to build a fire."

"It was not your right." For some reason those words popped out of Mica's mouth; he wasn't sure why at the time.

314

Gravely blinked, looking at Speth. The assassin shrugged, "The sap's been unblanked for a long time now."

"So that's what you call it," Mica said. "*Blanking.* It's appropriate."

The two intruders were taken aback. Speth had been conditioned by Gravely to wait for his signal, and they had both been ready for a brief, vicious struggle, not a conversation. It was unnerving, and Gravely now found himself wishing they had insisted more firmly on Dr. Railsbach's presence. Gravely remembered little things from the file which had seemed unimportant at the time; this was the one room in the house from which their scanning devices had been removed after the death of the wife and daughter, due to allocation of resources. Mica didn't use the room, and control had calculated nothing ever took place here. But now something was happening here, and the ever-present Felney had no eyes to see what was going on, no ears to record what was taking place, no command voice to prod and push translations over the edge. Perhaps that was even why Speth had chosen it.

two

Gravely forced down the tight little ball of fear which had formed in his throat.

"You know who we are?" he asked, lightly tapping the edges of his troublesome moustache. He saw Speth was beginning his maneuver as they had discussed, edging slightly to one side to cut off any possible retreat.

"I know you shouldn't be here."

"Pah!" Speth spat in his usual venomous way, his foamy spittle forming a white spot on the tile floor. "This space. That space. Who says we shouldn't?"

"Hey, no spitting in here. I meant by what I said that you have no right to be in my house. You have transgressed, as I clearly did not invite you in. You didn't even ask."

Gravely saw the sudden flicker of fear cross Speth's face. "Old bitches' tale," he said quickly.

Mica shrugged, "On your head." He felt remarkably calm. After everything he had been through, there actually was a *they*. True, they were devil-like aliens, they were weird and powerful, they had him and in a few minutes they would strip his memory, but he wasn't crazy, he hadn't lost his mind. He neatly sidestepped Speth and went to a carved oak sideboard where he poured himself two fingers of cognac from a dusty crystal decanter.

"May we have one?" Gravely asked, trying to back out of their mistake.

"Of course not. You're not invited. Do I make myself perfectly clear?"

"Pah!" Speth strode across the room and poured his own drink, and one for Gravely as well. Mica watched as his two uninvited guests sipped from their heavy tumblers.

"Will this hurt much?" he asked.

"You know why we're here?" Gravely was amazed at the rogue human's presence of mind.

"Of course. To replace the little silver cylinder. To make me forget." Mica gazed to where the white spittle continued to eat a small hole in the terra-cotta tile floor. "After what I've been through, I ought to be grateful...but...I can't talk you out of it, can I?"

Gravely saw Speth was ready to spring. He gestured, *wait a moment*. It was beginning to occur to him what an opportunity this was for him personally, to be the one to speak to an unblanked human, the first in centuries! The eminent Dr. Railsbach had chosen not to be here—fine, he and Speth would interrogate the *sap*!

Gravely raised one hand in a calming gesture. "I'd like to ask you a few questions," he said.

Both the human and Speth were staring at him strangely, as if he'd gone mad.

"All right," Mica finally replied. He pointed to himself, Speth and Gravely. "One each, to be answered with the truth, or..."

"Or crushed to dust," Gravely answered automatically.

Mica nodded, "Or crushed to dust. Go

317

ahead." He pointed to Speth, "You ask first."

Speth sneered, and yet he was suddenly feeling a *smallness*, a desire to not be doing this thing.   There was nothing more, he told himself, that he really wanted or needed to know about his enemies.   Fuming that his junior grade superior had locked him into this useless game, he spat out the first thing that came to mind, "This *mundungus* about us not being allowed in here. What do you know about us, anyway?"

Mica thought a moment, staring at the flickering flames shooting from the oak logs.

"I think you guys are aliens.   You've probably always been here.   In Medieval Europe, you were considered demons. There are Mayan drawings of creatures like you in spaceships."   He lifted a book from the table and turned to a pre-marked page.

"That's supposed to be *us*?!" Speth snarled.

"Not a very flattering likeness. Today, of course, every science fiction writer from King to Strieber and Spielberg has a story about you."

Gravely nodded, "Go on."   If the *sap* wanted to think of them as aliens, that wouldn't hurt anything.

"I guess I know four sets of things," Mica continued.   "First, there is legend and lore, of which I probably know more than most, because even if Horny is a cartoon, I researched him more than any of my fans realize. Second, there is personal experience; I've seen you guys shift and wobble and do your tricks, getting

318

inside people's heads. I know what you really look like, and at least some of what you can do. And third, the dreams..."

"Dreams?" Speth suddenly looked alert.

"Is that another question?"

"No," Gravely interjected, "Your answer is currently incomplete. You said *four* things."

Mica nodded. He sipped from his glass to calm his nerves. The glass shook as he held it to his lips, but he managed a small sip.

"Okay. I've had terrible nightmares since—since my family was killed. But lately I've dreamed some personal things about the two of you. And about others."

He pointed to Speth. "I've been seeing this guy in action. Killing people. Tearing them apart. Dragging their spirits down to *your dimension,* as you called it."

Gravely wondered how much of what Mica was referring to was official action, and how much Speth was freebooting on his own. Gravely's own mind was in a whirl; on the one hand, he was seeing the historic opportunity in this chance meeting and wanting to make the most of it. On the other, Mica was showing some disturbing indications of power. His clairvoyance, if that was what it was, in the form of what he apparently was convinced were dreams, indicated a new and unexpected strength. Was it possible that there was some form of psychic connection between him and his deceased wife and daughter? Gravely had read his *sap* socio-history back at the academy, and now thoughts of hearts and cupids with

bows, and images of men and women gazing
into each other's eyes crowded his mind.

320

<u>three</u>

Gravely might have done better, might have forestalled the turn of the slow wheel of events which were to come if at that moment he had pressed to know exactly what personal things Mica had dreamed about them; but he wasn't a professional interrogator, and he could see Speth's agitation, and so he hurried to ask, "What's the fourth thing?"

"And last, I'm convinced you're holding Sally and Anne Mae prisoners. I know it and I want them back."

"How could you possibly know that?" Speth spat into the fireplace and turned to glare at him, the coat of his face somehow perfectly matching the demonic expression Gravely knew lay under the surface.

"Now that <u>is</u> another question."

Gravely shrugged, forced by curiosity and the moment into his own question, "Alright. I'll ask it. How do you know?"

"A human clairvoyant saw them."

Gravely had never heard of such a thing. "You have to explain. That's not really an answer."

"That's exactly what happened. It's a person with special powers, a human who sees things. I held this man's hand, and he was somehow drawn to my wife and daughter. He actually found them, still alive. Sally told him to tell me they were waiting for me to come and rescue them."

Gravely felt a flash of reassurance. In spite

321

of his saying they were dead, Mica must believe they were still somehow retrievable. Perhaps the connection through this person with special powers had been a onetime, random experience. Still, the *sapiens* had spoken of his dreams. Were these dreams the same as the clairvoyant experience? How much more did he know? And did Railsbach know any of this? Gravely felt cheated, as if he'd wasted his question. He tried to draw out the human by rephrasing, "How could you possibly know she is waiting?"

"I already *told* you. My wife, Sally, through this clairvoyant. She told him, and he told me that she's waiting for me to come and rescue her and Anne Mae."

Gravely and Speth looked at each other, wondering why Railsbach hadn't reported this. Gravely was suddenly very relieved that Railsbach's experiments had been pulled back to the other side. Naturally suspicious as a race, he and Speth both instantly recognized that, if Mica was speaking the truth, then the foulest infamy was possible. If this *sapiens* had somehow actually penetrated through Dr. Railsbach's office and into the void to reach Sally Harris, could not a living, breathing human invade their homeland? Was it not possible that, just as his race longed for the holocaust which would burn and blow the noxious oxygen from this human dimension, that the lowly *saps* might desire and somehow be able to cross the other way to oxygenate the prime land, poisoning it for their own foul purposes?

four

Mica looked expectantly at the younger alien.

"Okay, my turn."

"We don't have to play this game," Speth shot out.

"Of course you don't," Mica replied. "But what does it matter? You're going to blank me anyway. In a few minutes, if you have your way, I'm going to be back to dreamland."

"What is your question?" Gravely asked, aware that even in the asking Mica might reveal something of what he did or didn't know. Even as he spoke, he was forced to hold one hand to his lips to hide the twitching of his blessed moustache which was betraying him once again.

"Just where are my wife and daughter?"

"They're gone," Speth sputtered impatiently.

"That wasn't my question."

Gravely signed Speth to keep his peace and shook his head. "We don't really know."

"You can do better than that."

"Alright," Gravely sighed, "If I understand the experiment correctly—and it was only an experiment—we managed to capture them." He chose his words carefully, not wanting Mica to know that they were truly, finally and forever dead to this world. *Save that spirit-crusher for a final play!* Gravely struggled for words to explain what had happened in terms of spaceships and aliens. "Look, *sapiens*. You already know there's this world, and our alien world. Our race crossed over the vast barrier of—of *space* once before, and would have owned this world...but you got...help. Okay, we learned our lesson, and we've quietly been coming back for centuries. We think we've been really proper and good about it; we don't think your helpers know. Or maybe they've gone away, or just don't care anymore. But lately, our science experts have been experimenting with another dimension. The best way to explain is to call it unformed matter. There's this—this empty space, and one of our doctors has figured out a way to store *saps* there for short periods of time."

"Saps?"

"Short for *sapiens*."

"And that's where Sally and Anne Mae are?"

"Like flies in a jug," Speth laughed, showing his teeth to be long, irregular and yellow.

The assassin was at the end of his tether. He moved in to backhand Mica unconscious so they could implant and be gone. But the human seemed to have eyes in the back of his head; he neatly sidestepped him, putting a chair between them.

"What are you doing, Speth?" he asked.

"You know my name!?" Speth's always steady coat betrayed him then, flickering just once back and forth between his human coat and alien form before he regained control.

"Of course. It came to me in a dream,

while I was sleeping in my office." He pointed to the assassin and then to Gravely. "Speth-who-has-no-earthly-name and his boss, the one earth-named James Gravely whose true name is Krel-Net-Ja-Nor, will come unwelcome into my house. They cannot touch me. I have the power to ask them to leave. If they do not, I can—what was your expression? Crush them into dust."

"Enough!" Speth shouted. He flowed into his assassin's stance, turning sideways with his left hand coming up in a smooth arc. He felt the power surge and build from the base of his carapace, *up from the hooves* as his father had taught him, and his anger and desire to smash all living things rose and then honed in on this one most undesirable of all beings.

And then, at the last possible second, when the power was blooming from Speth's fingertips, the *sap* raised the palm of his left hand towards him and Speth was jammed as if he'd been rubber gloved. With nowhere to go, the huge energy surge raced back through his body, cooking his human coat, frying his white-blond hair to gray ash, and melting his golden watch and turning his silk Armani suit to smoking rags. The assassin dropped like a stone with his flesh coat bubbling and running over his demonic face like Play Dough left on a car hood on a hot summer's day.

five

"Get him out of here," Mica said quietly. "You were not invited." Mica didn't understand why he had raised his hand, didn't really know why he now spoke as he did. It was almost cellular knowledge, as if he knew these things in his bones, in the makeup of his genes; somehow, his unconscious being had been aware of this possibility all along, and had known how to act in these circumstances. He wondered, as he stared down the remaining alien/demon, what else he might be capable of in his unblanked state. But for now, it would be enough to have these beings out of his house.

"You are going, aren't you." It wasn't a question, and he raised one hand as he said it.

Gravely blanched and took an involuntary step backwards. "Yes, of course."

Seeing no alternative, he took Speth under the arms and tried to drag him away. The assassin's still smoking coat felt loose like jelly, and he was far heavier than he looked. Speth began to twitch, bubbling froth running from his mouth.

"I can't do it alone," Gravely protested.

"Well, I don't want him dying in here."

"I don't think he'll ever be the same, but he won't translate."

Mica nodded to himself. "Translate," he repeated. They used the word translate for death, as in *translated to another mode of existence*. It was another little piece of

327

information that might prove useful.

"Well, I don't like him bubbling on the floor like that. Sally and I got these tiles from Baja. That trip is one of my good memories."

"Then you've got to help me."

Mica frowned his distaste, but he moved closer and gingerly lifted the legs, grunting as he felt the weight. The creature, who smelled like cooked meat, was heavier by twice what he looked.

"You guys weigh a ton," he said.

"Denser world," Gravely found himself replying before he could stop himself. Oh, what the heaven did it matter, anyway?

"Come on, together now."

Mica helped Gravely dump Speth in the backseat of the BMW, where his drool immediately started eating through the soft black leather seat covers. He carefully watched as the younger one backed down the driveway.

"Don't ever come back, Krel-Net-Ja-Nor."

"You have not seen the last of us."

Gravely drove off; in spite of his threatening words, he was bitterly aware of his defeat. He found his way down winding Zelzah Drive, moving slowly past the informal horse properties. He turned East on Rinaldi and caught the 118 at Balboa.

Speth's car handled like a dream, the engine purring and the lights cutting through the moonless night. Nothing like the little sputterers Gravely was used to on the other side. He decided he was going to have to get one of these for himself. He started to take stock in their situation, and the further he drove from the house, the better he felt. His enemy Speth had, through some strange malfunction, been delivered a blow that would take off some of his edge. Let Mica enjoy his momentary victory. After all, there still were two devils left in his house with every intention and opportunity to drive the poor sap into madness and despair.

CHAPTER 19
Demonic Affairs

<u>one</u>

After watching the BMW drive off, Mica walked around the outside of the house in the dark and entered through the back door. He kicked aside a drift of old newspapers on the floor in the hallway, and then froze as he heard a noise. He stood, quietly listening until he heard it again. Giggling and whispers from his bedroom. He picked up an old baseball bat that was leaning in a corner near the door. Sally had called the grizzled and battered bat her Enforcer; it had made her feel secure from the occasional wandering out-of-work beggar and the salesmen who thought to take the gravel drive to their isolated house. Mica fought the wave of shivers that ran down his back and forced himself to walk toward the bedroom.

He reached one hand around the corner and snapped on the light switch. And there, blinking in the sudden bright glare of the lamp, was his Sally. And the Doc, Doctor Bruce, the chubby, hairy, little fellow himself, still wearing his dark blue socks with the gray diamond pattern and apparently nothing else.

Sally started up, blinking in the light, "Mica! What are you doing home?!"

Doctor Bruce was not quite so composed. With the sheet wrapped about his tubby middle, he was awkwardly pulling his pants on, trying to be halfway decent. His left foot jammed in the wrong pants leg, and he sat back on the bed with a little thump.

"It's too late, Sally," he sighed. "We're caught."

The scene was real to the last detail, the illusion perfectly played even to the mole on Sally's shoulder and the freckles sprinkled over the tops of her white breasts and the sound of her voice with the little edge of fear on it. But after the first heart-stopping moment, Mica already knew it wasn't, it couldn't be his Sally. There had always been a nameless, fundamental attraction between them, something chemical and more, a feeling that they were drawn together by the force of their electrons, by the very essence of their being. What he saw and felt here was the moonlight reflection of Sally; it was like looking at a third dimensional model of her, perfect in every shape and attitude, but still a portrayal, a living hologram.

"How's it goin', Doc?" he said. He tried to keep his voice low, to conceal the terrible anger that was growing inside him. "I didn't know you made house calls."

"Oh, Sally, Sally," the Doc repeated as if he couldn't think of anything else to say, "He's caught us."

From his desk in the study of the Fern mansion, Felney decided it was time to make his play. He concentrated, the brow of his own coat furrowing as he sent the thought racing across the distance to Granada Hills and driving

331

like a nail into Mica's brain.

"Mica, you worthless vermin, can't you see she's cheated on you?!"

The voice thundered in Mica's mind, roared through his consciousness like God speaking through a waterfall, like the grand and groaning crash of onshore water spill in a tropical hurricane. Mica clapped his hands to his ears and looked wildly around the room. Nothing. No one. They had somehow gotten into his mind again! Was it hopeless then? Was there nowhere he could hide, be himself, be free of this mad invasion?

Silly little Mica, the voice roared, *I know what you're thinking. You can't get away. You're an ant, an insignificant worm. And you're going to end it all now.*

The voice boomed in his skull, sending lightning bolts of pain flashing through his awareness. He would do anything to make it stop, to find peace.

The gun, Mica. It's in your dresser drawer, right where you left it under your old Joe Boxers with the picture of the rainbow trout on them.

Moving like a robot, Mica reached for the old brass drawer handle, pulled the drawer open, and found his 9 mm automatic. The cold feel of the dark metal in his hand gave him a secure feeling. At least he had some control over his own destiny.

That's right, the voice boomed, *stick it in your mouth.*

A picture of Sally and Anne Mae, laughing

332

and dancing in the meadow, was framed on the bureau near him. He'd taken it from the last roll of film he'd found in his mangled camera after the wreck. It would be the last thing he would see, his last image from a life of pain and loneliness. And yet, even as the giant voice was commanding him to do it, to pull the trigger and get it over with, an odd little thought came to him, elbowing the huge and commanding presence aside.

two

Mica pulled the barrel of the weapon away from his open lips and pointed it at the Doc.

"Doc," he said, "I heard a rumor. Is it true that you have two hearts?"

The booming voice in his head went up an octave, *Put down that gun, you presumptuous little worm!*

"W-where did you hear that, Mica?" The Doc's face was pale, but steady. "That's ridiculous. It's really silly. Come on now, Mica—nobody has two hearts."

"Nobody *human,* Doc." It felt odd to be playing out the empty rhythms of their old word games.

"Well, *everybody's* human, Mica."

"Maybe not *everybody,* Doc."

Mica turned the gun on Sally. Her eyebrows began to twitch uncontrollably, first one, and then the other.

"Your coat!" the doctor warned.

"Coat," Mica repeated. "That's very good, Doc. You coat yourself with humanity."

"Pull yourself together!" the Doc thundered, but it was too late. Her face and limbs were beginning to chatter uncontrollably back and forth between her new coat and an older one, that of Janie, the secretary at Dr. Bruce's office, Sally-Janie, Sally-Janie, Sally-Janie.

"Why, it's Janie," Mica said.

"Put down the gun!" the voice in Mica's head thundered. But Mica had found a way to

burrow under that massive presence, to keep his own thoughts, much as the poor soldiers in the 50's had lain in foxholes a few hundred yards from experimental atomic blasts.

"Doc," he said, "just out of curiosity. If Janie here has two hearts and I shot one of them, do you think she might live?"

By now her control was slipping to where her coat was morphing between that of Janie and a dark presence that was clearly demonic.

"Now, Mica," the Doc warned, "that would be very dangerous."

"It's not my fault. It's the voice in my head that's making me do it. I think he wants me to kill her."

The voice had now risen to a needle-sharp insect whine, *I command you, drop that gun!*

The pistol bucked once in his hand and the dark form that had been imitating Sally gave out an inhuman yelp as it was thrown back on the bed. It shuddered and twitched, with greenish gray liquid oozing from a hole high on the left side of its torso.

Alright, human! The voice shrieked, full of menace, *You asked for it!*

A pain rose through Mica's body as if every cell were on fire and ready to burst. It was so intense that his cry of anguish became one with the animal howl from the wounded creature on the bed. Pain of that intensity couldn't last, and it didn't. Without another word, Mica slumped unconscious to the floor.

What happened next was yet another blunder of monumental proportions. There he was, the rogue sap himself, lying unconscious and ready for implant. But Maahg, grooved and clamped as he was for maintenance of demonic life at all costs, was already pulling the wounded Rethan from the house; and Speth, who had insisted on carrying the supply of silvery little blankers, was miles away—and worse, he was fried silly, babbling nonsense from the back of his own car. Felney contacted Gravely, and the young aide pulled over to the side of the road and went through what was left of Speth's clothing with no success. Though it cost an enormous amount of energy, Felney managed a temporary brain clamp which left the unblanked EMO in a drunken stupor. Against their wishes, Mica wandered away from the rancho and was last seen staggering across an open field. With the taste of ashes in his mouth, Felney grimly rounded up several emergency teams from other sectors and sent them out to find him.

CHAPTER 20
On Chewing One's Own Wrist

<u>one</u>

With no apparent interruption of time, Mica found himself on his knees in broad daylight, one hand on a punker's crotch. The punker, who had a yellow to green dye job on his hair, an open leather vest over bare skin and the tattered remnants of faded jeans cut off at the thighs, was holding Mica's other hand.

Mica's world was turned upside down. It had been night, and now it was day. He had been in his bedroom, and now he was at a bus stop in downtown L.A. People were everywhere, walking past or standing there waiting for the bus, and they were alternately shocked or amused at his performance.

His scream carried over from the other reality, turned into the word, "NOOOOO!"

The punker's scrawny biceps were like steel wires. He grabbed Mica's hair and jerked his head down into his crotch.

"It's okay," the punker laughed. "Stay here. I like it, lover boy."

Mica managed to jerk away. He tumbled backward into the street and was brushed by a beeping brown Plymouth Voyager that knocked him spinning to the ground as it rushed past.

On bloody hands and knees, he heard a snicker from someone in the crowd.

An unctuous minister made a strange sign,

more like a five-sided star than a cross, and shouted, "Filth and foul promiscuity everywhere!"

Mica managed to stand, but in his confusion, he stepped back into the street.

"Step forward," a soft voice said. Mica did, not knowing why, and it was just enough to save his life. Where had that voice come from? With that single step, he just cleared a dusty diesel-engined semi, an old blue Peterbilt with one crumpled fender that seemed to come out of nowhere. One dangerous second and then it was past, and it, too, had missed. Was that retreating image in the back of the crowd the old black bum who kept haunting him?

Mica stared at the gay punker's face.

"What's the matter, dude?" the punker taunted. "Got a fixation?"

Mica struggled to gather his thoughts. In his bedroom, he'd had a gun in his left hand. Now he had no gun. They didn't dare leave him with the gun, now that they knew he could and would use it. But that proved time had passed. They could somehow switch his consciousness on and off, but they had limits to their power. They couldn't just shift time. They had set him up, brought him here and set him up! That much would be easy for them!

But in his confusion, he was forgetting something; something important was retreating from him like time down a tunnel. His memories of the past few days were unraveling. For a moment he couldn't remember, but the maddening itch in his thumb gave it away. He looked at his hand in amazement. The swelling was gone and there was no more pain. There was no gaping, unhealed scar where he had removed—something shiny, whatever it was. They must have put it back! Soon he would forget everything; he would be totally blanked again, just like all the humans around him! Blanked, what did that mean? Even as these strange thoughts came to his mind, they were brushed away, like a magnetic sound tape that was being erased, line by line.

Could it be possible? His hand was totally healed over, there wasn't even a scar. He could feel it, the transplant under his skin. But even as he thought the word transplant, the powerful suggestion came to his mind that it was just an old piece of pencil lead, the remnants of a childhood accident. "Noooooo!" he shouted again. Without a second thought, he gnawed the back of his thumb, chewed like an animal caught in a trap, biting deep into his own skin until blood appeared between his teeth.

"W-what are you doing?" the punker yelled, taking a half step toward him.

Mica had the cylinder between his teeth. He could feel it warming quickly in his mouth. He glared and moved toward the punker, and the self-assurance drained out of the kid. "Hey! Get away from me!"

He took another step and the punker's face began to slip and slide between acne-skinned and the smooth, dark skin of an alien.

Mica spat the silvery cylinder at him, turning away and ducking his head as the tiny pellet became a small sun. It had stuck to the torso of the unfortunate punker, who had time for one choking scream before he was reduced to a bubbling green mass and then just a blackened spot on the sidewalk. Mica opened his eyes in time to see the reduction of the last sputtering remains, the melting eyes and gaping mouth having found their own horror, and then winking into nothing.

The minister was shouting, "You are damned—damned for all eternity!"

Stunned by what he had done, Mica turned in a complete circle, like a dazed fool trying to get his bearings. He stared at the people at the bus stop. Half of them were now frowning at him, shaking their heads in disgust. Some of them were trying their best to ignore him. But at least half of them were aliens, no longer concerned with their appearance, but totally uncoated and staring at him with their blank almond eyes. As if on command, they moved to encircle him.

"So many of you..." Mica said in a half whisper.

And then he turned and ran.

two

Somewhere in the long drain of his flight through streets crowded with a mix of common pedestrians and unmasked aliens, he saw the old black bum. It was the same man he'd bumped into several times before, he was sure of it. The old fellow was begging at a street corner with a crude sign crayon-marked on a worn scrap of cardboard, "Will Work for Food. God bless."

"Help me!" Mica cried. His hair was in his eyes and there were dark circles of sweat under his arms, and his shirttails were hanging out of his torn pants. He'd lost a shoe and was bleeding from patches at his knees and from the palms of his hands, one of which was also oozing blood from a tear on the thumb. Just another citizen of the lost city of the angels.

The bum looked him straight in the eye and shrugged.

"What can I do, man? I'm jist a broke-down ol' bum, tryin' to find Jesus for myself."

Mica saw there was no help for him; he ran on, his shirt flopping, heading west on Olympic Boulevard.

341

three

"Where's he going?" Gravely asked. He and Felney were in Gravely's new black Mustang convertible. Gravely had the amber warning blinkers on, and they were trailing the exhausted human by about a half a block. They had followed him all the way from the downtown high-rises, and were now approaching Robertson Boulevard in the rim of Beverly Hills.

"It doesn't much matter," Felney answered. "We shouldn't be inactive like this. We should have gathered him in hours ago, the minute our vehicles missed."

"That blanking should have taken hold!"

"Oh, now you're an expert on implanting!" Felney shot back. He was far more irritable than usual. Even though there was a sweet irresistibility to the smell of engine exhaust and the heavy blanket of yellow gray smog enwrapped them like spawnling pit scum, Felney didn't like being away from his position of control at his desk, and he liked even less being out in the actual field. Things happened out here that he could do nothing about, and he missed the multi-eye viewpoint which gave him the options to stay ahead of the game.

"Blodlick says I'm right." It was the only thing Gravely could think to say, and it got to Felney, making his lip twitch. With Speth half out of his mind and wandering the mansion like a maimed drunk, getting away from Sir Fern's nest had at one point seemed to Felney like a decent idea. But Blodlick, his replacement, had proven himself entirely capable in so short a time that now Felney worried his job was in jeopardy. And Blodlick was sitting at the desk happily translating and rolling over while Felney was out here, stranded in the field with this incompetent boy genius.

"Blodlick is a cowcatcher," he grumbled.

"That's a little harsh." Gravely couldn't resist a smile, recognizing Felney's problems with the new scratcher. "He can tell a *sap* from a bovine. Actually, I thought he was doing quite well. I don't think Sir Albert misses you."

"Don't start me up," Felney warned glumly.

"Anyway," Gravely said, going back to their earlier conversation, "We can't translate Mica Harris. He's got to do it himself."

"I thought we had him with that big, blue truck."

"Or the *merde*-colored car." Gravely nodded his agreement.

"He did step directly into the path of that car."

"Not far enough. You know the rules."

"We've got to get better drivers."

four

For a while they trailed Mica in silence, watching as he talked to someone on the street corner.

"He's made a contact."

"No, just some broken-down old sap."

"Trace him?" Felney aimed the scope, got a lock, and then his hands hovered over the portable screen on his lap.

"Couldn't hurt." Gravely nodded; it would give Felney something to do.

They followed Mica in silence. Felney, who had crosshaired and locked off the old bum, was not getting anywhere with his trace. Blodlick ran a deep scan and apparently there was no one who answered to the description; and that was impossible, because they knew everything about every existing *sap* right down to the genetic code. From what they had, this one could be anybody or nobody. Felney insisted Blodlick do a cross-border trace, and when that came up empty, he had the first thrill of joy in an otherwise frightening and gloomy day.

"Blodlick isn't all Fern thinks he is."

"Oh? Why?" Gravely had to brake suddenly as a big white trailer truck with giant decals of green vegetables, tomatoes and a slab of uncooked meat on its side backed in their way.

"What is this truck?" Felney shrieked, frantically typing the word VON'S in his laptop.

344

"Relax. It's a *sap* consumption supply vehicle. Even I know that."

Felney slumped back in his bucket seat. "I'll just be glad to get back to my chair. You may like Blodlick, but I say he can't even do a simple trace-track."

The VON'S truck finally cleared their path. Mica was nowhere to be seen.

"He's gone!" Felney wailed.

Gravely, who was so tired of Felney's behavior he was starting to wish for the return of the grim and relentless spitter, shook his head. "It doesn't matter. He's heading for the medical building."

"He wouldn't go back there. He'd be table meat for sure."

Gravely shrugged, "Don't bet your dusting." He couldn't remember exactly how much he'd told Mica of Sally and Anne Mae's location, but it couldn't have been much. Nobody, even Dr. Railsbach, was exactly sure where they were. And, of course, the lab had been pulled otherside.

"Nothing left for him to see there, anyway."

"He doesn't know that."

There was a moment of silence, and then Felney started up again, "Speth was right. We should have translated him when we had the chance."

"You had your moment to say so."

"I *did* say so! Nobody listens to a monitor translator."

"I guess you can see why," Gravely shot

345

back, showing the strain and suddenly more impatient and angrier than he would have liked.

"You're blaming *me* for not controlling him this morning?! That *sapiens* was totally reblanked! If he could get out of that, the great Bub himself in his glory days couldn't have controlled him!"

"He may be unblanked again, but he's like a *sap* baby. He doesn't know anything!"

"So, are you thinking you and I are going to take him alone at the medical building?" Felney's fingers were poised over his keyboard, ready to type in the necessary backup, including every assassin within three square miles, if they could afford it.

"No. I've got a better idea."

"You have another of your better ideas. Where did you get it, out of a textbook on inter-species relations?"

Gravely pulled the car within a few inches of a fuming school bus, took a deep breath, and cut impatiently around the sulphur-colored vehicle. He felt alone and vulnerable. Nobody realized how much he personally had at stake here. He had put his tail in the crack for Doctor Railsbach's dream of a glorious and victorious future. Sir Fern was giving him enough rope to lower himself into the magma, and now he had this little ferret Felney whining about their enormous energy outlay for the past day's excesses, while Speth was back at Fern's mansion, bumping into walls, ranting about seeing his bitch-mother and drooling spittle that was eating into his own black Florsheims.

346

Taking extraordinary measures, the ever-efficient Maahg, coated as Dr. Bruce, had managed to save Rethan from the effects of the metal pellet that had penetrated her carapace, getting her into pure nitrogen and flashing her to the other side for a replacement heart, but Railsbach hadn't been heard from for 24 hours and he, James Gravely III, on his first real assignment out of the academy, was stuck tailing an increasingly dangerous unblanked *sapiens* without the services of his own assassin.

He didn't figure it could get much worse. And then he stopped for the red glow of a traffic light and Felney snapped his computer shut and jumped out of the car, slamming the door behind him.

"You do whatever you want, Mr. 5.0 Mustang," the plump little translator said in his reedy voice, "It's obvious you don't need me anymore. I'll just run along."

Felney spat on the hood of Gravely's new car in a brave little imitation of Speth, and waddled off in his own direction. Gravely angrily eyed the spittle as it bubbled its way into the black enamel finish; he couldn't stand Felney, but he had to admit Fern's *Old Gurpler* had this oxygen-poisoned world at his beck and call. The translator hadn't taken ten steps before a yellow cab pulled up for him. He opened the back door and hopped in, waving the taxi in the direction of the Fern mansion.

Without Felney, Gravely decided to leapfrog back to Mica's rancho. If whatever help they could muster was able to detain him at the medical building, fine; if not, Mica would eventually return to the rancho where Gravely would provide the final unpleasantness. Gravely was glad he'd read Mica's dossier with such care. It seemed the only other things in the world the poor sap cared for were the horses he and Sally had owned.

CHAPTER 21
Family Ties

<u>one</u>

Mica stood in the late afternoon shade across the street from the medical building on 3rd Street. He pointed with his index finger to keep track as he slowly counted from floor to floor, "Eighteen, nineteen, twenty!!" He was crestfallen until he realized they never counted the 13th floor. There could be a 21st floor after all.

He was tired and sweaty and beginning to feel chilled in the late afternoon air, and his clothes smelled like they belonged in a high school locker room. But this building was the only connecting point he had left to Sally and Anne Mae.

The front doors hissed and slid open at his presence. Mica tucked in his shirt and raked his fingers through his damp hair. He figured they already knew he was here; still, he waited until the security guard had his back turned, and then he limped across the lobby to the nearest elevator. He hesitated and the doors started to close, giving him just time to dart inside before they slammed shut with a hollow clunk. There was a button with 21 on it, and he pushed it. It glowed; it was going to take him there.

The doors opened at the third floor and a hefty nurse wearing a knitted sweater of faded turquoise eased her weight into the elevator. She selected a button and then stood with her hands on her hips, staring at him.

"Snake bite," Mica muttered. He looked down at his shoeless foot. The sock was gone now, and the bottom of the foot was raw and bleeding. "I had to walk here."

"You smell disgusting," she said, retreating as far as she could to her side of the elevator.

"I thought you people took an oath to cure and heal."

"Not me. I do blood tests for people who are gonna die anyway." The elevator stopped at ten and she got off.

"Thanks for the empathy," he called after her retreating form.

Mica continued alone up to 21. The elevator shuddered to a stop, the doors opened, and he stepped into a confusion of new construction. The entire floor was going through a massive change. There were no walls, no doors, no ceilings. Everywhere he looked, he could see through framing studs to windows that looked out over Beverly Hills and West L.A. Nothing was as it had been. Now there were just open spaces between evenly spaced aluminum two-by-fours.

Mica settled to the floor with his back against several two-by-fours that framed a new doorway, and he held his aching head between his hands. He stayed that way while the shadows from the setting sun lengthened across the room, and finally left him in semi-darkness. They, whoever they were, had Sally and Anne

Mae, and he didn't know where. They were everywhere on the planet, their pale, lifeless bug eyes watching from behind their human forms. He alone out of all of humanity, could see them. There was no one he could go to for help. Police? The FBI? The CIA? They would laugh, call him paranoid, maybe decide he was dangerous and put him in jail. Meanwhile, where had the alien demons taken his wife and daughter, and how could he find them?

He finally admitted to himself that this thread had snapped, there was nothing more to this trail. He started backtracking, trying to piece together how he had gotten downtown. The night before, he had shot the Janie alien demon who had been impersonating Sally. The voice had risen in his head and then he woke and found himself midway through the next day. He was sure of the date; he'd glanced at a newspaper vending machine on his long marathon from downtown to this building. It was his luck that they'd implanted in the same thumb, right where they'd done it before, and that he'd remembered before the blanking took over. He stared down at the loose flap of skin on his thumb. It was bluish-white, the tear itself caked with a dirty scab.

He still had his wallet with a few dollars and some credit cards. His car keys, which he remembered leaving in the Alfa at the rancho, just like he always did, were now in his pocket. Could they have manipulated him like a puppet on strings, caused him to drive his own car into town without his knowing it? He knew it was possible; that powerful voice ringing in his head could make a poor *sap* do anything.

Why would they have done it that way? How many of them were there in the first place? He tried to count the ones he'd met, starting with the white-coated man, and Dr. Bruce, and Janie, and then Speth and the younger man, James Gravely. The voice in his head had to be somebody. And the little homeboy at city hall. There had been something different about him; he'd turned into a short little alien, and then into something more sinister, almost like a little devil-dog. The pattern seemed to be that they went from human to alien, but they weren't really aliens. Their final form was something more sinister and evil. Hadn't Janie, the one Dr. Bruce had called Rethan, also started to change into something demonic, just as he shot her?

There was another puzzling question; along Olympic Street, he'd seen dozens, maybe a hundred aliens. They had been everywhere, sitting on the benches at bus stops, looking in store windows, sipping iced tea under red-and-white outdoor cafe umbrellas. Everywhere he looked, it had seemed, there were seven or eight pairs of almond shaped eyes staring at him. But that wasn't what bothered him; something about each tableau seemed familiar, as if the pattern was repeating itself over and over again. He tried to re-create some of the scenes. A mix of people and aliens in a strip mall parking lot. The same in a 76 gas station.

And again outside a storefront run by the Jehovah's Witnesses.

And then he had it; in each group there had been a preacher of some kind. One was a rabbi, another a Catholic Priest who looked Scotch or Irish, another a Baptist minister black as the ace of spades. And there had been a plump mother carrying one child. First she was a black lady, then poor white trash, then a Middle Eastern woman. Two or three teenagers, he couldn't remember exactly. A middle-aged man, balding, who was always more or less disheveled in his various roles as window-washing bum, a plumber and a telephone repairman. The balance was always the same; he was fairly certain he had been seeing the same group of people over and over again. And, if that were true, perhaps it was the same aliens also, over and over again.

Mica felt bone tired, and yet a small core of hope and resolve was rebuilding in him. He was still free, and perhaps the aliens/demons weren't as pervasive as they wanted him to believe. They had enormous and strange powers, and yet they weren't all-powerful, and they did make mistakes.

Still, in a world of humans, he was the only one he knew who even believed these creatures existed. Well, maybe that wasn't exactly true. There was Jimmy, who also believed in dancing meadowland fairies and the Wicked Witch of the West. The whole fringe lunatic bunch, the X-Filers and the folks who flocked to see movies like *Cocoon* and *Close*

Encounters of the Third Kind would welcome
him with open arms.

two

Mica sighed and managed to get back on his feet, his joints stiff and aching. He retreated back to the elevator, taking care not to step on any nails. The door had remained open for him, and so he got in and pushed the button for the main lobby.

He should have known. The elevator again had a mind of its own, stopping on seven and refusing to continue. The stairwell exits were locked; there was only one path left for him. He traced the short walk down the hallway to Doctor Bruce's suite, shivering a little in the air conditioning, his one bloody foot leaving smudges on the gray carpeting. He knew they were waiting for him; but a cold anger was on him, and he trudged on with the growing certainty that they wouldn't be able to hold him.

The reception room was full, like always, with a smattering of bored humanity. If they *were* saps, Mica reminded himself.

The receptionist looked up. If it was Janie, she'd made a fast recovery. He decided it was her double. She gave him Miss Perfectly Cool; she was somebody who didn't know him.

"Hi," he said, "the elevator brought me here."

"Hi," she answered in the brush-off voice of Miss Frosty. "May I help you?"

"You don't know me?"

Her temperature definitely took a plunge, "Should I know you?"

"I'm Dr. Bruce's star patient. And I'd like

355

to see him, right now."

"There is no Doctor Bruce here." She tapped a testy fingernail against the sign on the wall behind her, snapping the names off as she went, "Fineman. Gold. Harrisburg. Kellerman. Butterfield. Definitely no Dr. Bruce here."

Mica fished in his wallet and handed over the appointment card she had given him.

She frowned as she reached for the card. "I already told you, we have no Doctor Bruce here." He held it just beyond her fingertips.

"Yes," he said, "but that's his name on the front of this card, along with Fineman, Gold and Harrisburg, which is also a city in Pennsylvania, just another coincidence." He turned the card over, "And here's a third. Here's your home phone number on the back, in your own lovely handwriting."

"Where did you get this?"

"You gave it to me. Out of gratitude."

"For what?"

"A good time, of course."

Her eyes shifted, and he looked up to see the crowd in the room was standing, as if on signal. Humans and aliens, in about the same ratio he'd seen before. The fat mother and her bratty kid. Three teenagers. The sloppy man, now dressed in a loose jumpsuit with an emblem for Pioneer Bread on back and the name Jake stitched in front in red letters. And the man of the cloth, this time with a shaven head and wearing bright orange robes. He swung around to face them. They had bunched together and were moving toward him like a room full of geriatric robots. They stared at him with expressionless faces, their eyes unblinking and hollow. And mixed among them, the aliens were of two types, tall and short, both with slick, grayish skin and huge unblinking almond eyes.

three

The aliens stood back, allowing the humans to move forward. Mica saw they could overpower him by the sheer mass of numbers. An old woman struck him across the back with her purse, and an even older man grabbed his arm, baring his teeth to take a bite.

Someone was punching him in the back and one of the teens had grabbed his arms from behind. As he struggled, he looked over the crowd to the line of aliens standing at the back of the room. If they were in control, why were they standing back? What were they worried about? Could they be frightened, and if so, of what?

He managed to break one arm free, and a shudder ran through the humans ganged up around him, and the aliens seemed visibly shaken. He fisted the Pioneer Bread man, feeling a crunch as he flattened the man's nose. He managed to twist around and glare at the teens trying to hang onto his other arm, and they backed away from him.

"Oh, sorry man, we made a big mistake," one of them said, holding his hands wide.

There was a momentary clearing, and he darted for the door, trying to get back to the hallway. But before he could make it, Peggy, the nurse who always accompanied him to his examination room, came out from the inner offices.

"Oh, there you are, Mr. Harris," she said cheerily, and she clamped her hand on his wrist with a grip of iron.

He took a deep breath and swung hard with his free hand. He caught her on the side of her chin, breaking her grip and knocking her into the Buddhist monk, who cursed him in a high singsong dialect. As he darted for the door, he glanced back and was rewarded with one last image of the large woman with the child, who looked to be a chunky four or five years of age. She was holding it by the legs, and was reared back, ready to swing it like a club. And then he stepped over the fallen Pioneer Bread man and was out the door and down the hall.

Somehow, Peggy had gotten through the crowd and beaten him to the elevator. He stopped dead in his tracks, now with nowhere to go.

"Come on, Mica!" she shouted. "I'm trying to help you!"

With humans and aliens boiling out of the reception room behind him, he darted into the elevator just as the doors closed.

"Down. Get us down!"

She pushed the button for the main lobby, and he slumped in one corner of the elevator in gratitude.

"I thought you were one of them," he said. He leaned back against the wall, closing his eyes and humming a ragged little hoot-hoot-hoot of the Stones' "Sympathy for the Devil" song in harmony with the sound of the elevator.

He would never know why he opened his eyes at that second, but he was just in time to throw up one protective arm as Peggy, eyes flashing, slashed down at him with a huge scalpel she had raised over her head. He wasn't afraid. He was filled with a sudden, blind anger. Without thinking, out of pure reflex, he swung his other arm in a crude attempt to backhand her. And to his astonishment, raw gouts of blue flame, of pure energy, leapt from his fingertips. The wave of energy cut through the silvery walls of the elevator like butter, and where it cut through the creature he had known as Peggy, she literally exploded into a mass of bubbling blue-green putty. Her last scream was cut short, and then she was in two parts on the floor. Her face twisted and assumed the features of an alien, and then as he stared in horror and amazement from her to his fingertips and back again, she went through another change and became so frighteningly demonic, so terrifyingly ugly that he had to look away.

Dying as she was, the creature could still talk.

"Look at me, *sapiens*," she hissed.

He had no choice but to do as she commanded.

"This is on your head. You'll die a thousand deaths for mine."

Even as his blood chilled with the threat and the horrible sight that lay before him, something in him hardened.

"I don't know how it is possible that I have done what I have done," he said simply. "But you should never have taken my wife and daughter."

CHAPTER 22
The Stuff of Dreams

one

Mica limped three blocks east on 3rd Street to a Sav-On drugstore where he bought thick, white cotton socks, a cheap pair of canvas shoes, Bactine antiseptic, a psycho-shock florescent orange and green T-shirt that shouted, "California Dreamin'". To this he added a black baseball cap celebrating the San Jose Sharks, a heavy blue sweatshirt size double-X that zipped up the front and had a hood and drawstrings and unmatched sweatpants, and a pair of swirl patterned blue-and-purple cotton swim trunks labeled "CrazyWear". His credit cards wouldn't work, but one of several hundred dollar bills he had folded and stashed behind his driver's license served the moment. He bullied the assistant manager into letting him use the employee bathroom. Once inside, he locked the door and doused his thumb and the bottoms of his feet in Bactine and changed into his new clothes. Then, when an employee used his key to come in the back door of the building, he managed to slip out before it slammed shut again.

He was less than a mile from his cubicle at the L.A. Weekly. By now it was dark; Jimmy wouldn't be home yet; she was probably tomcatting somewhere in West L.A., anywhere the action was. He trudged along 3rd Street, and when he reached his office, was surprised to find his own car parked in the lot. The back door next to the parking lot was still open, and he let himself in.

"Mica! You gonna work all the time?"

It was Jimmy, seated in his chair. Her long, chocolate-milk legs were up on the sofa he'd crammed in his little office.

"You sure are back in the zone," she purred.

"What do you mean?" He came uncertainly into the room.

"We'll, I'm not the judge, but this stuff is *gooood*, mon." She indicated the batch of Hornys on her lap.

He edged a little closer and looked over her shoulder to see for himself. In the top strip, Horny was calmly meeting an almond-eyed alien. The alien asks why he isn't afraid like others he's encountered. Horny replies that the people on his planet are advanced, and he ticks off a list of accomplishments to prove it: atomic power, the automobile, mass production, the airplane. The alien, who has had little thought clouds showing an atom bomb cloud, auto crashes, smoking factory chimneys and bombers dropping bombs, retreats in horror. Horny stares out of the last frame with an expression of bewildered wonder, *Why was the alien afraid of him?*

"How many do I have there?"

"Six..." She quickly scanned through the thick pages, "No, seven."

"I never did more than two in a day in my

life."

"You were here when I got in, workin' like crazy."

"What did I say?"

"Didn't say a word to nobody. Finished up at noon and you were out of here, like *gone,* mon."

He nodded, looking over the work. The strips each featured a cute little almond-eyed alien who was obviously Horny's new foil. All seven of them worked, the payoffs were right, and the drawings appeared in his shaky, Thurberesque style. His little cartoon creatures were all solidly in character.

He shook his head slowly from side to side. "Problem is, I can't remember doing them."

She gave him a speculative look. "You remember us going to see the channeler?"

"Malibu Ned? Sure." Lost in his own thoughts, Mica didn't say any more. So much had happened since Ned had been crisped in his La-Z-Boy, that experience seemed years in the past.

"He's gonna be alright. A few bad burns, is all."

"Who?"

"Mica! Malibu Ned!"

"Oh, yeah." Mica sighed. He'd been thinking of creatures who bubbled green when they were shot and faces that shifted from person to person and from person to alien and of the deadly killing power which had rippled unbidden from his fingertips to cut down Peggy

363

in the elevator. He stared at the strips for another moment or two before handing them back to Jimmy.

"Glad to see I'm back."

"Mica...Let's go catch a hamburger."

"No, I'm going home. I've got to get some Zees." He wandered out of the room, saying over his shoulder, "See you tomorrow, I guess."

"Yeah, mon. Tomorrow for sure." The disappointment was obvious in her voice. "Hey, mon," she called after him. "Where'd you get those clothes? You shoppin' at the flea market again?" But the only answer was the hiss and click of the back door closing as he left.

two

Jimmy sighed and frowned, the Horny strips lying forgotten on her lap. Mica Harris had her plenty worried. Not that he ever acted like himself, not since Sally and Anne Mae had died, but now there was a haunted look to him, and he seemed particularly distracted and distant. She hadn't seen him this way since the month and three days when she'd taken him in, right after Sally died. She wondered how much he remembered of that time; those days were probably nothing to him, the time that she remembered as the sweetest days of her life. She'd started by saying she was doing it for Sally, and then the guilt had set in, knowing she was enjoying him, slowly losing herself in him. At first it had been impossible for her to draw back, and then impossible to stop her long free fall into hopeless love.

It wasn't the same for him. He'd gradually come back from his worst times and had healed little by little until he started drawing again. And one day she'd come back to her apartment to find he'd moved out. He'd gone back to the rancho, to taking care of himself; maybe he thought he had gone on, but she knew he'd only retreated into his past. She'd lost him to his memories of Sally and Anne Mae, and maybe that was the way it was always supposed to be. She and Mica were still close, still friends. But they never talked about the special month and three days. For her part, Jimmy never did because she was afraid to bring it up. And

365

Mica, she was sure, because he'd pushed it so far into the back of his mind that he'd forgotten.

three

Mica took the service road to Zelzah and wound through the hilly back roads crowded by peppertrees until he came to his rancho. *Were his enemies tailing him? Waiting in ambush by the roadside? Sleeping in his bed?* He didn't care anymore. He didn't have anything left to fight with. He was drained, a dead battery. He seemed to be saying, *Come and get me. The shelves which held the pleasures of my life are empty, the cupboard of my memories is bare.*

The gravel crunched under the wheels as he pulled the Alfa to its spot next to the big live oak tree trunk, and it grumbled under his footsteps as he made his way around to the back entrance. He stopped on the back porch, reluctant to go inside the house.

He pulled a pile of folded blankets and some pillows from a musty old steamer chest and threw one over a worn stick chair that was his favorite. He settled into the chair and pulled another blanket over him. As he tossed and turned in restless slumber, the pale and silvery disk of a half-moon rose, climbing silently through the night sky until it was hidden behind the roof overhang above him. Spiders crawled and spun their webs in the wooden beams. A thin coyote, drifting like a nervous ghost, came within twenty feet of him. It paused and sniffed the air before wandering on to look for smaller, easier prey.

367

four

Mica dreamed a long, slow dream of Sally and Anne Mae, and of the good things that once had been. He was back in time, in his own bright kitchen in the good old days. Sally was doing the dishes, and sweet, bubbly Anne Mae was nearby, elbow deep in cookie dough. He cried out loud for her, for the girl who loved sugar and spice, who took early to baking with cinnamon and dark bittersweet baker's chocolate, first as mother's little helper almost before she was walking, and then branching out on her own, learning to read as much from Betty Crocker and the Better Homes & Gardens NEW Cookbook as from Dr. Seuss and Richard Scarry.

In his dream she was baking chocolate chip specials. She looked up, grinning, and handed him one.

"Here it is, Daddy," she said, "double-chipped, the way we like them." The cookie was golden brown, with the chocolate still gooey and warm, at the stage where you inhaled its essence as much as ate it.

He looked around the kitchen. In his dream, Sally was no longer wiping dishes. Now she was sitting at the table playing chess with a man in a white coat. It couldn't be—*It was the white-coated stranger, the man he'd met on the elevator!*

He wanted to warn her, to yell, to reach across the table and grab the man. But he couldn't move. His muscles were frozen and all he could do was watch.

Anne Mae winked at him and walked over to her mother and pulled her arm, trying to get her attention.

"Mom, I need to talk to you."

"Just a moment, honey-bird." Sally moved one of the chessmen and then moved to the sink. She picked up her towel and began wiping a yellow mixing bowl.

Anne Mae reached up like she was going to kiss her mother and whispered in her ear, "Daddy's here. I gave him a cookie."

"I know, sweetie. Do you think you could show Doctor Kelp your painting?"

Anne Mae grinned. "You mean dis-tract him, right?" she whispered.

"That would be nice."

Anne Mae walked over to the table and looked at the chessboard. Her mother's white army was firmly in control.

"You don't have a chance," she said happily.

"Well, I don't need to hear that from a spawnling—"

"Don't be grumpy." She took his huge hand in her own. "Come on, I want to show you my watercolor."

Railsbach, demon to the last, had a momentary vision of crushing that soft and friendly hand. But then he went along with the little girl.

In his dream, Sally looked directly into Mica's eyes. The wrinkles at the corners of her eyes bunched and her face lit in her special wry smile, so beautiful it made his heart ache.

"You have the power," she told him, speaking softly and yet very clearly. "We all do. They've hidden it from us."

His voice sprang from his throat, "But— but I killed somebody!"

"You did nothing wrong. Power and responsibility are balanced. You had no choice. Remember, this is *our* world. They are trying to take it from us."

The white-coated man looked up from his conversation with Anne Mae, aware for the first time that Sally was speaking. "W-What?!" he shouted, but Mica heard more fear than anger in his voice. "There's no way. It's not possible!"

"Of course, it isn't," she said, agreeing with him. She smiled over at Anne Mae, waggling her fingers goodbye to Mica in a gesture the white-coated man could not help but see.

Mica wanted to stay, but Sally and Anne Mae were moving away from him quickly, the objects of his affection in an infinite zoom lens that was inexorably pulling backwards. They were small as cats, as mice, as ants, and then the connection was broken.

five

Mica was lost in inner space, and he tumbled down, spinning like a cell in a bloodstream. Somewhere in his troubled dreams, Felney managed to lock on and input a steady stream of shattering scenes of violence. Mica shuddered under the impact of exploding shells, endured the crash that was fatal to his wife and child over and over a dozen times, relived every grizzly scene from every news flash he'd ever seen. It all came real and played before his eyes, and he was helpless to do a thing about it.

Gravely watched in silent admiration as Felney, working out of Albert Fern's study, called up scene after scene of bloody horror and flicked them at Mica's unwary mind. Gravely had pulled his Mustang deep into the shadows of a line of dark Juniper firs not a hundred feet from where Mica tossed in fitful sleep. From his portable viewpad, he could see Mica on one monitor set overhead in the rafters, although from time to time the view was obstructed by a busy spider's leg. Mica wasn't taking this well at all, from the facial expressions, the tossing and turning, and the faint groans which escaped from his lips. A night spent that way, Gravely well knew, would cause the *sapiens* to awaken in the morning feeling totally unrefreshed and dispirited. It was one of the first things they taught at the academy.

six

Sally studied Dr. Railsbach across the chessboard. The doctor looked tired and disheveled. They had set up another game, but hadn't started playing. Anne Mae slept on a couch nearby.

"It took courage to come back here, after what we did to your little friend," Sally said.

"Courage is a *sapiens* emotion," he replied. "We have no choice. We simply do the things we have to."

"No," Sally replied. "Everybody has a choice. Even you."

"You don't know anything."

"I know you're in trouble, Kelp. Deep trouble...or you wouldn't be here talking to me."

Railsbach eyed her for a moment, and then averted his gaze. He reached for one of the black pawns, and tentatively pushed it forward on the board. He checked his palm-sized communication device, carefully moving a small switch.

"I want to ask you something..."

"Shoot. I'm all ears." She smiled at his blank look. "I mean, you have my attention."

"Have you ever heard of a *good* devil?"

"What is that supposed to mean?"

"Good in terms of morality. Like you *saps* say, *he is a good person.*"

"Oh. I see." Sally thought about it while she moved one of her pawns into the neutral zone. "Well, I suppose Horny is a good devil."

"No, not a fictional character. I mean some example based in reality."

Sally shook her head. "No, I never did. But that doesn't mean it isn't possible."

Railsbach's features brightened visibly.

"How so?"

"Look—you've got good and bad people. And it's not black or white. Some good people do some really stupid and bad things. I suppose the same might be true for you...although I didn't see anything good in Snivler."

"Snivler is a very low form, compared to...well, someone like me. You have creatures on earth that you breed to kill."

"I don't think so."

He shrugged, "Pit bulls. Fighting roosters. Bears. Tigers."

"I don't know where this is going. What was your original question?"

"In theology at the academy we are taught that we must strive always towards darkness. Beautiful darkness. To succeed in that goal is to be a good demon. How could it be any other way?"

"That's right, that covers everything but the unthinkable horror."

"The unthinkable horror?" Railsbach repeated slowly, struggling to make himself ready to squeeze any heretic thought from his mind. But when it came, he found himself incapable of anything but an almost indescribable feeling of longing, what he would describe later as the first faint whisper of hope.

"Yes," the sap female said, brushing her

blond hair back from her face with a careless wave of one hand. "Suppose your people actually are *fallen angels*? Then, wouldn't the opposite of everything you've been taught be true?"

CHAPTER 23
Demon Tricks

<u>one</u>

Mica woke with a start when a peacock owned by his neighbors shattered the silence with its early morning call, the shiny dark blue bird's supernatural whistle ending in a frightening scream. He jumped up to find the bird eating dried hollyhock seeds from the base of a few tall stalks that were tipped in creamy flowers still standing in Sally's sadly neglected and overgrown flower garden. The bird turned on him, quickly spreading the incredible fan of its tail, and Mica tried to remember if it had ever attacked anyone. His thoughts felt disjointed and fuzzy and his bones ached.

"Nice birdie," he said, hoping the miscreant fowl wouldn't get the idea this was its home and that he was an intruder.

His voice seemed to satisfy it; the large fan lurched down to half-mast, and the bird went back to pecking at the hollyhocks.

A scratching noise began from inside the house. *So, it begins early,* Mica thought to himself. Pulling against every fiber in his body, he decided he had to go in and reclaim his home for himself. The kitchen was empty, bright with sunshine and looking cheery in spite of the neglected piles of dishes and the old piles of newspapers scattered everywhere. The living room was also deserted; he noticed the pockmarks where the alien had spit, now quiet and no longer smoking. He wondered if he could fill them in with colored grout. Slivers of sunlight glanced in under the porch overhang. *Where was that scritch, scritch, scratching noise coming from?* He moved into the master bedroom. And there he found Blumper and Thunderhead, the two beautiful horses he and Sally used to ride, filling the room with the sweet, sickly smell of death. Their blood was everywhere, sprayed on the walls, drenching the bed, settled in dark pools on the pale flowered tile floors. And everywhere he looked, the room was alive with feeding rats.

He slumped to the floor, whimpering, calling out for his lost sanity. "Noooo...I can't—I can't take this anymore."

Naturally, the 9 mm automatic was at his side. He took it in both hands, setting it on his lap. He brushed a few flecks of blood from the cut grill handle and took out the clip, studied it to see that it was nearly full. He put the clip back in and jacked a round in the chamber.

And then, when he'd resolved to end it all, he again saw Sally staring at him from one of the pictures on his dresser, looking across time from a bright day five years before. There she was in her eternal moment, the day captured forever in the photograph and his memory. Back then they were so young and carefree that all the joy in the world had seemed theirs for the taking. They had been like kids, romping through a flimsy reality that had come crashing to an end. There was a bullet hole in the

376

picture, and the glass was splintered and broken; still, the picture stirred old memories in him of dozens of picnics and beach parties, of quiet rides through their meadowlands. He remembered riding with her through the tans of autumn, the lush green in the spring, foggy days and misty mornings, and his eyes blurred with tears.

"Well, Sal, old girl," he said, addressing the splintered picture, "It looks like they want me to blow my head off. What say you to that?"

He waited in the bloody room, imagining what she would say. He listened, nodding as if in response, confident his enemies were watching and wanting to give them any discomfort he could.

"Yes, ma'am," he said finally, the way he'd always addressed her after he'd really made her angry and was trying to make up. He stood and ejected the round from the chamber, taking the time to stuff the pistol in his belt behind his back.

"Well, then, I better get going," he said, giving a little salute to the picture, "I know they've got a surprise or two in store for me, and I wouldn't want to miss out on that."

He paused for a moment, looking around the room at the red horror. "Give up, assholes," he said softly. "Because I'm coming for you."

two

Mica walked out of the bedroom, managing to get down the hall and out the door before he bent to his knees with the dry heaves. After a while he felt well enough to pull himself to his feet. He leaned his weight against one of the posts that held up the porch overhang. The early morning sun was just lighting the dew-heavy fields in gold. He looked at himself in the rusty Bianchi Gunleather promotional mirror that still hung on the porch. *Portrait of Mica in Hell,* he thought glumly. Sally's voice seemed to come to him then, *Get cleaned up, pal. At least you can look your best.*

That seemed like a good idea, so he stripped off his old clothes and headed for the back shower, away from the bedroom. But the shower water ran bright green gunk and smelled rank as a swamp, and his electric razor fizzled and popped dead in his hand. He rinsed the green slime off his body by jumping into the pool. He had time for one quick dive, and he got out just before the water congealed into thick gray mud. He scooped a handful and threw it against a tree where it stuck, already drying like quick-set cement. Big black spiders were crawling over the small stack of towels he kept in a small cabinet next to the pool, but he shook them off and used the towel to dry himself.

"Where's the plague of locusts?" he asked out loud. There was an old pair of beach

378

cutoffs and a somewhat muted Hawaiian shirt hanging from a wooden piece carved and painted in a replica of Pinocchio's face, the nose serving as a hook. He remembered Sally had found the old hook buried in an antique shop; it had been cracked and faded, but she had bought sandpaper, wood filling and enamel, and returned the puppet to its former glory. The moment he touched the pants, brown crickets hopped out of them. He found an angry little scorpion in the pocket of the shirt, but he turned the pockets and the pants themselves inside out, and shook them several times before putting them on.

The small bathroom just off the pool still had serviceable water. He found a rusty old plastic Bic shaver in a cabinet and managed to scrape his face with only minor damage. In the laundry room he found some decent, only used once jeans still threaded with a thick leather belt with a silver Zuni buckle done in the image of the mysterious rain man, who was dancing around, tooting on his inset turquoise flute, calling down rain on the fields of his people, thunder on their enemies. He traded the cutoffs for the jeans, found some decent socks in the drier and an old pair of Clark's walking shoes in a rack on the back porch. His grief over the horses had subsided into a hot, red wall of anger he felt for his tormentors. And something more; he was learning about the limits of their power. The strange special effects—the shower water turning to slime, the pool water to mud, and the bugs in his clothing—were all changes in appearance, all cut from the same cloth of deception. He suspected and hoped with all his heart that the horses were just another delusion.

He wasn't in top shape by any means, but it was noted by his watchers that he was hooting his low hoot, hoot, hoot, his abominable rendering of the old Stones' song, as he made his way to his Alfa. Felney, having heard that hoot hundreds of times, had long since determined it was conscious and derogatory. In the little translator's mind, that alone was enough to grind the rebellious EMO into dust.

three

Sir Albert had already called James Gravely twice for a special session in the large boardroom near the study. The last summons had come five minutes earlier, while Gravely was fussing around behind Felney's station, anxiously watching the monitors for the final crack in Mica's armor. The water tricks were simple variations of Jesus' old water-into-wine stunt, and the bugs were easy, but to maintain the corporeal presence of two huge bloody horses over time was costing them heavily. And he, Gravely, had to walk into a status meeting with nothing tangible to report.

He waited a moment longer, watching hopefully as Felney manufactured a deep pothole on the steep downgrade from Mica's rancho to Zelzah Drive. Mica swung the car recklessly around the mirage; his battered Alfa fishtailed badly and looked for a moment like it might slide over the embankment and tumble down a brush-choked hill, but Mica stayed in control and continued on toward the freeway.

Gravely clapped Felney on the shoulder. "Thanks. I know you threw that one in for me."

Felney shrugged, his glittering, beady eyes already on another monitor. A group of chubby young lawyers in fine dark suits were gathered around a table in a posh restaurant, arguing amiably about politics. One of them raised his fork and in that moment began to choke on a big bite of cordon bleu already stuffed in his mouth. Felney pushed the button, Translate.

While his well-mannered fellows looked on in horror, the lawyer slid to the floor, one hand gesturing wildly at his own throat, his eyes bulging. No one in the restaurant seemed to remember the Heimlich Maneuver or even moved to help him. Felney cleared the screen and was already on to a do-it-yourself mechanic who was whistling an old blues song from under his car, which he'd propped up with two cinder blocks. Albert made his impatient, throat-clearing sounds from the next room. Gravely sighed and reluctantly went to join his boss.

<u>four</u>

It was young James Gravely's first meeting with the entities whom Speth in his better days had referred to as the *musty dusties*. They were quite a sight; the twelve ancients wore coats so old they smelled fetid and rank. Their human flesh was tattered and worn through in spots, and their hair so ancient it cracked and fell at the slightest touch. Gravely knew it was pure formality; the only reason the old tails wore their coats at all was the immutable rule about not stepping earthside without a coat, the same one that, since universal blanking, nobody on hooves insisted on anymore, except fuddy old Sir Albert.

The twelve sat rigidly around the table, and their heavily wrinkled flesh spilled out of ancient fabric suits as they stared at Gravely with cloudy, unblinking cat's eyes, each laboring to breathe in the heavy, noxious atmosphere. These were the conservative blacksides, very old crawlers, most of them claiming veteran glory in the first conflict, a brag equally difficult to prove as it was to deny. They were unimpressed with the recent scientific gains which they saw as less than glorious and they were weary of the eternal fight with mankind and the constant outpouring of energy it took to maintain their portholes, their precious beachheads, in 47 of the most populous regions of the oxygen-poisoned planet.

Speth lurched back and forth in the

background, moving with a crippled, crab-like gait while spittle drooled from his mouth. He was exercising as he had done since he'd been stunned in the backwash of his own powers, flexing his lanky frame in a seemingly doomed but unyielding attempt to *gain back his edge*.

"HHHemm," Sir Fern coughed again, giving Speth an annoyed look before turning his attention back to his young underling. "Good of you to join us, Gravely."

"I'm sorry, sire. It's so exciting. We're so close now, sire; so very close. We've practically got him in the bag!"

"You're babbling like an underclassman, Gravely." Albert's eyes were like cold gray marbles.

"Ahhh, yes, sire."

"Perhaps you could explain for the good masters here what it is you have been attempting to do since taking over from Doctor Railsbach."

"I?! But—" Gravely bit his lip, realizing how neatly the old striker had him pinned. He patted the moustache, which had begun its damnable twitching, this time on both sides, until he had it under control. Perhaps he should just shave the blessed thing off, be rid of it once and for all. "Yes, of course, sire."

For the first time he noticed the charts on one wall. He could make out the energy peak from the unsuccessful flying saucer setup, and, of course, the recent enormous drains to keep the unblanked human on the defensive.

"James...You have something to report?"

Sir Fern's stern voice pulled him back to present realities.

"Why—why, yes, sire. There will be one more peak usage of energy. After which Mica Harris will again be under the blanket or he will be translated to his reward."

The oldest of the twelve spoke in a thin, sweet voice, "What equity do we have to this outcome, aside from your hopeful aspirations?" He was a spirit so aged his coat was more like a crust of dried sores than an actual coating of flesh, and his clawed hands shook as he strove to maintain presence in the foreign brightness and alien earthside atmosphere.

"Only that it is an excellent plan, revered one."

"Empty promises, spawnling."

"Sire. We do not have much choice. This unblanked human remains a threat of totally unknown dimensions."

The ancient waved one hand around, the gesture taking in the mansion, "Surely not a danger to...to everything we have established here?"

"We just don't know! You know what they are capable of better than I. You saw unblanked humans in the last glory."

"Oh, yes...*And here they now ascend, the howling jackal beasts of earth, shrill and frightful laughs tumbling out from between their ears. Large and small, their flaming biters mow down the chosen righteous sons of darkness...*" The old one nodded, drifting into silence as his thoughts turned inward.

Speth was muttering in the background, taking up the old chant from the legendary First Coming, *"Krath Net Lo Jun/Rath Let No Sum/Hath Met Fro Gun/KALE! KALE! KALE!"*

"Oh, don't get him started," Sir Fern muttered. "Is there any chance you'll transfer me a new bone-biter before next moon?"

"No chance, not even in a full twelve-cycle. Every sector's stretched to the snap. Why do you think we're here?"

The twelve stared at him, awaiting his answer. Albert sucked in a big gulp of oxygen and slowly blew it in their direction. No way around it; no matter how he slipped or slid, it was still his quadrant to win or lose. Were it not for young Gravely's father and the fondness of the olden times, he would have had his spawnling properly blamed, strangled and oxidized days before. Now he snapped his jaw shut, his long teeth clacking together, and then spat out words as if he were chewing them, "My man Gravely will snatch the heart. I side with his plan." His choosing not to respond in mother-tongue could have been held as a spite, but no one rose to the bait.

"Be it, then," the eldest said after a long pause. As he spoke, he made a level motion with the palm of his hand, the lid-over-brimstone sign which meant the matter was now settled until magma rose once again. Then he stood and snapped his briefcase shut.

"One last thing…"

"Yes?" Fern hoped his face didn't show how eager he was to have them all out of the room.

"Has Dr. Railsbach said anything about a mutant named Snivler?"

"No. Should he have?"

"Praise be to the dark," the old one said, ignoring Albert's question with a farewell nod of his ancient head. He walked with stiff and careful precision from the room, headed as if on autopilot for the huge fireplace in the study. The others, without another word, rose from their seats and followed after him.

five

The overheads picked up Mica Harris as he pulled on the 118 at Reseda and headed west. Felney decided he was probably going to DeSoto and the off-ramp that led to Brown's Canyon, to the ramshackle spread owned by the old couple who boarded horses. And because it wasn't in anybody's best interest that Mica see with his own eyes that his horses weren't really chopped into sections and lying in bloody chunks in his bedroom, and also because they were now desperate for the *sap* to be netted, Gravely decided they should wait no longer, and that the major burn was to commence. It was a traditional ploy, the old day-for-night flop; Felney applied it with his excellent touch from the monitor board at his desk, and it came down classic, just like the book-feed.

One moment Mica was driving along the freeway in his Alfa, squinting in the morning sunlight. The next, he was still driving, but in another car and at night. He was on a mountain road in the fated Fiat Spyder just moments before his crash.

"No, Mica!" a familiar voice screamed in his ear, and he blinked stupidly, realizing Sally was at his side and Anne Mae was behind him, leaning forward over the seat back.

"You're just plain selfish, Mica! Mica Monster-Man! All you ever think about is yourself and your career! Me, me, me— MICA! You never have any time for Anne and me!"

"You're not really here!" Mica screamed. "This isn't really happening!" He tried to find some shred of calmness and not rise to the bait, even though he'd had a similar argument and shared words such as these with Sally once before. But that had been back before Horny, back before the money had started flowing in a bright and steady stream, years before the moment of their car crash.

"That's what you always say!" she shouted, just as she had in that long-ago time.

"No. I don't mean that. I mean we're not really here. It's daytime, not night. I'm in my Alfa, not my old Spyder. You're not Sally. You're not really here."

He took his eyes off the night road, glanced over to see her features start to waver. In another moment—he was sure of it—the sunlight would break through again and this cruel test would be a thing of his past, but then Anne Mae screamed, "Daddy, look out!!"

There it was, perfect in every last detail, the huge silver grill bearing down on them, the giant trailer truck almost graceful in its leap over the center divider.

"Selfish!" Sally's cry was a needle in his ear, "Selfish, selfish, selfish man! See, now you've killed us!"

"Noooo! This isn't the way it happened!!"

Knowing he was rocketing through an illusion was one thing; but it was so *real*, so very much a devious blend of fiction and the actual way he remembered it, that he couldn't avoid taking his hands off the wheel and holding them up in front of him, as if his two mortal hands could ward off tons of steel shooting in his direction.

And in that instant, the black of night once again became the bright gold of a sunny morning. He was back in the Alfa, and Sally and Anne Mae were gone. There was no semi bearing down on him; just the whistle of the wind and his battered sportster rocketing along at close to 85 miles an hour. He grabbed the wheel and took his foot off the gas, but it was too late.

He felt as much as saw the blinking red and white lights, and heard the insect-like siren wail behind him. *To survive all that illusion and fakery, only to be pulled over by the highway patrol!* He wondered if they had a code for driving under the influence of aliens. As he glided over to the center divider and pulled to a stop, he noticed the pistol on the passenger seat. *Great, a cocked and loaded 9mm pistol!* He had just enough time to shove it under his right thigh.

The CHP officer approached, wearing bug-like wrap-around sunglasses. How appropriate, he thought, wondering if it took less energy for them to shift into something that looked closer to their real appearance. The officer stood at his side of the convertible, looking down at him. She was a smallish woman, natty in her tailored tans. She held her citation book on the ready with her left hand, while her right was behind her, resting on her hip within easy reach of her own weapon. Her partner stayed behind, leaning against the patrol car. The traditional backup, he was a lumpish fellow with a natty moustache, and he also wore the huge black sunglasses. *The bugsy twins,* Mica thought.

"You were weaving all over the road, sir," the lady cop said. Her mouth was pushed into a look of stern disapproval. Mica was distracted by the thin layer of frosted pink on her lips.

"I—there was a—a bee—attacked me. I lost control for a moment."

"A bee attacked you while you were rocketing no-handed down the freeway at 85 or 90 miles an hour?"

"Yes, a bee. See, this bee—somehow the air currents behind the windshield trapped him. And he got mad. I think he was a killer bee."

"Let me see your eyes." She put one hand on his head and turned it so he was staring directly into her dark glasses.

"Dilated pupils."

"They are not."

"Are you taking any medications, sir?"

"No, of course not; this is silly."

"Would you please step out of the car, sir?"

Mica hesitated, thinking about the pistol. "I—I can't..."

Their relationship deteriorated at once. Convinced that she had *a hot one*, she went hard in a flash, "I said, *Step out of the car, sir!*"

Mica's vision went blurry, and his eyes stung.

"Just give me a moment, here." He rubbed his eyes, trying to clear them. It didn't seem to help, but when he looked up again, he saw the

CHP lady in uniform was really just another bug-eyed alien.

"You!!" Mica shouted, grabbing for the pistol at his side, "I know who you are!"

She was good with her stubby little police .38, pulling it from her holster and getting off a wild round that zipped past his head and buried itself in the worn black leather upholstery of the passenger side door of his Alfa before he could get his hands on his own 9mm. But then he had the pistol up and blasted three quick shots into her chest before she could correct her aim. The force of the bullets knocked her back against the concrete center partition dividing the freeway. She slid to a sitting position on the ground, staring blankly ahead. Mica stared, waiting for the transformation he was sure would come.

But it didn't. She didn't turn into an alien or a demon. She was still a downed CHP officer, head to the side, almost certainly dead.

"Change, damn you—change!" he screamed. Shots rang out behind him, and the windshield in front of him went opaque as it cracked into hundreds of little squares. The second officer was running up behind him. Mica dropped his own pistol to the seat and hit the gas as shots whistled around his head and took out nearly all of the windshield which remained.

The Alfa leaped forward and he was back in traffic, accelerating as a lemon yellow Corvette bore down on him from behind, horn blaring in a Doppler effect as it swept around him and away into the distance.

Behind Mica, the second CHP rushed up to the downed officer.

"Phillips! Christ, Phillips!"

The CHP lady groaned and tried to sit up, the dark glasses sliding crookedly down her nose until one eye was looking over the steel rims. "Score one for Kevlar," she groaned.

"How do you feel?"

"You take a bullet in the nipples and tell *me* about it."

She coughed and rolled over on her side. Still spunky, she looked up at him, "You get— his number?"

"Got it."

"Well, stupid—call it in!"

CHAPTER 24
And Then There Were Two

<u>one</u>

Gravely claimed it a success and even Felney said it was at least a partial victory; Mica was now a hunted man, wanted by the law-keepers of his own species. As such, he couldn't possibly last more than a few hours. But another huge energy spike had been consumed, and even Gravely had to concede the *sap* was not yet *in the bag* as he had promised. Fortunately, he'd had the forethought to gather up Speth with a flood of sweet promises relating to the dissection of the unblanked human, and they were far away from the manse, speeding over the Sepulveda Pass toward the San Fernando Valley in Speth's BMW at the same time that Mica made his escape from the police.

As the morning wore on, the study at the Fern mansion was not a happy place, and everyone knew it. Lollypop, the little white dog, was hiding out somewhere, and Nilch and Zilch found the foul mood of the place reason enough to go outside and torture toads in the pond. Railsbach was supposedly back otherside, busy with his void experiments, and days late for his promised return. Sir Fern's discreet inquiries as to who Snivley was and what he might have to do with Railsbach went nowhere. Speth and Gravely hadn't so much as checked in.

Even Felney left off from his workstation, making vague rumbling excuses about some dealings with the kitchen staff. Sir Albert knew Gurpler's rumbling invariably whiffed of petty prevarication and dissembling; he granted him a few hours leave back otherside; and without so much as a word of gratitude, the little translator leapt through the gateway in a sudden boil of dust and ashes and was gone.

two

That left Sir Albert Fern conveniently alone to deal with the special accountant, a tall, spare gray-skinned spirit with the dour politician's face of an ancient Roosevelt, Wilson, Jackson or Nixon, who came stooping through the fireplace to waver his glum expression around the study until his eyes fixed on the silent form of the master of the house, seated in his favorite wing chair, waiting for him.

"And have you bottled for me one James Gravely?" he asked without so much as a formal introduction or even a petty signal of greeting.

"Bottled? Why?" Fern sputtered, pretended indignation.

"The promised netting of Mica Harris did not occur. The energy has been burned. You're taking this failure on your own back?"

"My ship, my responsibility."

In that moment, Felney surprised Sir Fern by returning from his little vacation. On seeing the special accountant, he dusted himself and sat nearby. The little translator said nothing, but Fern knew he was doubtless imagining the worst, dreading an assignment to someplace north and cold, or flicker knows worse, bottled for pounding or even a remold.

"I have come for James Gravely," the special accountant insisted, opening his briefcase and waving a still-smoking paper in his hand.

Felney surprised everyone, speaking up in his thin, reedy voice, "The elders exceed themselves."

"And what do you know?!" The thin man turned like a viper, ready at the lash.

Felney gathered his small frame. "I have come from the den of the Admiral, himself. He says to tell you that—and I quote his words—*If the paper-men were allowed to run the effort, we would all be horns-within-hole by now.*"

Sir Albert's eyebrows shot up at the crude pictogram Felney's words drew, demons with their heads up their butts. It was a heavy insult, and the accountant flared from within, slightly singeing his own coat.

Albert recognized the moment Felney had given him and moved to the offensive, "I can assure you, *paper-man,*" he said, his jaws chewing out the words, "our energy expenditures have been—*and will for the foreseeable future*—continue to be of the utmost necessity. We are on the front line. We are the cutting edge of technology applied. How do you think we got this far? Sitting back bar somewhere mincing over how many thrusts it takes to split a *sap* whore?"

"You wouldn't want to...volunteer for audit?"

Sir Fern stepped back at that, deeply offended. For a long moment he didn't say anything. Then he spoke in a low, hissing voice, "So, it's come to that." Another long pause, thinking it over. "Who is it? TELL me!"

The accountant hesitated, "You've always had your...detractors."

Again Felney spoke from his seat in the corner, his reedy voice carrying across the room, "Unfortunately, Sire, it is Gravely's father, Old Bacchalius, himself."

The accountant gave a startled leap backwards before he could compose himself. His features went passive, and he was again unreadable, "I have dealt as instructed, and now you are warned. The bottom line is all that counts. All that is wanted are favorable results." He gave them a last bleak stare, and backed out of the room.

Albert Fern hardly saw him leave. His mind was spinning with the implications of what Felney had said. If Gurpler was right, perhaps his old friend Bacchalius had hoped his son would fail. Had he anticipated it? Even precipitated it in some way?

Felney interrupted his jumbled thoughts. "It is whispered among the inner circle that Gravely presented a certain ungraceful public amusement about the frequency with which he attracted his father's lovers."

Sir Alfred paused to consider this. "Male or female?"

Felney shrugged, "Female, I would assume." On the surface, it was a question of little consequence; inherent sex roles were vestigial and nearly useless. In heating moments, the dominant partner assumed the male organs and role as a traditional right of might that was as sacred as the glorious

398

mysteries of the pitch-black night and the secrets of the seventh seal.

"But he was the favorite, the shining spawnling! His father told me as much, and many, many times over. I have letters, rambling in their praise."

"And if the boy was sent here in our time of complicated circumstances, and in these difficult times he failed?"

"He would suffer the mold, of course."

"And does passion's demon smile on the remolded?"

"Of course not. The scars..." Sir Fern saw it more clearly then, "Thank you Old Gurpler. Well thought through, indeed. When the winsome lad returns, send him to me."

Felney saw the staunch old stabber had stopped puffing on his pipe and was looking at the glittering tips of his retractable fingernails, which were gleaming in the flickering light from the fireplace. James Gravely's time earthside could now be measured in hours rather than days.

three

Mica moved aside a stack of books and sat at his kitchen table, staring at a cup of coffee in front of him. There was a knock on the door and after a moment's hesitation Jimmy came in.

"We were down to one last Horny," she said. "But don' worry, now we got the new ones, they can hold us until next week."

She took one look at the mold growing on top of his coffee and swiped the cup from in front of him.

"You got things growin' in here, Mica. Why don' I just make another pot?"

The morning light streamed through the room, hitting a small stack of new Hornys piled on his art director's desk next to Anne Mae's smaller one. "I've been busy..." was all he said.

Jimmy deftly knocked the dry grounds from the basket in the coffeemaker, inserted a new filter and ground the last of the Colombian beans. Once the coffee was started, she took a look at the new drawings.

"Police officers stopped by the office this morning..." She said it casually, letting it drop into the sunlight slanting across the room between them.

"They've been here, too. I hid in the barn." His head came up, a ghost remaining of his old, quick curiosity, "Jimmy, would you...?"

"What, hon? Sure. Anything for you, Mica. What?"

"See if there are any bodies in the bedroom."

She shrugged, taking it in. "In her prime my auntie back down on the islands lived through worse weird than this."

"You don't *have* to look, if you don't want to."

"Hey, this is me, Jimmy. You got me my job at the paper, remember?" And all the time she was thinking, *And we slept together for a month and three days, the sweetest time of my life, remember, remember?* But she didn't say it. She wandered down the hallway to the bedroom, wondering what she would find. The room was messy, but nothing special, except for the holes in the plaster.

She walked back to the kitchen. "It's a room some the worse for the bullet holes in the walls, but no bodies in there. No blood, even."

Mica sagged back in obvious relief. Jimmy drained off enough coffee from the still-brewing pot to half-fill two cups. She brought them to the table and set one in front of him; then moved the newspapers and books from another chair and slumped into it.

"We seem to have got a recurring theme here. Aliens. Mysterious happenings. Events which cannot be explained by science. The Twilight Zone meets X-Files and Strange Luck."

He sipped his coffee, staring at nothing, wrapped in his thoughts. After a while, he said, "They can do anything. Be anybody."

"Who can?"

"The aliens."

"Ohh..." She waited, but he didn't say

anything more. She stood and took his arm. "Come on, Mica. We should get some help."

"I got nothing but help. Almond-eyed friends everywhere. Can't wait to get that silver capsule back in me."

"Mica, come on now..."

He pulled away from her. "By the way, where's *your* capsule?"

"My capsule? What are you talking about?"

"Most people don't need them. They just get their brains nulled, by electrical waves or something; I don't know how they do it. But a person like you. You figure in this somehow." He stood and walked towards her.

"Mica, you're scaring me." She retreated until the small of her back was against the slant of his drawing table.

"Give me your hand," he said suddenly, reaching out to grab it. He felt along the bone on the outside of her thumb for a moment, then impatiently thrust it aside. "No, your other one."

He did the same with her other thumb, stopping at a point where he felt something small move under his thumb.

"What is this?" he asked.

"It's just a piece of pencil lead," she said, staring wide-eyed at him. "I fell on a pencil when I was a kid."

"No, it isn't," he said, reaching for an X-ACTO knife on his desk.

<u>four</u>

"Mica," she protested, trying to pull away from him, "You're not gonna—NO!" She pulled her hand away and tucked it under her arm. "I ain't gonna let you just cut me like this!"

"Jimmy, I trusted you with that crazy clairvoyant. You've got to do this one for me. Please. It's me, Mica."

She reluctantly extended her hand to him, holding her other hand over her eyes. "You're the doctor, hon."

The X-ACTO blade was sharp and new, and this time he knew more about what he was doing. He could feel the quiver run through her body as he cut into her skin. There was still plenty of blood, but the silver cylinder was there, just as he had imagined it.

"Look, now!" he commanded. The object stuck; then fell from her hand and rolled on the tile floor.

"What is it?" she asked, still wincing from the knife.

"Your implant. That's how they dull our minds." He set the silvery knife back on the table.

"It's glowing!"

"Shield your eyes!"

There was the same brief blue-white glare he'd experienced in the Doc's office, and then all that remained was a six-inch burn spot on the tile. It was just a little thing, in the light of everything that was happening, but it angered him to see another blemish on the tile he and Sally had handpicked and laid in the house.

"I better get a band-aid..." Jimmy's voice sounded vague and forlorn. He grabbed her as her knees buckled.

"You'd better lie on the couch in the living room. Can you make it?"

"Colors—so vivid. Everything rushing by."

"I know what it's like. That's how I crashed the Alfa. Though I did have a little help..."

He had his arm around her and supported her to the living room, where she collapsed on the couch. She lay there, staring up at the ceiling.

"I'll be right back."

He didn't have to worry; she hadn't moved in the short time it took him to find a roll of gauze and a tube of disinfectant. He daubed half the tube on her incision and then bandaged it, and took a moment longer to rub some of the remaining gray-green jelly into his own thumb, which was still swollen and discolored.

"Mica, hon," she said, "we really gotta go see this guy I know."

"You sure you can—?"

"Mica, now!"

And so, instead of heading West as he had planned, towards DeSoto and Brown's Canyon to check on his horses, Mica drove East over the La Crescenta Pass and through Pasadena, and then south on the 605, shaking Jimmy out of her trance whenever he needed instructions on the next leg of their journey.

At the same time, Gravely and Speth, who had pulled off to the side of one of the dirt roads leading to Brown's Canyon, waited and waited with that sinking feeling that comes from knowing you've gotten a complicated guess dead wrong. At least Gravely felt that way; Speth wandered around aimlessly, fast-drawing on little rodents that popped up alongside the road and blowing them away while he spit a steady stream of jumbled threats and profanity. Positioned as they were in a pocket of extremely bad transmission, they were out of contact for nearly three hours and so failed to hear the unfortunate news that now, instead of one, there were two unblanked saps wandering the arena of this strange and noxious planet.

CHAPTER 25
The Holy Man from Jersey City

<u>one</u>

Once control saw that Mica intended to remove Jimmy's implant, they had sent a rolling thunder of shock waves to confuse and bewilder him. But everything they did was stopped well short of the mark. Mica's abilities were continuing to grow with bewildering speed; it appeared that now the unblanked human had built some sort of a wall around himself. Whatever he had done, he wasn't putting any effort into defending himself; it was just that Felney couldn't get through to him anymore.

Sir Albert put in an urgent demand of his own, that Railsbach stop whatever foolishness he was up to otherside and get back at once. That done, there was little more the mighty Krath-Net-Ja-Pur could do but stoke his pipe and sit back and watch his little problem, which had now doubled itself, as the two unblanked humans headed for an unknown destination.

Mica drove while Jimmy slept in the passenger's seat. It was easy to follow their progress, once the bug's-eye spotter in the tree in front of Mica's house picked up that they were driving the black girl's little Japanese car. The two unblanked *saps* made their way East on the 118 and the 210 and then South on the 605 through the field of huge open-pit gravel mines in Irwindale, and then they wound up a small two-lane road in the old, wooded section of Hacienda Heights. Even off the freeways, they were not hard to follow.

There was even the blessing of a high overhead shot from a rock outcropping as they pulled up a long, winding private road. Mica parked the Civic in front of a wrought iron gated stucco wall that ran around a huge home, the faded pink walls of which seemed to squat under a topping of heavy rust-red tile. The house wore rococo fluffs daubed in white under its overhanging eaves, and graceful palm trees reached overhead to dust the pale blue sky.

"Worms within worms. What *is* this place?" Albert muttered softly, sucking on his pipe.

Felney was busy with coordinates and a map overlay. "I'm way behind with my regular workload," he complained.

"This has precedent, old Gurpler. For the time being, they'll all have to get to Hell the old-fashioned way."

Felney gave his sharp little snort of displeasure. His brows were twitching and fingers flying over the multiple keyboards without success.

"It doesn't figure. This place simply does not exist. Nobody owns it. It isn't even there."

"Isn't *there?!*" Fern roared in outraged astonishment, "Railsbach and his fellows assured us we would know every single—"

"—*Sapiens*." Railsbach finished the sentence as he stepped into the room, coat still steaming from his quick entry. "No ordinary human lives there."

"Well, ignite my bliss, you've decided to return."

"Recalled by yourself," Railsbach corrected him. "At great inconvenience to the critical work which I am—"

"Save it for the auditors, Kelp. Do you know the uproar your EMO project has caused around here?"

"What, that my one bitsy little EMO is still running around the great earth entirely unblanked? That is not my business; I'm really not a field assassin."

"Dr. Railsbach. You personally begged us not to translate Mica Harris!" Albert got to his feet in such a state of upset that his favorite pipe spilled to the ground, breaking the stem and causing the tobacco to spill onto the priceless Persian carpet where it began to fume in a brown circle the size of a silver dollar.

"You shouldn't be shouting at me, Sir Albert. The authorities otherside are quite aware it is your team which has bungled." Railsbach smoothed his white coat and looked around the room like an old houseguest who was happy to be back. "To say nothing of you personally..."

"Meee?!" Sir Albert fairly shrieked his rage.

"You were at Copenhagen. You could have translated him then, if that was your wish."

"You're playing a dangerous game, Dr.

Kelp."

In spite of his strange showing of confidence, the normally diffident and cautious Railsbach couldn't keep himself from retreating a pace or two. Fern was a notorious slasher, and everyone on his staff bore the scars to prove it. "No. Do not think of harming me in any way. I am not here entirely at your request. The timing was such that they selected me."

"Selected?! For what!?" Albert's hand was raised, the silvery nails fully extended.

"Please. I'm just the messenger, sent to tell you you're being recalled."

"Recalled..."

"Yes. And remolded, I think; I heard it whispered in council."

Albert Fern seemed to shrink in size. He stepped back as if he'd been physically punched, and fell backwards into his favorite chair.

"How long...?" He spoke in a voice that was faint with fear, "How long do I have?"

"Seven days to clear your affairs." The doctor rose from his chair and turned to leave.

"Where are you going?"

"Back. I have real work to do."

"No you are not. You are here now, with me now. And those unblanked humans are your responsibility."

"Humans? More than one?"

"Two, as of this moment. Who knows how many more to come? How shall the history books title this chapter—Kelp's Folly?"

"How could—?"

409

"Felney will fill you in. I have seven days to right this incredible wrong which has been pitched against me." He glowered at Railsbach, "And I charge you to help me."

"But there are no orders cut, Sir Fern, and no smoking threat to cause you to act in this fashion."

"I decide that. This is my territory. Were I you, I would assist willingly. Seven days could easily be a lifetime. Maybe your lifetime."

Railsbach returned his bitter stare as calmly as he could. He had thought he would simply pass along the word of the high council and try to slip away, to disappear somehow into this noxious world. But that was not to be; now Sir Albert had neatly conscripted him, and the old lord had nothing left to lose.

"Come look at this," Felney hissed from his position behind his desk. He gestured to the main monitor where they saw Mica and Jimmy meeting a turbaned young man at a shiny white-painted wrought iron gate.

two

"May I help you?" the young man asked with a barely civil politeness, the words more a statement of denial than a question.

"Jimmy." Mica shook her arm. "Why are we here?"

Jimmy started out of her reverie, "Oh, yes. The Maharishi. He said I could come here any time I needed him."

"His reverence has been known to say that to many beautiful young ladies."

"Yes, but he gave me his address. How else did I know to come here?"

The servant held his hand through the bars. He was dressed in tight-fitting knickers of red satin and a buttonless, billowy open-fronted tan shirt of brushed cotton.

"What's he sticking his hand at us for?" Mica asked.

"Give him some money," Jimmy said.

"This is a *holy* man?"

"Just his assistant. Don't be a problem, Mica. I'm really feeling dizzy."

Mica took a crumpled twenty from his pocket and handed it through the grill.

The servant looked disdainfully at the bill, but he didn't refuse it.

"Follow me, oh cheap ones."

He swung the gate open and padded off, his bare feet making no sound on the dull red-orange paver tiles. Mica had to support Jimmy with an arm around her waist as they walked through a courtyard that was overhung with blooming hyacinths and pleasant with the splash of water in a circular fountain.

Where the courtyard was all light and shadow, the Maharishi's inner chamber was dark by contrast. It had high ceilings with squared beams painted in primitive Indian designs. Ancient rugs hung from the walls. Candles glowed from iron stands positioned throughout in the ornate room, and the heavy, sweet smell of incense hung in the air. The high tinkling sound of small silver bells was punctuated at intervals by a deep, brassy gong.

The great person himself sat in the center of this room with his legs crossed and his hands together at his lap. He was thin and middle-aged, but he looked fit. He had olive brown skin and a rim of dark hair around a shiny bald head.

The servant indicated that they were to remain silent and could sit on pillows across from the holy man. The servant looked at Mica as if he were expecting a second tip; he pouted when he didn't get it, retreating a few steps to stand behind them with his arms folded across his chest.

After some moments, the man broke his concentration, indicating he recognized their presence. "Ahh, and so," he sighed. "And what is it that I may be in the doing of for you?"

"You're not the Maharishi," Jimmy muttered. "This guy's a fraud."

"True, I am not the Holy Man, himself, in person. I am his valued first helper."

"Sort of like a cameraman has all his assistants," Jimmy chortled, still on her high ride as she fell back on her pillow, convulsing in silent laughter.

"Come out with it, strange peoples. Why are you here?"

"Come out with it, mon!" Jimmy said to the ceiling, mimicking the man's East Indian accent.

Mica could see she was going to be of no help, so he plunged in without her, "I... uhh, have to rescue my wife, who has—incredible as it sounds—been abducted by aliens and taken to another planet."

Frown lines appeared on the assistant's calm brow. He stood up, ready to take his leave. "I am very, very sorry, unusual peoples. You see, Unidentified Flying Obstacles is not our usual line of occupation."

Jimmy's eyes popped open. She sighed, and held her hand out for the twenty Mica had given the servant. "My, my, my. Refund time. Sorry, Mica, my dude can't deliver."

The servant sniffed and moved a step or two back from Jimmy. It was clear there would be no refund. But Jimmy lurched to her feet, "Hey. These are inflationary times, but I believe in *a little value* for the dollar."

The assistant looked his disgust. "Alien space fliers, indeed. We are not common dogs, to sniffle for drugs and such-not in the baggage of life."

Jimmy had the servant by his baggy shirt before a voice came out of the darkness.

413

"Akmet. That's enough." This new voice was heavy with a New Jersey accent. The man who spoke stepped forward into the candlelight. He was a short, dumpy little hot dog of a man, a rumpled roly-poly fellow complete with Polish T-shirt and a stubbly chin. He looked like a short-order cook on his way to Mel's Diner, an aluminum siding salesman the morning after an all-night Super Bowl party, or the slimy little auto mechanic who is everybody's nightmare.

"Maharishi!" Jimmy cried, rushing across the room and flinging herself into his chubby arms.

414

<u>three</u>

The newcomer seemed annoyed and swiftly moved to disentangle himself from Jimmy's embrace.

"Just who are you?" Mica asked.

The question seemed to irritate the bristly little man, "I'm the Holy Man, for Chris'sake! Can't you tell?"

Without waiting for an answer, the little man plunked himself down on the pillows vacated by Akmet.

"Now, what the hell's your problem?" he asked angrily.

Mica gave Jimmy a doubting look, but she seemed satisfied; in fact she looked radiant at the sight of the little man.

The Holy Man continued, again not waiting for an answer, "Hey, it's a tough job I got here, being the one and only Holy Man— but somebody's got to do it."

Mica tried to pull Jimmy to her feet. "Come on, pal, let's hit the road."

"Hey, hey, HEY!" the Holy Man shouted. "Sit down! Give us a break, here; you come in flashin' a fast twenty and talking a bullshit story about space aliens. How do I know you're not on a Beverly Hills scavenger hunt?"

Mica was still intent on leaving, "Come ON, Jimmy!"

The Holy Man jumped to his feet. "Hold ON, oh ye of little faith!" He marched around Mica, poking him in the ribs with a plump forefinger and looking up at him as he did so.

"I could tell you one thing, right now. She ain't on no distant planet. She's right here, sort of."

Mica was stunned. He managed a weak word, "Who?"

"Your wife, schmuck."

"Where?"

The Holy Man lowered his heavy eyebrows and narrowed his eyes. On him, the expression looked heavy-lidded and daffy. He indicated the air around them with a wide sweep of both arms. "Right here. Here. Here. Here. Everywhere, double-schmuck."

Mica wasn't convinced. He'd seen too much over the past few weeks. He had his arm around Jimmy's waist and was gently but firmly pushing her to the exit. The little man took Mica by the arm, pulling him back, "Wait a minute. You paid for the whole show, you stay for the whole show."

From their station by the door, both the young man in the billowy shirt and Akmet showed signs of alarm. "Master," Akmet warned, "You say you not do this thing, not anymore."

The Holy Man laughed him off with a wave of one pudgy hand, "Ahh, bullshit, Akmet. You only live once..." He gave a small, ironic chuckle, "...that is, once at a time."

four

With no further conversation, the chubby little man plunked himself down cross-legged, trying to get as close as he could to the lotus position. It was impossible for him; he was too chunky.

"Hell with it," he grunted. He gave up and sat with his back against the wall of pillows, feet straight out. He was wearing Nike shorts, a black T-shirt featuring the Chicago skyline in threaded gold, and chartreuse rubber bathroom clogs.

"Come here, kid." He beckoned to Mica; he closed his eyes and felt the end of Mica's shirt for a moment. A tranquil expression spread across his cherubic face. He began to hum. After a few moments, the hum began to intensify. It rose, became singsong, deepened to a low, guttural groan which began at the base of his throat and then rose higher and higher into a terrible scream.

The Holy Man's eyes blinked open. He was sweating, his eyes wide with terror. Akmet stepped forward with a white towel stitched in green letters with the words Holiday Inn and wiped the sweat from his forehead. The chubby little man himself appeared befuddled.

Mica leaned forward, "What was it?"

"I—I can't remember."

"What did you see?"

"A—a room. It looked like a kitchen in some fancy suburb, like Westlake Village. Horse country. There were some people there.

A blond woman."

"Was she in danger?"

"I don't know."

"Why did you scream?"

The Holy Man gave him an indignant glare, "I didn't scream. Look, sometimes it doesn't work."

"But you—"

The Holy Man waved him silent, turning to the Maharishi, "Akmet, give them their money back."

The Maharishi hesitated, looking at the servant. The Holy Man yelled at him, "DO it, boonsaba of the underbelly of the Orient!"

"Wait a minute." Mica was now certain that there was something more to be learned from the Holy Man's unpleasant experience.

But the little fellow had already risen to his feet and started toward an inner door. "Nope. Interview's over. I got to meditate, and stuff." And with that, the door slammed behind him and he was gone. There was nothing Mica and Jimmy could do but gather in their twenty dollars and leave.

418

CHAPTER 26
The Noose Tightens

one

Once Felney and Fern realized the rogue humans had contacted *presences of unknown identity,* the circumstances were quickly upgraded to critical status. Gravely and Speth had returned from Brown's Canyon empty-handed and looking foolish. But now, just when he was needed, Gravely dashed back otherside for a few hours on what was logged a *personal effects* run before anyone could stop him.

Fern would have given plenty to know what was going on between father and son, but he could only fuss and fume and make do with the personnel he had. So Speth, who had recovered well enough to drive in a jerky sort of fashion, was sent in his BMW, with a reluctant Railsbach along to try to keep him in check. The two of them, in Speth's dark gray car, arrived at the destination in Hacienda Heights and were watching from a vantage point several hundred yards away as Mica and Jimmy came out of a heavy wrought iron gate and headed toward Jimmy's Civic, which was parked along the side of the driveway.

Speth no sooner spotted them than he put his car in gear.

Railsbach gave him a fearful glance. "You know we are not supposed to translate him."

"Kelpie, I was eatin' human emotion when James Gravely was still jelly in the pod." Speth's words were slurred and his attempt to spit at the window failed. A glob of spittle bubbled on his lip. Speth wiped it on the sleeve of an expensive woolen suit. Railsbach could see the sleeve of the otherwise impeccably tailored suit was tattered. And even as the doctor made this observation, Speth jammed the accelerator to the floor and the big car lurched forward.

Mica looked up, seeing the now familiar dark BMW racing toward them. Jimmy, on the driver's side of the Civic, was in the direct path of the oncoming car. Mica dashed around to her side and pulled her off her feet. They both tumbled into a nearby ditch.

Jimmy stood slowly, brushing the dust and weed stickers from her outfit.

"There was something, wasn't there?" She stared at him. "I saw...like a blur."

"I could kiss you, all dusty and scratched up the way you are." Mica was looking back down the road, in the direction the BMW had taken. "They're stopping. Get behind me."

two

Jimmy could make out the wavy image of a lean and dark man, stepping from what looked like a big, foreign car. The man raised one hand from a distance of about fifty yards away, and there was a sudden blossoming of energy, like a rocket fired in their direction. Mica quickly raised one hand and the strange blossom was stopped, as if by an invisible shield, and went winging back toward its source. The distant man quickly ducked behind the open door of his car, which took the full force of the blow, except for the bottoms of his pants. He looked down at the ruins of his expensive leather shoes, spitting and chewing out an unintelligible string of curses. And then, as he saw Mica raise his own hand in a crude approximation of a shooter's stance, the man jumped inside his BMW and quickly drove away.

three

"I feel like a monkey on a long chain." Mica was driving Jimmy back to the L.A. Weekly office.

Jimmy had enough control of her senses that she was now sitting up and studying the startling new world around her. "How can you be sure they know where we are?"

Mica swung next to a parking meter on the street in front of the L.A. Weekly. "They found us at the Maharishi's place."

He hopped out of the Alfa on his side, and saw that the old black bum had once again set up his cardboard house near the parking meter.

"What, you waiting for me?" Mica asked. At the same time, he fished hopelessly in his pockets for money for the meter.

"Plainclothes police across the street," the old bum said quietly. "They gonna catch themselves a cop-shooter."

Jimmy, who hadn't heard the bum, came around from her side of the car. "I've got a few quarters."

Mica motioned, "Give them to this man, here."

"But the meter..."

"Do it, Jimmy."

She handed over a small handful of change. The old black man accepted the coins, nodding and poking around at them in his hand. "Thank you, thank you kindly, missy." He paused, reflecting, "Was me, I do believe I'd get around the back of the building an' jump in the

422

dumpster."

Mica gave him a curt nod, and took Jimmy's hand, pulling her along with him. "Do you think you can run?"

"I think so."

"Get ready," he told her. They were about ten feet from the front door of the Weekly when he cut into a narrow opening between the newspaper building and the one next to it, running for the alley with Jimmy right after him.

Out of the corner of his eye, Mica saw two men jump from a late model plain brown sedan. The two started to sprint across the street, but were temporarily held back by a string of cars.

Felney watched from his seat in front of the monitors, poised to help the plainclothes men in any way he could. But the moment Mica and Jimmy dashed for the rear of the building, Felney's reception was replaced with fuzzy gray static. He was out of touch for thirty seconds at the most, and then all the micro-cameras clicked back on at once. Felney frowned as he scanned the wide-angles of the street, the narrow opening into which Mica and Jimmy had darted, and the alley itself. Mica and Jimmy were nowhere to be found. The two detectives were looking around like lost sheep. One of them stirred in the lone dumpster with the broken end of a broomstick, holding one hand over his nose as he did so.

"In here?" he asked.

"That's really bad," the other said. There was movement at one end of the alley, and they both headed off in that direction. After a brief pause, two heads popped out of the garbage. Jimmy crawled out of the dumpster and helped Mica out.

"This way!" the bum whispered from the shadows. And, having nowhere else to go, they hurried after him.

CHAPTER 27
An Even Dozen

<u>one</u>

Los Angeles's indigent alley thrives in the shadow of the city's great public buildings, a cardboard town within walking distance of the mission soup lines and three or four gritty liquor stores that stay open all night. Weather permitting, it offers a tenuous shelter for the night, and every morning, by the time the sun slants between the tall buildings, it is gone. Each evening after dark it springs up again, its architecture adhering to the classic rule of shelter, *Form follows function.* The prized spots for tenancy are the grills from which exhale the heated air from the great buildings towering overhead, for in the City of the Angels, night is often bitter cold, no matter how hot the day has been. The cardboard city features, within its temporary walls, an occasional flashlight glimmer, muffled groans, muted conversation, a bark of momentary laughter and the dense hush of men and a few women waiting for luck, for tomorrow's breakfast at the mission, for the rare dregs of a pint of bourbon, sick-sweet muscatel or cheap red, or a needle-pointed vial of yellow forgetfulness to come their way. They wait for the weather to change, for the police to come, or a rusty knife or heavy boot or .38 slug to materialize out of the darkness. For whatever comes next. *Delivering spirit, come take me away.*

Jimmy was sleeping, tucked in a curl in the cardboard Motorola box. Mica and the old bum sat on the sidewalk with their backs against a brick wall. They were on a side street, a quiet suburb somewhat disconnected from the main run of Bum Town. The advantage was, the old black man had told Mica, that they could spot a patrol car from some distance. The disadvantage was an inquisitive and persistent night wind off the ocean that could be counted on to nicker at their one thin blanket and chill their buttocks in spite of their seats of doubled-over cardboard.

"My name's Jim Crow," the old man said.

"Sure it is," Mica said easily. He handed back the small, flat bottle of whiskey and sucked in a breath of air, feeling the bite of the drink on his tongue and the inside of his mouth. He unwound the bandage from around his thumb, and frowned when he saw the festering yellow-black wound.

"Well, you could call me Ol' Black Joe, if you want."

"Jim Crow is okay."

"Here, le' me see that hand of yours." Jim carefully poured whiskey on the infected thumb. "Don't wrap it back up. Better to leave it open." He took a pull from the bottle and sighed gratefully, "You was tellin' me your wife an' daughter is passed through the veil."

"I was there when it happened. There's no question in my mind."

426

The old man gave Mica an intense look, but when he spoke again his voice was as calm as before, "Well, there must be some question on your mind..."

"I'm just crazy," Mica said, his voice flat with defeat.

The old black man shook his head. "Nope. They's something more than that working here. You know, souls have to fly to the light when it be their time."

Mica yawned. "That's a nice bedtime story. But this is—more complicated, somehow."

"How you mean?"

"I know they died, but somehow I don't think they...left. Somehow they're still around somewhere."

"How come you feel that?"

"A channeler contacted them. And a holy maharishi."

The old black man shook his head sadly. "New Age <u>and</u> Eastern, right here in the heart of Jesus' people. Whatever happened to dat ol' time religion?"

Mica spoke from a great distance away, drifting off to sleep, "Gimme dat ol' time religion."

"Yas sir, boss." When Mica didn't respond, he continued in a low voice, "I think we go git ourselves some, first thing come tomorrow."

The old black bum found the cap and screwed it back on the whiskey bottle, which was still over half full. He sat upright for a long time, quiet and careful. He wasn't as blown away on alcohol as he seemed, and he wasn't going to drink any more that night. He took several pinches of powder from a small cloth tobacco pouch and allowed it to trickle from his fingers in an uneven semicircle around their perimeter. He was just a simple watchman, not really cut out for action. He knew he would need all his wits and all his powers if the dark ones came rogue-stalking between the little cardboard tents that night.

<u>two</u>

In her kitchen of what she had come to think of as the non-place of chaos, Sally was resting on her favorite couch when she heard the heavy knock on the door. Anne Mae, who was increasingly restless and tired, had finally fallen asleep on her lap. It required more of Sally's attention to hold Anne Mae together, and the room itself was showing signs of neglect. Sally wasn't aware exactly how the false environment around them worked, any more than the average person could discuss the mathematics of nuclear fission or quantum theory, but she knew the room's dingy look was somehow a direct reflection of her and her daughter's worn emotional state.

"Who is it?" she asked.

"Twelve patriarchs," a reedy old voice replied from the other side of the door. "May we come in?"

"If you have to ask, the answer is 'no'." There was a moment's pause and angry muttering from the other side of the door, followed by a burst of more insistent knocking.

"We must come in," the voice insisted.

"At your own risk," Sally said.

There was more arguing, and then the knob was turned and the door slowly opened. A parade of twelve very old and tattered-looking men walked into the kitchen. They wore ancient suits, each one in the style of the generation from which they had taken their coats, from the American Revolutionary period

429

through the 1800's and into the 20th century. The oldest, who wore a wide-lapel coat of faded royal blue with yellowed piping and double rows of tarnished metal buttons, also carried a dusty cocked hat.

"We have come," the oldest said politely, "to inquire into the translation—that is, as you would say it, the death—of one with the given name of Kelmekth—"

"We don't know anybody like that." It was Anne Mae, sleepily rubbing her eyes. "Gosh, you guys *stink!*"

"Kelmekth, also known as Snivley, a short, perhaps dog or badger-like creature." The ancient motioned with his hand, indicating a creature who was less than waist high. One of the others, wearing a charred tweed suit and a frayed high collar from the 1890's, opened his briefcase. He pointed to the open lid, but nothing happened. There was a brief exchange in a coarse, brutal tongue, and then the eldest spoke to Sally again, "There is some problem with bringing you an image of Kelmekth. We must proceed without."

"Proceed to do what?" Sally's eyes narrowed, and she held tighter to Anne Mae.

"The punishment to a *sapiens* for knowingly translating any demonic spirit is ground-into-dust."

The realization jolted Sally. "You're talking about killing us?"

"Not translated; the spirit ground-into-dust. You will become nothing. The law is clear. You, certainly will go. As for your daughter, you may claim the right to take her first; that is, before we do."

"That vile little creature attacked my daughter."

"And so you somehow managed to translate him."

Sally stared at them for a moment. *They didn't really know what happened!*

"I am trying to be patient," the old man said. "Are there mitigating circumstances?"

"I already told you, he threatened my daughter."

Plainly frightened, Anne Mae threw her arms around Sally's neck, "What's happening, Mom?"

"They're trying to punish us for what happened to that wicked little beast Dr. Railsbach brought in here."

"Well, I did that..." Anne Mae's voice trailed off as she saw the twelve pairs of eyes glitter.

The ancient in the tattered colonial greatcoat pointed his cocked hat at her. "So. The daughter first," he said.

The ancients circled them and began a low, wordless hum, rich and chordal as a Gregorian chant. After a moment, Anne Mae's face turned white, and her teeth began to chatter.

"Mom!" she wailed.

The intensity of the chant began to increase nearly imperceptibly, the chords thickening and intertwining. Anne Mae began to shake involuntarily. "Mooom! It hurts..."

"Stop it!" Sally stood, enveloped by her

431

own blooming kirlian halo. But, whatever energy she had, it couldn't break through to her daughter, who had now drifted away from her into the air and was racked with shudders, buffeted by forces designed to pull her apart.

Panicked, Sally poured every ounce of her attention to breaking through the hold the circled twelve had on her daughter. But it was useless. She was powerless to save Anne Mae. In a mindless rage, she turned on the closest of the twelve and pounded at him. Before she could touch him, twin bolts of blue energy left her fists, blowing the unfortunate demon to smoking nothingness.

Sally was startled, but only for a moment, by what she had done. The remaining eleven still chanted, locked in their infernal course of action, and unaware of the disappearance of one of their kind. They simply closed the hole in the circle made by their fallen comrade. Anne Mae's screams were all Sally could hear. She obliterated the next closest demon with a single bolt from her fist. And then, stalking around the circle, she took them out one by one until only the eldest held Anne Mae aloft in the chant of his high, sweet old voice.

"Stop!" she commanded. "Stop in the name of Krath-Net-Ja-Pur!"

The old one hesitated, and in that moment, Sally broke through and caught her daughter before she fell to the floor.

three

While Sally held Anne Mae in her arms and tried to comfort her, the remaining elder wandered about the kitchen in bewildered confusion.

"What—?" He started, glaring at her.

"Translated," Sally replied quickly in the calmest voice she could muster.

"All of them? *All?!* But that's not possible!"

"By whose rules?"

"The most ancient laws say nothing of..."

"Laws which apply in <u>your</u> land. This is <u>not</u> your place."

"All to dust?" He stared about the room like a fumbling old human, seemingly overwhelmed by the turn of events.

Sally had no room for pity, with the vision fresh in her mind of Anne Mae with blood running from her nose and ears. "Get the concept. I told you, 'Enter at your own risk.' I told you that."

The ancient nodded in silent assent, turning in a full circle to see if there was anything he had missed. "And may I now leave?"

"You know where the door is."

Had it not been for the stunning loss of his brothers, had he taken time to reflect on what he was doing, had his kind not ruled so firmly for so many centuries over their docile herds of well-blanked *saps*, the ancient elder certainly would not have attempted single-handed vengeance on the female *sapiens*. But it had been too much lava over the precipice. The old demon took up his briefcase in one hand and his cocked hat in the other, and in the same fluid motion pointed the hat at the woman and her child and unleashed in their direction every ounce of fury he could muster. He was a wily lasher, but her aura easily blunted his effort. Worse for him, his massive blast of energy was deflected directly back in his direction, translating him to dust as efficiently as if she had expended her own resources.

Anne Mae complained of a terrible headache, but she was a tough kid, and Sally thought she would recover. After comforting her daughter as best she could, she laid her on the couch to rest. Sally opened the windows to air out the house, and then took a broom and dustpan and swept up the few balls of lint and fur which remained. The one demon briefcase that had been opened was empty. For the moment, she left it lying in the corner where it was. She couldn't open the other cases, so she threw them out the front door. One by one, they went spinning into the pearly white fog, each dissipating into nothingness with a buzzing crackle.

For a long time after that, Sally and Anne Mae stayed on the couch, Sally trying to give her daughter strength and to figure out what to do next while Anne Mae shuddered and whimpered on her lap. The air slowly cleared, but the light seemed even more dingy than it had before the appearance of the twelve vengeful old men.

There was a small popping sound, and a long crack ran through the plaster on one of the walls. Sally dutifully mended the crack and hugged her daughter and told her over and over that Mica would soon be there and everything would be all right. But in her heart she knew they couldn't keep this up much longer.

<u>four</u>

Gravely came back through the roaring fireplace into Sir Fern's study sometime after midnight to find Zilch and Nilch wrestling on the rug while Felney worked endlessly in front of his monitors. In response to Gravely's request for Railsbach, Felney simply nodded once in the direction of the open window. Gravely took a shallow breath and stepped out into the night. He found the doctor seated on a stone bench at the end of a long gravel path. Below them, the light-web of the Los Angeles basin winked and glittered, while a low cloud layer was revealed above them, colored in a wash of dull, yellowish gray.

Gravely nodded, and sat the respectful distance, just beyond lash length. "I'm glad to find you alone, Doctor."

"And why is that?" Railsbach was fidgeting nervously. He had to know at least something of what was coming.

"Enormous news from home."

"They found my missing assistant?"

"Worse than that, Doctor. They went into your experiment to avenge his loss."

"They *what!? Who did?*"

"The Council of Twelve."

Railsbach could hardly bear to breathe. Suddenly, there were no other options for him; he very clearly saw himself doomed into exile on this barren, oxygen laden planet. And that was if he was lucky.

"And—?"

"None of them came back. Not one."

"No one asked me—I would have warned them—"

"You've been put on the list."

"No!" Railsbach jumped up, looking wildly around him.

"Relax," Gravely said, holding both palms forward to show no claws. "I put a seven-day restraint on it."

"Why would you do that for me?"

"Let's say I have a need of allies right now. You help me control the old Speedballer, and I'll see what I can do to buy you out of it altogether."

"They'll never go for that."

"Don't be so sure. My father has connections. And the Twelve had their share of detractors. *What's dumber than a dozen saps playing with their own joysticks?* You've heard the old sly talk."

"Still, they were the old slitters."

"Gone and already replaced. Sure, they're blaming you, but it's just routine. I asked for a delay and nobody even spit twice."

Taking care that Gravely was still seated a safe distance from him, Railsbach now fitfully marched back and forth on the patio.

"What of my project?"

"EMO is being reviewed. Some of the paper-men would like to plow it under, but there's a dozen ambitious young science-meisters itching to replace you. By the way, is there any chance those *sap* women can get loose?" Gravely dared not raise his eyes as he

437

asked the question.

"Of course not," Railsbach snapped.

"You're sure of that...?"

"Absolutely sure."

__five__

Sally came out of a deep, foggy sleep thinking that there was something she was supposed to be doing, some step that she had to take for herself. *There had to be a way out. But how? Couldn't they get out of this void into which they had been bottled?* In a strange world like this, where energy burst from her fingertips and demons were everywhere, anything was possible. Anything at all. And so thinking, she fell into a shallow, fitful sleep and dreamed about the open suitcase that was still lying in the corner. Only it was a suitcase no longer; it had been transformed into a giant sea oyster. She moved closer, swimming underwater in her dream, and saw that in the heart of the oyster there rested a large black pearl.

CHAPTER 28
That Old-Time Religion

<u>one</u>

Dawn in downtown Los Angeles found Speth once again behind the wheel, studiously ignoring James Gravely, who was nattering him for what seemed seven times seven for attempting to translate Mica Harris without direct orders. *As if he, Speth, hadn't had his own shoes fried off in the attempt!* Wagner's *Die Valkyrie* was coming in loud and clear over the speakers and Bub should have been in his boil, but here was the young squeaker, blabbing on and on about tradition and taboos, the translation sanctions, disturbing the balance, clamps and dustings, the Book of Clear Lines, and the penalties for countermanding his own personal orders. And all the while Gravely's little moustache was twitching like crazy, tempting Speth to reach over and rake it off, along with half his face.

Get a life, little bug-man!, Speth thought. He tried unsuccessfully to spit at the window, and, failing that, turned up the volume on the music so he wouldn't have to listen to his companion anymore.

Gravely glared while Speth watched him out of the corner of his eye. Speth had seen Gravely's request for his remold within hours after it had been placed, and had called up a few favors owed. He had managed to derail the request. The clamp job would be delayed for six months, at a minimum. To a snufter, six months was a lifetime. Speth was sure something would take young Gravely out long before then, and Speth would have a new assignment, be working another sector somewhere halfway around the noxious globe, while Gravely's old request tablet would be quietly ground into clay and forgotten.

Railsbach, even quieter than usual, hadn't said a word from the backseat as the three of them followed Mica, Jimmy and an old bum down 4th street. The three *saps* were slowly walking along the cracked and tilt-slab sidewalks in the direction of the mission soup kitchen, where presumably they hoped to get a free meal. Gravely had called in to ID the old bum, but again, Felney boiled over when he failed to lock on the *antique ebony sap*. They all figured it was the same old black man who had interfered when they'd tried to grab Mica at City Hall, but beyond that, no one had a clue as to his actual identity.

The humans entered a gritty, brick-faced building with wire fence window guards, a huge three-story building that looked like a warehouse or an old gym.

Speth gave a look of alarm, slammed on the brakes, and spun around to look at Railsbach in the backseat. "What you think, Kelpie?"

"Not good," Railsbach replied, the concern rising in his voice. "I think we don't want to go in there."

441

"What? Don't leave me in the slag." James Gravely lightly slapped Speth's shoulder, and was rewarded with an angry growl.

"Not now, Old Spitter!" Railsbach did his best to calm Speth from the backseat. He pointed out the blue neon cross hanging above the doorway of the building. "It's a sap groveling den."

Gravely felt the ends of his moustache slip out of control again, "W—we can't go in there."

The smell of Gravely's fear decided it for Speth, "Nothing more than old bitch's tales. Come on." Speth swung the BMW diagonally into a spot between two cars that was too small to allow it to be parked correctly. He butted the two cars until he had the space he needed, and then slammed the door and stalked across the street without waiting to see if they would follow. The spitter's expensive gray pants were burned off halfway between his knees and his ankles, the gray of his carapace showed through the tattered remains of the flayed and cooked *sap* coat which was stringing from his shins, and his burned shoes flopped as he walked.

"What happened to him?" Gravely asked Railsbach.

"He tried a second time to take out our favorite EMO, and it backfired again."

"Did he come close?"

"No. Not close."

"So now he knows his limitations."

"Not our Speth. He thinks it was just another case of Lucifer's luck." Railsbach warily eyed the building in front of them.

442

"Looks like one of those broadcast wailings."

"Are we safe to go in there?" Gravely indicated the entrance into which Speth had disappeared.

Railsbach shrugged. "I don't think even Felney knows very much about it—or the old Speedballer, for that matter. He just went in there because he smelled fear in your coat."

"I admit to that. What do we know for sure?"

"The basic slag is that the sap invokers who put on these ceremonies do it for the money. But the distant stench is that there have been actual cures here and there."

"Cures!?"

Railsbach waved his hands in the air, a weak imitation of Aunt Jemima. "You know—*Thank you, Lordie, thank you—I been healed!*"

"I suppose we'd better see for ourselves, before Speth gets into more trouble."

two

As they crossed the street, they suspiciously eyed the backlit sign of faded blue plastic hanging over the door that read, "The Latter Day Church of Jesus Christ Incarnate". Some athletic wag had inked the two "t's" in Latter to make it read "Ladder".

Gravely blew out a breath of the noxious air, "Well, let's go do it." They carefully slipped in the door, ready to retreat at the first sign of trouble.

Once inside, they saw that Mica, Jimmy and the unidentified old black *sap* had made their way up the aisle. A slide-in plastic sign on a small iron stand said REVEREND DICKIE. The Reverend was a middle-aged Negro with smooth mahogany skin and a monk's fringe of curly black hair around his bald pate. He was in a magnificent frenzy, into the act of curing with the power of his hands and his magnificent voice. The cameras consisted of two chunky old network outcasts, and the crew was grubby and non-union. The audience was made up of vagrants and elderly black people, with a salt sprinkling of old white folks. They sat on metal fold-down chairs on the floor of what looked like an old basketball gym.

The Reverend Dickie was sweating heavily. It took energy to work a crowd like this into the spirit of the Lord. He shook an old white man by the shoulders, his voice rising, "All together, now—Praise God, Praise the

444

Lord! *Demons, Out NOW! Leave this man's soul!*"

As the Reverend shook him, the old man gave a hollow "Whoo-UP!" sound. He rolled his eyes wildly and collapsed into the arms of Dickie's assistant, who was strategically positioned behind him.

<u>three</u>

Standing in the rear of the big room, in the shadows under the flickering red EXIT sign, Gravely was openmouthed in astonishment.

"Exorcism..." he whispered in awe.

Railsbach said nothing. He was poised for flight, ready to dart out the door at the first sign of trouble. Even Speth was feeling a blend of raw emotion—shock, fear and curiosity welting up at the same time in a curious bittersweet mix, somehow not unlike the time he'd bitten his first *sap* throat.

Speth chanted in a low undertone, clearly baiting Gravely, "Remember <u>what</u> they <u>taught</u> you <u>at</u> the academy, spawnling. The saps <u>have</u> to <u>believe</u> or it's <u>not</u> a <u>true</u> con-<u>nect</u>-ion."

As if making Speth's point, the audience responded with various halfhearted cries that were clearly false and premeditated.

"Yeah!"

"Yeah. Amen. Yes to that."

"Praise the Lord."

"Jesus, Jesus, Savior Lord."

The Reverend Dickie pounded the limp old man's chest, "Out Demons—OUT!" He thwacked the man on the ears, a double palmed one-two punch, "Out, OUT, I say!"

And the old man responded, cupping his ears and yelling in a screechy voice, "I kin hear you! I kin hear you! Oh, Lordy, thank you, *thank you*—I kin hear!"

"All praise the Lord," the Reverend cried, "This mortal soul is cured!"

A mild swell of applause rippled through the chairs. Again, the three demons in the back of the room consoled themselves with the unconscious mockery of the audience.

"They don't really believe it," Gravely said, hoping for the best.

"Maybe it's because they're blanked," Railsbach whispered. "They just can't reach for a connection."

"Well, they seem to know what they're supposed to be doing."

Gravely wasn't at all sure they were on solid footing. "Empty habit. The shell without the substance," Railsbach reassured him.

"I, for one, would prefer to see this residual behavior gone from the sap population."

Railsbach smiled, trying to hide his recent doubts. "Once EMO takes over, there *won't be any humans.*"

"All gone? I didn't know that."

"Completely wiped from the face of the earth." Even as he spoke, he hoped Gravely couldn't detect the trembling in his voice.

four

Mica, Jimmy and the old black man who called himself Jim Crow stood in a line behind two others waiting to be cured.

"You sure we should be here?" Mica asked.

"Wuz you baptized?"

"I'm not sure. I doubt it—"

The bum made a rapid sign at Mica, slicing the air horizontally and then vertically in front of him. He rattled words like a shotgun, "I-baptize-thee-in-the-name-of-the-Father, the-Son, an'-th'-Holy-Ghost!" In one continuing motion, the bum spit on his hand and slapped Mica across the forehead. "There. Done." He looked over at Jimmy.

"No, I already been shielded by th' Lord," she said quickly.

Watching from the back of the room, Dr. Railsbach was consumed by a dull fury. "No, no, no—not my primary EMO!"

James Gravely was astonished, "Surely, that wasn't *legal?!*"

"Will you two Weak Wigglers shut up?!" Speth shook until he had to spit out his fury. But scornful as he was of his two companions, he wasn't quite sure, himself.

The Reverend Dickie was working over an elderly black woman, the last sinner between Mica and his blessing.

"Bless this woman," the Reverend wailed, "Oh Lord, bless this woman!"

"I feels it!" she cried. "I feels de blessing."

448

This was a low point in the ceremony, and it earned no more than a few scattered claps and amens. And then Mica was next.

"Fellows," the Reverend said in a low whisper. "What we got here?"

Nobody answered, and this did not reassure Rev. Dickie. He had grown up in services like this one. He had spent his life in the Lord's Work, singing and haranguing the flock along the good path. There had been comforts and rewards along the way, but there had been complications as well. In short, Rev. Dickie knew trouble when he saw it. He'd also noticed the small group that had entered and was hanging around the back of the hall. Troublemakers—he called them *Devil Brewers*—always hung to the back. They were the ones afraid of the light of the Lord. But the studio lights were bright in the Reverend's eyes; he could only make out three shadowy figures, huddled back near the exit sign.

When he looked their way, Speth was the first one who spooked. He automatically took the stance, turning and raising his arm. Gravely noticed and put his hand over Speth's arm. "Wait. He can't see us."

"He senses something," Speth replied. "I know danger when it prickles."

Across the room, under the eye of the cameras and in the lights, the Reverend turned his attention to the old black man standing with Mica and Jimmy.

"Come on, brother. Answer me. What gives here?"

"Devils." The old black bum spoke the one word and gave a little nod. A small ripple of understanding passed between the two men. "Come on, do it, brother."

Rev. Dickie nodded back, "Okay...okay, but this don't look like no believer to me."

"He been dunked." Jim Crow glanced back at the three men in the shadows, and looked back at Rev. Dickie. "If you don't want to, okay. But you de minister. I say this be your job; but I can't tell you what to do. Follow your heart, Rev'rend."

The cameraman on Camera B, which had a large red light glowing on its hood, spoke in a low and urgent voice, "Rev. We burnin' tape here."

Rev. Dickie sighed and nodded. He pointed an accusing finger at Mica and his voice rose to fill the room.

"What is this I see before me?! A white boy UNBELIEVER!! A lost one come here from the slam dance halls of Hollywood, the whore bars of Beverly Hills, the crack dens in the Valley, the filthy holes of the devil hisself! You dare to come here, to the holy temple of God Almighty?! Don't tell me you BELIEVE, man! You be a follower of Satan!!"

Mica forgot for a moment that he was on camera. He was stunned silent by the force of the minister's attack.

The bum nudged him, "Mica. Your turn."

"Ahh, no," he stuttered. "I—I USED to follow Satan."

Rev. Dickie took it from there, "So, you

come here to MOCK us, to RIDICULE the Lord's work, to MAKE A FOOL of God's People!!"

Again, the bum had to nudge Mica.

"Ahh, no. Not at all. I USED TO BE that way. Not now."

Rev. Dickie sighed at the weakness of Mica's performance, taking a moment to shoot a glare in the old bum's direction. Jim Crow shrugged. Mica obviously didn't know the script; Dickie was going to have to carry a little more of it himself. The Reverend sucked it up and cranked his delivery a notch, "What is it you are feeling, you poor, hopeless, shrivel-souled little white boy? Is there some small shred of remorse? Some tiny little scrap of hope? Are you tellin' me you want the 'demption of our Savior, Jesus Christ?!"

Mica sneaked a look at the old bum, who quickly nodded yes.

"Yes, I do," Mica said in a small but clear voice.

In the back of the room, Speth stepped back from Gravely, giving himself a clear field. Railsbach looked over at Gravely, the uncertainty clear in his voice, "I would prefer him alive, but he is unblanked. We could be in terrible danger here..."

Speth hissed, bubbling a string of incomprehensible words from his lips.

"What did he say?" Gravely, alarmed, was concerned the situation was slipping beyond his control.

Speth had decided he would wait no

451

longer. The assassin had resumed his shooter's stance, and his arm was coming up.

"No, wait!" Gravely again moved to block his aim and pull his arm back down. But Speth moved back and away from him, staying one step clear as Gravely stalked him.

Meanwhile, across the large room on the low, one step platform stage, the Rev. Dickie had turned the corner. "Praise the Lord!" he shouted. "I DO see repentance here! Oh, Lord, thank you, thank you for the soul of this man. With these consecrated hands, dedicated to the service of the Master, our Lord Jesus Christ Incarnate, will I rescue yet another lost and hopeless soul into the flock! Oh, SAVE him, Oh Jesus!"

With these words, the Reverend laid both hands on Mica's shoulders.

"Never!" Speth cried from the back of the room.

And at this same moment, as Mica felt the clap of Rev. Dickie's hands, a bolt of roiling red force boiled towards him and the Reverend. There was an electric crackle and a boom of thunder as the writhing electrical bolt wrapped itself around the Rev. Dickie, who lurched backwards with the full force of the blow. Dickie's body stiffened, captured in a pod of roiling energy. In seconds, the Reverend was boiled alive and then crisped into a smoking skeleton. For a moment, the bones seemed to stand of their own volition. The stench of burning flesh was heavy in the air, and all that remained was a few burnt crisps of flesh

452

clinging to the too-white bones. The bones, still held together by tough tendons, swayed for a moment and then collapsed in a puppet heap on the platform.

<u>five</u>

Mica was devastated. The minister had clapped him on the shoulders, and then had been blown apart. He heard the screams from the crowd. The stage lights flickered unevenly and people began milling and shoving as the audience tried to make its collective way to the exits. Mica realized Jimmy was next to him, staring at what was left of Reverend Dickie. And the old bum was on the floor, blood welling from his side.

"Did he touch you?" the old black man managed to gasp.

"Who?"

"The Reverend. With the blessing?"

Mica dumbly nodded yes.

"Good. Go on, get out of here!"

"But he—you—" Mica looked from the skeleton smoking at his feet to the black man and back again.

"I be okay, boy! Move out, quick!"

From the back of the room, Speth raised his hand again. Gravely saw him, and managed to shout, "No! Sir Alfred Fern distinctly said—"

Railsbach, who was closer to Speth, lunged forward and knocked Speth's avenging arm off its aim. But in doing so, Railsbach redirected the brunt of the new blast of energy from Mica to young James Gravely. It happened so fast Gravely had no time to say anything. His eyes widened and then popped as the charge of energy hit him. In the next moment, he

454

crumpled silently to the ground. By the time Gravely's body reached the wooden gym floor, he was transmogrified back into his true form. It had been a brief blast, but they could see by the jellied eyes and by the green-black fluids draining from around the fangs and from his facial orifice that Gravely was a hopeless loss.

"Bub's balls..." Railsbach stared. "You've translated him."

"No, Kelpie," Speth spat. "YOU'VE translated him. YOU knocked my hand. You, and you alone. They'll grind you into dust for this." He stared at Railsbach, letting him know he was sure he could make it stick. Inside, the assassin was singing the old chants. *Still only about 80% of his former self, and he'd managed to take out the two demons he detested most in the black world, both James Gravely and the cowardly Kelp!* The white-coated fool believed him, because he gave a whimpering sigh and ran from the room without a word. Speth let him go. Even while he was breathing the short-form warrior's incantation for Gravely's respect, Speth took a small capsule from the inner lining of his belt. Breaking the outer shell of the silvery capsule with a nip of his teeth, he dropped it on what remained of Gravely. A heat shield spread over the fallen body, becoming hotter and hotter until James Gravely dissolved into nothing in a blue-white flash of light. The wooden floorboards burned in a neat circle of flames where his remains had been. *That'll teach you!* Speth thought in light-headed glee. *That'll*

CHAPTER 29
Ned's End

one

Mica and Jimmy hid among the rocks just below the highway and above the sandy sweep of Malibu's coastline. The night wind was cold and their hiding place was damp and uncomfortable. Mica had parked his Alfa in a lot on a paved pad that was just south of Alice's Restaurant, and he and Jimmy had managed to mix in the crowd on the pier, and then with the patient fishermen hanging their long lines down into the water. Finally, when the pier was deserted and about to be closed, they'd thought to sleep in the Alfa. But when Mica saw how alone and vulnerable it looked with the fog swirling around it in the middle of the empty lot, he decided camping out might be a better idea. Jimmy, who had figured out that sleeping in the Alfa would be warmer and more comfortable, tried to argue her point, but Mica snagged a blanket and the 9mm pistol from the trunk, and grabbed her by the wrist and grimly set out for the beach. They argued for a while, and finally set up for the night among the huge boulders halfway between the lot and the water's edge.

Jimmy soon drifted off into a fitful sleep. Mica sat next to her, ticking off the slow hours while the phosphorescent rollers crested and spent themselves on a thin line of sand forty

457

feet below them.

It was after two in the morning when he heard a clinking sound. He checked the 9mm automatic and shoved it back in his belt. After a few moments, he saw the outline of two black-helmeted SWATS moving up the steep slope. Whether through luck or skill, he had chosen their hiding spot well. Squeezed in a small, sandy patch, they could only be reached by crabbing sideways along a dim trail through the field of boulders to their left.

With his heightened senses, Mica could see the two black-suited SWATs clearly; he could even make out part of their whispered conversation, "...no-good cop killer..."

The second whisper answering, "He didn't exactly *kill* her, Charley..."

And the first voice answered, "Didn't exactly...stop to ask if she had a vest on, either..."

Mica waited until they had climbed up to and over the lip of the slope and were out of sight, presumably moving in on his empty car. Then he woke Jimmy and they made their careful way down to the beach, and then jogged on the wet sand under the pier toward Malibu Creek.

two

They were about a half mile from the Alfa when the police hit the lights. Someone started shooting, and the night air was punctured with a ragged volley that ended in a small explosion.

"I really liked that car," he said.

"Are you sure you know where we're going?" Jimmy was looking up the slope. "The houses all look pretty much the same from this side."

"Easy. It'll glow with Ned's aura."

"You don't have to be snippy."

"I'm serious. Everybody has a different aura. You'll see in a couple of days. There. That one." He confidently left the wet sand, trudged across a short span of thick dry sand, and mounted a set of worn wooden steps which led to a first floor balcony. Jimmy trailed after him, catching up on the balcony just in time to see Mica letting himself in a screen door.

"Shhh," he whispered. They crossed the living room, and a short hallway, and entered Ned's bedroom. They both could make out a sleeping form on the big bed. Mica grasped the handle of his automatic and placed one hand over Ned's mouth. Ned panicked, flailing wildly about. He caught Mica with a wild punch, and it was all Mica and Jimmy could do to keep him from darting out of the room.

"Ned! It's Jimmy!"

Mica managed to get him in an armlock and a half nelson. "Turn on the light," he ordered.

Jimmy turned on a small reading light, and as soon as Mica released Ned, he cowered near the far wall, as far from them as he could get.

"I'm not going to hurt you," Mica said, shoving the pistol in his belt.

Ned's voice was mostly whimper, "Don't ask me. I'll never go back there. Never. You can shoot me."

"Just tell me about it."

Ned shook his head like it was full of snakes. "There's nothing to tell."

Mica palmed his pistol and tapped Ned gently on the head. "I know one way to send you back there."

Ned remained silent.

"I forgot; you have nothing to lose, right? You'll just skate off somewhere else with another life."

three

A half mile south of Ned's, Speth pulled off the road, parking his dark gray BMW next to the black Mustang that had been Gravely's. He and Railsbach tumbled out of the BMW and ran up to Felney, Zilch and Nilch, who were watching Mica's Alfa burn in the parking lot across the street.

"Did they get him?" Speth spoke directly to Felney, ignoring Zilch and Nilch.

"I—I... I'm not an expert," Felney said.

"Blodlick has your screens covered," Speth yelled impatiently. "Did these *sap* policemen translate Railsbach's EMO?!"

Felney hitched up his pants. "I'm not sure..."

Zilch was at Speth's side, whispering like an idiot savant, "Did they get him? Did they get him? Did they get him?"

Nilch gave him a broad shrug and a funny little giggle.

Felney ignored the dwarves, talking directly to Speth, "I don't think so."

Nilch picked up the chant, whispering, "I don't think so."

Speth angrily poked Felney in the chest with the first two fingers of his left hand. "You're supposed to know." Felney felt the prick of the spring-mounted steel blades, and was faint with the knowledge of how close he was to translation.

Zilch grinned and whispered, "You're supposed to know. You're supposed to know."

461

Speth idly backhanded Zilch, bowling him over, and then spun on his heel and headed back to his BMW. "Shut up, idiot," Speth said to the dwarf. And then, to Felney, he said, "I know where he's going."

As Zilch was scrambling to his feet and dusting off his homeboy pants, Nilch whispered to him, "I know where he's going."

With quick, catlike reflexes, Zilch backhanded Nilch, bowling him over. "Shut up, idiot," Zilch said.

four

"My real name is Harry Morrison," Ned said. "From Iowa. I took acting classes at State. Had a local TV show in Davenport. *Harry The Clown and His Girlfriend Bimbola.* Pretty hot shit, for Davenport. Pretty soon I got the big head, moved to L.A. I bummed around, hit all the studios, got a few little gigs but couldn't get a break until I thought up my channeler routine."

Mica interrupted, "You couldn't have faked what happened that one time with me."

"No, I couldn't. But that was the *only* time. I faked everything else."

"Go back through what happened. Play-by-play."

"Do I have to?" Mica tapped his head with the pistol, and he continued. "Okay. Near as I can figure, I *hooked into something.* I still don't know what. I was flying, really flying. At least I thought I was—"

Ned paused, seeing Speth's dark shadow as it filled the doorway. "What is this, some public bathhouse?"

At that moment, Mica was already springing up.

Speth pointed his hand and spoke in a voice like doom, "Nala or Ned, prepare for translation!"

In that moment, Mica grabbed Jimmy's hand and dove for the window. As they crashed through in a spray of glass shards, a fiery reddish-orange blast rang out in the room behind them. They hit and rolled down a hillside covered with squashy and slippery ice plant. Behind them, Ned's harsh scream became a bubbling gargle. There was a second blast of energy, and the night was silent.

Mica ran up the bluff beside the house with Jimmy close behind him. He carefully made his way through a wooden gate which only opened from the beach side, and they found themselves at the front of the house, on the sidewalk next to the highway. They crouched beside some huge clay pots filled with blossoming oleanders. Two police cars came screaming up to the front of the house. Four officers jumped out and crashed through Ned's front door, leaving their car doors open and engines running.

Mica waited a moment more, and then sprinted for the nearest black-and-white. From inside the house came flares of reddish-orange light, yelled orders from the police, shrieks of pain, and random pistol shots. Mica was about to slide in behind the wheel of the nearest squad car when he spotted Speth's BMW in the same inviting condition.

"Come on!" he shouted to Jimmy. "We can't pass up this one!" They slipped into the black leather bucket seats, slammed the doors, and Mica hit the gas.

Mica was just in time; the big car fishtailed away as Speth came rocketing out the front door, his burnt leather shoes flopping around and fighting for traction on the sandy sidewalk. Speth saw what was happening immediately, and ran for the nearest police car. He raced after Mica and Jimmy, who were speeding away, heading south toward the Topanga cutoff. Speth was breathing heavily, his bellows neatly siphoning off the poisonous oxygen and pouring the regenerating carbonates into his system. He felt fully alive and confident; it was two common *sapiens* against a semi-immortal who was also a seasoned snufter with a thousand translations in his bag. Could there be any doubt about the outcome?

<u>five</u>

Speth hit the overhead lights on the squad car he was driving and pulled alongside his own BMW, oblivious that he was on the wrong side of the road and running a steady stream of oncoming cars into the cliff wall and each other. He dropped back and came up on the other side of the BMW, nudging Mica toward the center divider. But the BMW was much heavier, and the police car Speth had commandeered was a primitive piece of junk by comparison.

They reached a straight stretch of highway just past the slide area known as Big Rock, and as Speth pulled alongside the BMW, he motioned Mica to wind his window down. Jimmy was cringing low in the seat with her hands over her head. Mica seemed to follow his instructions, but by the time Speth flipped his hand up and blasted from his own half-opened window, the BMW's window was back up and the blast of orange energy glanced off the specially glazed dark glass and back at the black-and-white, blowing out all the windows and roasting Speth's forehead. Speth reached up to feel the blood on his cheek. It irritated him that he was going to have to go back otherside for a re-coat, but then he realized he was going to have to go anyway for his legs.

Speth looked back over at Mica in time to see the *sap* was grinning at him, giving him the scornful gesture known as *the finger*. In the millennium of his earthside adventuring, no human had ever dared gesture him. Rage mounted up in Speth, solid and black as obsidian. He turned his attention entirely on the rogue *sapiens,* certain now that he was going to translate this human with slow, exquisite tortures.

But Speth had taken his eyes off the road, and, in that moment, Mica hit the gas until he had a fractional edge, and then swung the wheel, jamming the squad car and forcing it off the road. They had reached the end of the straightaway. Here the road curved gently left, while on the right shoulder it dropped away in a steep, boulder-littered slope to the surf which was crashing a hundred feet below. Speth had nowhere else to go but off the road. And so his police car lifted gracefully in a short little arc and nosed down into the rocks just shy of the sand, then flipped over a short stretch of dry sand to come to a halt in a shallow tide pool. There was a brief hesitation, and then the car erupted in a ball of flame. After a count of no less than ten seconds, though it was impossible, a smoking body crawled out of the wreckage. It was Speth, looking like a creature from a horror movie with the broiled flesh of his *sap* coat hanging from his battered and dented exoskeleton. He crawled for a few feet, and then pulled himself upright and dusted the sparks off what remained of his expensive gray suit.

CHAPTER 30
Out of Limbo

<u>one</u>

Dr. Bruce and his assistant Janie were assigned to take over Dr. Railsbach's laboratory. Since Railsbach had been secretive even by demonic standards, there were no notes or files to work from, and the newcomers had to work carefully, step-by-step, to reconstruct the simple direction and purpose of many of the energy expenditures for which they were now responsible. The hybrid and mutant brain experiments, almost entirely failures, were easy enough to follow, and Dr. Bruce had summarily terminated all of them except for the rage-driven offspring of a *sap* and the demonic equivalent of a pit bull.

The limbo experiments were entirely another matter. There was a video disk recording of the violent end of the *Dusty Dozen*, and Dr. Railsbach had required the help of an assistant for his own retrieval when he ventured into the void itself. Under dire threat of the clamp, this assistant had stepped forward and ventured the process. Doctor Bruce, taking no chances, had the unfortunate demon clamped immediately after the draining, but it netted no new information as the poor fellow apparently had already revealed all.

Sally and Anne Mae could be seen huddled together on the screen of the single monitor playing in the isolation chamber, which seemed no more than a brightly lit but empty, glass-walled room in the center of the laboratory. Dr. Bruce and Janie sat on stools, and recorded the slow disintegration of the space occupied by Mica's wife and daughter in the void. The now-removed assistant had been following their case and had measured the steady dimming of the light, noted the plaster as it cracked and fell from the walls, the furniture as it sagged and split apart. At this stage, even windowpanes were breaking with a sudden and unexpected pop, or simply vanishing into nothing. The assistant, in his last wailing shrieks, had revealed that they could expect Sally and Anne Mae to ultimately unravel and disappear.

They had been gauging the *sap* termination with scientific curiosity for several hours when Dr. Bruce looked up from his notes with an air of expectancy. "It'll be any time now. She's going a lot faster than I would have expected."

"You say *she*," Janie asked with an air of deference.

"It seems obvious to me, the mother is the key. The spawnling is draining energy."

"Don' trust 'er," Speth snarled from behind them. The assassin was lurching back and forth, practicing his shooter's stance and getting his arm up in the quick draw. The remold on his human coat wasn't fixed, but he refused to sit quietly and let it take hold.

Dr. Bruce shot him a hateful look; he'd always disliked Speth because of the disrespect he'd shown Railsbach.

"Look, the *sap* woman is muttering to herself again." Janie brought him back to the current experiment.

"I told Kelpie, an' now I'm tellin' you," Speth slurred, "You can't accomplish anything this way!"

"The assistant we clamped insisted that when they finally let go they are utterly dissolved in the void," Janie said, doing her best to ignore Speth.

Dr. Bruce nodded, rubbing his hands together, "What a weapon, if we could control the process!"

"But I don't think he really knew," Janie added.

The room Sally had created in the image of her earthside kitchen was now showing signs of rapid decay. Mother and daughter huddled under the kitchen table, around which they had assembled much of the furniture from the kitchen. Although they weren't directly visible on the monitors, the spawnling gave a little squeak of alarm as a huge chunk of plaster crashed down onto the table from the kitchen ceiling.

From the safety of the laboratory, Janie laughed as one might chuckle over the antics of a frightened dog.

"I wouldn't go in there for the biggest set of wings in Hades," Dr Bruce muttered.

"Dr. Railsbach got away with it," Janie ventured.

"Got away with it is right…"

Dr. Bruce had Dr. Railsbach figured as a fairly rash scientist. Railsbach had apparently ventured into the void not once, but in a series of experiments. None of it was recorded, but Railsbach had purposefully encountered the *sap* females, attempting to discover their secret of survival.

"Nothing short of *Grind Into Dust* would persuade me to follow in his hooves," Dr Bruce added.

Janie shrugged and pretended to be interested in her notes. They both knew that if he was gobbled by the void she was next in line to take over the EMO project.

<u>two</u>

While they watched Sally and Anne Mae with scientific detachment tinged with demonic anticipation, because they were unwilling to follow Dr. Railsbach's lead, the demons were not in a position to understand what was happening on the other side of the monitor. For the moment, they couldn't even see the two *saps*, hidden as they were under their makeshift little den of tables, chairs and painting easels. Had Dr. Bruce thought to harness Janie to one of Railsbach's electronic tethers and thrust her into the void, they would have realized the *sap* captives had not lost all hope. Out of view of the camera lenses, Sally was concentrating on the open briefcase left behind by the twelve ancients.

"Remember, hon," she whispered to Anne Mae, "the white-coated man always carried a briefcase when he came to visit."

"So what, Mom?" Anne Mae peeped out from under the table in time to see one wall fall away from the kitchen. Instead of sunny mountain meadows, she could see nothing but a pearly fog.

"Things are going to happen fast now," Sally warned.

"You better put that old briefcase down and do something, Mom," Anne Mae warned, her voice verging on panic.

"I've figured this all out, kiddo," Sally muttered from the corner of her mouth. "Hang on to my arm."

From their vantage, Dr. Bruce and Janie stared as the remaining walls and ceiling dissolved into nothing. Next, the pile of furniture hiding them vanished. Sally and Anne Mae were alone, standing on a small patch of the tile floor that remained.

Sally had strung the strap from the briefcase around her neck and was staring directly into the monitor.

Speth was the first to realize what was happening. "The *sap* bitch figured out the tether!" he screamed. He lurched around the laboratory, looking in closets and knocking over tables and chairs.

"Get it under the lid," Dr. Bruce barked at him. He was fascinated to watch as Sally and Anne Mae dissolved and then disappeared entirely from view. "Gone to nothing..." he whispered in awe. "The first actual witnessing of a sap spirit ground into dust."

They both gaped. "Where *are* they?!" Janie cried in disbelief.

"Old bones," Dr. Bruce replied with a sage nod of his head. "Just a part of history."

"Ahh, Ahh, AHH—" Speth was trying to spit out some words from behind them and bring his arm up at the same time. But before he could do either, he was hit by a bolt of violet-colored energy. His body flew halfway across the room and crashed against the plate glass, and then slid down to the floor. He scrambled to his feet as quickly as he could manage and bolted out of the room. *Better to fall back and live to thrust another day.*

three

Dr. Bruce was bewildered. Impossibly, the two *sap* female spirits stood in the center of his lab. Janie lost her composure, and began to flicker back and forth between her coat and her demonic form.

"Shape yourself, little maggot," Dr. Bruce commanded, backhanding his assistant across the face. He couldn't do anything to retrieve Speth, but with all the presence of mind he could muster, Dr. Bruce turned to face the subjects of Dr. Railsbach's latest failure.

"Allow me to introduce myself. I used to be your husband's physician, after your...unfortunate accident."

"Is that what it was, Maahg?" Sally said, using his personal demonic. "An *accident*?" She moved closer to him, pushing into his claw space as if she hadn't a care in the world, with her daughter directly behind her.

He blanched and stepped back from them.

"Don't be afraid, Maahg," she said, stepping forward to close the distance between them again. "I need your help."

"And how may we help you?" he asked politely.

"You're going to get us out of here."

"I'm afraid that's not possible."

Janie had stepped to the side. Now she was able to rush headlong to the attack with her nails fully extended. But she was not within two feet of either of the humans when she was repelled and hurled back into the same glass wall with which Speth had recently made violent contact. She snarled and gathered haunch, but Dr. Bruce, seeing the futility in it, gestured her back into a wait-and-watch pose.

Sally didn't even give her a glance. Her attention was fully on Dr. Bruce. She gave him a thin smile. "Let me say it a different way. Take us to your leader, if it's not too much to ask."

Dr. Bruce passed them both his most benign and radiant smile, the one he'd used with such great effect over the years on Mica. "And who might that be?" he asked. The comforting smile as well as every shred of his confidence left him as he heard her response.

"His name is Albert Fern," she said. "*Sir* Albert Fern, to a lower spawn like you."

"I'm afraid I don't know any—"

"Oh, yes, you do. You will take us to the one known as Krathnetjapur."

Dr. Bruce paused, thinking through his options. He tried to stall, complaining, "That would be a journey of some difficulty."

"We will be going *now*," she said calmly.

He gave Janie a warning glance and then nodded in slow and methodical assent. With that high and sacred name, Krathnetjapur, set firmly in his brain like a steel hook caught deep in a blue-skinned, big-eyed tuna's mouth, the demon known as Maahg, who for twenty years had always enjoyed wearing the coat of a chubby little Jewish doctor, had no choice but to reluctantly comply, even though he knew the price for his assent would be his own corporeal

475

reality flayed-into-dust.

"Well, come on then, let's be going now," he said softly. "The gate of Hell is a very long way from this place." He kept talking as they left the laboratory and started down a long and dimly lit corridor. His voice assumed the low, singsong chant he'd practiced so often at the knee of the dark masters.

four

They hadn't gone but half the distance down the hallway to the waiting elevator before the woman's steps became dull and plodding. Soon, her eyes glazed under his spell.

"Mom, watch out! It's some trick!" Anne Mae shook her, trying to bring her back.

"The locket...where's the locket?" Sally mumbled. Anne Mae took it from her own neck and placed it in her mother's hand. Sally gave her a vague little smile, but holding onto the locket didn't seem to change anything. And in another few paces Anne Mae, too, was caught in the soft web of chanting.

Plump little Doctor Bruce glanced back every few moments, but he wasn't worried. He could see the silver threads of his chanting continuing to weave tight and unbreakable cords around their wills. *Saps had such weak and foolish spirits—the victims of their own inflated egos!* It was no wonder they never ever could escape the hellside bond.

There was no protocol for what he was doing, but he had no choice. The *sap* female had commanded an audience with Sir Fern. He would escort them both back to his Lord and benefactor, and claim his just reward. He, Maahg, a few days before nothing more than the great and lofty Dr. Railsbach's humble understudy, would be the hero of the darkside for webbing the two *sap* women and escorting them away from the homeland, where they might be capable of immeasurable harm. He would bring them to Sir Fern, who could grind them to dust as he saw fit.

It was laughable, really. Sally and Anne Mae would be the first spirits since the legendary Orpheus and Staggerlee to make their way back through the gates of Hell. The irony was, caught as they were in the web of their past lives, they would never realize what they had achieved. Nor would anyone else. It wasn't good for the human experience to allow such rumors to take wing. For the dark empire to remain strong, the ancient rule had to stand: *Abandon hope, all ye mortal beings who enter here.*

CHAPTER 31
Fire from the Sky

<u>one</u>

As Mica cut through the late night traffic in Speth's BMW, he knew the elation that killer whales feel when gliding through a pack of lesser beings. He slowed out of old habit when he spotted a CHP patrol car, but the two chips ignored him.

The winding two-lane up through Hacienda Heights woke Jimmy. After a moment, she recognized where they were.

"Mica, we're not—"

"He knows more than he's saying."

"He won't even be there."

"I'll bet he is. For a Holy Man, he had a lot of baggage to pack."

He wheeled the big BMW to a stop in front of the Maharishi's place, behind a taxi which had its lights on, the trunk open and the motor running. The taxi driver tried to wave him away, but he and Jimmy ran past, and so doing, crashed into the Holy Man, who was waddling along with a heavy suitcase in each hand.

"Jeeeez! What are you doin here?!"

"We came to see you."

"Get out of here! It's dangerous!" The pudgy little man yelled impatiently over his shoulder, "Akmet! Come on, we're gonna miss the show!" He reached up to shove a finger in Mica's chest. "Can't you hear me? You! Get out of here! You're the last thing I need!"

He tried to get around Mica and Jimmy, but the walkway was narrow, and with the suitcases it was impossible.

"You've got to help us," Jimmy implored. "For old time's sake."

A sudden smile lit the Holy Man's face. "Those were some good times, weren't they?" The smile vanished as quickly as it came. "But, look, I'm out of town, bud."

"Why?"

"There ain't enough good vibes to hold L.A. together anymore. She's gonna go up like Sodom and Gomorrah." He managed to push past, suitcases and all. "And, on top of that, they're on to me. My little piece is gonna blow, that's sure."

"Who is on to you?" Mica asked.

"You know who, schmuck."

Mica followed after him, pleading his case, "My wife needs me. I've got to go to her!"

The Holy Man stopped for a breather, setting his heavy suitcases down by the side of the cab.

"Look, dummy, there ain't nothing you can do."

"I saw her abducted!"

"No you didn't. And your wife ain't on no so-called distant planet. She's dead."

"Dead." Mica looked at him steadily, as if that wasn't enough of an explanation.

The Holy Man rolled his eyes, gesturing to the heavens, which were already overcast with incoming coastal fog. "Why do I get all the crap details?" He eyed Mica. "Your daughter, too. Look, I feel sorry for you, but there's nothing I can do. Dead is dead."

"Dead," Mica said again.

The Holy Man threw up his hands, "Yes, *dead* as in *gone forever*!"

"But not as in *died and gone to Heaven*."

"Oh, now you want guarantees." The Holy Man looked back over his shoulder. "Akmet," he called, "Leave the fuckin' carpet!"

By now the cabbie had the suitcases in the trunk, and Akmet showed up, dragging a rolled-up carpet. They had to unwind the back window, so the end could stick out.

"Would you please move your car?"

Mica threw Jimmy the keys to the BMW, and then he opened the back door of the cab and squeezed in with Akmet and the carpet.

"You can't come with us," the Holy Man protested.

"I've got to! My wife needs me."

The Holy Man threw his hands up in despair, and whacked the driver with his hat like he was driving a mule.

"Step on it, I said!"

The Holy Man had good reason to want to hurry, and to be afraid.

481

two

As the yellow taxi and the gray BMW made their way out of the eastern canyons and east on the 210 freeway in the direction of the Burbank Airport, the overhead micros maintained their easy surveillance. Felney kept them in the upper corner of his desk monitors, giving them an occasional glance while he whisked through his regular agenda of translations. And Sir Albert Fern himself judged the matter to be in control.

Dr. Bruce was the man of the hour for bringing the two *sap* females under control. Speth, who seemed to have more lives than an obsidian *felis domestica*, had been banned by the master of the house from the study. It would be some time, if ever, before they would trust him indoors, or to drive a car, but he was busily ruining another of his fine dark gray suits with his spitting and drooling as he jerkily hitched himself about outside on the patio, keeping busy practicing his fast draw. Zilch and Nilch had a running bet going, how long it would take the assassin to shoot himself in the hoof.

If there was one thing that bothered Fern, it was the absence of Dr. Railsbach. Now that Railsbach was wanted on both sides for a string of crimes linked to his EMO experiments, Albert Fern could see why he would make himself scarce. But with their web firmly in place *from the mountains to the sea*, tracking him should have taken minutes, not days. Fern just didn't understand how a demon could disappear like that.

three

Akmet whiled away the time in the airport cafe, sitting at one of the small tables with fixed chairs. He and Jimmy were playing a game of war with a deck of tarot cards.

Mica sat at the next table with the Holy Man, who was gobbling the remains of a pepperoni pizza and guzzling it down with his third long-neck Coors.

"Hey," Jimmy complained, "You're cheating."

"I will not accept the 'hand of death' card. It is in my rules." Akmet slipped the card back into the unused portion of the deck.

"Hey, hold it down," the Holy Man said. "We're talkin' serious stuff over here." He took another huge bite of the pizza. "Look, here's what I do." He gobbled at a long string of cheese, trying unsuccessfully to eat it before it dropped to the table. "I clear my mind, like, sweep it clean of thoughts like hot babes with long, smooth legs, or fancy cars, or winning the lottery. That's the clean page, the so-called fuckin' *tabula rasa*. Then, if you got the gift, you write your own ticket. You could go anywhere. Do anything. Except, I got it, and apparently you don't."

"Got what?"

"The gift."

"How do you know?"

The Holy Man gave him a lofty look with his brows arched and his mouth pursed into a little round pucker. "You been unblanked how long now? If you had it, you wouldn't hafta ask." The Holy Man broke out in a sympathetic grin and reached for another piece of pizza. "Pepperoni was one of God's gifts to this world, don't you think, Akmet?"

"Ah, yes, most assuredly so, Master," Akmet replied, intent on the field of cards growing on the table in front of him.

"Look, Mica," the Holy Man muttered around a new mouthful of pizza, "don't get pissed just because you don't have my gifts. You got your own gifts. Everybody does."

"Right. Sure I do."

"Come on. You got an aura big as a rhino's butt."

Mica eyed him dejectedly, sure he was being conned, or, at the least, that they were speaking different languages.

"Yeah, I can see it. What am I supposed to do with it?"

The Holy Man raised his Coors instructionally. "St. Stephen himself should have been so lucky to have such a radiation—he could have warded off all those arrows." He swigged the beer, thinking about it. "Of course, then he wouldn't have become a martyr, and probably not a saint, either." He shrugged. "See, it's all choices. You never can tell."

"A radiation."

"Yeah, that's right. Didn't you tell me you turned one of them into chopped liver in an elevator? How did you do that?"

"I don't know. It just happened."

"No, no, no, no, no. Nothing 'just

485

happens'. That was your aura at work." The little man glared at Mica. "You think I'm nuts, don't you?!"

"Yes. I'm the guy who sees flying saucers, and yet you are the total whacko."

The Holy Man put his hand on Mica's good hand.

"Pick up the water," he said. He nodded to a water glass that was five inches from Mica's fingers.

"How can I—?"

"Pick up the fuckin' water glass, oh ye of little faith! Do it with your mind, dummy!"

Mica narrowed his gaze and stared intently at the water glass. It seemed to tremble slightly, but that was all. Maybe even that was his overworked imagination.

The Holy Man shook his head sadly. "Constipated spiritually."

Mica was upset. "I'm tired of all these stupid half-truths—"

The command in the Holy Man's voice was like iron, "The glass, you ass—the glass!"

Mica glared at the common glass of water on the table in front of him. In a second, the water was boiling fiercely, and then the glass shattered in a thousand fragments.

"Hey, my cards!" Akmet complained from the next table.

The Holy Man shrugged, reaching for another piece of pizza. "Interesting. If you could control it, you could boil eggs."

The last call for a Denver flight came over the intercom speakers. Akmet scooped up his cards and hurried to the door. The Holy Man stood, took a last bite of pizza and a gulp of beer. He indicated the few pieces left on the platter, "You want the rest?"

"They'll have more food on the plane."

The Holy Man, plainly irritated, took another huge bite. "We're never going to get to eat it," he muttered through his stuffed cheeks, speaking low so Akmet couldn't hear.

"What? What are you talking about?"

"Hey, get a life. You don't think they're going to actually let us go?!"

"But—?"

"It's for Akmet, schmuck. I gotta keep him busy, right up until the last second. Somebody's gotta be the shepherd." The Holy Man slung his carry-ons around his shoulders, took yet another last bite, and walked down the corridor, with Akmet beckoning him to hurry.

"Wait," Mica called after him. "What can I do besides cheap parlor tricks?"

The Holy Man turned, hesitated, and then came back for the rest of the pizza. He stacked it three pieces high, and then stood close, jabbing his chubby finger in Mica's chest.

"The human race has forgot almost everything it ever knew. Forget what it says about angels in the Bible. We used to be our own angels..." His voice ran down, as if grounded in awe at the vision of how great humans used to be. He turned to go, and then turned back to Mica. "'Vengeance is mine, sayeth the Lord.' If you ever point your hand at anyone in righteous anger..."

"Yes?"

Akmet was interrupting, calling from down the hall, but the Holy Man waved him off with an impatient shake of his hand.

"Just make sure," he said, "that you got the right guy."

With that, he scurried down the corridor toward his departure gate, waddling like a tourist penguin loaded with travel gear. He paused and spun around in a little half-circle, raising his voice so he could be heard over the foot slap and buzz of voices in the terminal, "You might want to practice on tin cans in the backyard."

"What?"

"He said—" Jimmy started.

The Holy Man put a hand to his mouth like a megaphone. "Hone your skills," he shouted.

He saw Mica still didn't appear to get it. "Ask your girlfriend. Or go see Old Black Joe. He always was better than me with the spiritual retards." Seeing that Mica was still staring dumbly at him, he gave one last wave of disgust, as if he was waving off an enormous mess.

"Aghh. Forget it." And with that, he waddled off towards his new Holy Man life in Denver.

four

Mica and Jimmy hurried back down the long corridor and out the front doors, intent on making their way back to the parking structure where she'd parked Speth's BMW. They were about to cross the street when Mica was detained by a worn-down looking, middle-aged security officer, who asked to see his identification.

"Caught me at last," Mica said with a sigh of relief. "I don't know how we've stayed free so long."

"Some joker," the security man said, leafing through his wallet. After several moments of silence, he handed the wallet back.

"You two run along," he said.

Mica and Jimmy stood at the passenger crosswalk, waiting for the green light. A plane took off, and from the sound of it, would pass directly overhead.

"That would be the Holy Man's plane," Jimmy said. "The Hegira of the Holy Man, to his promised lands east of the Rockies."

"You know, he told me he never expected to make it."

Whatever Jimmy was about to reply was lost in the flare and shattering sound of an enormous explosion. The plane overhead lost its sleek form and expanded into a red-orange ball of flame. Mica seemed frozen in time, staring up at the fiery image dropping towards them. Jimmy grabbed his arm. "Come on, Mica! Run for it!" They raced across the street as flaming debris pelted the ground around them. They'd just made the overhanging cement lip of the structure when a huge jet engine fell to the ground behind them, obliterating the security guard who had detained them.

"Over there!" Jimmy pointed, and they ran toward the BMW as a sheet of flaming jet fuel came after them like a fiery river. They gained the door, ripped it open and managed to slip inside and slam it behind them as the wave of flame roared and rolled over the car.

Mica beat on the steering wheel in frustration. "They can kill anybody they want."

"They didn't get us," Jimmy said. "We're getting help from somebody."

"I don't know what to do."

"The Holy Man said your old black friend is still alive."

"Jimmy, he had a hole in his side this big." He raised a fist to show her. "I could see through him."

"I say we go look for him. We got nothin' better to do, Mica-boy, til the Messiah come..."

Mica sat for a moment longer, thinking about it. And then he started the engine, snapped on the headlights and drove off into the night. As they went, the 7 series BMW, fresh from its fiery bath, steamed and smoked like a true hell-car.

CHAPTER 32
The Lure

<u>one</u>

Doctor Bruce took the elevator down to the main lobby, where he was met by a small squadron of heavily armed black troopers.

"Where are the unblanked *saps*?!" the leader shouted.

"I have no idea," the pudgy little doctor replied, pushing past the troopers with his small group. "Stand aside, we're in a hurry." Janie looked a little wild-eyed, but Sally and Anne Mae followed dutifully after like *sap* drones.

"Wait!" the demon called after him.

"Yes...?" Dr. Bruce hissed, turning slowly at the half claw.

"It's nothing, sir," the trooper said, falling back at this unexpected show of impatience. "Someone reported an incident up on the 21st floor."

"Then you should go up to 21 and check it out."

"Yes, sir!" the man barked. He gathered his men and started for the elevator at a squad trot.

While he was busy with the soldiers, Sally was preoccupied with her own thoughts. She was lost, but not in the way Dr. Bruce believed. She had tricked him neatly, relying on the golden locket to retain her consciousness even as he wove his seductive incantations around her. But the chants did more than enslave the human spirit; they broke down the bonds of forgetfulness that separated past lives and without which most humans would go mad from loss and despair. Even an unblanked human was spared the weight of his past lives. Because she was conscious as she fell through the layered stories of her existence, Sally gaped and gagged as the speck of her consciousness swam through the vast parade of her past lives, tempted to stay with every twig and flower and passion newly remembered, to caress again all the lovers, to hold once more all the children. And so too, the shock of old pain and suffering she had endured, of rape and torture and murder, were again hers.

And in the moment when she felt totally lost, when the layered weight of all her experiences would snuff her out like a candle, she heard Mica's voice calling in the distance.

"Sally, I'm coming," he said. "Hang on for me, I'm coming." And she knew that, of all her loves in all her lives, this one had been the most unexpected and precious. It didn't matter that it was the last love, she was certain it was absolutely the best one. And with that knowledge, the flame of her awareness flared up and was made whole. She knew she could live with her past, purified by his love.

And so, singing her own song, she marched along with her daughter to the cadence of Dr. Bruce's chant. Only now, she could feel the silver bonds corroding, the hold he had over them wearing away. Even with her eyes to the floor and in the middle of her shuffling gait, she sent a thought to Anne Mae, *Be careful he doesn't observe us.* And as they moved along at Dr. Bruce's side, she began to unwind the cords that bound her daughter. *Don't worry, honey-bird,* she said. *They're taking us where we want to go.*

two

A few hours before dawn, recognizing that Dr. Railsbach would not be uncovered as easily as they had thought, Albert Fern, Speth and Felney held a council of war in the big study of Fern's mansion. Zilch and Nilch, reprimanded for flicking glowing coals at frazzled little Lollypop, were nearby on a love seat, bickering over who would get to hold the dog.

Speth, who had returned from otherside moments before, was sporting a new navy blue suit accented with elegant thin pinstripes, over an extensive new temp patch-job to his coat.

"You look your old self," Sir Albert had complimented him, even though Speth seemed somewhat distracted and for that reason definitely *not* himself.

Speth was pleased. He did, in his own mind, resemble the violent and legendary assassin of old, except for the fresh scars lining his face, arms and legs, and one arm hampered by a sling, which he couldn't remove yet for several hours under the dire threat that the coating would fall off.

To the entire party's chagrin, Mica Harris and the Jamaican girl had evaded their most costly trap yet; and even though they had found and then translated a pudgy little *sap* they had figured to be one of the last partially unblanked Elevated Ones on the planet, Albert Fern was in dangerous high snip.

"Explain it to me yet again, Felney," he lashed out with his accusing, superior tone.

"You plan the vectors, convince me to expend the enormous amount of energy it takes to bring down a fully loaded passenger jet airplane, there is a veritable fiery fountain of debris and we still miss the EMOs."

Felney threw his arms wide, "Unblanked is unpredictable."

Speth tried to interrupt, "If you had just let me—"

Albert Fern cut him with a look. "And we still have the first two unblanked light-spawn since Buddha, that pesky Christ-character or mumbling Mohammed, and they're wandering about at will."

Speth spoke again, "I could have—"

"*Speedball! Shut up!*"

Speth felt the hot, dry flash of rage, but he bit his feelings. *Sir Fern had lately shown an unaccustomed impatience towards his old favorites. He should be more careful. He, too, could feel an assassin's sting.*

"Don't even think it, Speth," Fern snarled. He turned his back in a gesture of scorn, tempting the assassin further. But it was a quick motion, the formality rather than true superiority, and Speth retracted his claws, seeing he had no chance to lash.

"And," Fern continued, "these two saps are *motivated and dangerous*, particularly the man, who thinks we killed his wife and daughter."

"We did kill his wife and daughter," Felney muttered.

"It's all Kelp's fault," Speth interjected.

"And have you been able to find the good

doctor, Gurpler?" Sir Fern snarled.

"Well, no I have not. But don't think I have not been trying!" Felney stamped his foot like a little *sap* kid who'd been told he couldn't go out and play, prompting Zilch to hop off the love seat and stamp his own foot.

Sir Fern quenched whatever the little dwarf was about to say with a withering look. He cleared his throat, "Fellows of the darkness, these are serious times. In spite of the Gravely loss, a tragedy which affects me personally, I am now prepared to call in the auditors. The whole sector's in danger. I don't see how I can justify any alternative."

"But, Sir Fern—you'll be clamped and remolded, at the very least." Felney was suddenly ringing his hands in despair.

"Maybe even dusted, Old Gurpler," Fern nodded grimly.

"They'll turn this place into a barracks," Felney complained. "They'll bring in a dozen like Speth, shooters from around the world."

Fern eyed Speth, who, for once, resisted his age-old and detestable spitting.

"What, Speth?"

"I say, the women...?"

"He's madness," Felney said scornfully.

"No, let him speak," Fern said. He encouraged his assassin, "You've been around a long time, old shooter. You know rogues and topside lore with the best. What about the women?"

"We use them to lure Mica Harris."

"Lure him here?! Inside the stronghold?"

496

"Yes, here. They come badly outnumbered. We translate Mica and boot them all back-side. Give me one day."

Sir Fern was intrigued. It was the first time Speth had ever volunteered a plan. "Exactly how do we get him to come here?"

The blank look on Speth's face told them he didn't have a clue. But at that moment, fate intervened.

"I think I've found someone who can help us," Felney said. He snapped a minor monitor up to main screen center. There, huddled and shivering in a huge storm drain that emptied into the Los Angeles River, was the missing Dr. Railsbach.

<u>three</u>

It was a sleet-in-your-face night on the Scottish moors, and Mica and Sally, wearing cloaks and 17th century clothing which seemed familiar and yet odd at the same time to them, were riding in full gallop from a band of dark beings who clanked and gibbered in their armor. He heard distant shots and felt the tug of a bullet as it ripped through his woolen cape. They topped a rise in the rocky landscape, and a gale force wind hit them.

"We can't go on!" Sally cried.

She slipped down from her horse, took out her brace of pistols.

"Ride on! Take Anne Mae with you while I hold them off!"

Suddenly, Anne Mae was with them. She scrambled up on the horse behind him.

"No!" he screamed. "I'll never leave you!"

"You must save our child!" But, even as Sally spoke, she slipped, her feet going out from under her on the uneven, rocky ground. She came to a brief pause at the edge of a brink. The pistols had tumbled from her grasp. She looked back up at him one last time.

"Go! I'm lost, but you can still make it!"

Lightning flared, frightening Mica's horse, which reared on its hind legs, all flaring nostrils and lean flanks ready to run. He couldn't leave; he stared in horror as Sally slowly slid toward the edge of the precipice. He heard behind him the thundering sounds of the band of creatures coming for them and saw their pistols blazing.

As Sally slowly lost her grip, he jumped down from the horse.

"Anne Mae," he cried. "You've got to take the horse. We'll catch up later."

"No, I'm not going, either," Anne Mae said. "You're no good outdoors. You can't rescue her without me."

"Hold on, Sal," he shouted. "We're coming for you!"

And he reached down for her through fuzzy layers of gray fog. Only down was up and he was underwater, swimming up, up, up as beasts with large teeth swam after him.

He heard a voice calling, "Mica, Mica..."

four

Mica woke to realize he was sitting with his back against the brick wall in Indigent Alley, with Jimmy sleeping at his side. The old black bum was leaning over him, shaking him.

He started, instantly awake. "Jim Crow. Old Black Joe. Whatever. We've been looking for you."

The bum settled himself down to the ground next to Mica, hitching his legs around like they might have been made of wood. He gave out a deep sigh and held his head in his hands.

"You're not in such good shape," Mica said.

"That be an understatement," the old bum said, "But better than the last time you saw me." The bum opened his shirt and Mica could make out ragged healing marks across his chest. "It's jist a temporary patch job. Anyway, what kin I do for you?"

"Remember you told me about souls fluttering to the light after they die?"

"Yes. The good ones." The bum looked at Mica, his ancient yellow eyes showing no emotion.

"Well...could anything make you stay behind? I mean, if you were a soul?"

Jim thought about it for some time. He scratched his head and then moved his feet to a more comfortable position. "Well, maybe...some souls be too heavy with grief or despair. They could get left behind. But if that

500

happens, it could be a dangerous time."

"Why? They're already dead."

"They's things worse than dead. Their souls could be dragged down. It's that possibility they would have to worry about."

"I don't remember anything about that in the Bible."

Jim Crow gave him a shrug of his thin, old shoulders. "The debil be gettin' bolder by the minute."

Mica sat straighter, trying to puzzle it out. "Okay. Say that's true. But Sally was strong. She was good and decent. See, she would have beamed right up to that light. Anne Mae, too."

The old bum eyed Mica for a moment, hesitating before he spoke, "Unless she chose to stay behind...'cause of somebody else..."

"Because of somebody..." Mica whispered, thunderstruck.

Jim Crow nodded his agreement. "Sure. Somebody she cared for. A great love could do that. You know, there ain't nothin' so powerful in the known world as the true love of one human person for another."

Mica jumped to his feet. "I've got to save them!"

Jim put his fingers to his lips, "Shhh, you gonna wake your friend." He shook his head. "They's no way you can rescue them, young man. And if you could; say here, for a moment, that you could—still, there ain't no way back, no way to get them back, no way to get any of you back. Think Orpheus. Think Dr. Phibes."

The next thing that happened was so dramatic, Mica would wonder later if it had been planned, or preordained. For at that moment, the man in the white coat stepped out of the shadows, his foot clanking an empty bottle as he did so. "Not Dr. Phibes," he said. "Will Dr. Railsbach do?"

<u>five</u>

Mica jumped to his feet, ready to protect Jimmy and the old man.

"Don't touch us!" he warned.

The white-coated man stepped forward, unconcerned. "You've grown a bit past that. As for him..." He shrugged, his voice trailing off in a way that suggested there was more to the old negro than met the eye.

"What do you want?" Mica shouted, loud enough so a chorus rose from the alley to quiet him down.

"My name is Dr. Railsbach."

"Your name is Kelp," Jim Crow quietly corrected him.

"Well, yes, my *given* name."

"It don't matter." The old black man's voice was gentle, "How may we help you?"

"Why should we—?"

"Mica, let him talk."

Railsbach went into his pitch, "I've become an outcast. They're going to get me, sooner rather than later. I nearly didn't make it here."

"What did you do?" Mica asked.

"Nothing, really. It's unfair, but there's nothing anybody can do to save me. I'll be dirt by morning, but I'm making a choice now, maybe the only one I ever made in my life." He nodded to Mica, gesturing down the street, back the way he'd come. "I can take you to your wife and daughter. I can get you there."

"Why should you?"

"You're looking at desperation. I—I have

503

nothing more to lose."

The old bum nodded, and then staggered to his feet. "I think it's worth a try."

"Is it far?" Mica asked.

"You'll make it, but not him; Jim here will never get there, in the shape he's in," Railsbach said.

"Maybe it be for the best," Jim Crow said, looking relieved. He gave Mica a brief hug. "You go on with Kelp. I'll take care of Jimmy for you. 'Member now, you don't know what to do, give 'em *Righteous Anger*."

Mica stared back, recognizing it was the same advice given him by the plump little Holy Man before he got on his last plane to Denver.

Jim waved Mica on. "Make sure Jimmy's okay. I got to talk to the good Dr. Kelp, here." When Mica moved out of hearing, Jim pulled the doctor close to him with fierce strength, "You be good, now."

Railsbach nodded and tried to pull free, but the bum was holding his arm, and now Jim Crow spoke in an even lower whisper, "You do have a choice."

"What choice?" Kelp's voice was a sharp hiss.

"They say, every once in a while, a dark one learns to fly."

"You know who I am?"

"I tell you, you got one chance here to save yourself."

The white-coated man gave Jim a sardonic little smile. "Right. From your mouth to the ear of the Great Being."

"Yes," Jim gently agreed, a look that could have been resignation or sadness on his face, "I say a prayer. I will do that for you."

Railsbach pulled his arm away, as if he'd touched ice. He moved quickly into the shadows, only taking the time to call back over his shoulder to Mica, "Come on. We're almost out of time."

CHAPTER 33
Showdown at Ferngate

<u>one</u>

Dr. Bruce was certain he had an easy departure until he was stopped by one minor hoof after another on his way to Ferngate. He finally realized the paper-men were doing everything in their power to hold them back, not because they had any specific plan, but because it was unnatural to take *sap* spirits back out any gate. And there had been all that recent trouble in Sir Fern's sector. Too much trouble not to go without comment.

Not that anyone actually dared a lash; but regulations had to be met, questions answered and forms filled out. Thankful he had been strong in incantations, he fumed, and fussed and sputtered, but there was little else he could do to speed the process. And all the time he worried what was going on inside the mind of the woman and her daughter who walked along at his side.

At the final departure check, he had to leave Janie behind to satisfy the paperwork, while he and the two *sap* females took a slow conveyer belt for the gate itself. It was mildly interesting that, while there were nearly seventy belts running into Hell, and these were crowded with doomed souls in all states of panic and crushed disorder, there was only one narrow belt leading back the other way. And this was barely used; Dr. Bruce had to squint in the semi-lit corridor to make out the form of the departing demon who was nearly 200 meters in front of him, and there was no one at all behind them.

As their transportation belt jerked them along, he double-wound his silky incantation, just to make sure. Was there a flicker of intelligence behind the elder female's blank-eyed stare? *No, it couldn't be.* He but he did a special little heavy-threaded weaving, just to make sure.

<u>two</u>

Dr. Railsbach drove in the dark Mustang convertible that had until recently belonged to James Gravely. Mica sat quietly at his side, trying to prepare himself for the conflict he knew was now inevitable. The car rumbled as they wound their way up into the Hollywood Hills. Railsbach parked along the road, about 200 yards outside the high-walled gates of a large estate.

"We don't want to announce ourselves," he explained quietly. The night was overcast, and eerily lit with the city lights reflected off the low cloud overhang. Even the metal thump of their car doors seemed too loud. At Railsbach's direction, they slipped in through the open gates on foot and ran across a wide lawn to the shadows of a great, brooding, Tudor style mansion.

They crept into a darkened study through French windows open to the night air. At one end, a fireplace burned brightly. The other seemed bathed in soft blue light, which was coming from behind a huge desk.

"What is this place?" Mica whispered.

"Entry and departure. Follow me, quietly."

They walked toward the fireplace. Two small, gnomelike dwarves were sleeping on a rug in front of the crackling blaze. A little white dog sleeping between them stirred and began to bark. Railsbach wagged a finger at her, and she whined once and settled down. One of the dwarves moaned and sighed, but did not waken. The other reached out and slapped the dog, and then found a new sleeping position with his head on the dog's side.

They inched past the dwarves, heading toward the fireplace.

"Where to now?" Mica whispered.

Railsbach pointed to the roaring fire. "Through there." He saw Mica's look and shrugged, "It's just for show." And without another word, he stepped directly into the fire. He took two more steps and was gone.

Mica looked around uncertainly. After a moment, Railsbach returned, his pants cuffs smoking.

"Come on," he urged. "This is the only way to Sally and Anne Mae." And he stepped back through the sheet of flames and was gone.

Still, Mica hung back, unwilling to take the three steps which would carry him through to whatever lay beyond. And again Railsbach returned. This time he had to beat out the small flames starting at the bottoms of his trousers.

"Mica, *come on!* You do want to see your wife and daughter, don't you? This is your only chance!"

"I don't think so," he said. "The whole thing feels too easy."

And with that, the overhead chandeliers went on, illuminating the huge room in a blaze of light. The dwarves jumped to their feet, yawning and grinning at Mica. And an elderly man sat in a wing chair not thirty feet from where Mica stood.

"Thank you, Dr. Railsbach," the man said.

"You may now return to your reward."

Railsbach paled, and his face chattered several times, *doctor-alien, doctor-alien,* before he got it under control. "But, Sir Fern," he started to complain, "you promised—"

A raking blast of energy surged past Mica and would have struck Railsbach except for the fact that he dove headfirst back through the fire.

<u>three</u>

The bolt of red flame had come from a tall, dark-featured man who stood behind the elderly one.

"Speth," Mica said, recognizing him from their last meeting. "You've recovered from our last meeting, then."

"This time I do you permanently," the assassin sneered.

"Time enough for that," Sir Fern said, waving him quiet with a flip of his hand. "Mica Harris. Your wife and daughter wait on the other side of the portal. Why do you not walk through and reclaim what you believe is yours?"

Mica took a step toward Sir Fern, and the two dwarves bared their teeth and showed their nails, which had grown long and steely.

"Zilch. Nilch. Step back for a moment. We have the rogue sap quite in hand." Fern took an ornately carved pipe from his breast pocket and began to fill it from a small leather pouch. His nails slowly extended as he waited for Mica's answer. "Are you going to make me repeat my question?"

Mica inched his way past the two little monster-men until he was within a few feet of Fern. "Either they are not there, or you would be sending me to a place from which I could not return."

"Is that what the sapiens order calls deductive logic?" When Mica didn't answer, Fern tamped the tobacco with a small silver

511

device and then snapped flame to his pipe. "You're not very talkative tonight."

Mica walked past Fern and Speth to the other end of the room, where he could see Felney working the monitors. Speth started into his shooting stance, but Fern impatiently motioned him to stand down.

"Interesting, isn't it?" Albert Fern said from across the room. "Your brief glimpse into our operations means you now have seen more of us than almost any other human since…the first round."

"I want my wife and daughter."

Fern puffed peacefully at his pipe; then gave a brief, negative toss of his head. "You don't think there's any way we could persuade you to come along peacefully? There's no need, really, to grind you into dust. We can have you re-implanted and back on the streets by morning."

"My wife and daughter," Mica repeated.

Fern indicated the fireplace with his pipe. "Right on the other side."

There was a brief commotion, and Railsbach came through the fireplace again. This time, his clothes were dirty and disheveled, and he had with him a blond woman and her daughter. In seconds, he was followed by a strongly protesting Dr. Bruce. But his venting was more like the barking of a small lap dog, and it was easy to see he respected Railsbach's lash, if not his authority.

Fern clamped his pipe between his teeth and gave Railsbach a series of slow, derisive claps. "Well done, Kelp. To Hell and back in under a minute. Somewhat of a castle coup for you."

"Well, I nearly had them at the gate," Dr. Bruce protested.

Zilch and Nilch began to clap, whistle and stomp their feet.

"Jolly good show," Zilch squeaked in his best pompous Fern imitation.

"Hurrah! Hurray!" Nilch added.

The master of the house glared, and the two of them stopped instantly.

Fern again had to restrain Speth, "In a moment, Speedball."

"Sally! Anne Mae!" Mica was nearly across the room before he realized something was wrong.

four

Sally and Anne Mae were wearing the same blouses and skirts they had worn when he'd seen them in Copenhagen. Sally looked at him politely, and spoke in a strange tongue.

Albert Fern transmogrified himself into the professor whom Mica had last seen on a chilly but sunny day, sitting by the Gefion Fountain in Denmark.

"She's speaking 17th century Nordic, I believe..." Albert repeated with a crisp little professorial laugh. And then he easily shifted back into his Fern form.

"One of their past lives," Railsbach said.

"Enough, Kelp!" Speth shouted.

Railsbach had moved away from the fireplace. Now that he was too far from the portal to make another dive through it, he slid behind Mica.

"Let them go!" Mica shouted. "I want my wife and daughter!"

"You are boringly repetitious." Fern shrugged his shoulders. "I don't see why I should be motivated to do any such thing."

Speth stepped forward, spitting as he came. "You don't seem to understand, you vile little *rogue sap*. You're just a number, up for translation."

Fern nodded his agreement. "I'm afraid that's so. You've been bothersome, I will admit, but you're just a tiny part of the grand plan. Although our good Doctor here doesn't agree, you are easily expendable, easily

514

snuffed."

"What grand plan?"

Fern sniffed, "How can I simplify?"

Railsbach cut in, "It was a project. We took away everyone who—who cared for you."

"EMO?"

Railsbach nodded grimly.

"The Doctor here did you, actually." Fern's smile was cruel. "The one who's hiding behind you right now. He's the one who killed your wife and daughter."

Mica turned to Railsbach, "You...killed them? How can they be here?"

Railsbach pointed to Felney. "Well, actually *he* had them—"

"Oh, Kelp," Fern cut in smoothly, "Of course our little translator pulled the actual trigger. But EMO was your project from the first."

"How can they be here?" Mica repeated impatiently.

Fern shrugged. "The body corporeal. Life, death; here, not here. The spirit lives. Doesn't anybody on your planet read their catechisms anymore?"

Mica walked over to the two who looked so like his Sally and Anne Mae. He looked into the woman's eyes. She stood erect and proud, staring back at him. But she didn't seem to recognize him.

Mica spun around to face Fern again. "I demand you let them go! You have no right to do this!"

Speth sneered, "You demand."

Fern was curious to see if the human actually knew anything that could harm them, "Under what covenant?"

Speth interrupted before Mica could reply, "Where are your angels now, when you need them?"

"We are our own angels."

"Were," Railsbach corrected. "Not now. Not with your minds wiped, your vision blanked, your abilities nulled."

Fern turned on him like a furious cat, "It is forbidden to talk to light-spawn of this!"

Speth moved away at an angle from Fern so that, in order to keep Mica between them, Railsbach was forced to expose himself partly to Fern. The portly old man raised his hand, pointing it at Railsbach like an executioner. "Kelp, for this latest transgression, for the death of the Dozen Elders, and for the translation of James Gravely—"

Railsbach managed to shout, "Wait, I didn't—"

Speth stepped forward. "Allow me, sire." He raised his hand in one swift, fluid motion, boiling Railsbach's body with a brief emanation of blooming, deadly energy.

CHAPTER 34
Firestorm

<u>one</u>

The doctor fell to the ground, reverting to his alien and then his demonic form. He lay there, shuddering and moaning.

A thought formed in Mica's mind, *They die as easily as do we.* He felt raised to another level, strangely alive, radiant with energy and emotion. He didn't know why; all he knew was the flood of pure, raw anger that was flooding his being.

He shouted, "I demand you set my wife and daughter free!"

Fern eyed Mica coldly, then looked at Speth. Neither of them had ever seen a human in a heightened state. Speth shrugged. It obviously didn't matter to him. He was itching to translate. Again Fern gave him the *wait* sign. He wanted to know what the *unblanked EMO* knew, or perhaps he just wanted to play with the *sap* a little, like the dwarves with their little white dog, or the dog itself with a cornered mouse or a small gray bird.

"And what are you prepared to give in return?"

Speth, who misunderstood and thought he was actually prepared to deal with the rogue sap, dove across the room and took the blond woman, holding her in front of him. He grabbed the daughter in his other hand and began inching for the fireplace.

"No deals!" Speth shouted. "Come on, Zilch! Nilch! Do your job!"

The two dwarves, silly court jesters no longer, shifted into doglike aliens, and then into demonic devil-dogs, and stood on either side of the hellgate.

Mica was beside himself with fear for Sally and Anne Mae. His mind felt clotted with rage. Having come this close, he was still nowhere, as now he stood to lose Sally and Anne Mae forever. He didn't fully understand what was happening to them, but he knew it was wrong. He was their champion, and yet he felt he could do nothing. Out of sheer frustration, he raised both hands, perhaps to beg, perhaps to shake his fists. Whatever his intention, he was unable to complete his action as enormous blue bolts of energy unfurled from his hands, lashing out and destroying half a wall between Speth and the fireplace.

"Careful, *sap*," Speth taunted. "You'll destroy everything you love." Speth was ready to retaliate, but in that moment he lost his concentration. He looked down to see that the bubbling green mess which was all that remained of Dr. Railsbach had quietly crawled over to him and now had him by the ankle in a last death grip. Speth had to stomp his foot on Railsbach's torn and blistered face, and when that did not work, to waste a blast of energy to finish off Railsbach so he could pull his leg away.

This was all the diversion the blond

woman needed. She may not have known Mica, but she knew the situation well enough to understand her future didn't lie with Speth. She quickly grabbed her daughter and pulled away from the assassin, moving to a position behind Mica.

Albert Fern motioned to Felney, and they both began to inch quietly toward the roaring fireplace. Dr. Bruce, who had dropped to the ground at the first sign of violence, was creeping on his belly towards the portal. Fern looked back at Speth and spoke in a quiet and yet commanding voice, "Speth. Come."

But the assassin was beyond lash; Speth let out a cry of rage and leapt sideways to roll across the floor, loosening bolts of energy at Mica as he went. His shots went wild, blowing out windows and walls, but at least, due to his dive and roll, the one or two energy blasts which glanced off Mica's radiance like light off a mirror did not reflect back to strike Speth. Yet, clearly, the assassin was having no negative effect on the rogue human. Speth unleashed his best shot, a tremendous roiling orange mass of energy, in Mica's direction, but it was simply deflected.

Mica, in turn, was no longer acquiescent. Now he was sending blue energy snapping back at Speth.

two

While Mica and Speth's personal battle was engaged, the woman and her daughter seemed to be moving as if in an atmosphere of heavy liquid. Dr. Bruce recognized the first signs, and it sent a chill through his carapace. *Impossible, but the sap woman and her daughter were somehow unwinding the incantations!* They could regain their conscious spirits at any time. It might be days, it might be seconds; there was no way to know just when. He redoubled his efforts to crawl to the fireplace.

Speth was making little headway. Fern impatiently raised his own hand in Mica's direction to end the matter once and for all, but the woman moved directly into his line of fire. Now turned into some beautiful and yet terrifying elevated version of herself, Sally glared balefully at him. Her hair floated in her own brilliant aura. She raised one hand to stop Sir Fern, while her other sent an almost negligent and somehow graceful flick of energy racing across the room.

"Speth..." Albert Fern warned, but it was too late. The assassin was first singed, and then blown apart. Speth trailed off to dust, a last little cry of despair escaping his tortured, blackened form as he fell to what was left of the ornate parquet floor.

Felney and Dr. Bruce, deciding it was every demon for themselves, quickly stepped through the fireplace and were gone. Albert

Fern gave a short, ceremonial bow, and prepared to step through the gate. But this formality gave Mica time enough to raise his hands. Fern, who never thought he'd see the day, now had doom steadily pointing in his own eyes.

Mica's voice was a ragged howl, "My wife and child! Now! I want them back, the way they were!"

"That, I'm afraid, is impossible." Fern sputtered, "Truly, honestly, impossible."

"At least, you must let them know me!"

"Under what covenant? You don't even know my name!"

"Yes, I know your name. Krathnetjapur, let them know me!"

Albert Fern showed his teeth in a silent snarl. He gave an almost submissive but hateful little nod of assent. "Take them and be dust!" he shouted as he leapt and disappeared through the fireplace.

three

As Albert Fern passed from view, there was a quick and fiery wind. In that moment, all trace of the Fern mansion wavered and then vanished into the night. The many rooms with their classical paintings, and even the formal study, were snuffed into darkness. The ornate black iron gates and thick red-black lava walls, the formal gardens and the statuary were all transformed back into the native California hillside of sandy rock and dense, dry brush. The hot wind blew even stronger. Flames roared and sparks flew; Fern's last gift to Mica and his family was a California firestorm.

<u>four</u>

Mica turned away to shield himself from a wave of sparks which stung his face and hands. He was in a wild, bushy area, surrounded by a stand of pines, with umbrellas of eucalyptus trees towering overhead, bending before a high wind. The trees all around him bloomed into flame as the fire roared out of control.

"Sally!! Sally!! Anne Mae!!" He yelled, darting around like a lost soul.

And, at last, they came; his wife and daughter came running out of the flames to him.

Mica and Sally and Anne Mae hugged and kissed and spun around in joy, oblivious while the hillside burned around them. At Anne Mae's bidding, they held hands in a circle and danced with high, kicking steps, just as they had done on that happy afternoon of their final day together in Northern California before the accident. They came together in a close family hug. It was a last joyous moment shared by their three lifetimes. For his part, Mica was at peace, rejoined with the ones he loved, the center of his existence, the ones he cared for most in the world.

But this time couldn't last. A huge, burning tree fell nearby, narrowly missing them. The heavy crash brought Mica back to reality; there was danger here, a different kind than that which they had been facing, but still real.

"Come on, this way!" he yelled. He

scooped up Anne Mae and caught Sally's hand, ready to lead them to safety.

But Sally paused. She gently pulled back, brushing his hair from his face in a tender gesture.

"Mica, no..." she said.

He stopped with Anne Mae in his arms, staring at her.

"We've got to get out of here!" he shouted.

"Mica, we can't go with you. In your heart, you know we can't."

"But, I don't know that. I don't know any of this!"

"Mica, we must go."

"Then I have to come with you," he cried.

"No, Daddy," Anne Mae whispered in his ear. "You must stay here for now...It's a rule; you have to wait until it is your time."

They both were looking at him, their eyes full of love, and yet they were both shaking their heads, denying him the one thing he needed most in the world.

"Please," he begged. "There's nothing for me here anymore."

They looked at him, saying nothing.

He pleaded, "Please, Sally. Anne Mae. I won't have anything. There's nothing for me since the two of you left."

Sally gently took Anne Mae from his arms.

"No, Mica...Mica, my dear and eternal love. This is how it always is. This is what it means to be human. Everybody's always saying good-by."

Mica felt his heart breaking. "But I don't

know WHY..." he whispered.

They came together for a last time, for a last tender hug while the intense heat of the forest flared all around them. For a few seconds, the three of them glowed. Then two of them, glowing brighter and brighter, separated from Mica. Their light rose in the air, joining the sparks rising in the night.

five

Mica was standing alone in a small clearing surrounded by fire, still looking at the sky, when a team of firefighters broke through the wall of flames.

"Jerry, we got one over here!" a fireman shouted into his walkie-talkie. He listened for a beat, and then spoke again, "I donno, maybe a hiker."

Mica was still staring at the sky as they led him away. They were gentle with him, but firm, too. They thought he was blinded, or dazed by smoke inhalation.

"Get him out of here; this whole place is going up!"

"Come on, Mister—you're gonna be okay, now."

And so they led Mica, half carrying him away from the place that had been the study of Albert Fern's mansion. They went a few hundred yards through dense smoke and a snowfall of white ashes, until they stumbled out of the smoldering black brush at a road end.

A volunteer shoved a drink of Gatorade in Mica's hand. Someone else took his arm and led him to a group of blackened survivors.

"Lost a couple of houses..." Mica heard a voice say. He shucked off the helping hands and walked on his own through the little group. He stared at each person, but he failed to recognize anyone.

Mica sat alone on a log at the rim of the survivors. After some time—he didn't know how long, because time was meaningless to him in his despair—after some time, he spotted two pairs of reddish eyes peering from the darkness just outside the rim of light which illuminated the small group of survivors. They were glaring at him! He took a closer look, and made out the outline of two huge dogs, sitting on their haunches.

"I don't understand," he muttered weakly. "It should be over."

"Wind can always shift," a woman in a robe with red cabbage roses on it said. "Never trust a fire."

Mica studied her, but she looked just like everyone else. He stood and turned in a slow circle, trying to figure out what was happening. And he saw the small spark, fluttering feebly around his own shoulders.

"Railsbach," he whispered in a hoarse voice. "Railsbach, you're free, now. Go, Kelp. Fly up to the light." He gently waved the spark off. "Go on. You earned it."

The spark hesitated for a moment, and then began to labor higher, like an overloaded airplane clawing for altitude.

A dazed, half-crazed and fire-blackened man came staggering over with a cup of water.

"Embers!" the man shouted. "That's how it spreads! Here, I'll get it!" He reared back and made ready to heave his water at the spark, acting as if their lives depended on it.

Mica knocked the cup from the man's hand. The fire-blackened man glared at Mica, just for a moment. And then whatever emotion was behind those eyes suddenly snapped, and the man was an empty shell, just another *sap* set adrift. "What's happening around here, anyway?" he asked, before wandering off into the night.

The two dogs howled bitterly as the spark fluttered higher, now out of reach. Mica looked at the dogs. They were still in the same spot, glaring at him, with the red fire reflected in their eyes. He raised one hand in their direction, two fingers pointing. They yapped in fear and ran away into the darkness. By now the spark was firmly on course, heading higher and higher.

Mica looked skyward, toward the stars. And he saw, or thought he saw, the spark joining two others, and the three of them streaking away like comets. *Gone to the light,* he thought, and he stared up into the inky black night until the fire victims were shepherded into ambulances and taken down off the still-burning hill.

EPILOGUE
Who's Gonna Save Your Soul?

It was twelve years later, just another day in *The City of the Angels*. The micros looked down through the smog of early summer, picking up the jet-black Porsche Boxster as it smoothly crossed lanes and made its way off the 405 and onto the crowded and slow-moving Santa Monica Boulevard, heading in the direction of the Mormon Temple. Mica, dressed in an expensive sports jacket, pulled to a stop at the red light at Westwood Boulevard. Jimmy, in the passenger seat beside him, smiled.

"Already a hot morning. How about a shaved ice, Mica-boy wonder?"

"Raspberry, raspberry!" the boy in the backseat said, grinning at them both. He was nearly nine years old now, nearly the same age as Anne Mae when—Mica brushed the idea out of his mind. His heart was full. He didn't want to remember. Joey was so quick and bright; he was first in his class and a natural-born leader.

"You guys buy yourselves some shaved ice," he said. "I've got to get to the office and earn the big bucks."

"Mica's got curls," Jimmy teased, running her fingers through his ash-blond locks.

"Ladies have curls," he responded, "That's just bent hair."

Mica would be seeing the new scripts on this season's Horny Show, which had become a smash hit and was now in its fifth season. He was feeling great, just great, as the CD blared Jewel Kilcher's "Who Will Save Your Soul?" He beat his hand on the side door of the panel of the car and let the mixed bag that was Los Angeles pedestrian traffic pass in front of him on the crosswalk.

"Dad," Joey asked, "How come you always listen to this song?"

"Ahh, jaded youth," Mica replied. "Come on, I thought this was a really *with-it* song."

"Last week is history, Popster. And what's there to it, anyway? Just *Who's gonna save your soul?*, over and over again...whatever the heck a soul is, anyway..."

"Look out, Mica," Jimmy warned as an old black bum with a cardboard sign WILL WORK FOR FOOD approached on his side of the Porsche. Not really paying attention, Mica reached in his pocket with one hand and gave the bum a bill.

"Hey, Dad, that was a fiver," Joey said.

Jimmy smiled, looking back fondly at their son. "Money doesn't buy what it used to, my boy."

"Have a nice day," Mica said to the old black bum, jiving a little with the beat of the music.

"Thank you, boss," the bum said softly. "I be here when you need me."

"I'm sure you will," Mica smiled.

He looked past the bum, waiting for the light to change. The bum stepped back, still looking at him.

Mica's hand rested on the steering wheel. Without consciously thinking what he was doing, Mica idly scratched the back of his thumb, a characteristic gesture, and then put his hand back on the steering wheel.

"Something wrong with that thumb there, you know," the bum said softly, his voice hardly above a whisper.

"Yeah, pencil lead or something." Mica vaguely remembered something about falling on one of his school pencils when he was a kid, the tip of the pencil breaking off and getting stuck inside his skin. Something like that. But he really didn't think about it much.

"Naw, something worse. You should try to dig it out, sometime," the old bum said.

"Yeah. Sure. Thanks."

Mica was thinking how funny it was; you gave a bum a tiny grubstake and they thought it gave them license to pass on advice. The light changed to green, and he drove on, eager to turn the car over to Jimmy and little Joey, and to get to his scripts and his drawing board. While sitting at the intersection, he'd had a great idea for a new Horny. America's favorite hornhead meets a bum camped out next to his parking spot and the little horned guy has to decide whether to feed the meter or give his last quarter to the bum. Horny says, *Why don't you work for a living?* Mica couldn't remember what the bum says next, but it was there, the thread of an idea right at the tip of his mind. And then it was gone, just like that. Oh well, he'd think of it a little later, or, if not, he'd come

up with something else that was just as great.
He always did.

About the Author

John Klawitter

John Klawitter has worked as a writer, producer and director. Based in Hollywood, he's worked for major studios, indie companies and run his own production company. He's written and produced for CBS, NBC, Disney, The Disney Channel, Paramount, Universal, Atlantis Productions, and many others. He's also worked on animation projects for Disney, Warner Bros. Animation, Hanna-Barbera, Phil Mendez Productions, Zoiyu Productions (Japan), Pink Planet Productions (Holland) and Franke Films (Finland). He has directed short films featuring a wide range of stars and personalities, including Bill Cosby, Ali MacGraw, Jane Alexander, Jacqueline Bisset, Ray Bradbury, George Plimpton, Leslie Nielsen, and many others.

His film writing includes the political documentary Scene: Politic (EMMY AWARD); the Television Specials The Great American Dreammobile, Le Mans, The Adventures of Sports Goofy, and Here comes Sam (The Olympic Eagle). He has also adapted several novels to screenplay format, most notably HOBBERDY DICK by K.M. Briggs, STYX by Christopher Hyde, MONSTER TALES by Phil Mendez, and his own novel CRAZYHEAD.

One of his short stories, "Jack's Boat", won a prize at the Key West Hemingway Days festival. A collection of his short stories, TOUCHED, won a special mention from the prestigious Flannery O'Connor Short Fiction Awards. Klawitter's first novel, an action/thriller titled CRAZYHEAD, came out in 1990 as an Ivy imprint published by Ballantine Books. He co-wrote HEADSLAP, the biography of the life and times of Deacon Jones (the NFL Hall of Famer and self-proclaimed King of Sacks), published in 1996 by Prometheus Books. Other published works include THE BOOK OF DEACON (Seven Locks Press, 2001) and TANS (a collection of recollections by the Old Spooks & Spies).